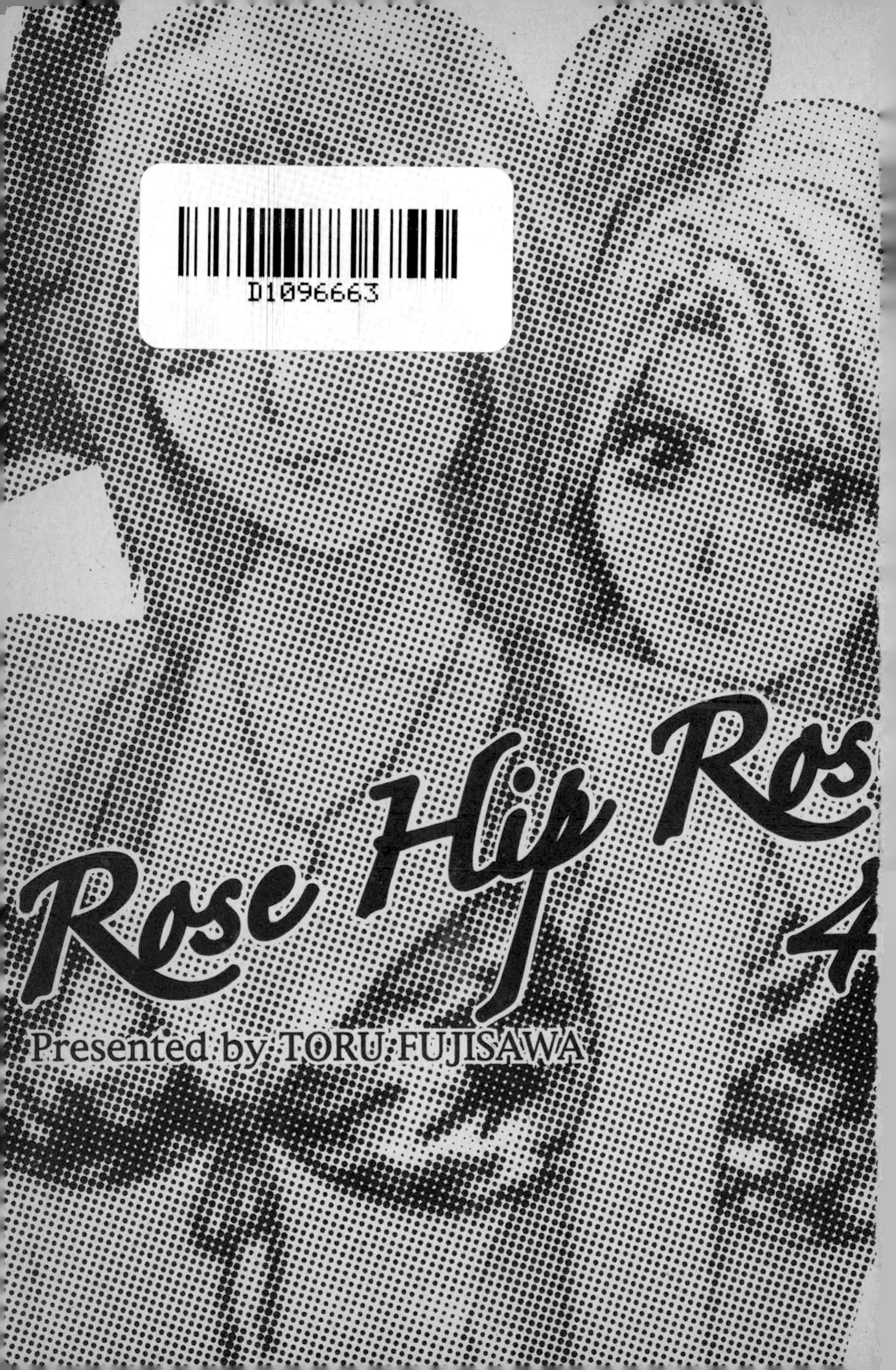
Rose Hip Ros
4
Presented by TORU FUJISAWA

Rose Hip Rose Volume 4
Created by Tohru Fujisawa

Translation - Nan Rymer
English Adapation - Michael French
Retouch and Lettering - Star Print Brokers
Production Artist - Aska Tun
Graphic Designer - Colin Graham

Editor - Alexis Kirsch
Pre-Production Supervisor - Vicente Rivera, Jr.
Print-Production Specialist - Lucas Rivera
Managing Editor - Vy Nguyen
Senior Designer - Louis Csontos
Senior Designer - James Lee
Senior Editor - Bryce P. Coleman
Senior Editor - Jenna Winterberg
Associate Publisher - Marco F. Pavia
President and C.O.O. - John Parker
C.E.O. and Chief Creative Officer - Stu Levy

A  Manga

TOKYOPOP and ☺ are trademarks or registered trademarks of TOKYOPOP Inc.

TOKYOPOP Inc.
5900 Wilshire Blvd. Suite 2000
Los Angeles, CA 90036

E-mail: info@TOKYOPOP.com
Come visit us online at www.TOKYOPOP.com

ISBN: 978-1-4278-0874-5

First TOKYOPOP printing: February 2009
10 9 8 7 6 5 4 3 2 1
Printed in the USA

VOLUME 4

by Tohru Fujisawa

HAMBURG // LONDON // LOS ANGELES // TOKYO

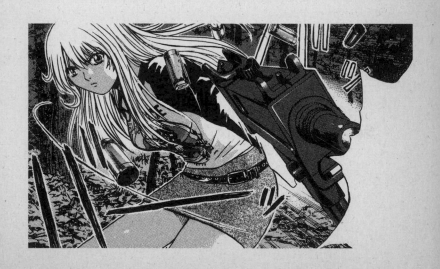

STORY SO FAR...

ROSE HIP ROSE

KASUMI AND NATSUKI ARE ONE BADASS CRIME FIGHTING TEAM! AND AFTER STOPPING A CRAZY SERIAL KILLER AND A HIJACKING ATTEMPT, THEY GET WHAT SEEMS TO BE A MUCH EASIER JOB OF HELPING POP SINGER MAYUKO WARD OFF A POTENTIAL STALKER. BUT PERHAPS THE SITUATION IS MORE SERIOUS THAN IT SEEMS. WHO ARE THESE MEN IN BLACK WHO ARE FOLLOWING MAYUKO AROUND...?

Rose Hip Rose

ローズ・ヒップ・ローズ

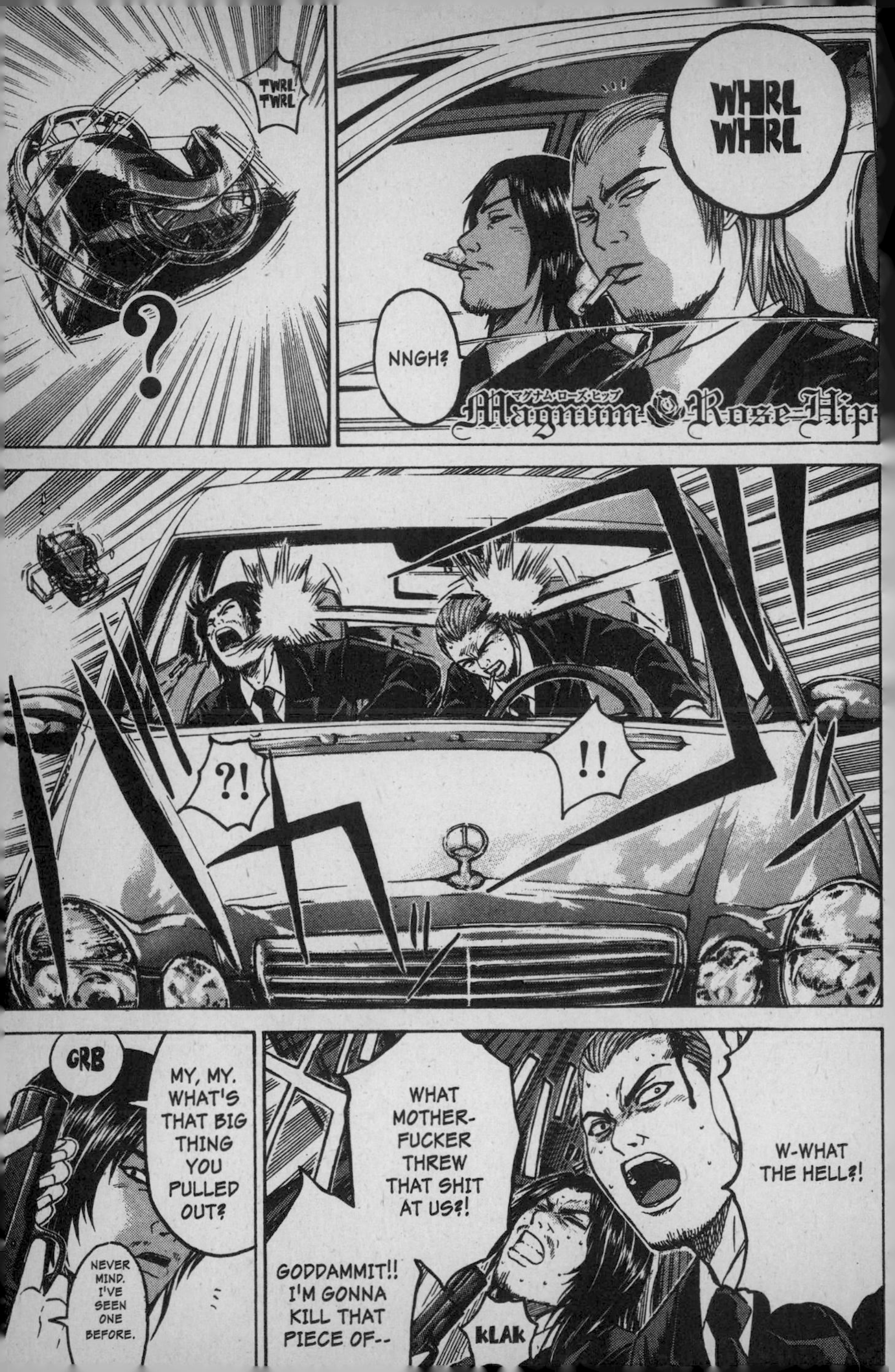
WHRL WHRL
NNGH?
マグナム・ローズ・ヒップ
Magnum Rose Hip
TWRL TWRL
?
!!
?!
W-WHAT THE HELL?!
WHAT MOTHER-FUCKER THREW THAT SHIT AT US?!
GODDAMMIT!! I'M GONNA KILL THAT PIECE OF--
KLAK
GRB
MY, MY. WHAT'S THAT BIG THING YOU PULLED OUT?
NEVER MIND. I'VE SEEN ONE BEFORE.

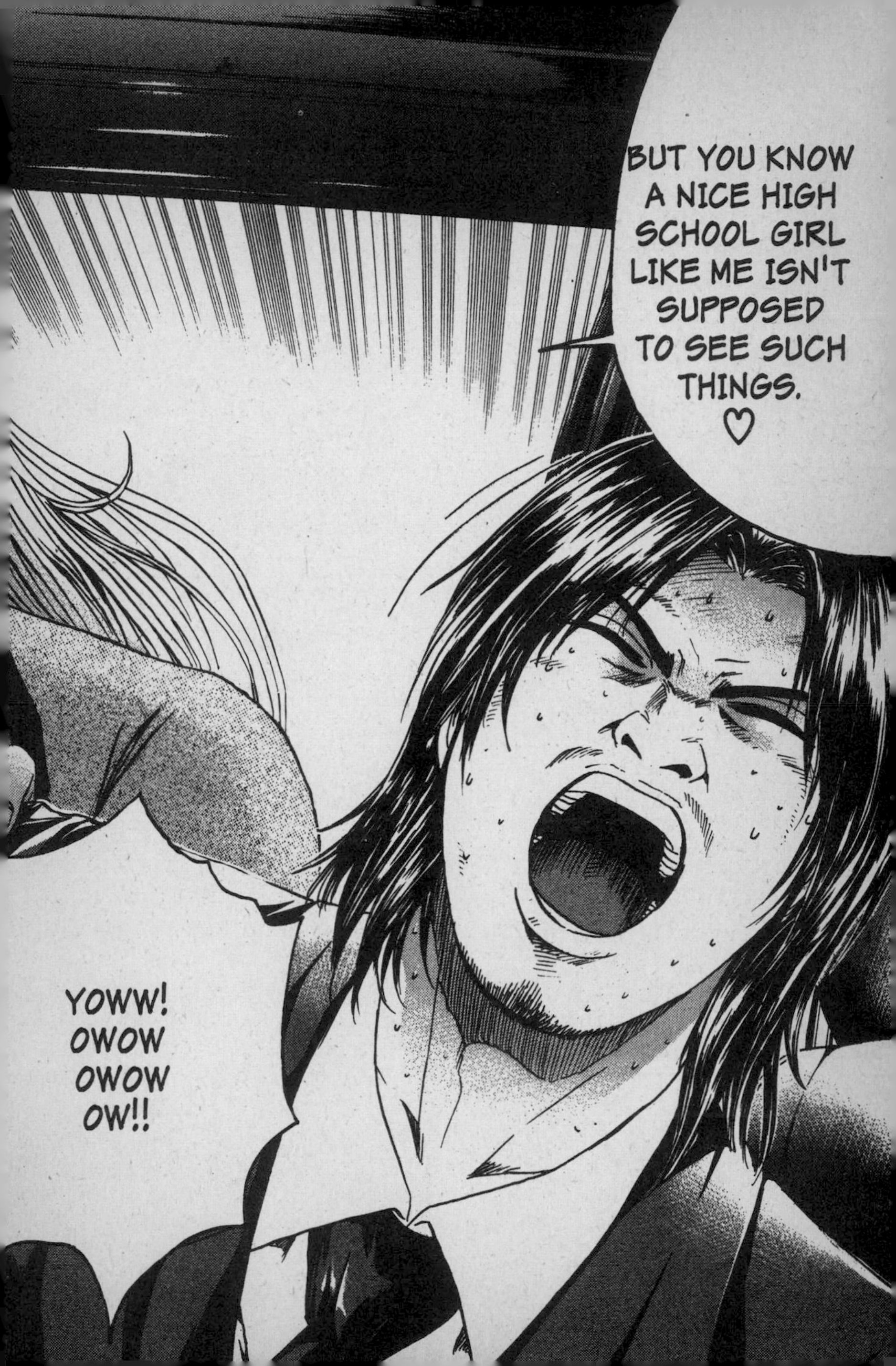
BUT YOU KNOW A NICE HIGH SCHOOL GIRL LIKE ME ISN'T SUPPOSED TO SEE SUCH THINGS. ♡
YOWW! OWOW OWOW OW!!

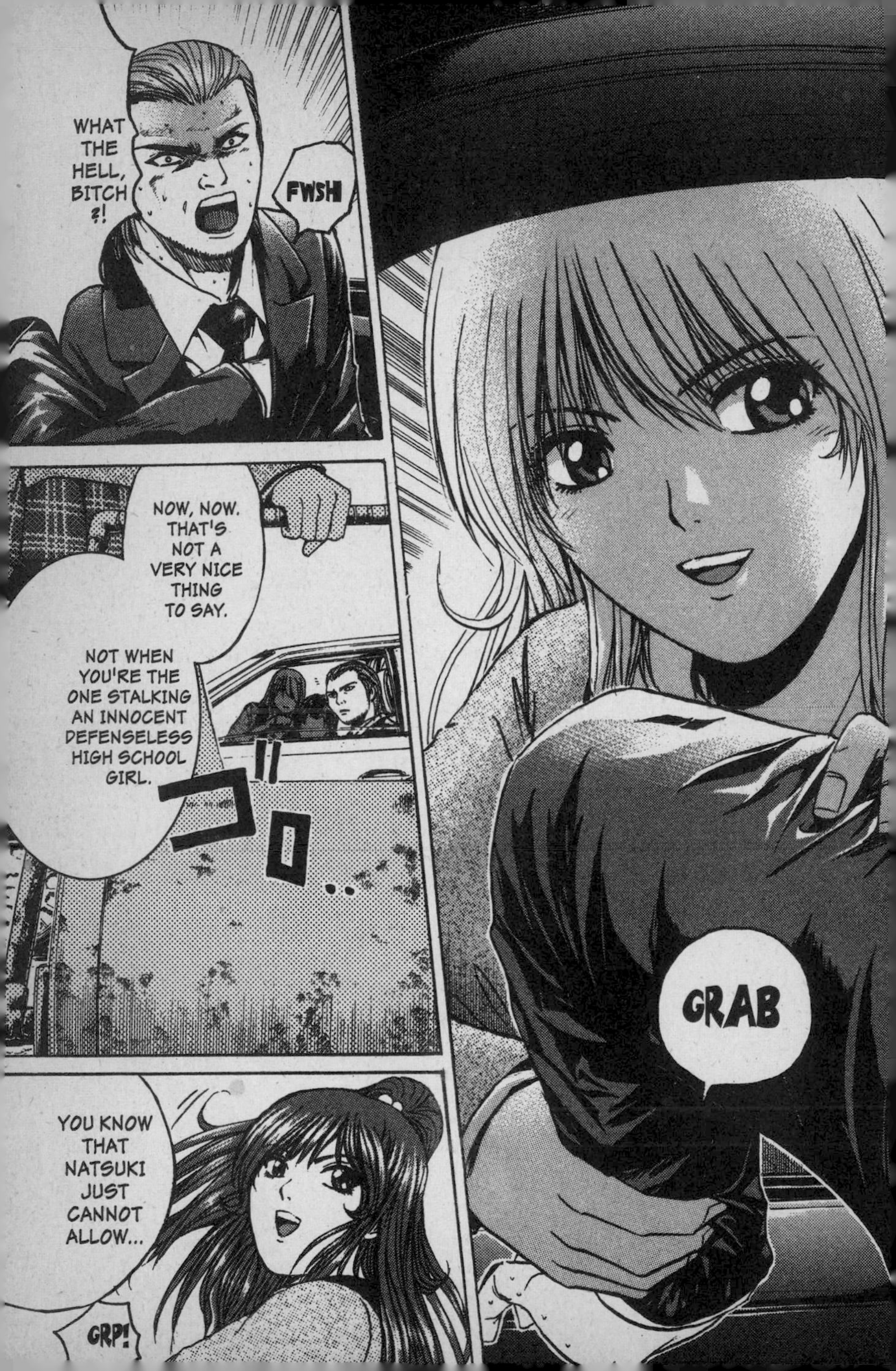
GRAB
FWSH
WHAT THE HELL, BITCH ?!
NOW, NOW. THAT'S NOT A VERY NICE THING TO SAY.
NOT WHEN YOU'RE THE ONE STALKING AN INNOCENT DEFENSELESS HIGH SCHOOL GIRL.
コロ..
YOU KNOW THAT NATSUKI JUST CANNOT ALLOW...
GRP!

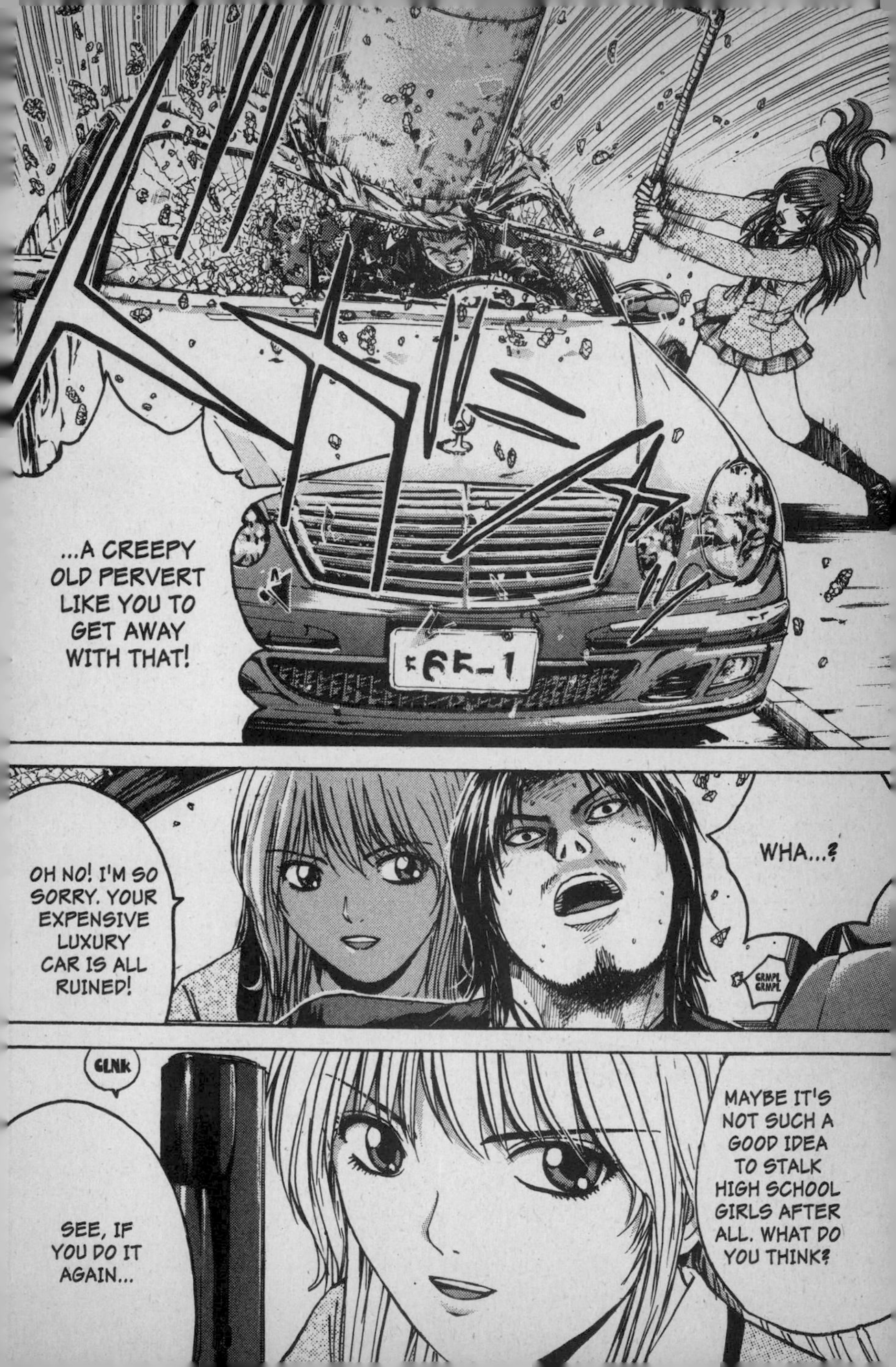
...A CREEPY OLD PERVERT LIKE YOU TO GET AWAY WITH THAT!
WHA...?
OH NO! I'M SO SORRY. YOUR EXPENSIVE LUXURY CAR IS ALL RUINED!
GRMPL GRMPL
MAYBE IT'S NOT SUCH A GOOD IDEA TO STALK HIGH SCHOOL GIRLS AFTER ALL. WHAT DO YOU THINK?
GLNK
SEE, IF YOU DO IT AGAIN...

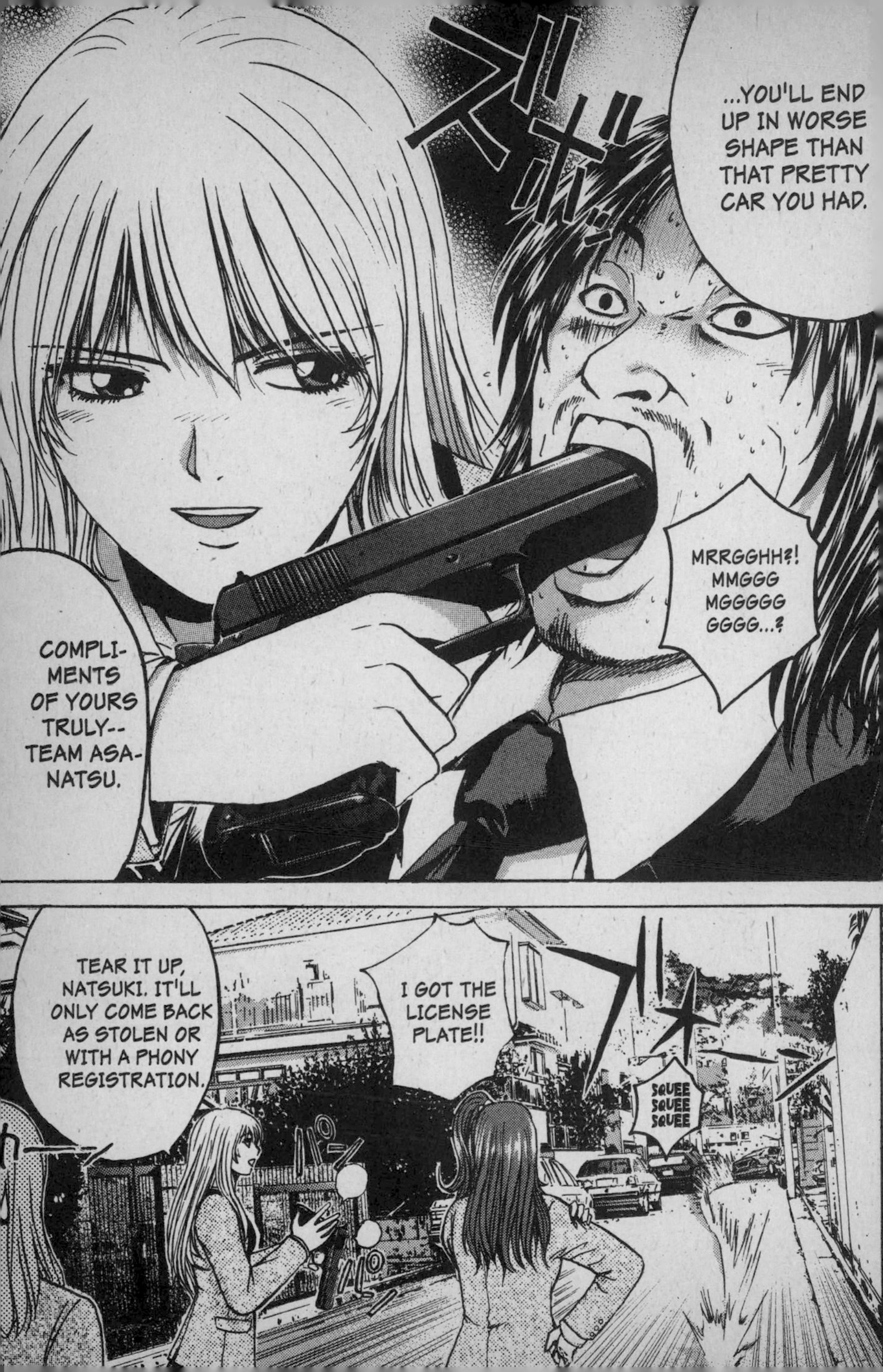
...YOU'LL END UP IN WORSE SHAPE THAN THAT PRETTY CAR YOU HAD.
MRRGGHH?! MMGGG MGGGGG GGGG...?
COMPLI-MENTS OF YOURS TRULY--TEAM ASA-NATSU.
SQUEE SQUEE SQUEE
I GOT THE LICENSE PLATE!!
TEAR IT UP, NATSUKI. IT'LL ONLY COME BACK AS STOLEN OR WITH A PHONY REGISTRATION.

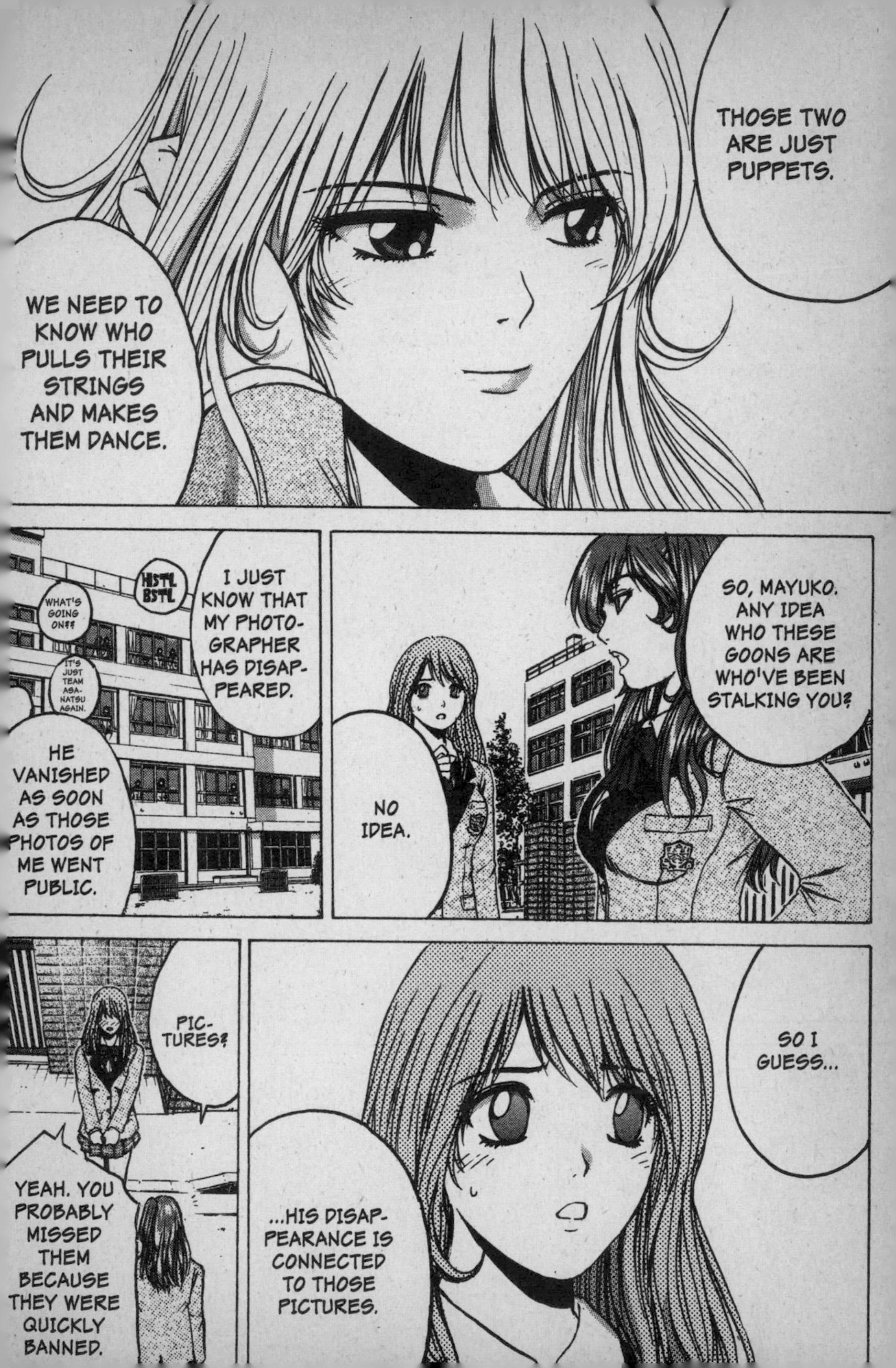

THOSE TWO ARE JUST PUPPETS.
WE NEED TO KNOW WHO PULLS THEIR STRINGS AND MAKES THEM DANCE.
SO, MAYUKO. ANY IDEA WHO THESE GOONS ARE WHO'VE BEEN STALKING YOU?
NO IDEA.
I JUST KNOW THAT MY PHOTOGRAPHER HAS DISAPPEARED.
HSTL BSTL
WHAT'S GOING ON??
IT'S JUST TEAM ASANATSU AGAIN.
HE VANISHED AS SOON AS THOSE PHOTOS OF ME WENT PUBLIC.
SO I GUESS...
...HIS DISAPPEARANCE IS CONNECTED TO THOSE PICTURES.
PICTURES?
YEAH. YOU PROBABLY MISSED THEM BECAUSE THEY WERE QUICKLY BANNED.

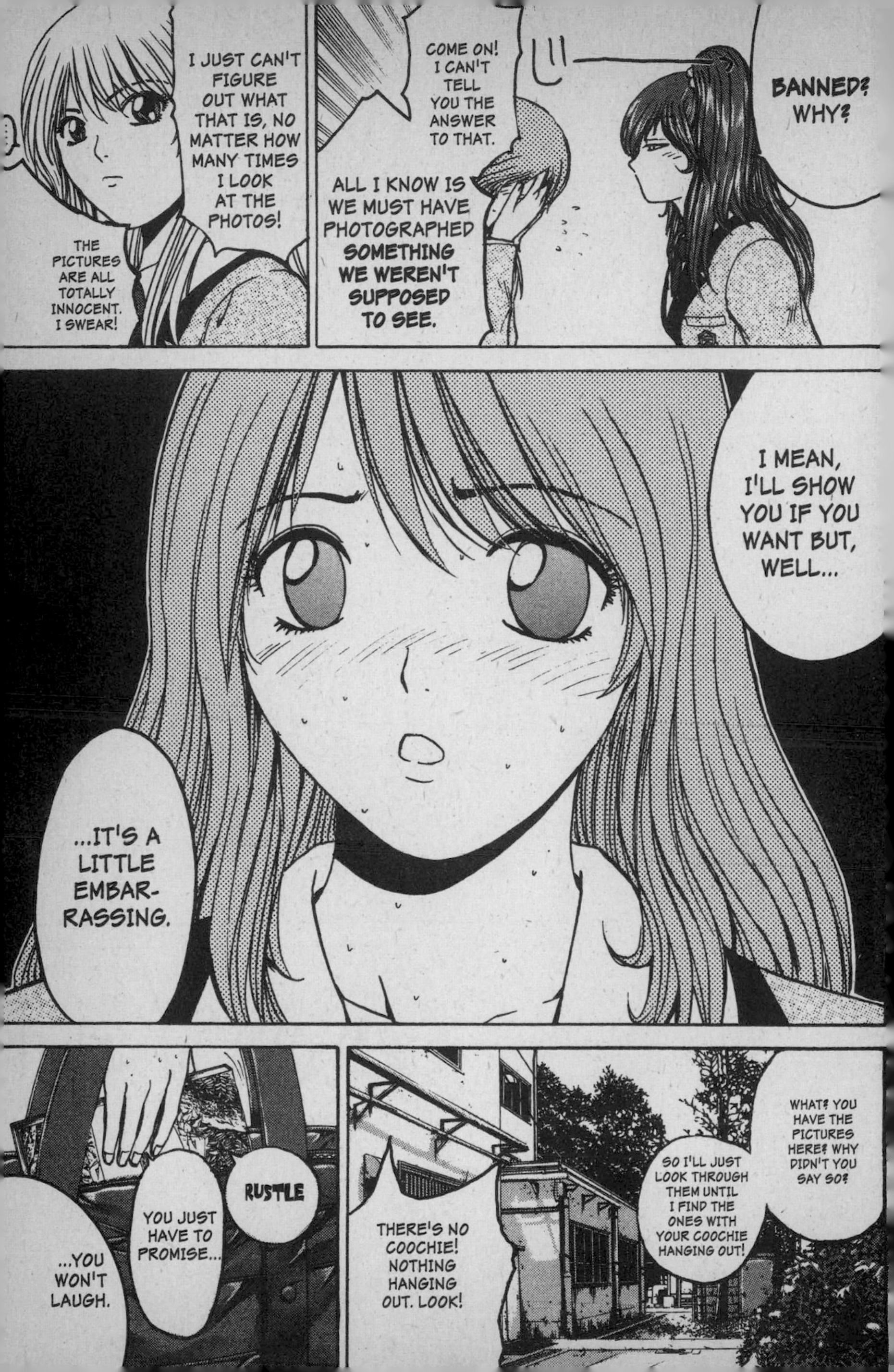
BANNED? WHY?
COME ON! I CAN'T TELL YOU THE ANSWER TO THAT.
ALL I KNOW IS WE MUST HAVE PHOTOGRAPHED SOMETHING WE WEREN'T SUPPOSED TO SEE.
I JUST CAN'T FIGURE OUT WHAT THAT IS, NO MATTER HOW MANY TIMES I LOOK AT THE PHOTOS!
THE PICTURES ARE ALL TOTALLY INNOCENT. I SWEAR!
I MEAN, I'LL SHOW YOU IF YOU WANT BUT, WELL...
...IT'S A LITTLE EMBARRASSING.
WHAT? YOU HAVE THE PICTURES HERE? WHY DIDN'T YOU SAY SO?
SO I'LL JUST LOOK THROUGH THEM UNTIL I FIND THE ONES WITH YOUR COOCHIE HANGING OUT!
THERE'S NO COOCHIE! NOTHING HANGING OUT. LOOK!
RUSTLE
YOU JUST HAVE TO PROMISE...
...YOU WON'T LAUGH.

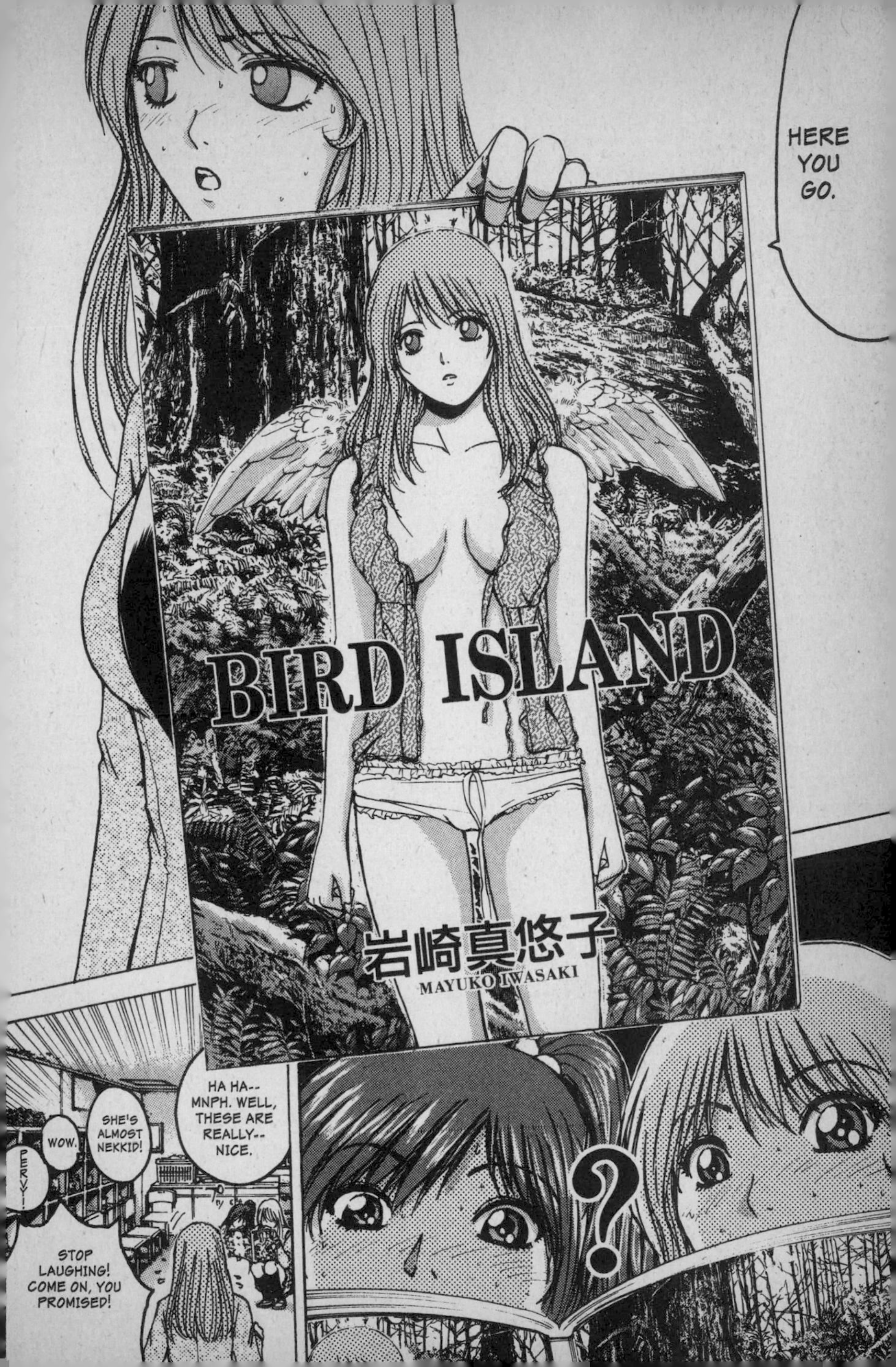
HERE YOU GO.
BIRD ISLAND
岩崎真悠子
MAYUKO IWASAKI
?
HA HA-- MNPH. WELL, THESE ARE REALLY-- NICE.
SHE'S ALMOST NEKKID!
WOW.
PERVY!
STOP LAUGHING! COME ON, YOU PROMISED!

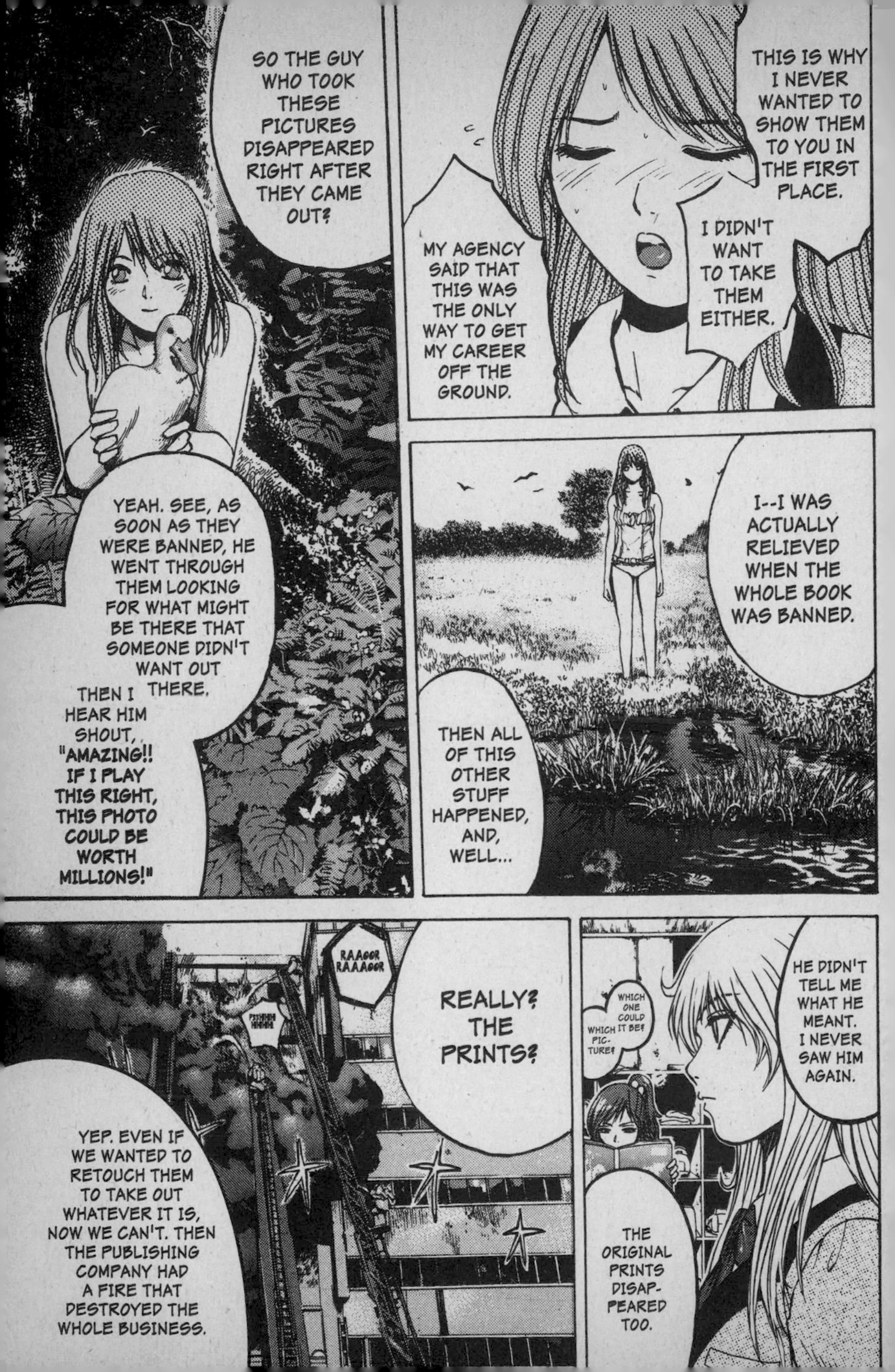
THIS IS WHY I NEVER WANTED TO SHOW THEM TO YOU IN THE FIRST PLACE.
I DIDN'T WANT TO TAKE THEM EITHER.
MY AGENCY SAID THAT THIS WAS THE ONLY WAY TO GET MY CAREER OFF THE GROUND.
I--I WAS ACTUALLY RELIEVED WHEN THE WHOLE BOOK WAS BANNED.
THEN ALL OF THIS OTHER STUFF HAPPENED, AND, WELL...
SO THE GUY WHO TOOK THESE PICTURES DISAPPEARED RIGHT AFTER THEY CAME OUT?
YEAH. SEE, AS SOON AS THEY WERE BANNED, HE WENT THROUGH THEM LOOKING FOR WHAT MIGHT BE THERE THAT SOMEONE DIDN'T WANT OUT THERE.
THEN I HEAR HIM SHOUT, "AMAZING!! IF I PLAY THIS RIGHT, THIS PHOTO COULD BE WORTH MILLIONS!"
HE DIDN'T TELL ME WHAT HE MEANT. I NEVER SAW HIM AGAIN.
WHICH ONE COULD IT BE?
WHICH PIC-TURE?
THE ORIGINAL PRINTS DISAP-PEARED TOO.
REALLY? THE PRINTS?
RAAGOR RAAAGOR
YEP. EVEN IF WE WANTED TO RETOUCH THEM TO TAKE OUT WHATEVER IT IS, NOW WE CAN'T. THEN THE PUBLISHING COMPANY HAD A FIRE THAT DESTROYED THE WHOLE BUSINESS.

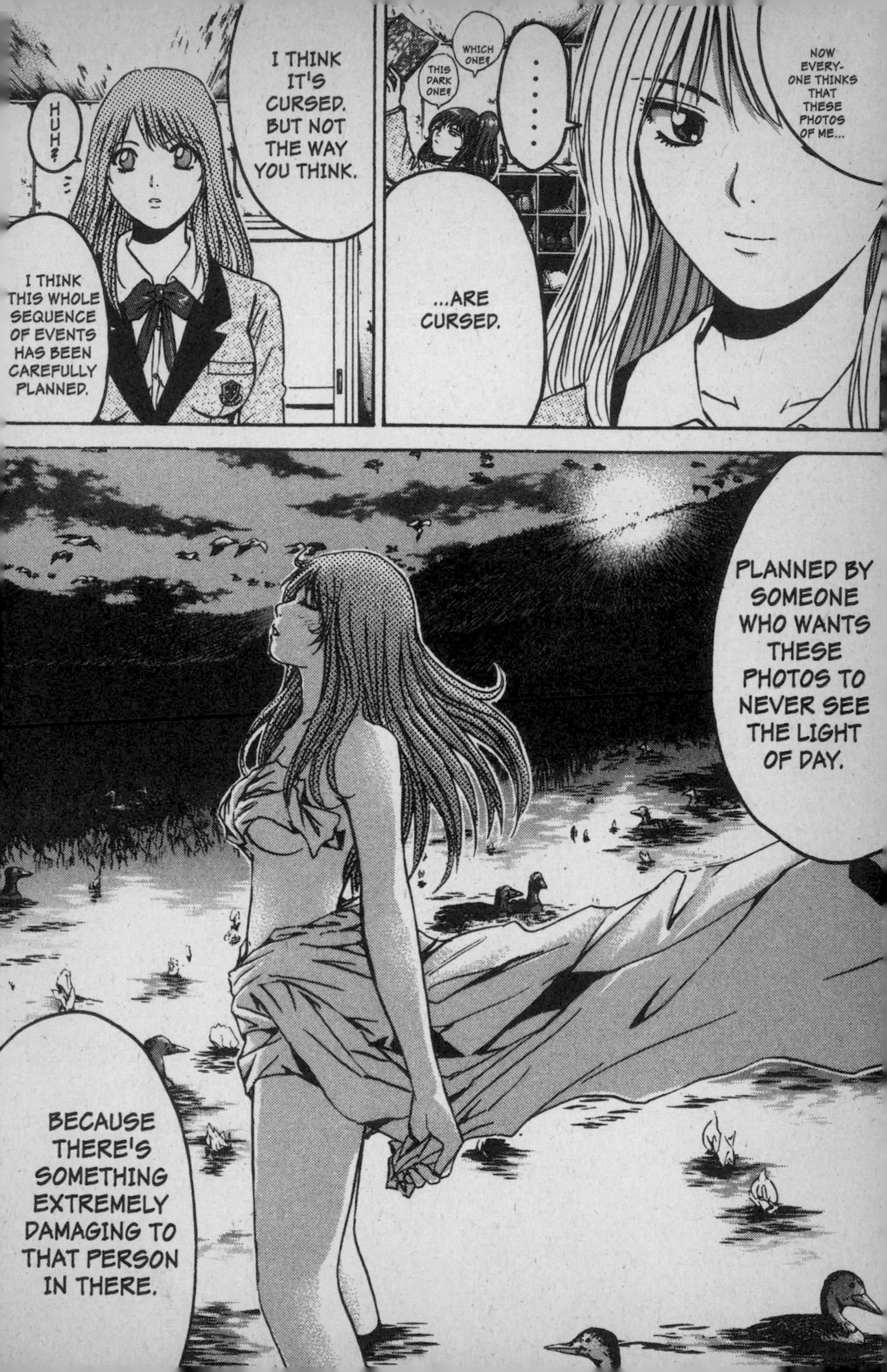
NOW EVERY-ONE THINKS THAT THESE PHOTOS OF ME...
......
WHICH ONE?
THIS DARK ONE?
...ARE CURSED.
I THINK IT'S CURSED. BUT NOT THE WAY YOU THINK.
HUH?
I THINK THIS WHOLE SEQUENCE OF EVENTS HAS BEEN CAREFULLY PLANNED.
PLANNED BY SOMEONE WHO WANTS THESE PHOTOS TO NEVER SEE THE LIGHT OF DAY.
BECAUSE THERE'S SOMETHING EXTREMELY DAMAGING TO THAT PERSON IN THERE.

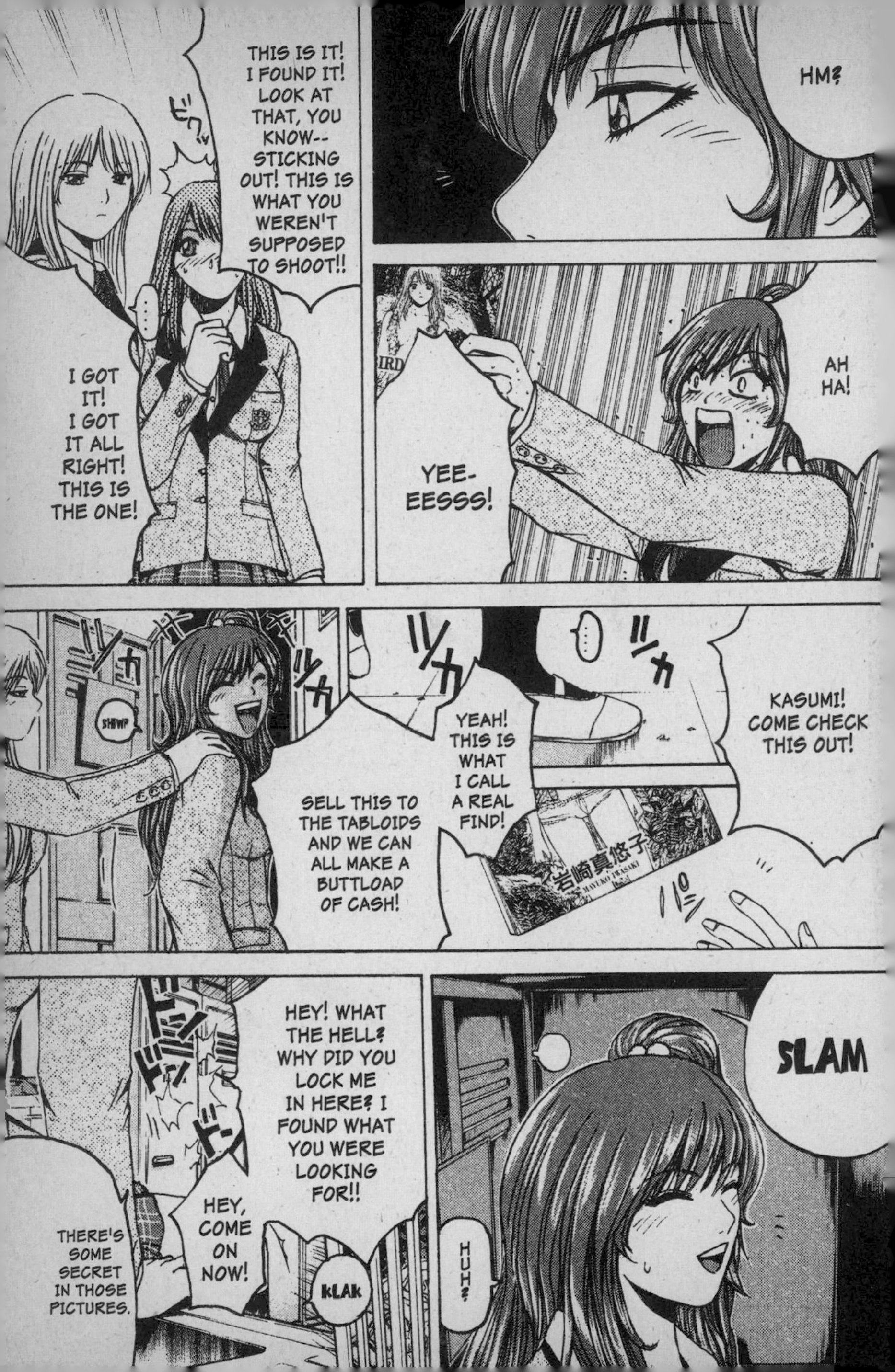
HM?
AH HA!
YEE-EESSS!
THIS IS IT! I FOUND IT! LOOK AT THAT, YOU KNOW-- STICKING OUT! THIS IS WHAT YOU WEREN'T SUPPOSED TO SHOOT!!
...
I GOT IT! I GOT IT ALL RIGHT! THIS IS THE ONE!
KASUMI! COME CHECK THIS OUT!
...
YEAH! THIS IS WHAT I CALL A REAL FIND!
岩崎真悠子
MAYUKO IWASAKI
SELL THIS TO THE TABLOIDS AND WE CAN ALL MAKE A BUTTLOAD OF CASH!
SHWP
SLAM
HUH?
HEY! WHAT THE HELL? WHY DID YOU LOCK ME IN HERE? I FOUND WHAT YOU WERE LOOKING FOR!!
HEY, COME ON NOW!
KLAK
THERE'S SOME SECRET IN THOSE PICTURES.

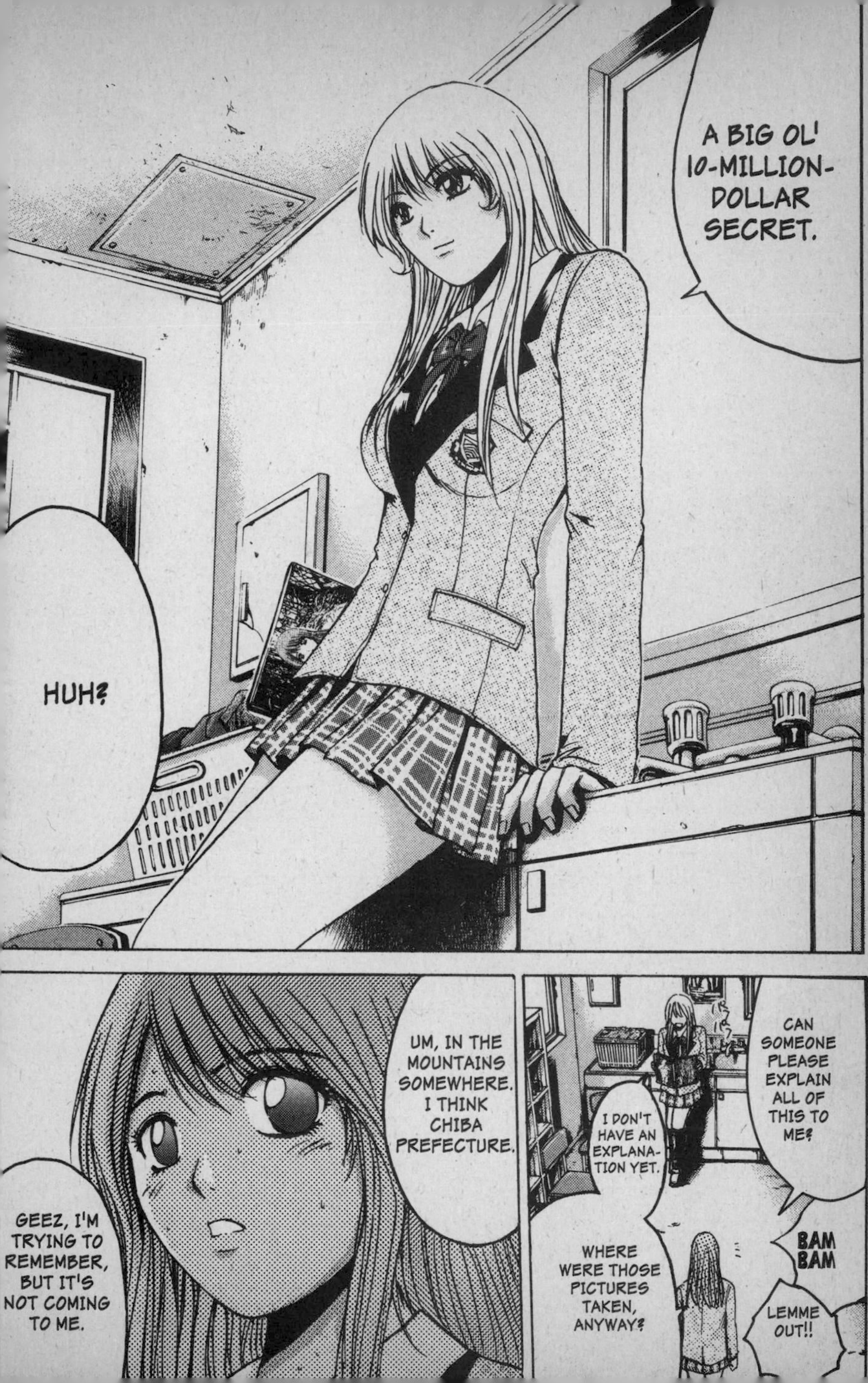
A BIG OL' 10-MILLION-DOLLAR SECRET.
HUH?
CAN SOMEONE PLEASE EXPLAIN ALL OF THIS TO ME?
I DON'T HAVE AN EXPLANATION YET.
BAM BAM
LEMME OUT!!
WHERE WERE THOSE PICTURES TAKEN, ANYWAY?
UM, IN THE MOUNTAINS SOMEWHERE. I THINK CHIBA PREFECTURE.
GEEZ, I'M TRYING TO REMEMBER, BUT IT'S NOT COMING TO ME.

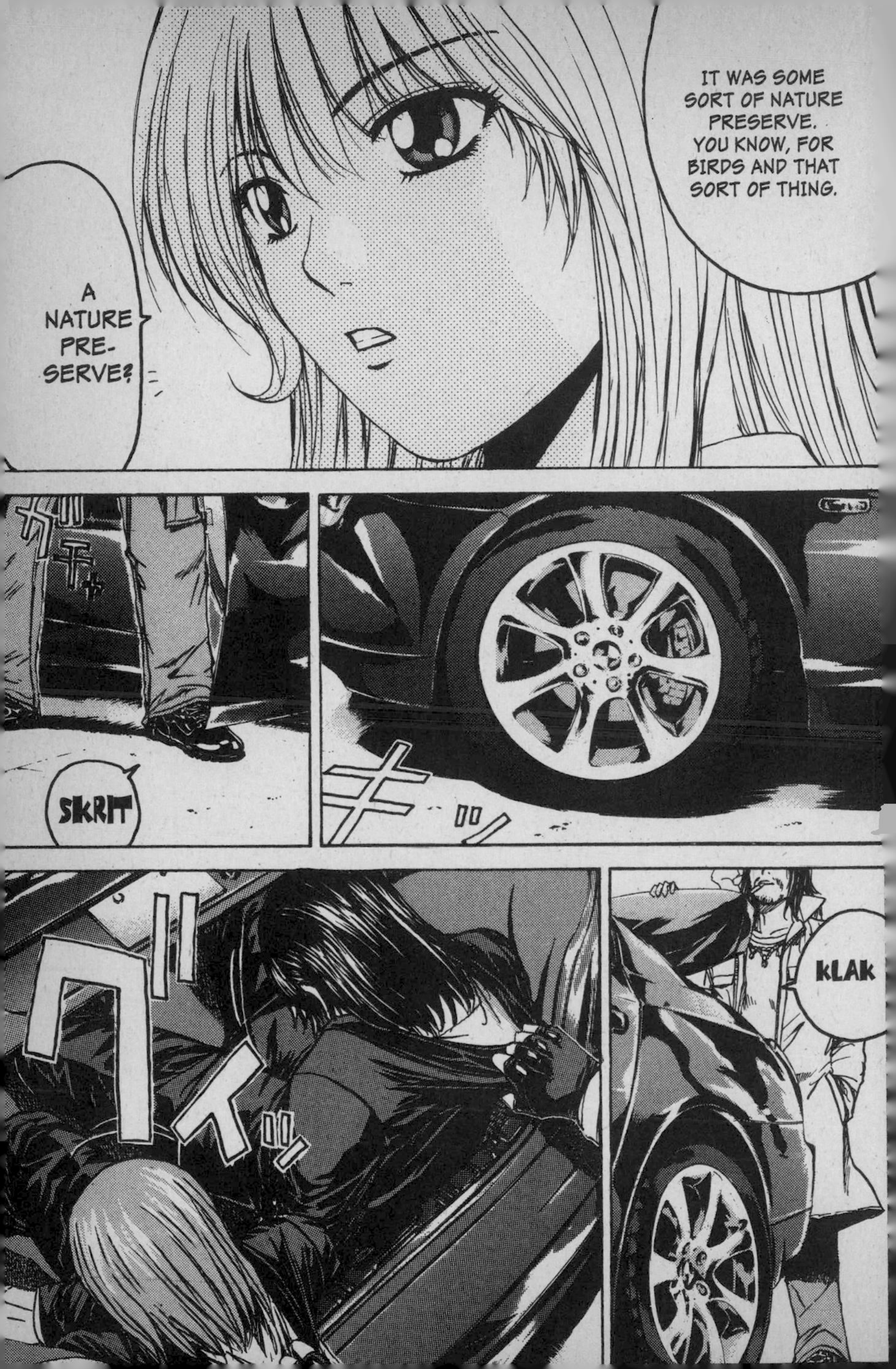
IT WAS SOME SORT OF NATURE PRESERVE. YOU KNOW, FOR BIRDS AND THAT SORT OF THING.
A NATURE PRE-SERVE?
SKRIT
KLAK

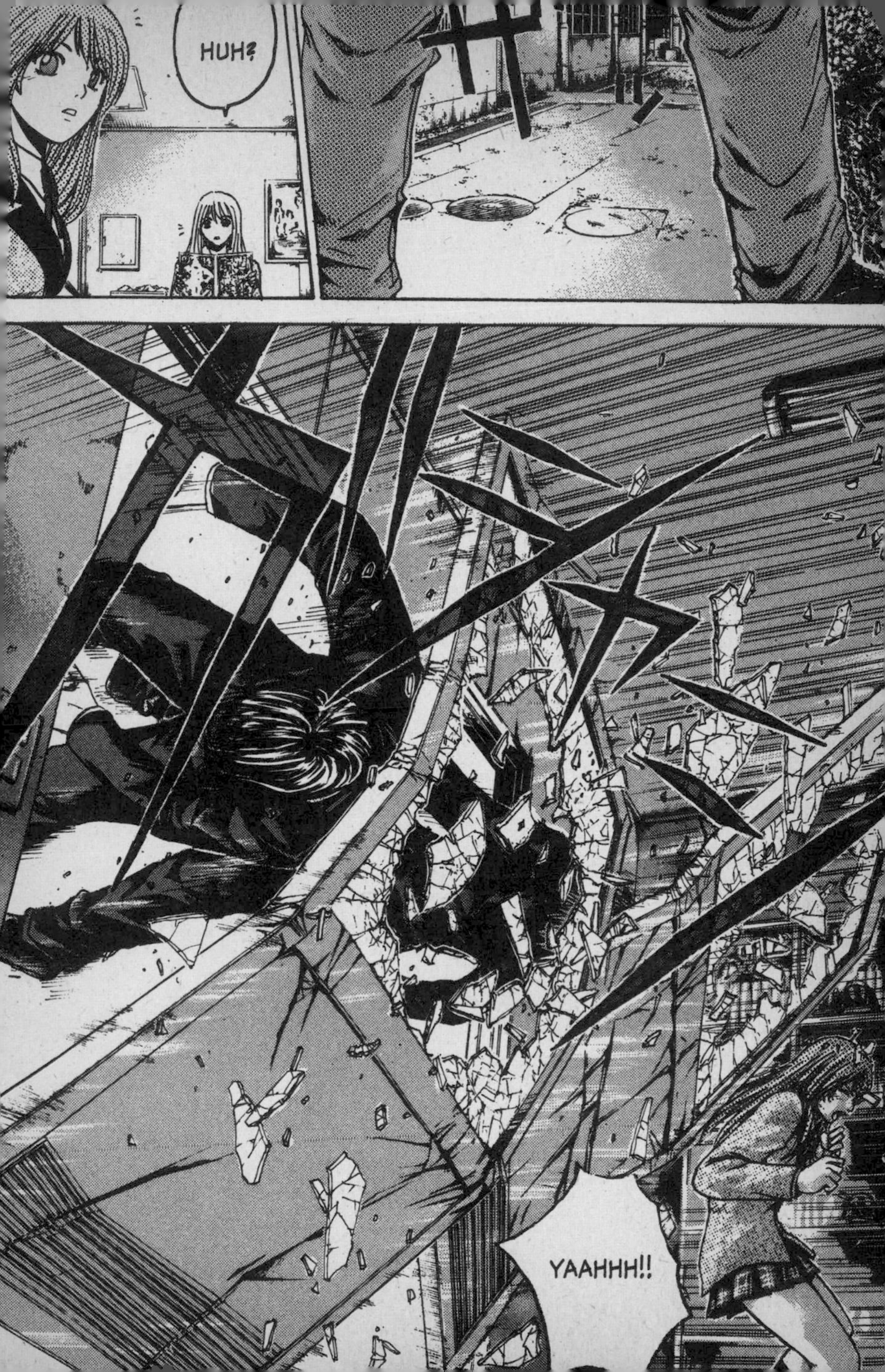
HUH?
YAAHHH!!

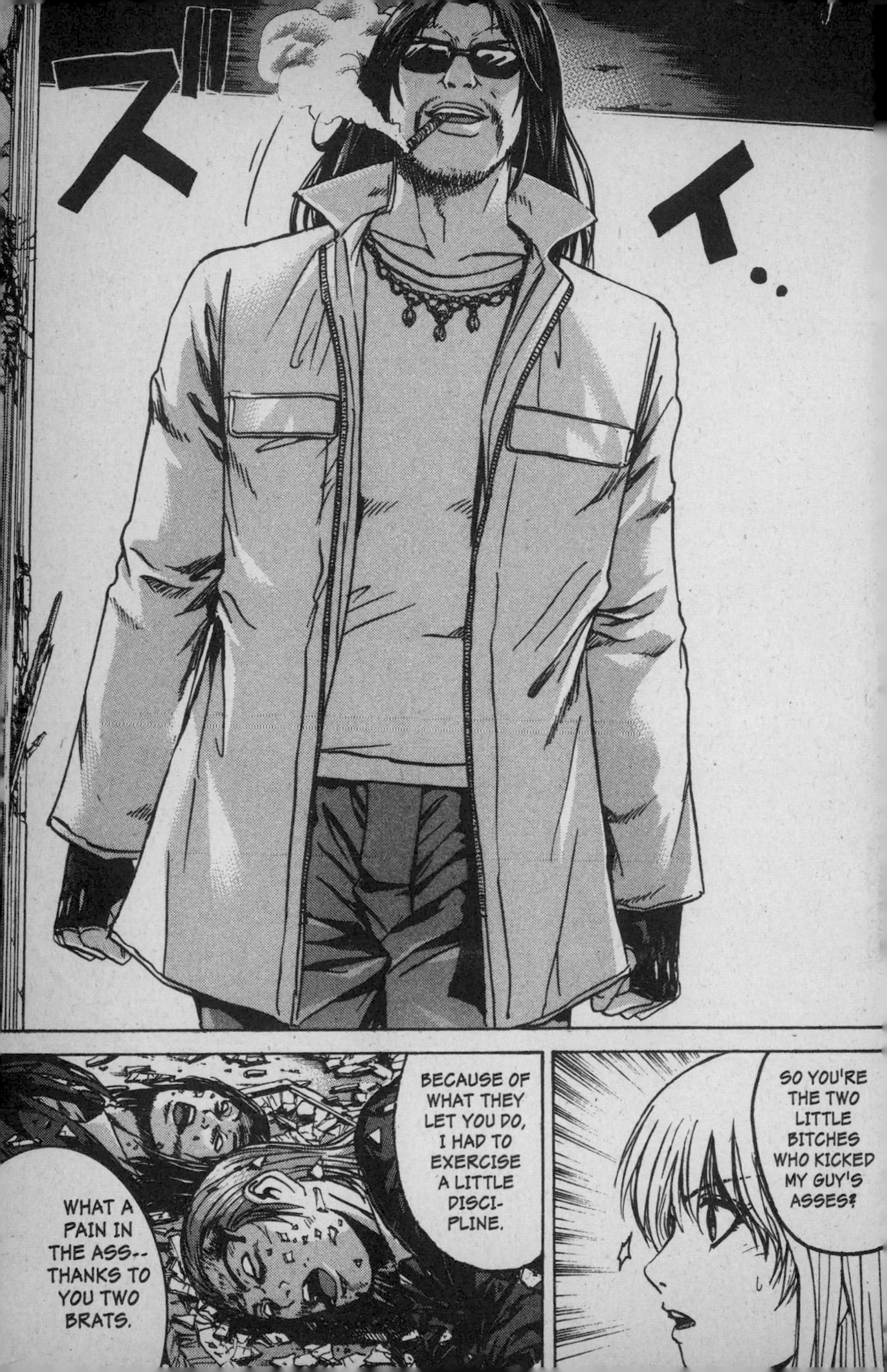
ズイ..
SO YOU'RE THE TWO LITTLE BITCHES WHO KICKED MY GUY'S ASSES?
BECAUSE OF WHAT THEY LET YOU DO, I HAD TO EXERCISE A LITTLE DISCIPLINE.
WHAT A PAIN IN THE ASS--THANKS TO YOU TWO BRATS.

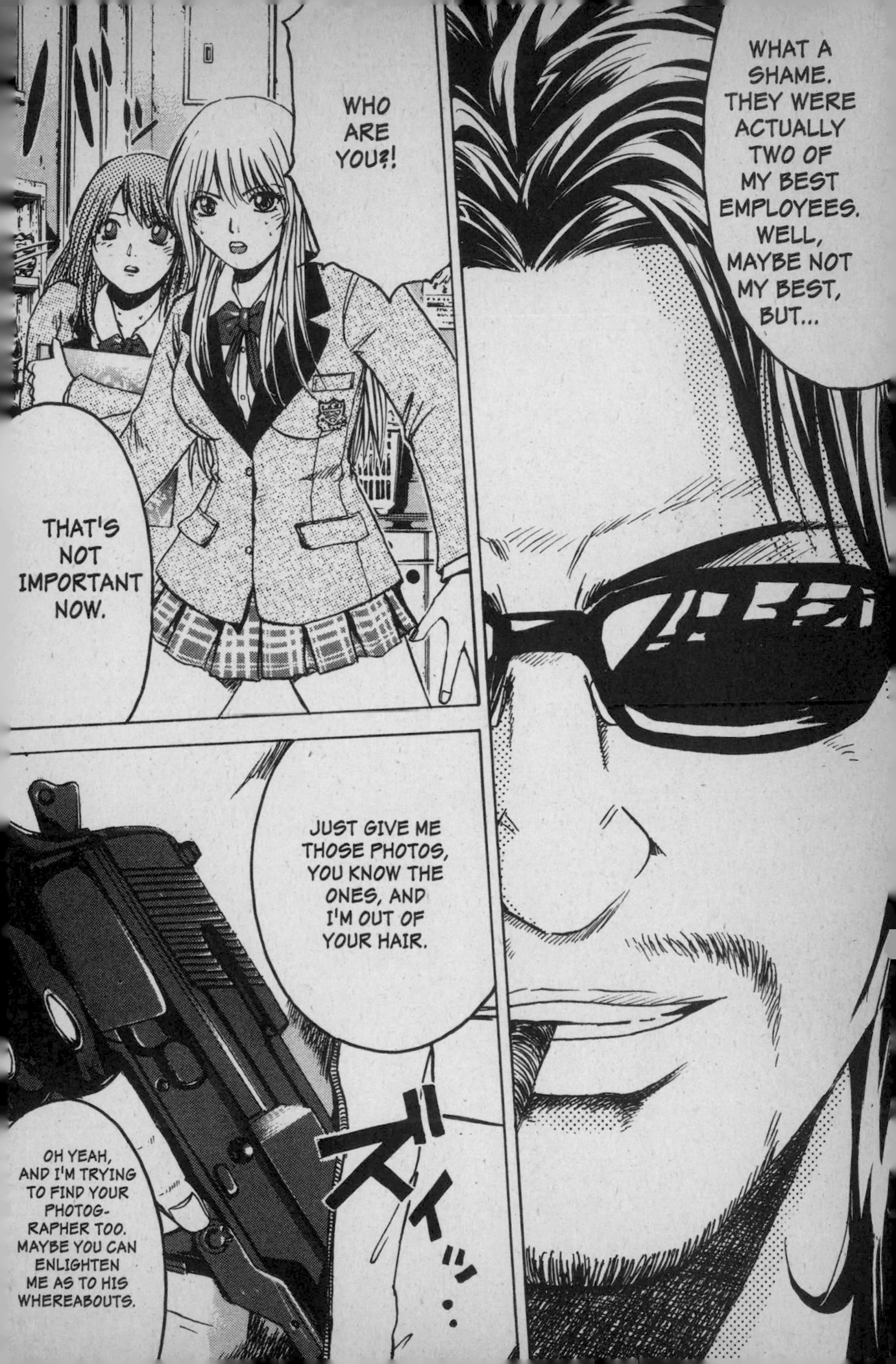
WHAT A SHAME. THEY WERE ACTUALLY TWO OF MY BEST EMPLOYEES. WELL, MAYBE NOT MY BEST, BUT...
WHO ARE YOU?!
THAT'S NOT IMPORTANT NOW.
JUST GIVE ME THOSE PHOTOS, YOU KNOW THE ONES, AND I'M OUT OF YOUR HAIR.
OH YEAH, AND I'M TRYING TO FIND YOUR PHOTOG-RAPHER TOO. MAYBE YOU CAN ENLIGHTEN ME AS TO HIS WHEREABOUTS.

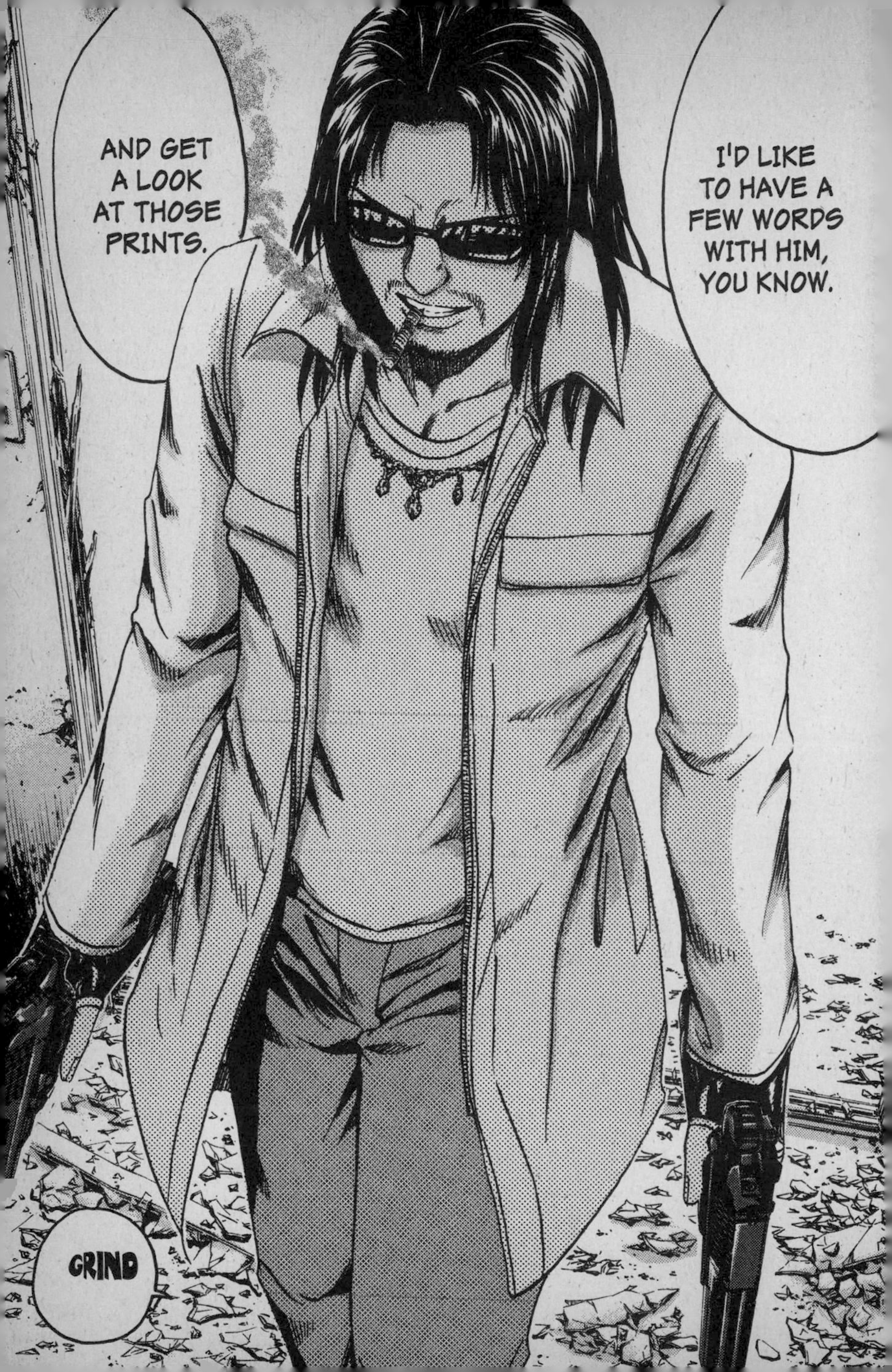
I'D LIKE TO HAVE A FEW WORDS WITH HIM, YOU KNOW.
AND GET A LOOK AT THOSE PRINTS.
GRIND

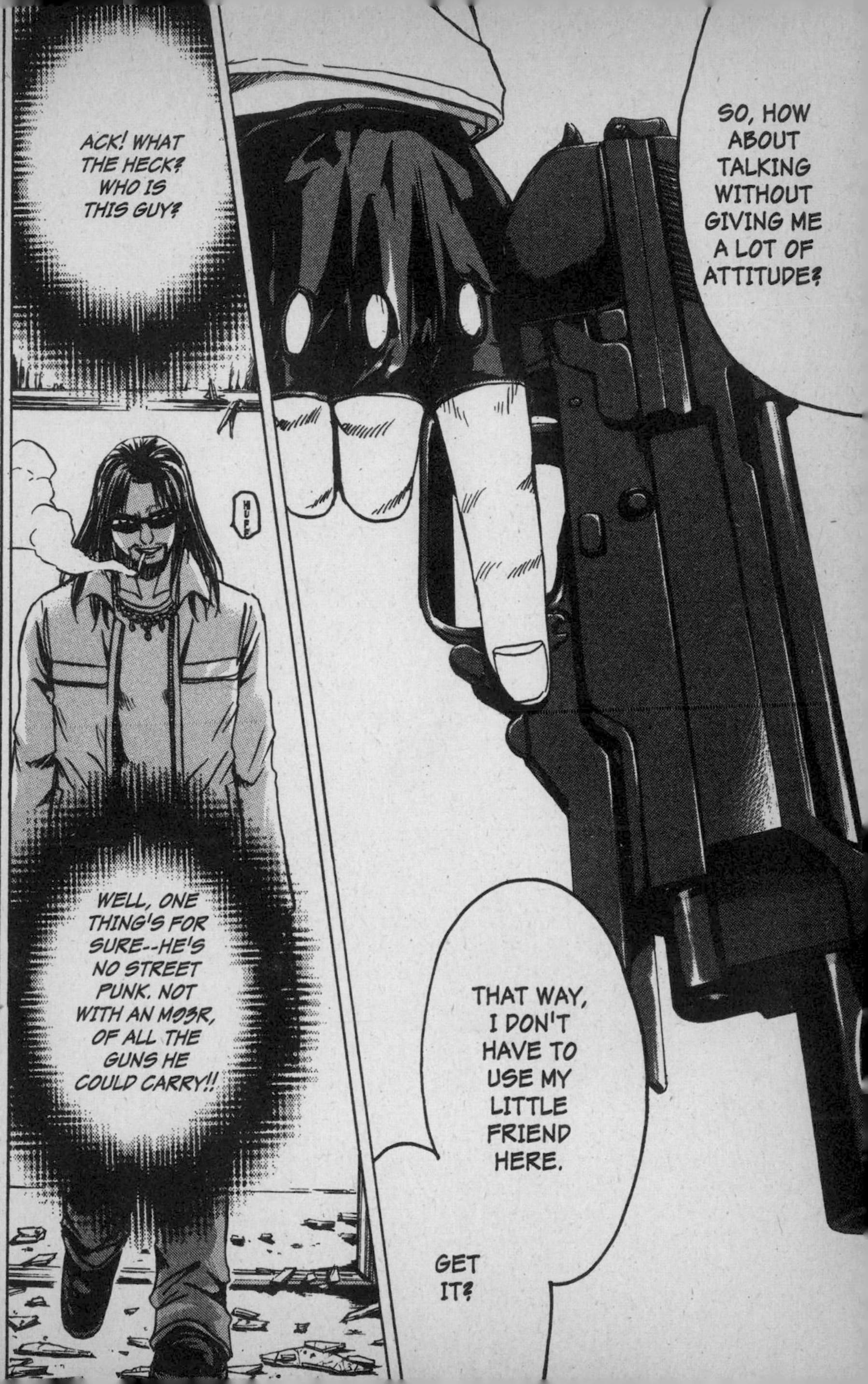
SO, HOW ABOUT TALKING WITHOUT GIVING ME A LOT OF ATTITUDE?
THAT WAY, I DON'T HAVE TO USE MY LITTLE FRIEND HERE.
GET IT?
ACK! WHAT THE HECK? WHO IS THIS GUY?
HUFF
WELL, ONE THING'S FOR SURE--HE'S NO STREET PUNK. NOT WITH AN M93R, OF ALL THE GUNS HE COULD CARRY!!

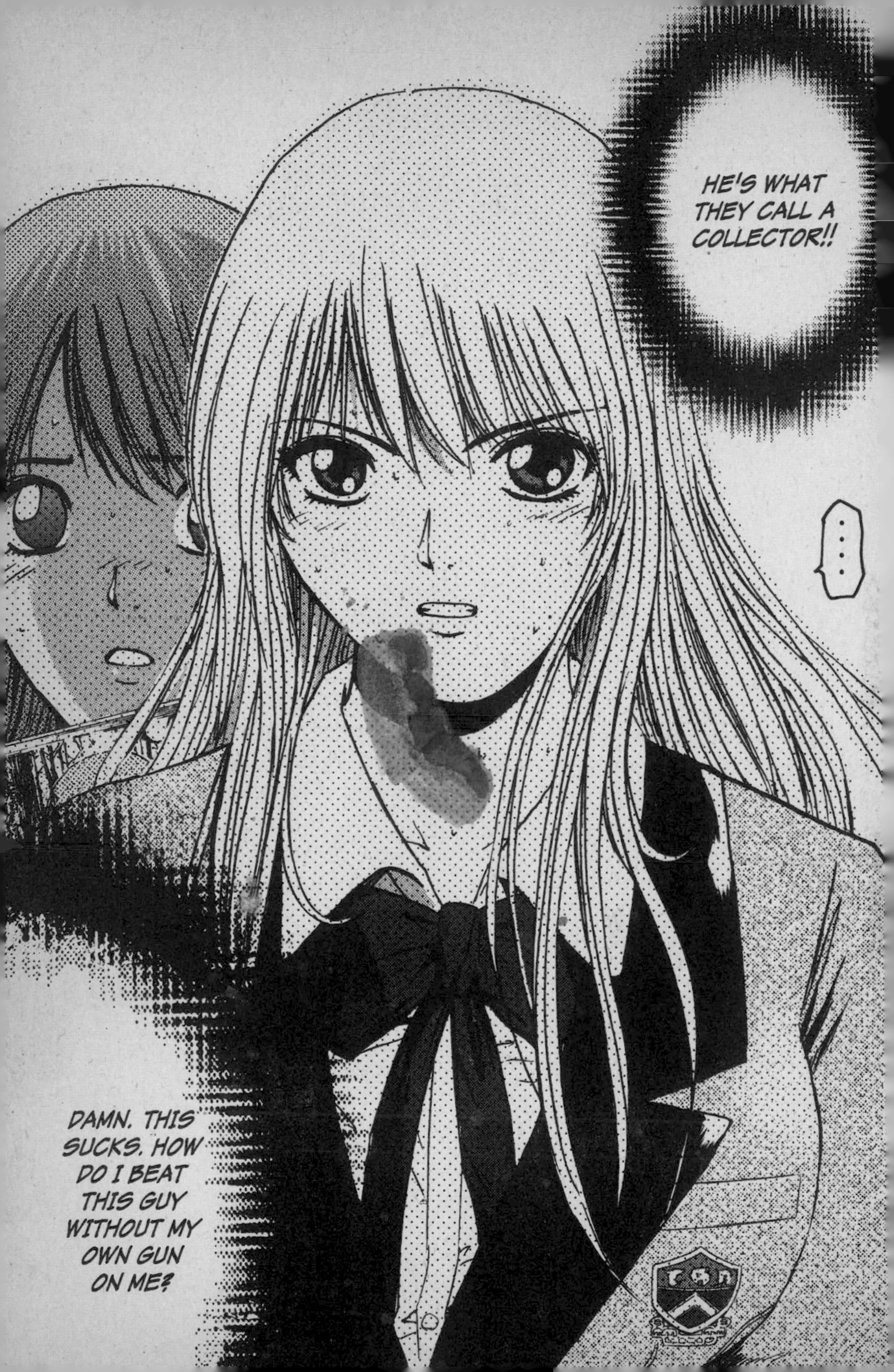
HE'S WHAT THEY CALL A COLLECTOR!!
...
DAMN. THIS SUCKS. HOW DO I BEAT THIS GUY WITHOUT MY OWN GUN ON ME?

Rose Hip Rose

ローズ・ヒップ・ローズ

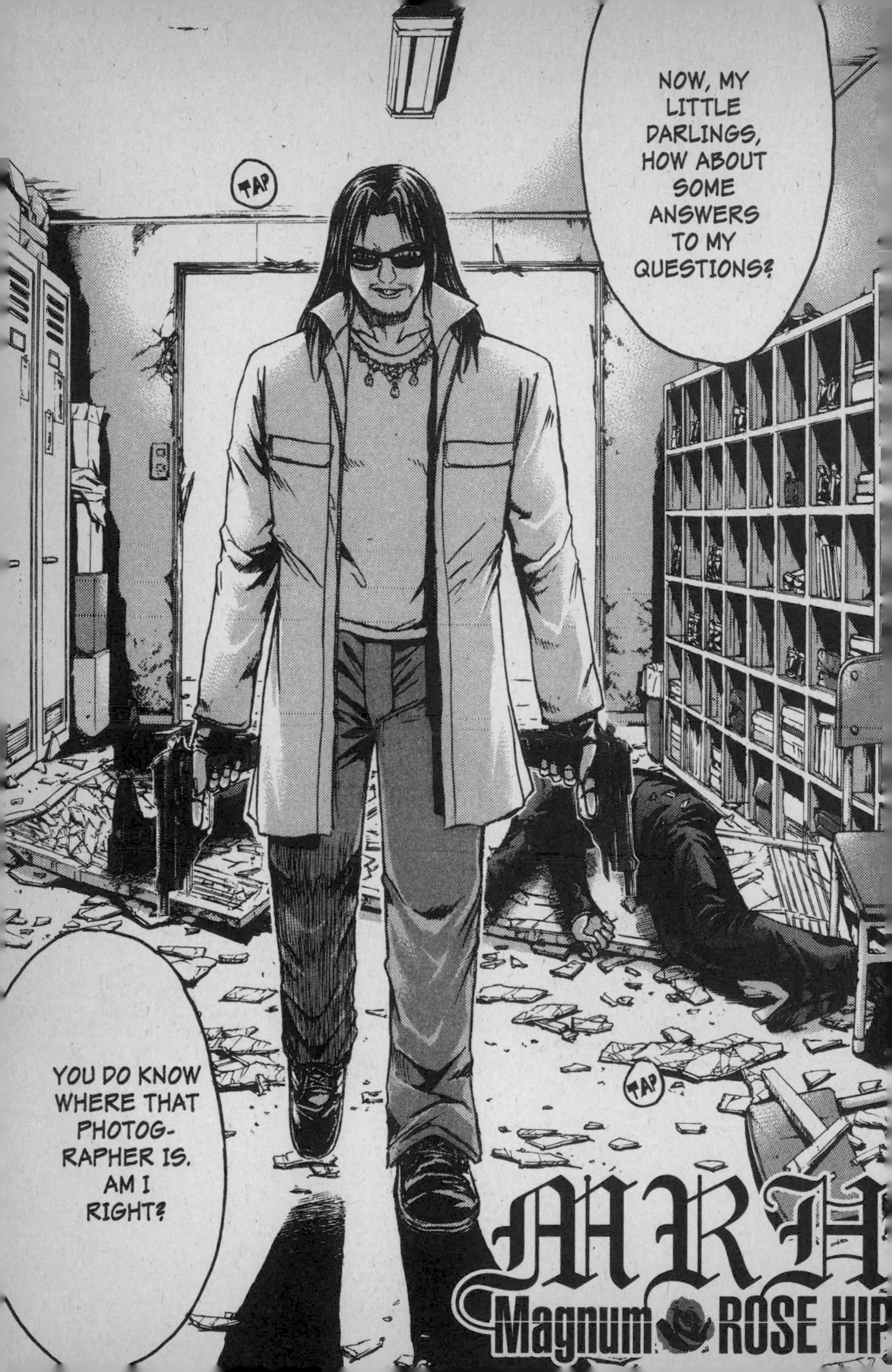
NOW, MY LITTLE DARLINGS, HOW ABOUT SOME ANSWERS TO MY QUESTIONS?
TAP
YOU DO KNOW WHERE THAT PHOTOG-RAPHER IS. AM I RIGHT?
TAP
Magnum ROSE HIP

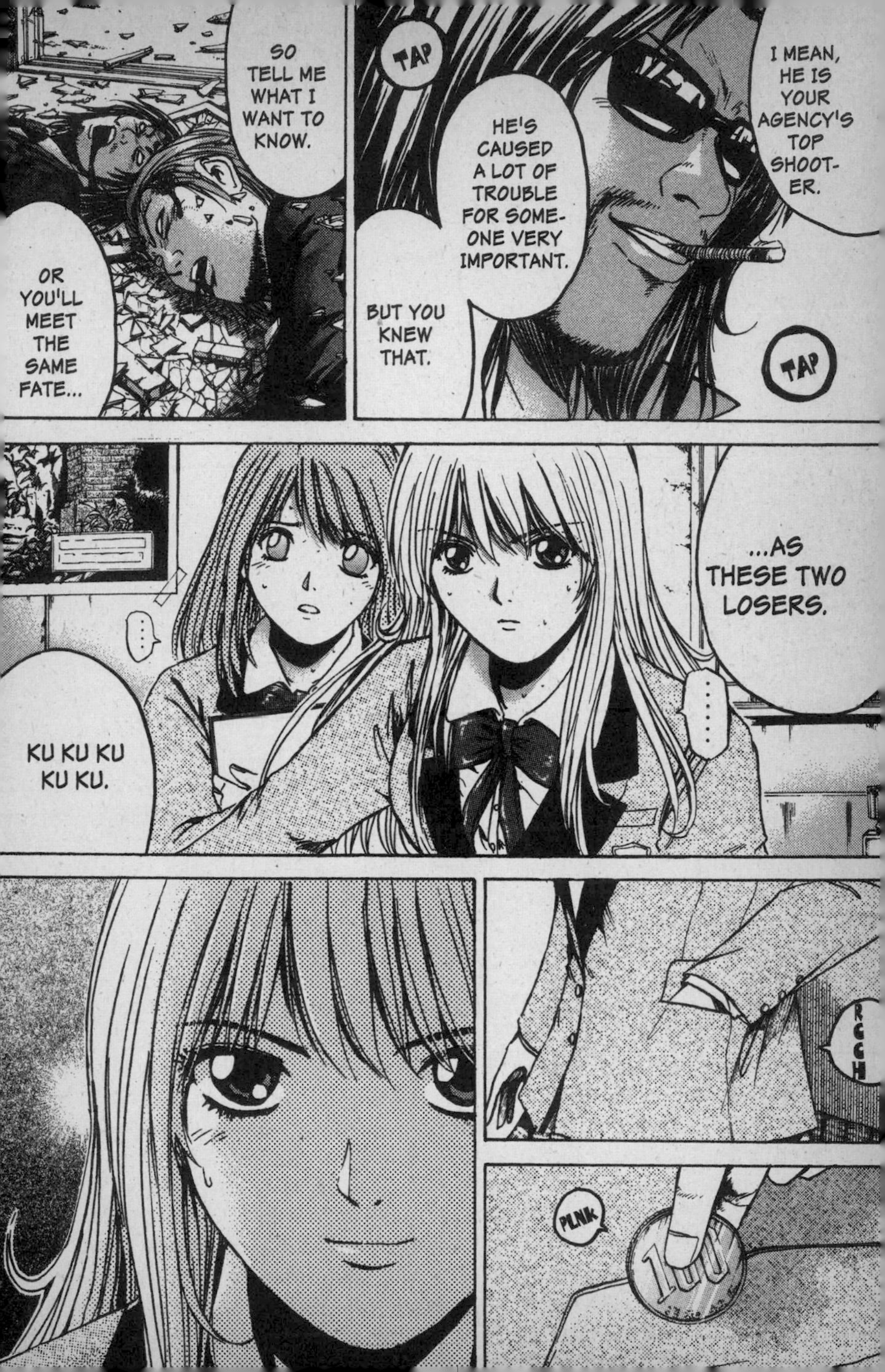
TAP
I MEAN, HE IS YOUR AGENCY'S TOP SHOOT-ER.
HE'S CAUSED A LOT OF TROUBLE FOR SOME-ONE VERY IMPORTANT.
BUT YOU KNEW THAT.
TAP
SO TELL ME WHAT I WANT TO KNOW.
OR YOU'LL MEET THE SAME FATE...
...AS THESE TWO LOSERS.
......
....
KU KU KU KU KU.
RGGH
PLNK

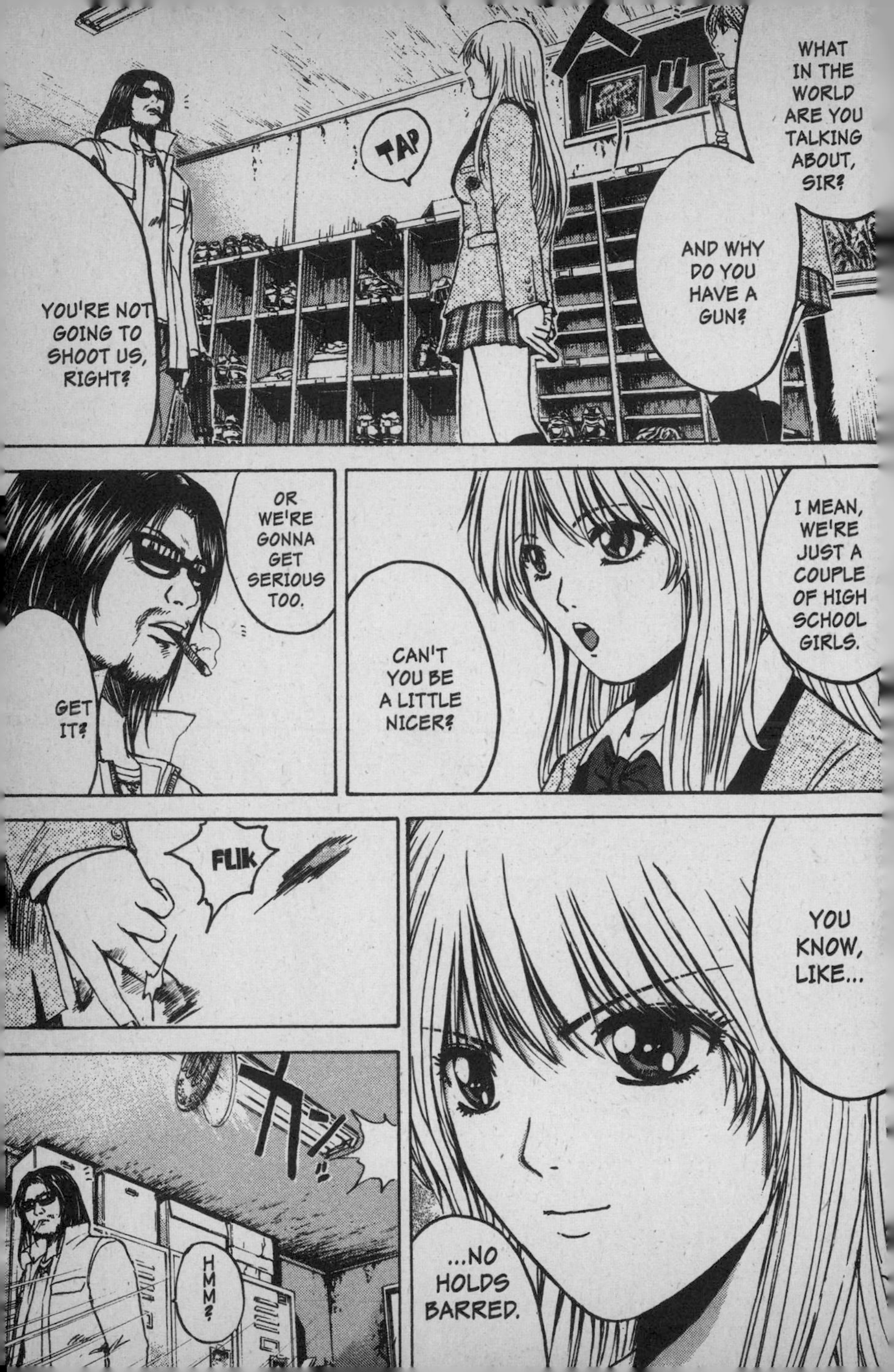
WHAT IN THE WORLD ARE YOU TALKING ABOUT, SIR?
AND WHY DO YOU HAVE A GUN?
TAP
YOU'RE NOT GOING TO SHOOT US, RIGHT?
I MEAN, WE'RE JUST A COUPLE OF HIGH SCHOOL GIRLS.
CAN'T YOU BE A LITTLE NICER?
OR WE'RE GONNA GET SERIOUS TOO.
GET IT?
YOU KNOW, LIKE...
...NO HOLDS BARRED.
FLIK
HMM?

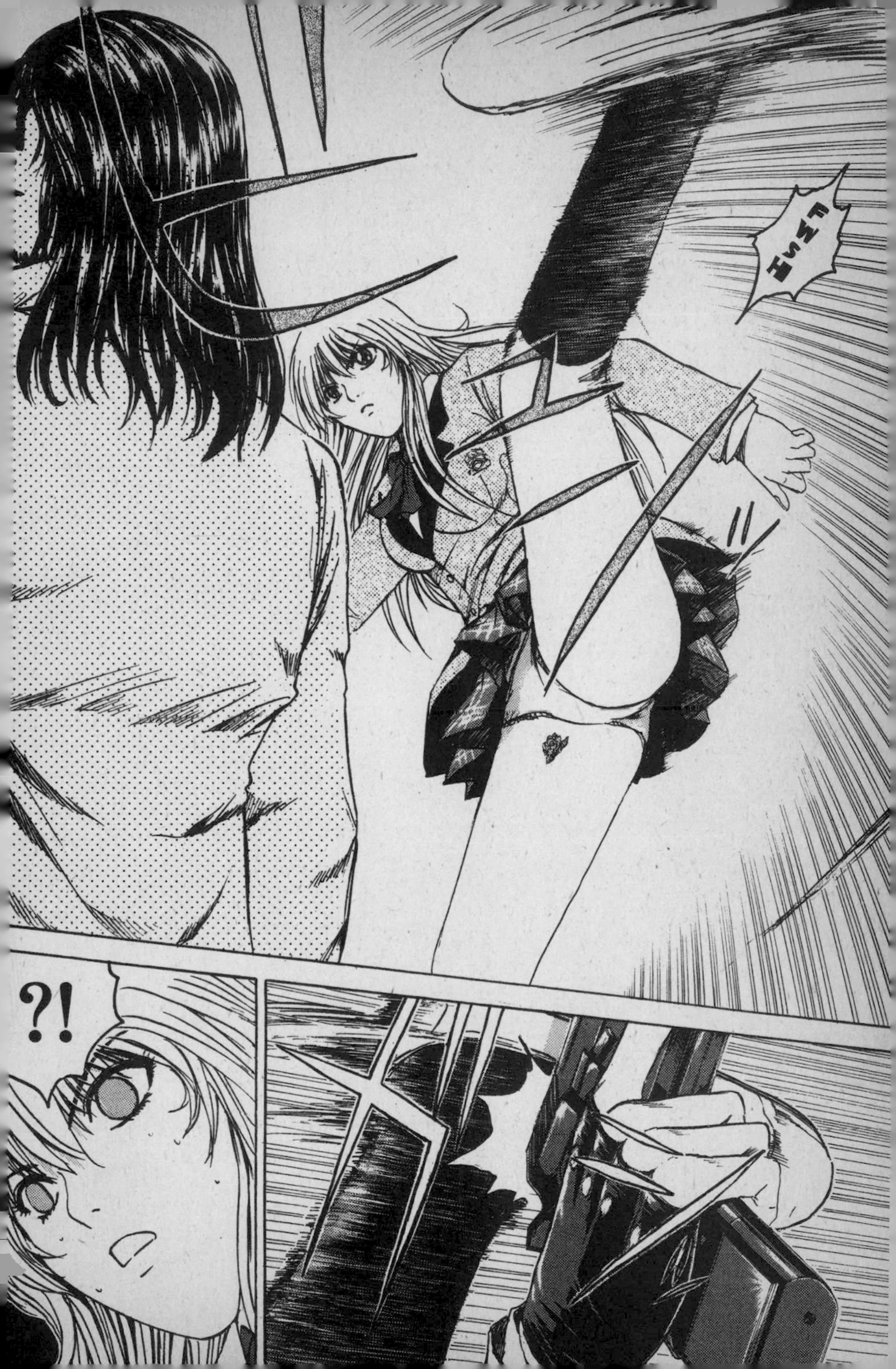
FWSH
?!

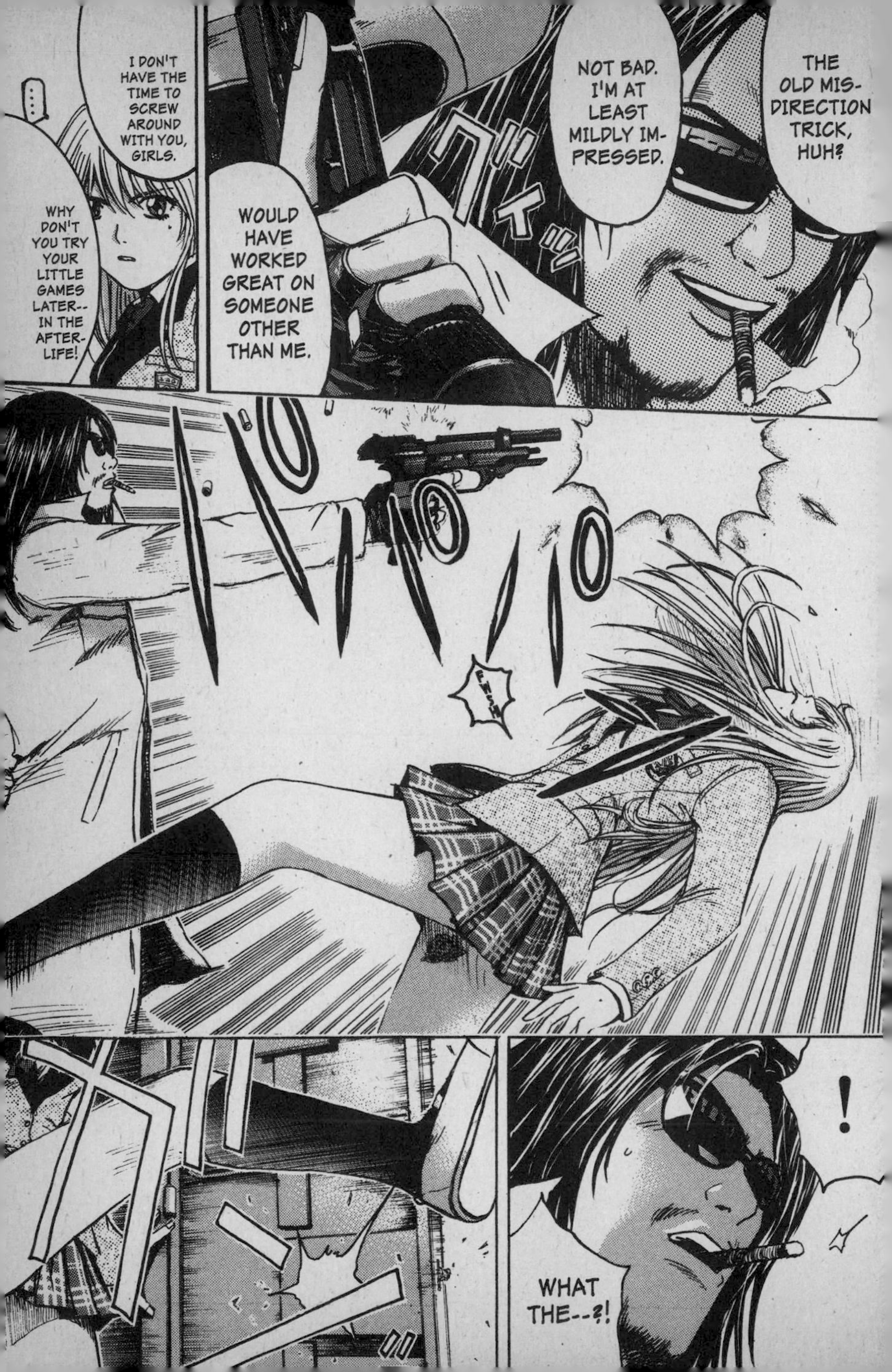
THE OLD MIS-DIRECTION TRICK, HUH?
NOT BAD. I'M AT LEAST MILDLY IM-PRESSED.
WOULD HAVE WORKED GREAT ON SOMEONE OTHER THAN ME.
I DON'T HAVE THE TIME TO SCREW AROUND WITH YOU, GIRLS.
...
WHY DON'T YOU TRY YOUR LITTLE GAMES LATER--IN THE AFTER-LIFE!
FWSH
!
WHAT THE--?!

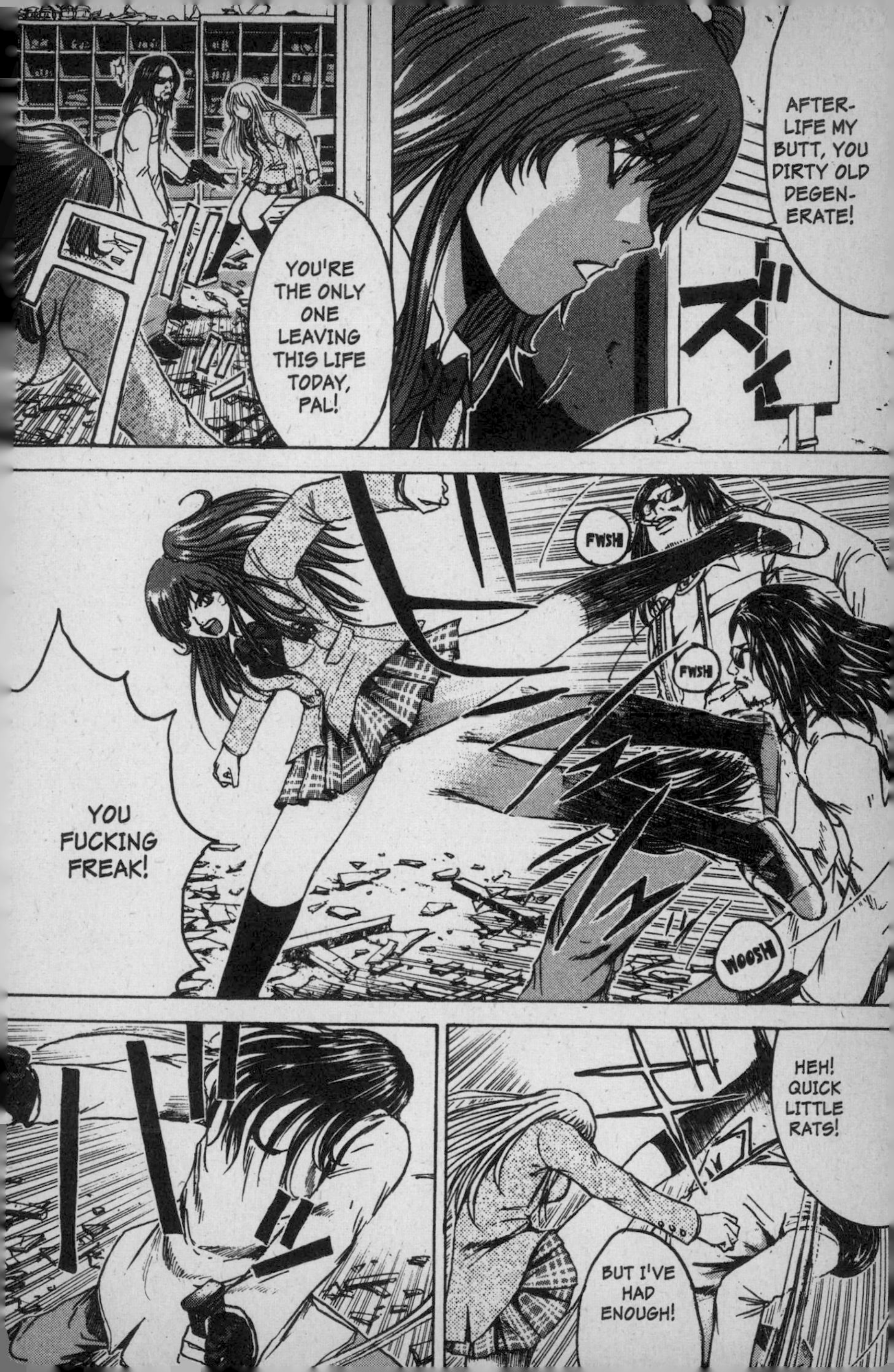
AFTER-LIFE MY BUTT, YOU DIRTY OLD DEGEN-ERATE!
YOU'RE THE ONLY ONE LEAVING THIS LIFE TODAY, PAL!
FWSH
FWSH
WOOSH
YOU FUCKING FREAK!
HEH! QUICK LITTLE RATS!
BUT I'VE HAD ENOUGH!

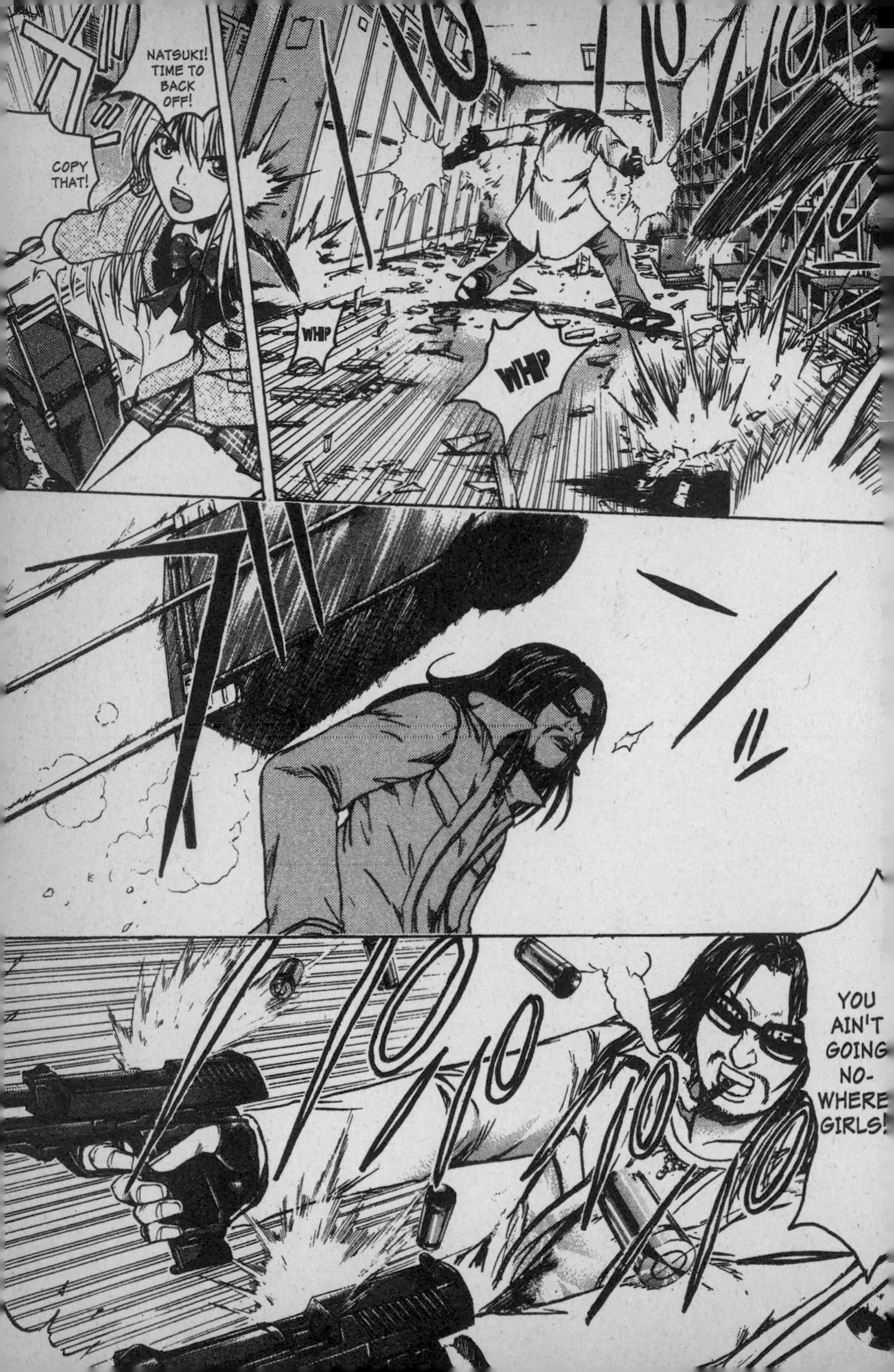
NATSUKI! TIME TO BACK OFF!
COPY THAT!
WHP
WHP
YOU AIN'T GOING NO-WHERE GIRLS!

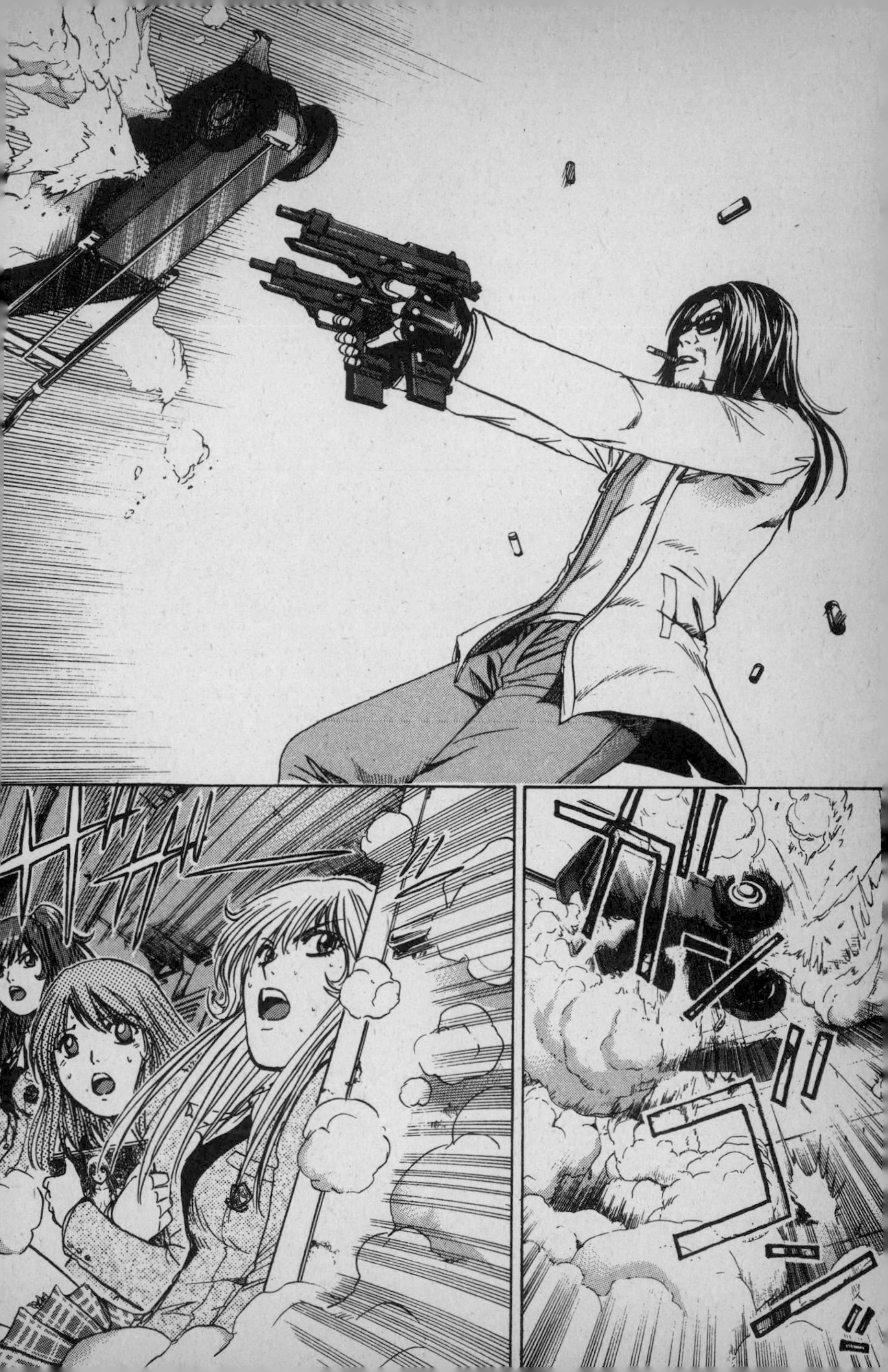

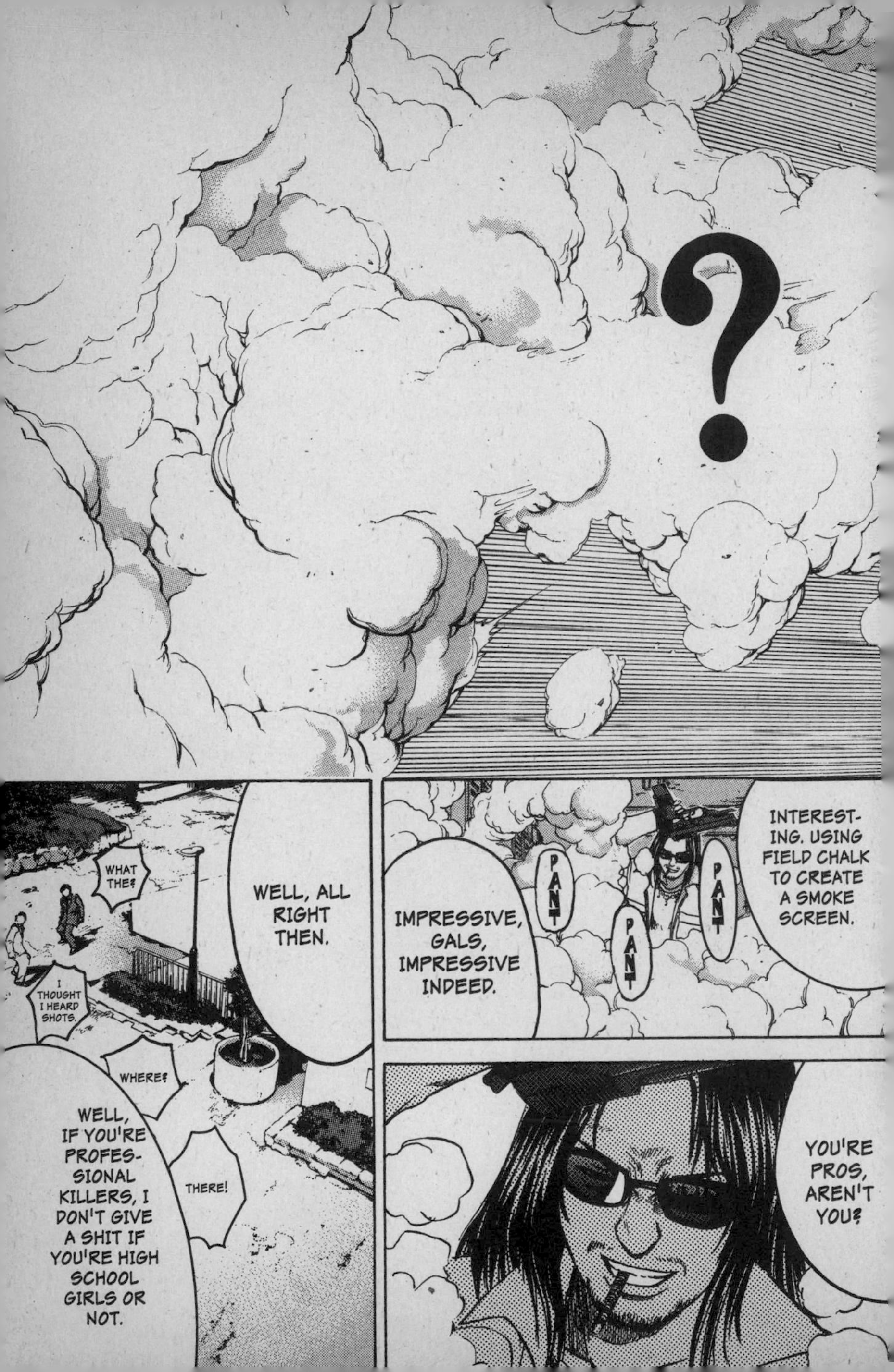
?
INTEREST-ING. USING FIELD CHALK TO CREATE A SMOKE SCREEN.
PANT
PANT
PANT
IMPRESSIVE, GALS, IMPRESSIVE INDEED.
YOU'RE PROS, AREN'T YOU?
WELL, ALL RIGHT THEN.
WHAT THE?
I THOUGHT I HEARD SHOTS.
WHERE?
THERE!
WELL, IF YOU'RE PROFES-SIONAL KILLERS, I DON'T GIVE A SHIT IF YOU'RE HIGH SCHOOL GIRLS OR NOT.

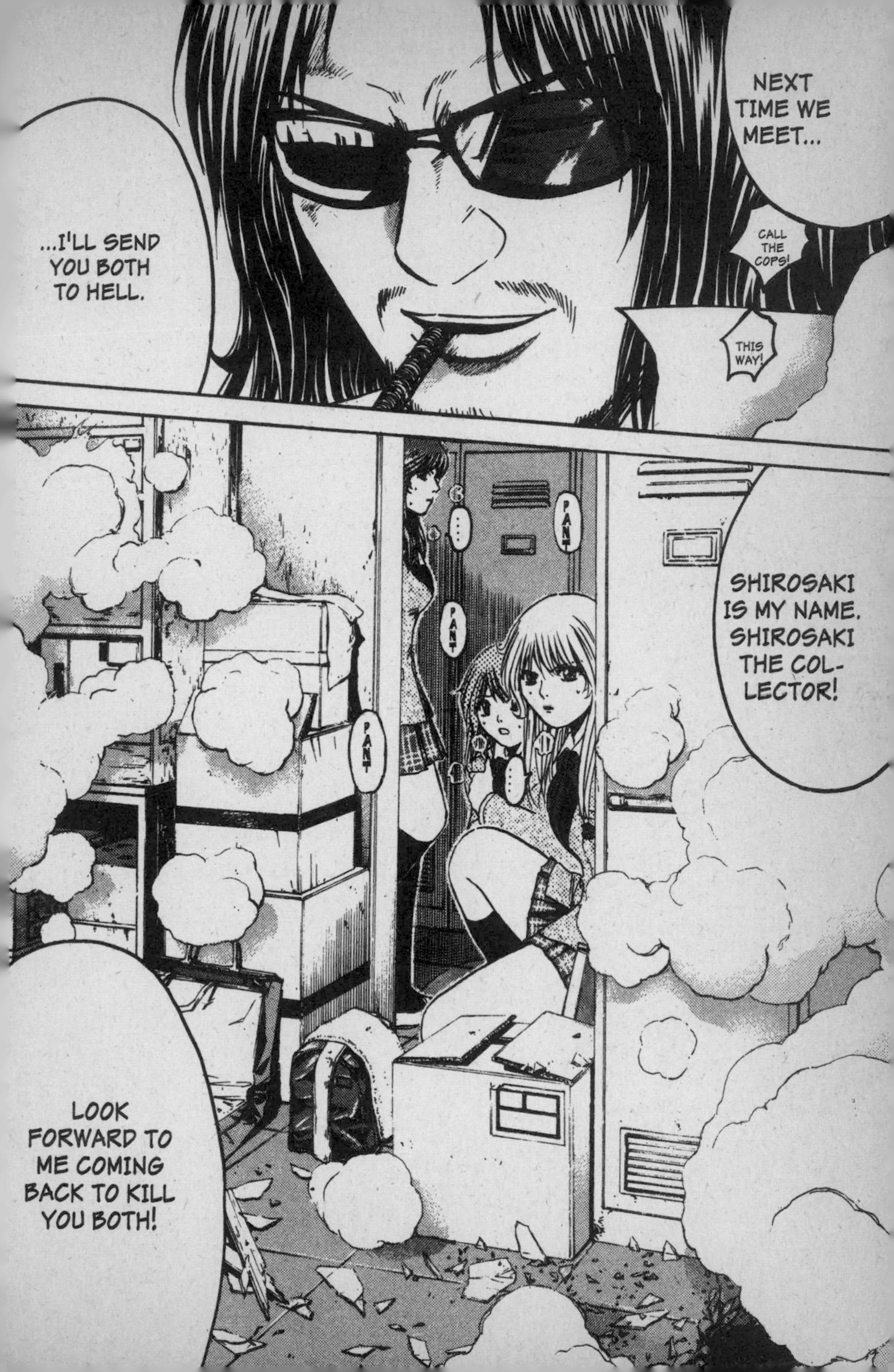
NEXT TIME WE MEET...
CALL THE COPS!
THIS WAY!
...I'LL SEND YOU BOTH TO HELL.
SHIROSAKI IS MY NAME. SHIROSAKI THE COL-LECTOR!
PANT
...
PANT
PANT
...
LOOK FORWARD TO ME COMING BACK TO KILL YOU BOTH!

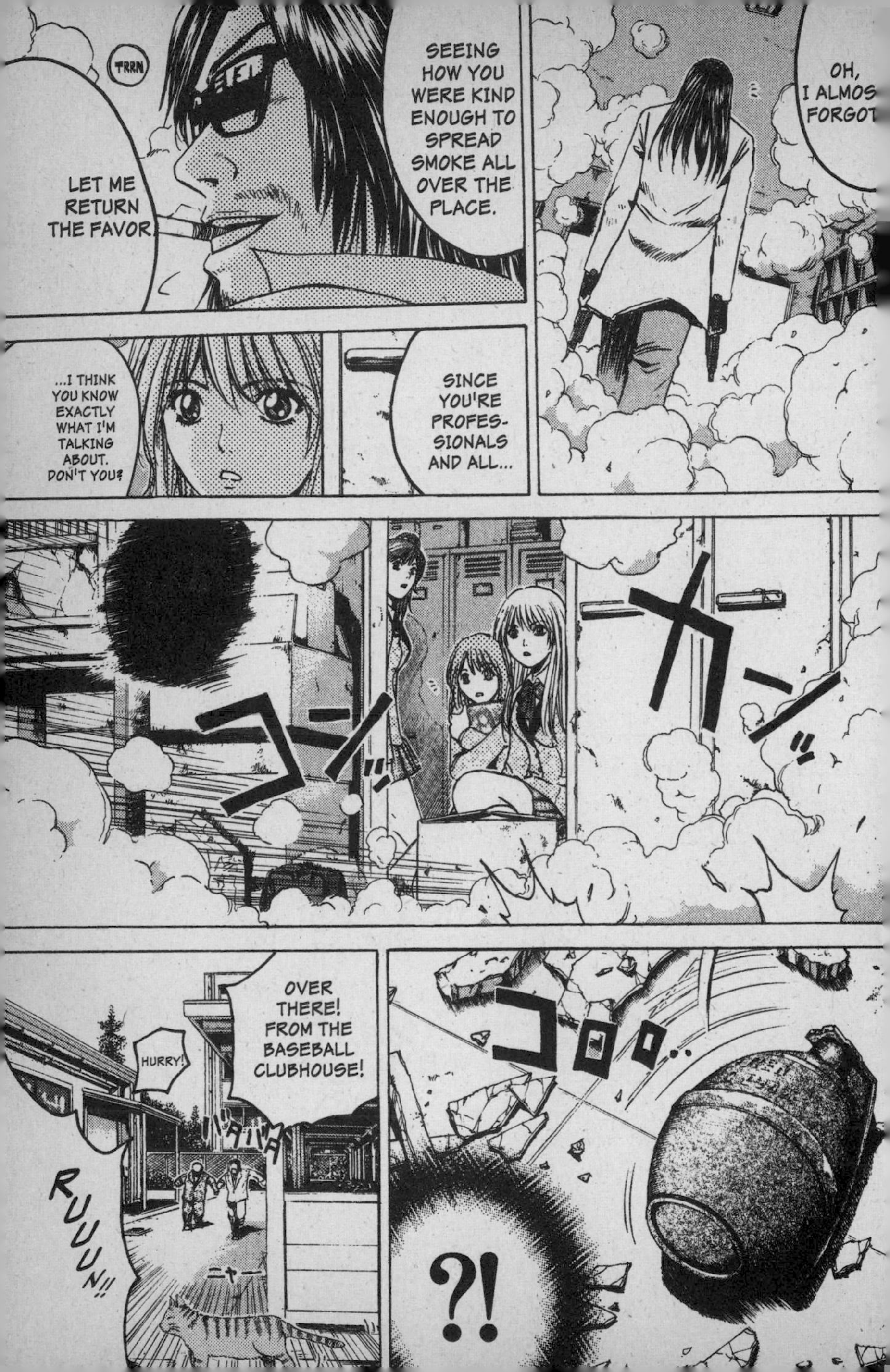
OH, I ALMOS FORGOT
SEEING HOW YOU WERE KIND ENOUGH TO SPREAD SMOKE ALL OVER THE PLACE.
TRRN
LET ME RETURN THE FAVOR.
SINCE YOU'RE PROFES-SIONALS AND ALL...
...I THINK YOU KNOW EXACTLY WHAT I'M TALKING ABOUT. DON'T YOU?
?!
OVER THERE! FROM THE BASEBALL CLUBHOUSE!
HURRY!
RUUUN!!

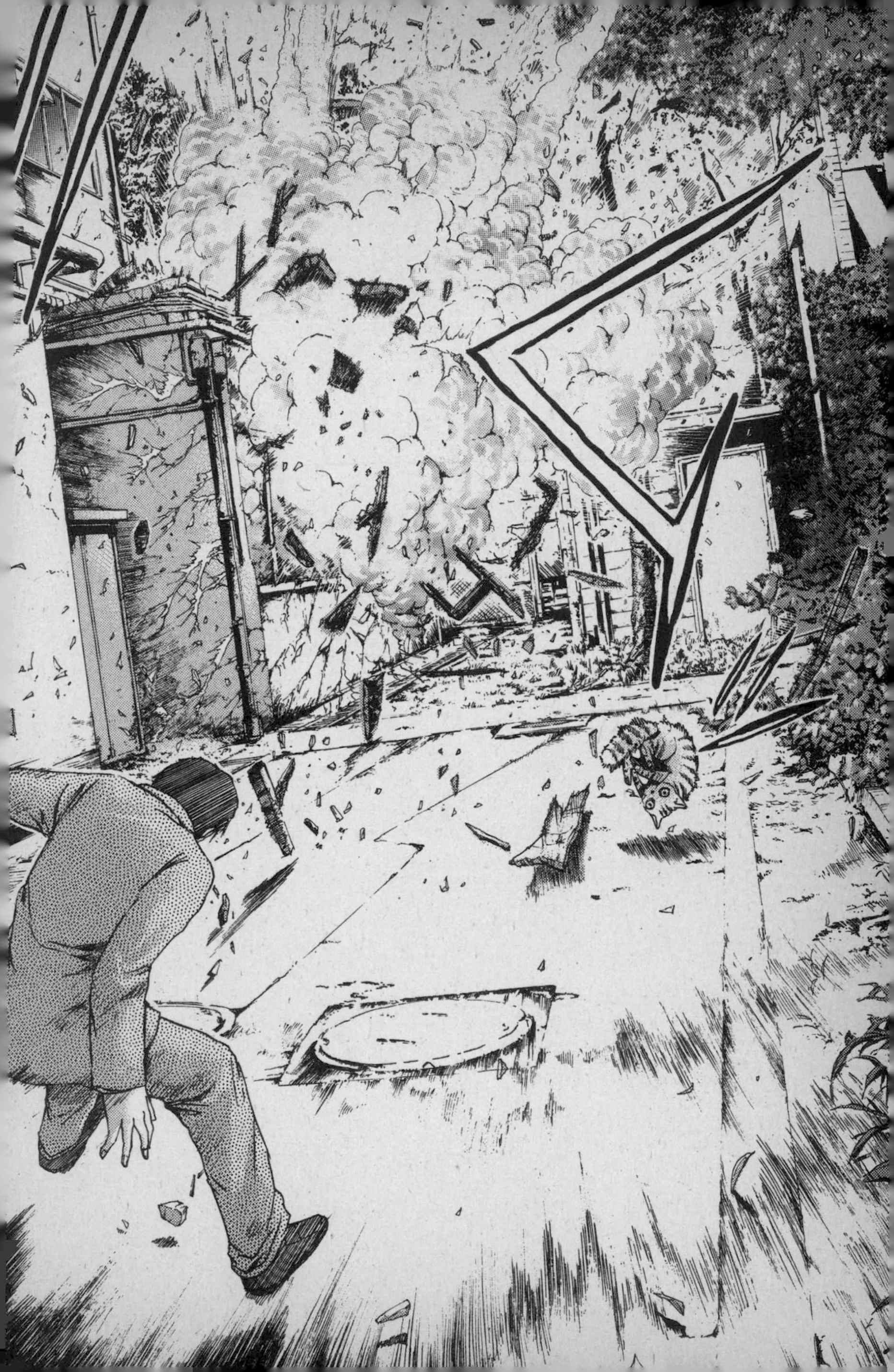

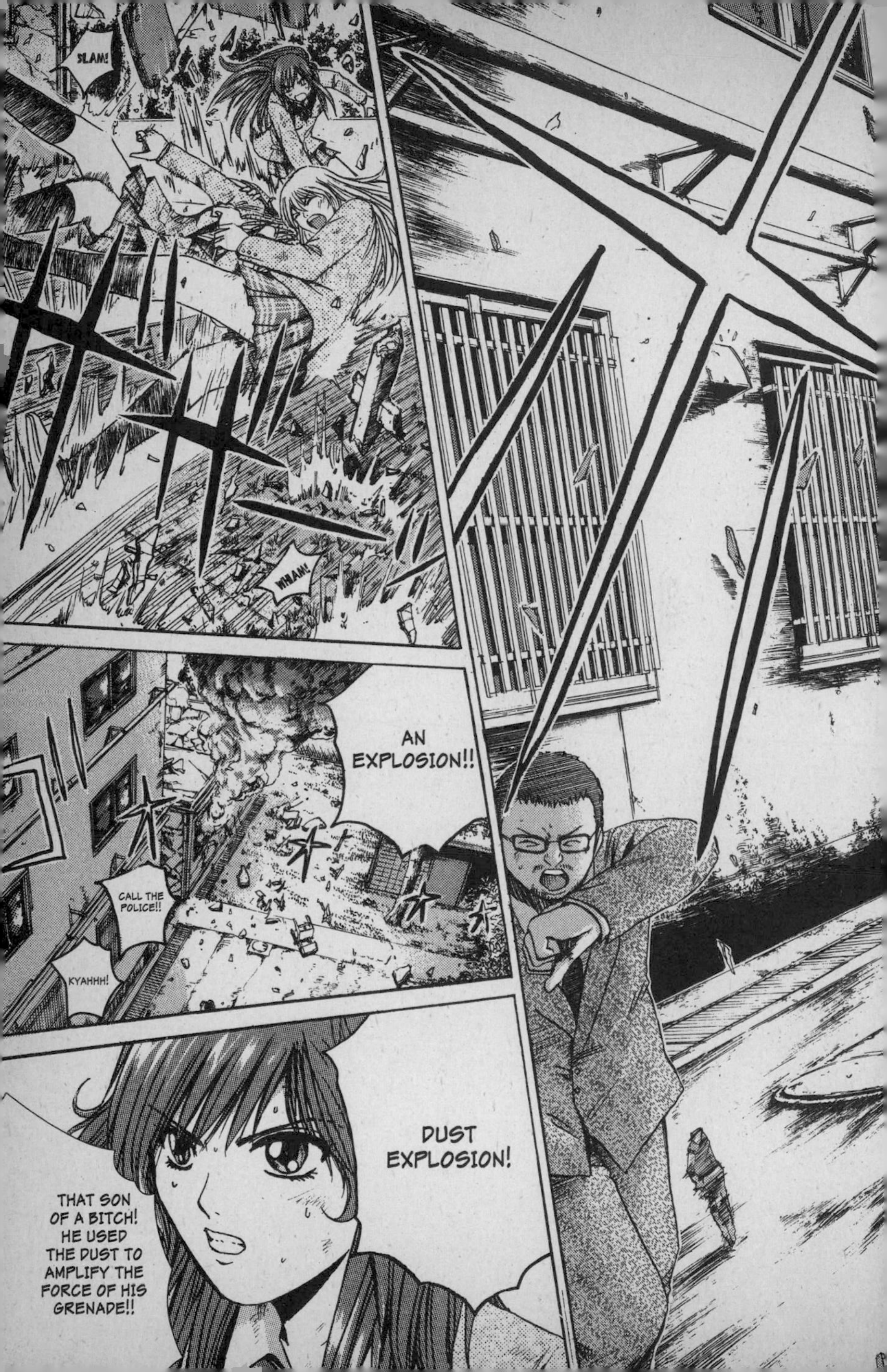
SLAM!
WHAM!
AN EXPLOSION!!
CALL THE POLICE!!
KYAHHH!
DUST EXPLOSION!
THAT SON OF A BITCH! HE USED THE DUST TO AMPLIFY THE FORCE OF HIS GRENADE!!

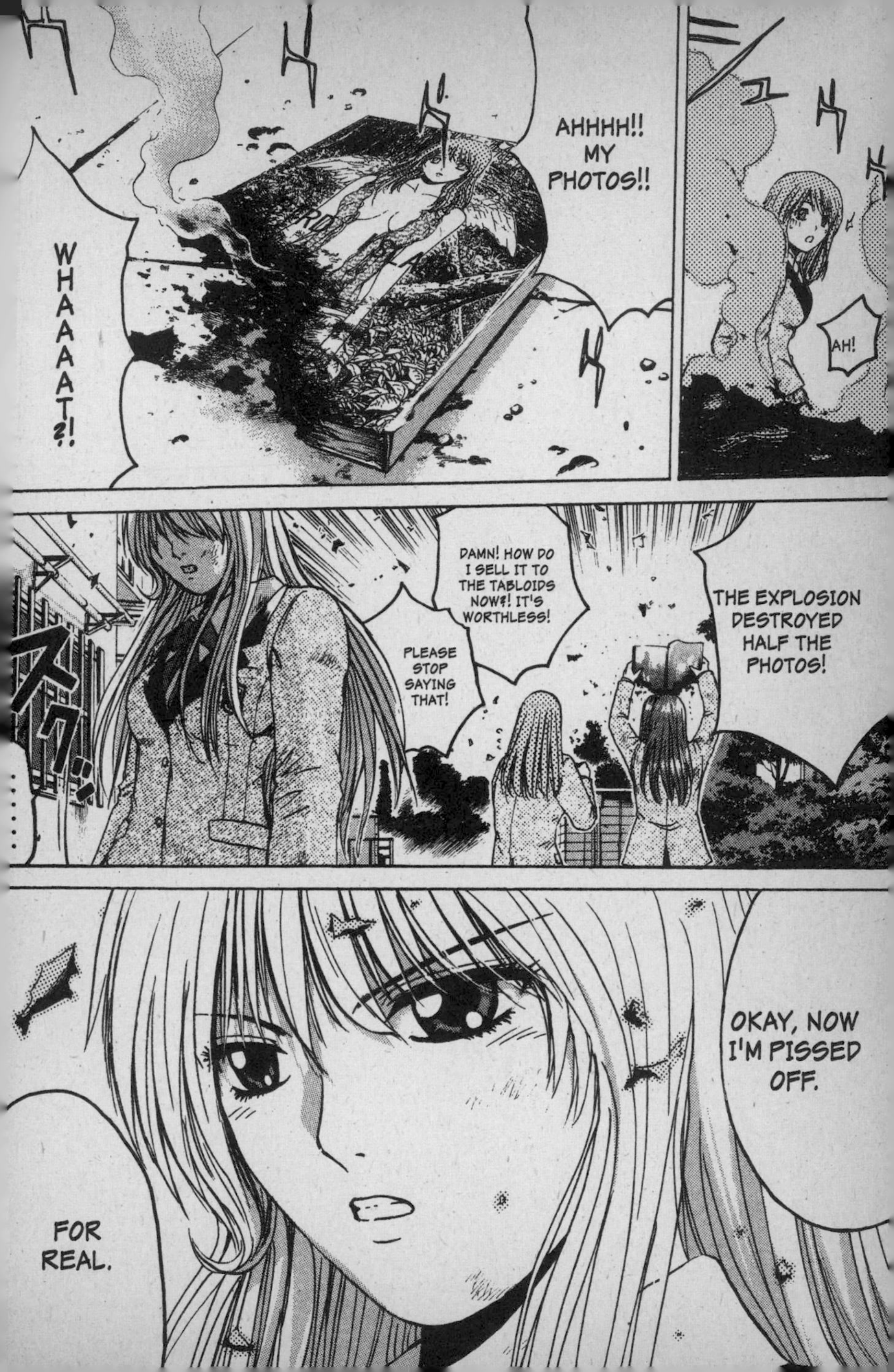
AH!
AHHHH!! MY PHOTOS!!
WHAAAAAT?!
THE EXPLOSION DESTROYED HALF THE PHOTOS!
DAMN! HOW DO I SELL IT TO THE TABLOIDS NOW?! IT'S WORTHLESS!
PLEASE STOP SAYING THAT!
OKAY, NOW I'M PISSED OFF.
FOR REAL.

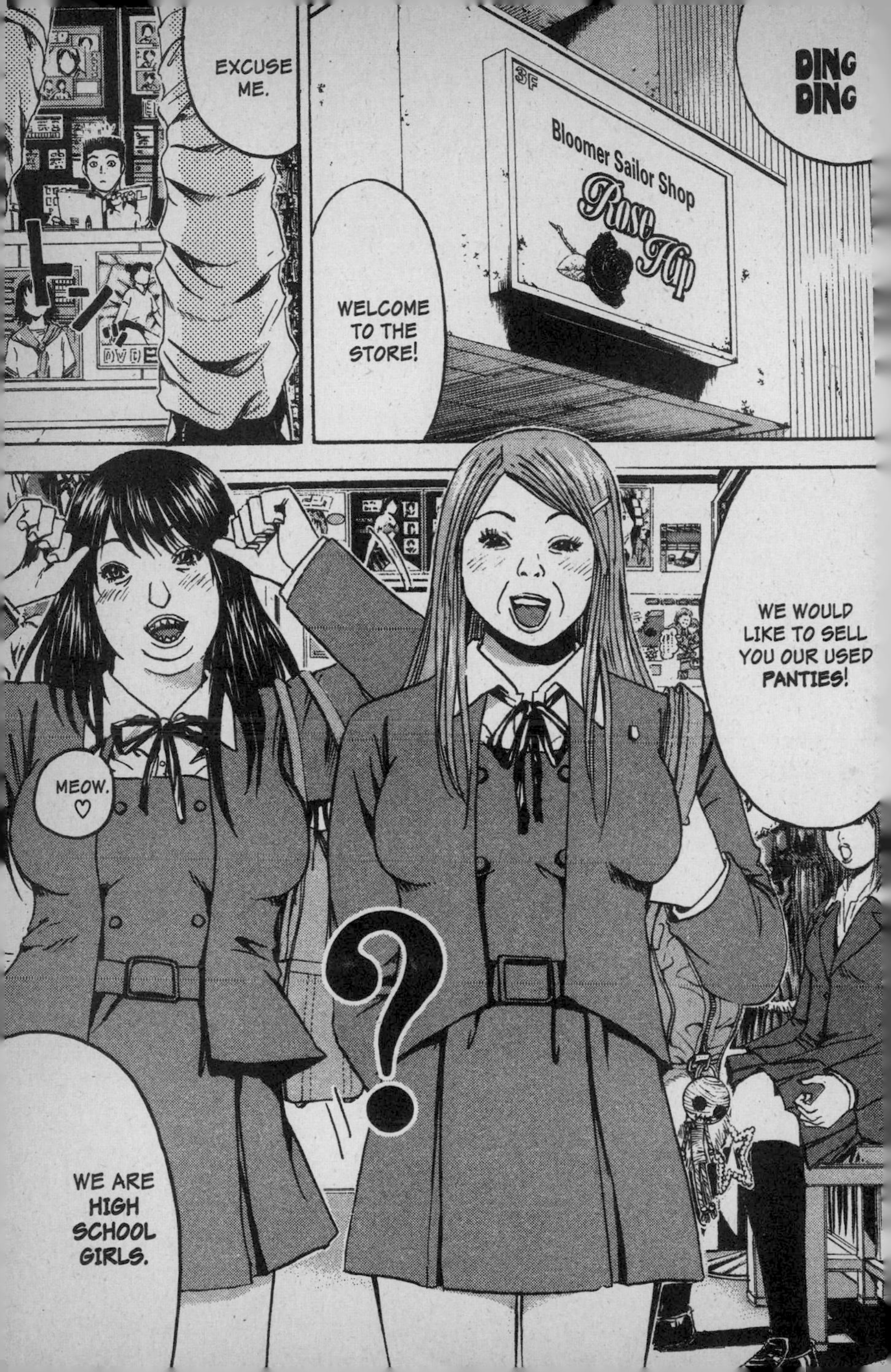
DING DING
3F
Bloomer Sailor Shop
Rose Hip
WELCOME TO THE STORE!
EXCUSE ME.
WE WOULD LIKE TO SELL YOU OUR USED PANTIES!
MEOW. ♡
?
WE ARE HIGH SCHOOL GIRLS.

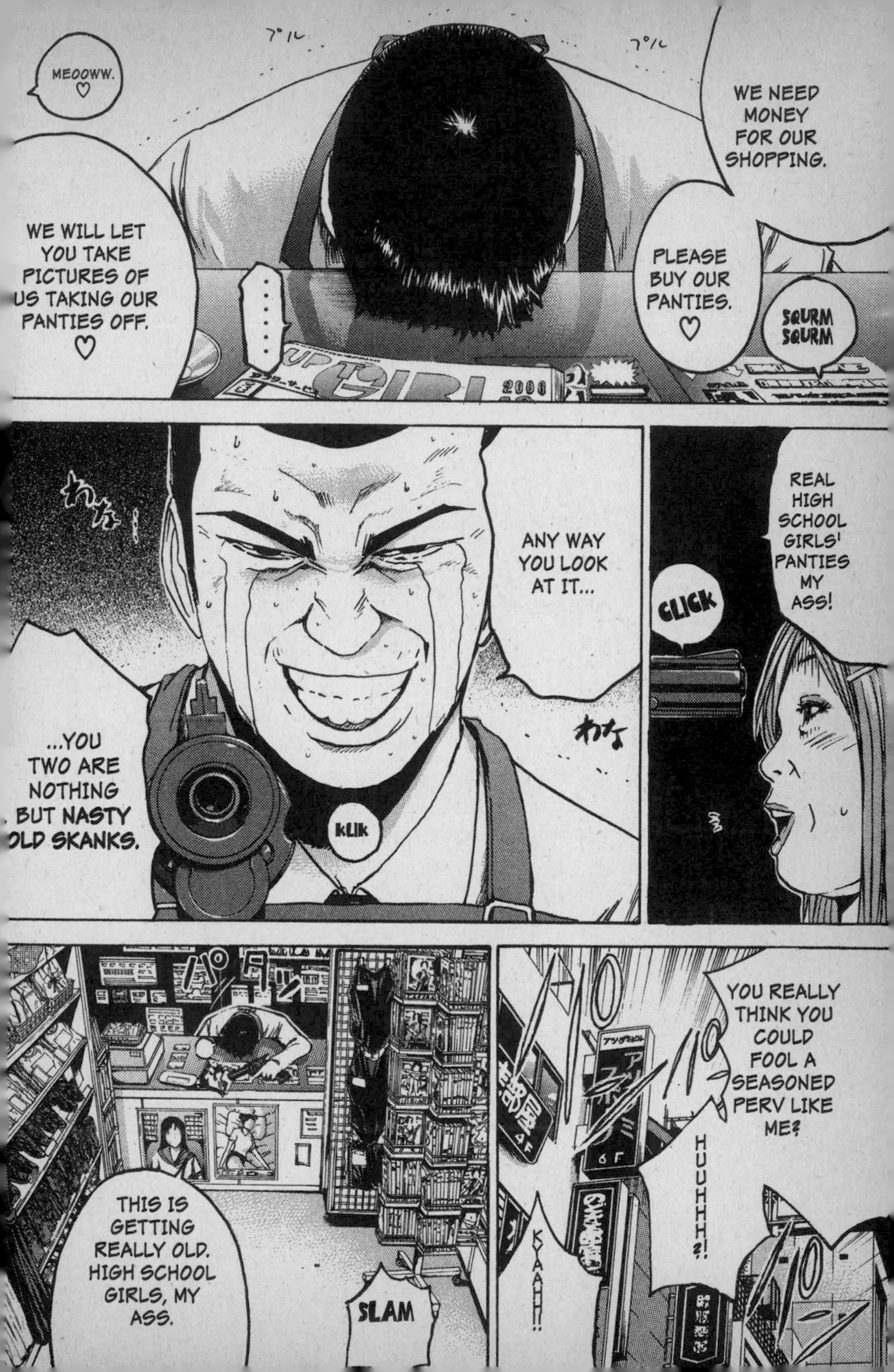
WE NEED MONEY FOR OUR SHOPPING.
PLEASE BUY OUR PANTIES. ♡
SQURM SQURM
MEOOWW. ♡
WE WILL LET YOU TAKE PICTURES OF US TAKING OUR PANTIES OFF. ♡
......
REAL HIGH SCHOOL GIRLS' PANTIES MY ASS!
CLICK
ANY WAY YOU LOOK AT IT...
...YOU TWO ARE NOTHING BUT NASTY OLD SKANKS.
KLIK
YOU REALLY THINK YOU COULD FOOL A SEASONED PERV LIKE ME?
HUUHHH?!
KYAAHH!!
THIS IS GETTING REALLY OLD. HIGH SCHOOL GIRLS, MY ASS.
SLAM

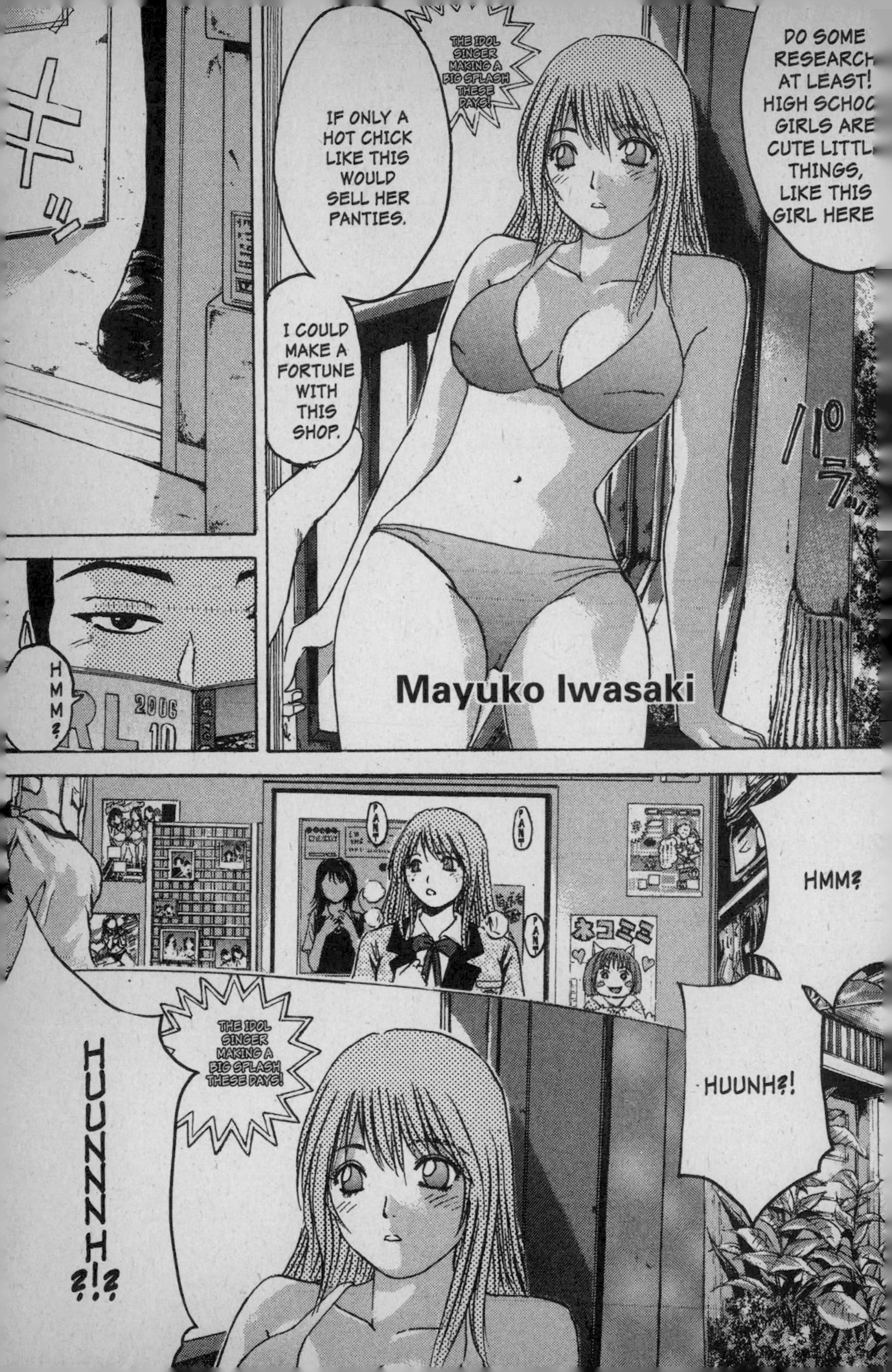
DO SOME RESEARCH AT LEAST! HIGH SCHOO GIRLS ARE CUTE LITTL THINGS, LIKE THIS GIRL HERE
THE IDOL SINGER MAKING A BIG SPLASH THESE DAYS!
IF ONLY A HOT CHICK LIKE THIS WOULD SELL HER PANTIES.
I COULD MAKE A FORTUNE WITH THIS SHOP.
Mayuko Iwasaki
HMM?
HMM?
HUUNH?!
PANT
PANT
PANT
THE IDOL SINGER MAKING A BIG SPLASH THESE DAYS!
HUUNNNH?!?

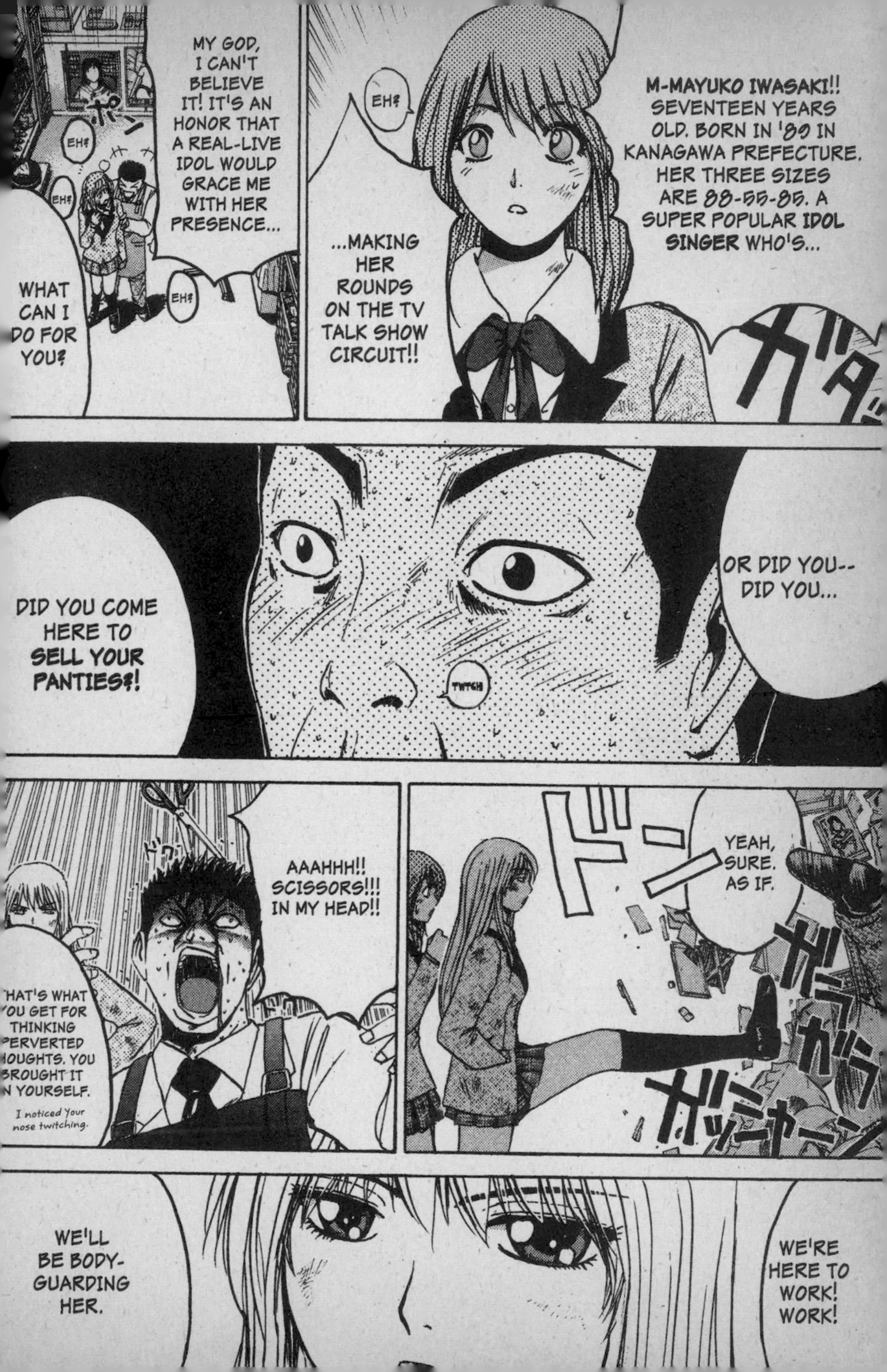
M-MAYUKO IWASAKI!! SEVENTEEN YEARS OLD. BORN IN '89 IN KANAGAWA PREFECTURE. HER THREE SIZES ARE 88-55-85. A SUPER POPULAR IDOL SINGER WHO'S...
EH?
...MAKING HER ROUNDS ON THE TV TALK SHOW CIRCUIT!!
MY GOD, I CAN'T BELIEVE IT! IT'S AN HONOR THAT A REAL-LIVE IDOL WOULD GRACE ME WITH HER PRESENCE...
EH?
EH?
EH?
WHAT CAN I DO FOR YOU?
OR DID YOU-- DID YOU...
TWTCH
DID YOU COME HERE TO SELL YOUR PANTIES?!
ドーン
YEAH, SURE. AS IF.
ガラガラ
ガッシャーン
AAAHHH!! SCISSORS!!! IN MY HEAD!!
THAT'S WHAT YOU GET FOR THINKING PERVERTED THOUGHTS. YOU BROUGHT IT ON YOURSELF.
I noticed your nose twitching.
WE'RE HERE TO WORK! WORK!
WE'LL BE BODY-GUARDING HER.

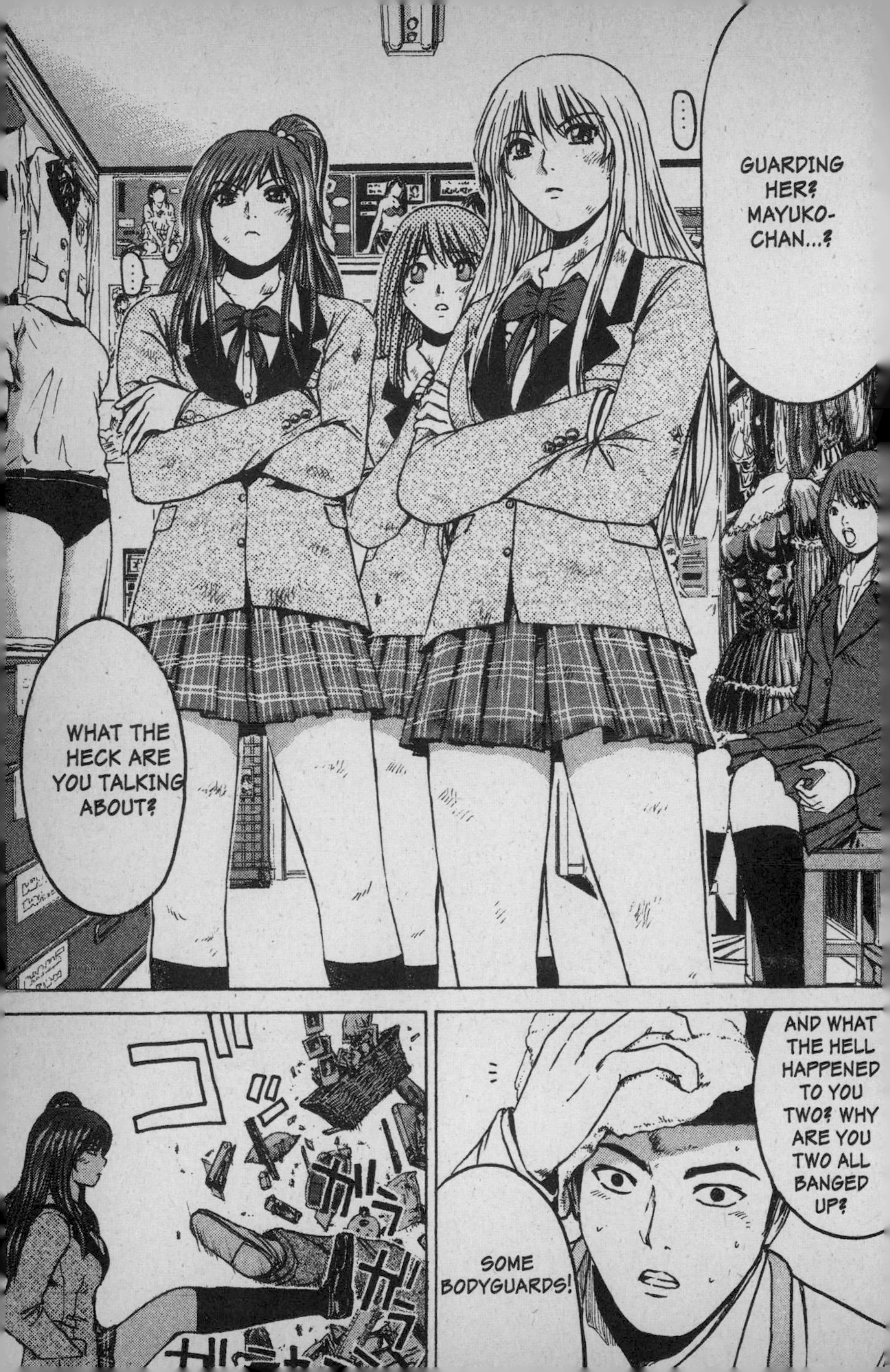
....
GUARDING HER? MAYUKO-CHAN...?
...
WHAT THE HECK ARE YOU TALKING ABOUT?
AND WHAT THE HELL HAPPENED TO YOU TWO? WHY ARE YOU TWO ALL BANGED UP?
SOME BODYGUARDS!

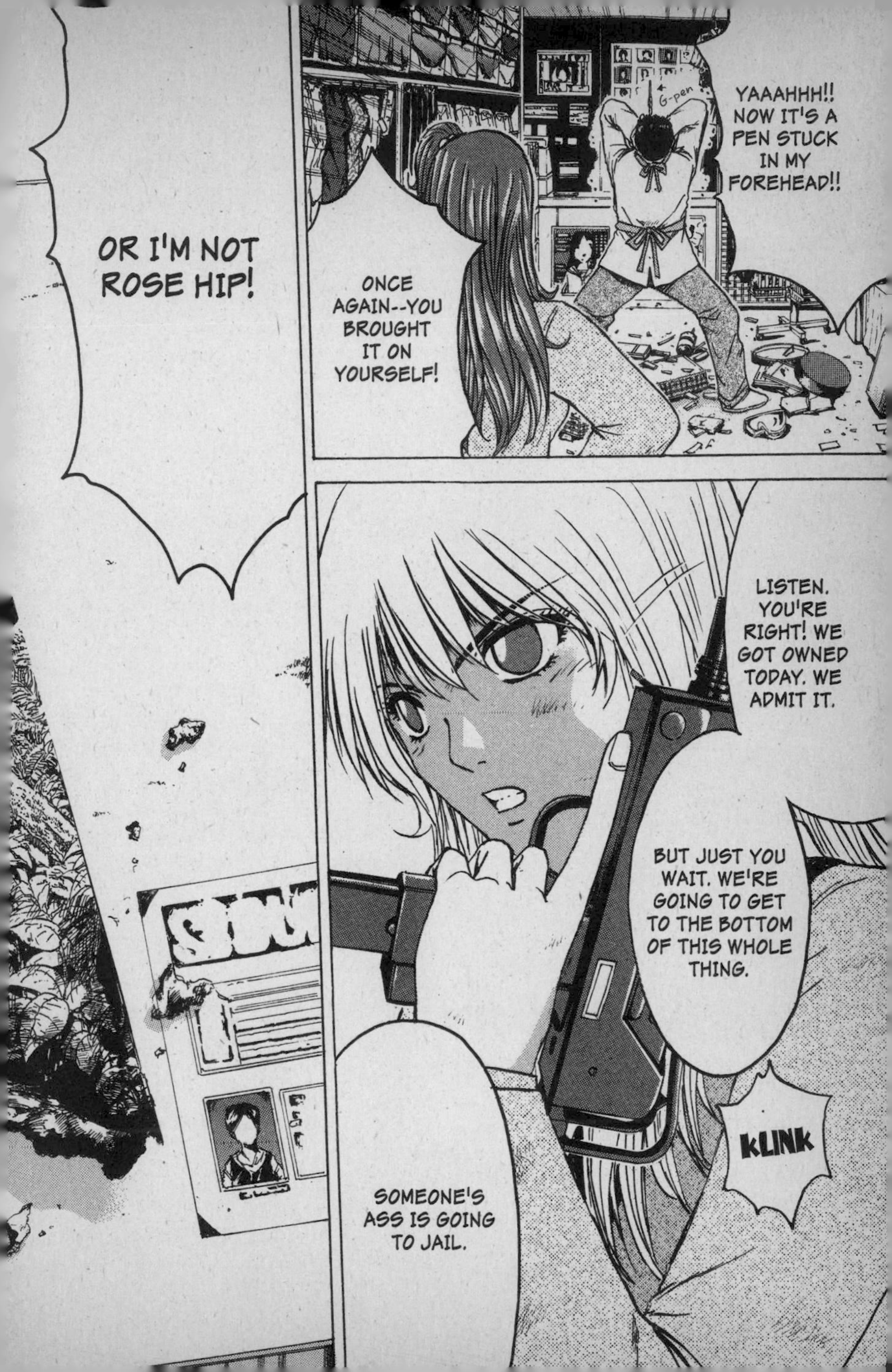
G-pen
YAAAHHH!! NOW IT'S A PEN STUCK IN MY FOREHEAD!!
ONCE AGAIN--YOU BROUGHT IT ON YOURSELF!
LISTEN. YOU'RE RIGHT! WE GOT OWNED TODAY. WE ADMIT IT.
BUT JUST YOU WAIT. WE'RE GOING TO GET TO THE BOTTOM OF THIS WHOLE THING.
KLINK
SOMEONE'S ASS IS GOING TO JAIL.
OR I'M NOT ROSE HIP!

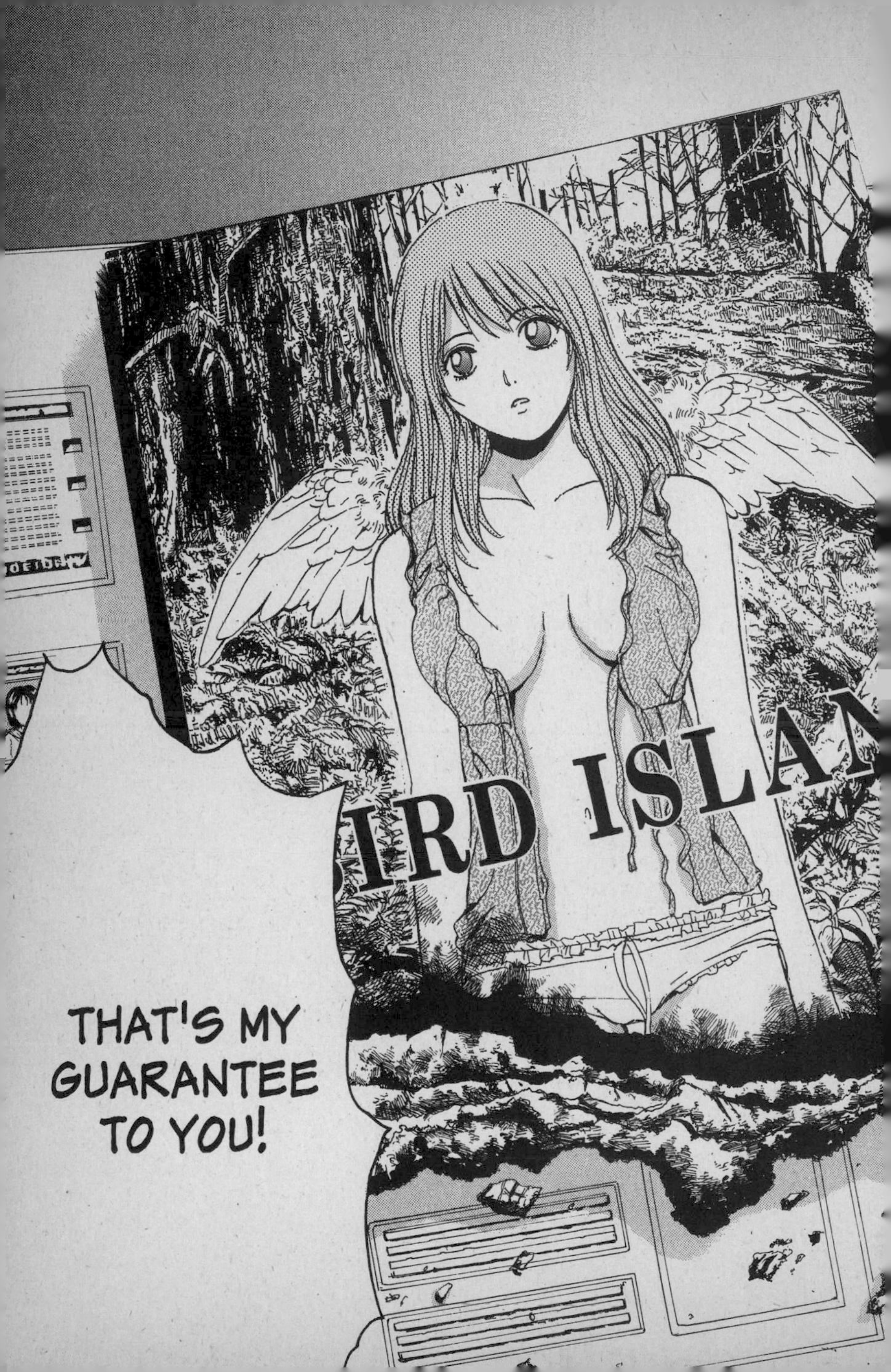
IRD ISLAN
THAT'S MY GUARANTEE TO YOU!

Rose Hip Rose

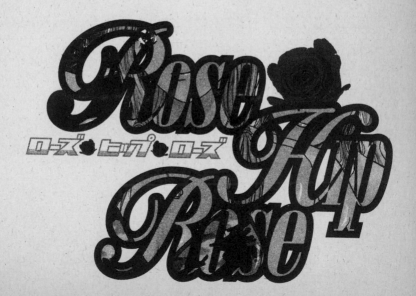

ローズ・ヒップ・ローズ

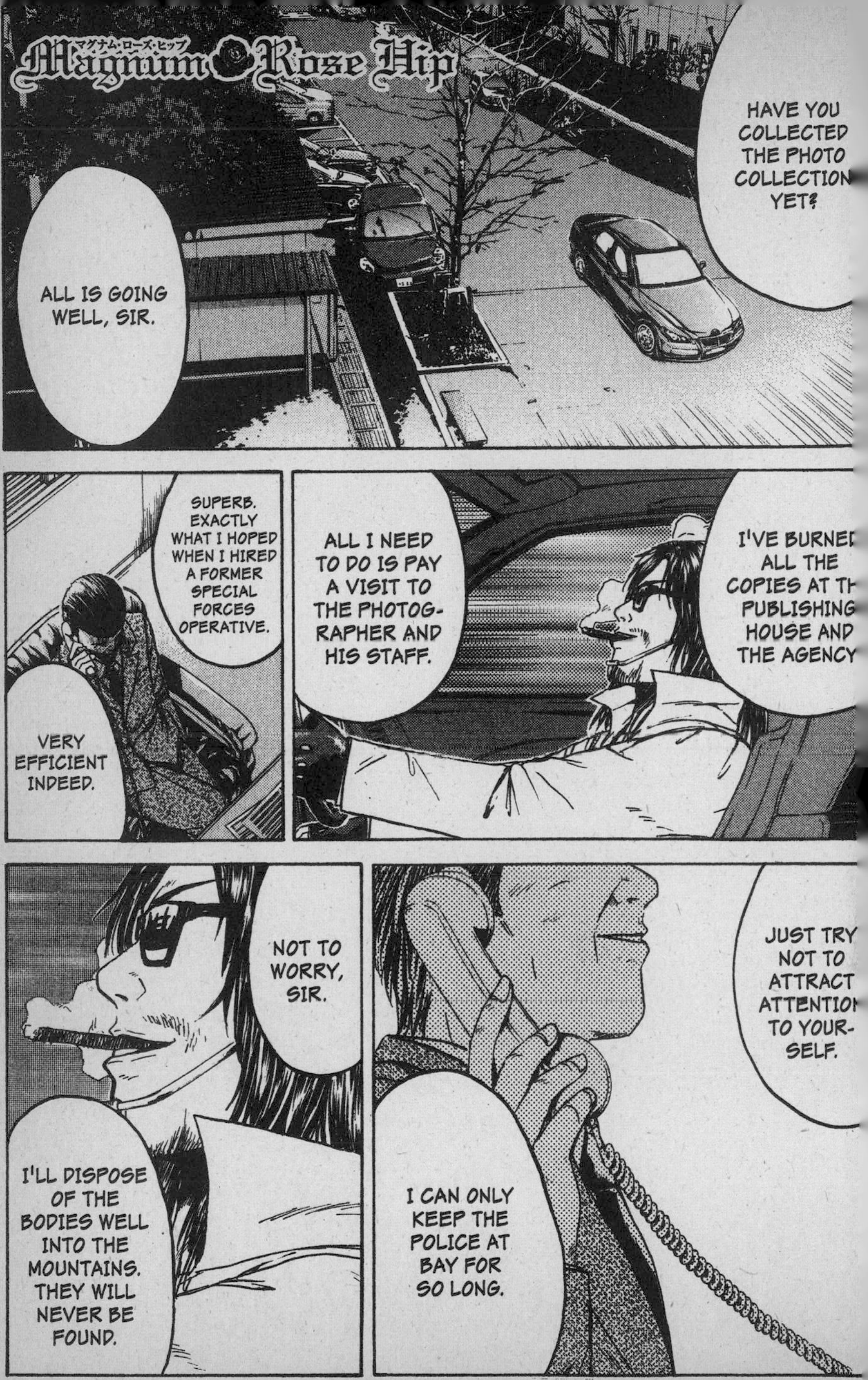
HAVE YOU COLLECTED THE PHOTO COLLECTION YET?
ALL IS GOING WELL, SIR.
I'VE BURNED ALL THE COPIES AT TH PUBLISHING HOUSE AND THE AGENCY
ALL I NEED TO DO IS PAY A VISIT TO THE PHOTOG-RAPHER AND HIS STAFF.
SUPERB. EXACTLY WHAT I HOPED WHEN I HIRED A FORMER SPECIAL FORCES OPERATIVE.
VERY EFFICIENT INDEED.
JUST TRY NOT TO ATTRACT ATTENTIO TO YOUR-SELF.
I CAN ONLY KEEP THE POLICE AT BAY FOR SO LONG.
NOT TO WORRY, SIR.
I'LL DISPOSE OF THE BODIES WELL INTO THE MOUNTAINS. THEY WILL NEVER BE FOUND.

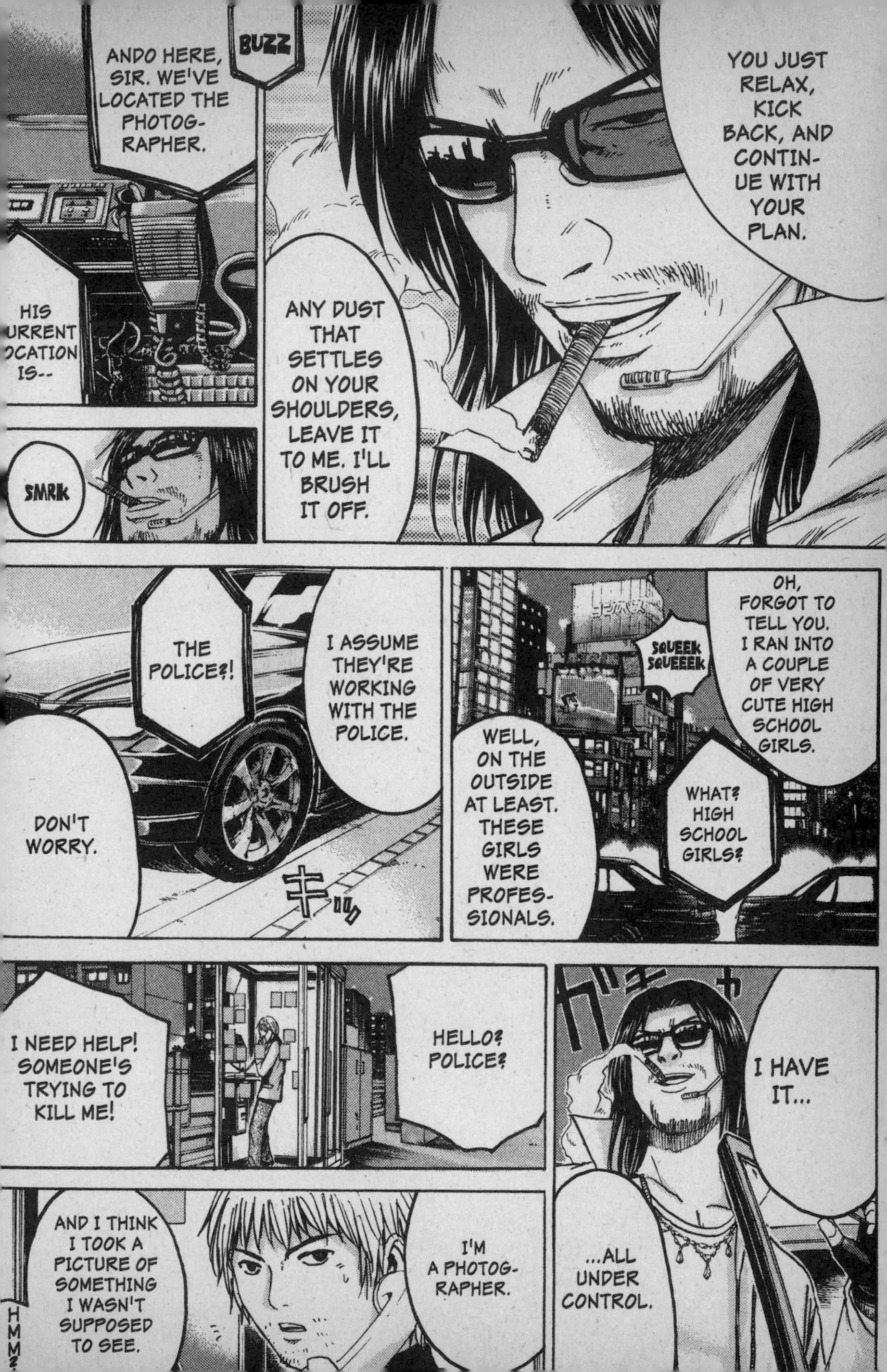

YOU JUST RELAX, KICK BACK, AND CONTIN-UE WITH YOUR PLAN.
ANY DUST THAT SETTLES ON YOUR SHOULDERS, LEAVE IT TO ME. I'LL BRUSH IT OFF.
BUZZ
ANDO HERE, SIR. WE'VE LOCATED THE PHOTOG-RAPHER.
HIS URRENT OCATION IS--
SMRK
OH, FORGOT TO TELL YOU. I RAN INTO A COUPLE OF VERY CUTE HIGH SCHOOL GIRLS.
SQUEEK SQUEEEK
WHAT? HIGH SCHOOL GIRLS?
WELL, ON THE OUTSIDE AT LEAST. THESE GIRLS WERE PROFES-SIONALS.
I ASSUME THEY'RE WORKING WITH THE POLICE.
THE POLICE?!
DON'T WORRY.
I HAVE IT...
...ALL UNDER CONTROL.
HELLO? POLICE?
I NEED HELP! SOMEONE'S TRYING TO KILL ME!
I'M A PHOTOG-RAPHER.
AND I THINK I TOOK A PICTURE OF SOMETHING I WASN'T SUPPOSED TO SEE.
HMM?

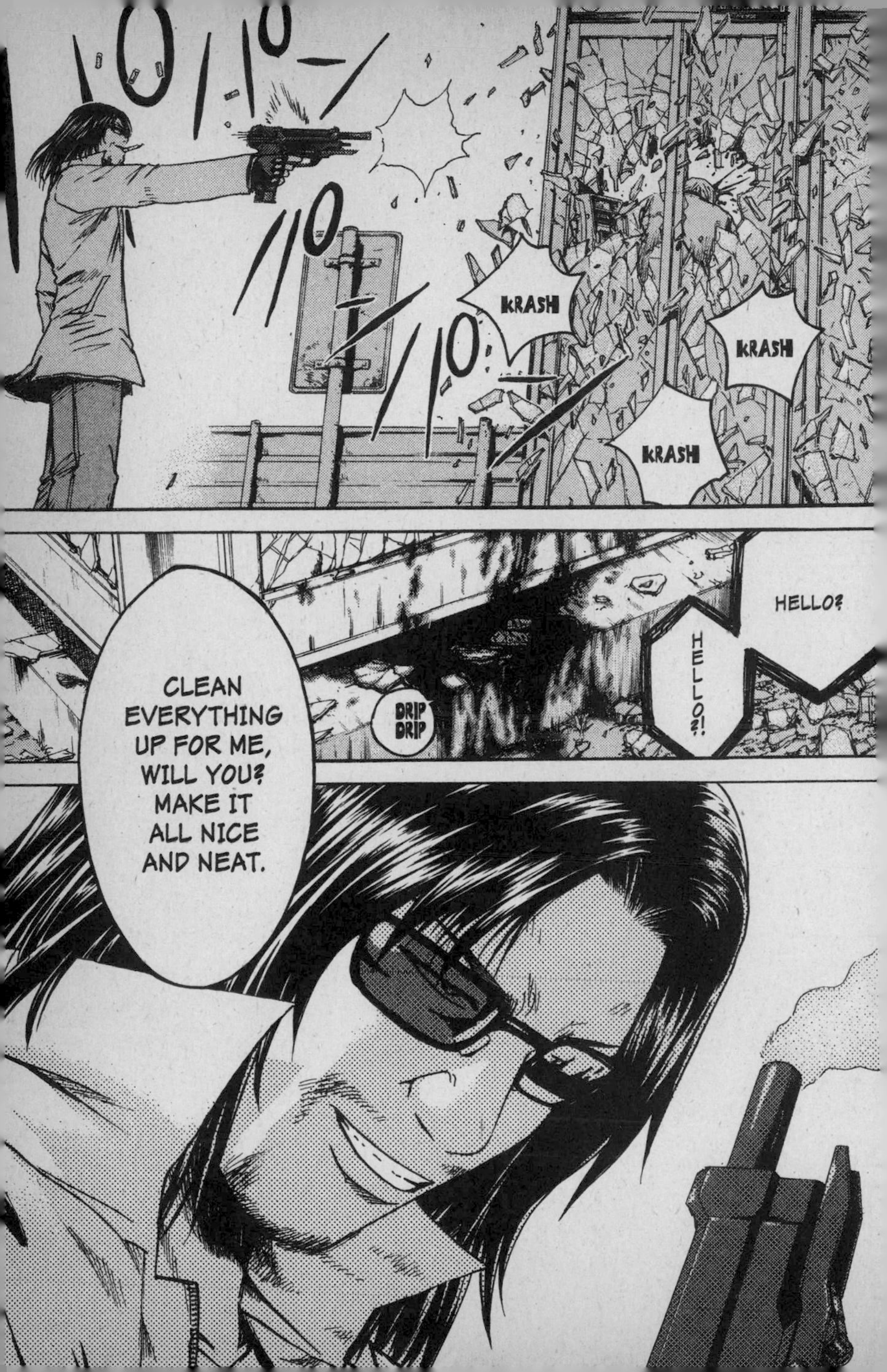
KRASH
KRASH
KRASH
HELLO?
HELLO?!
DRIP DRIP
CLEAN EVERYTHING UP FOR ME, WILL YOU? MAKE IT ALL NICE AND NEAT.

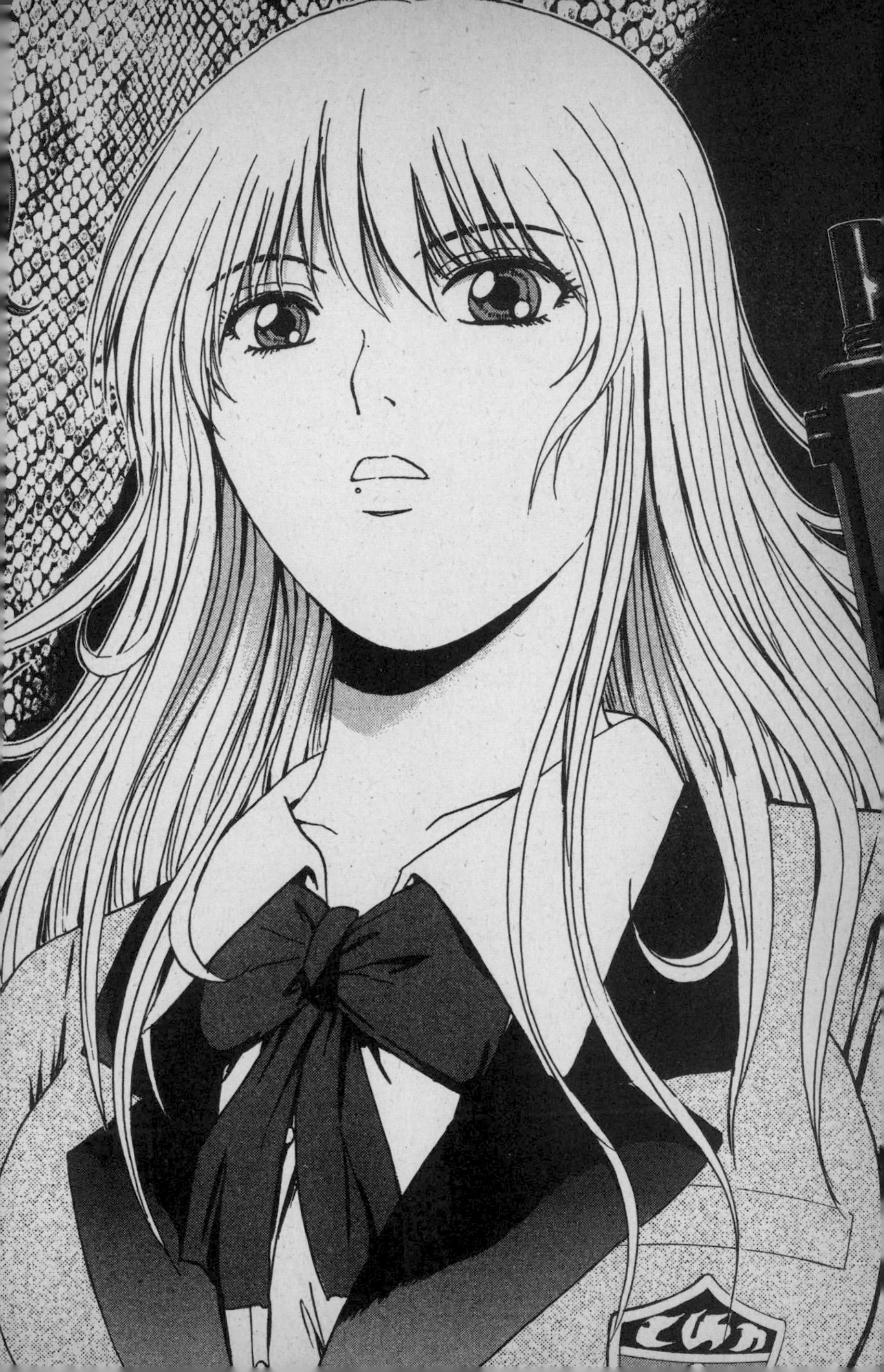

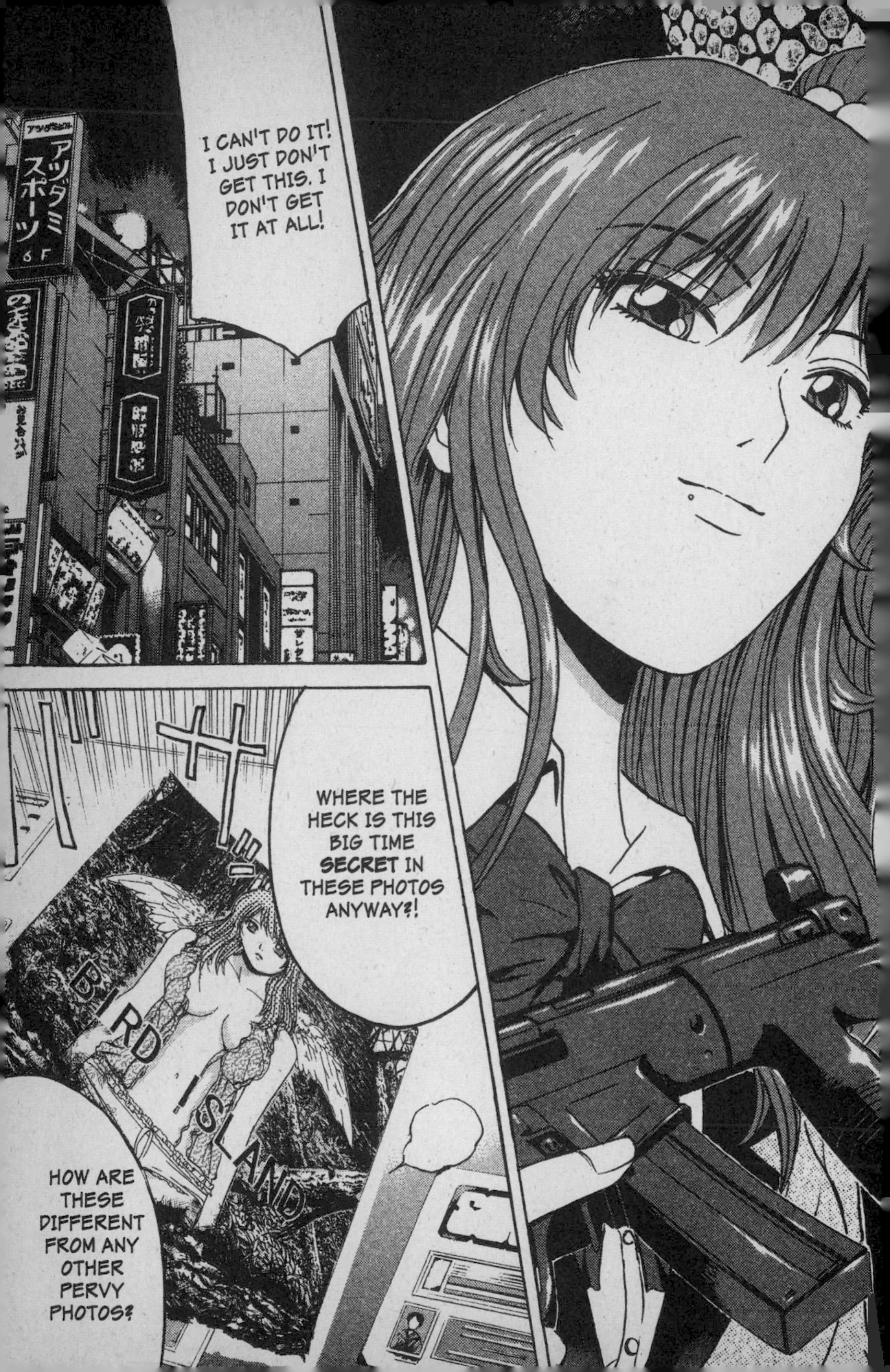
I CAN'T DO IT! I JUST DON'T GET THIS. I DON'T GET IT AT ALL!
アツダミ
スポーツ
6F
WHERE THE HECK IS THIS BIG TIME SECRET IN THESE PHOTOS ANYWAY?!
BIRD ISLAND
HOW ARE THESE DIFFERENT FROM ANY OTHER PERVY PHOTOS?

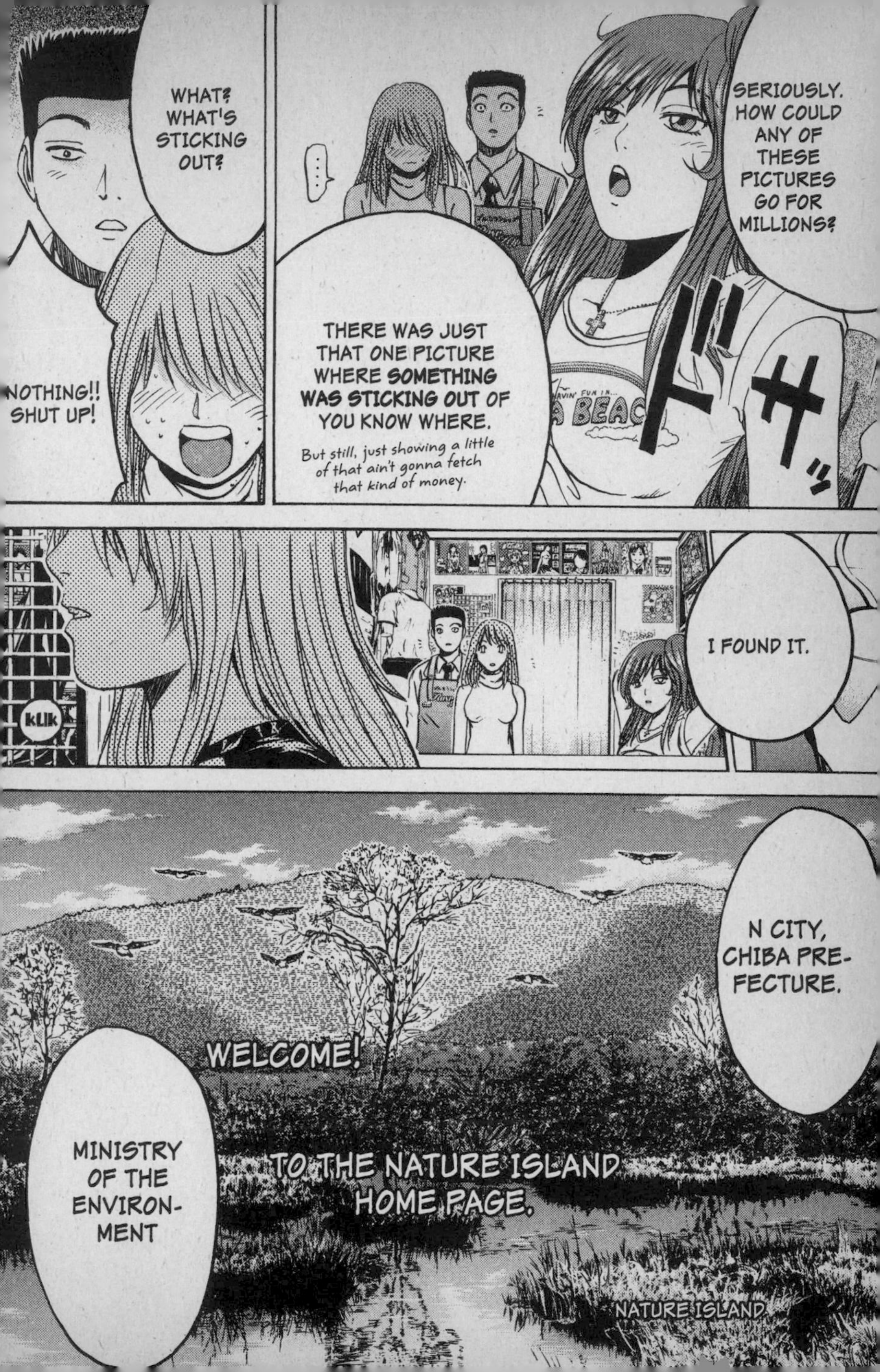
SERIOUSLY. HOW COULD ANY OF THESE PICTURES GO FOR MILLIONS?
ドサッ
....
THERE WAS JUST THAT ONE PICTURE WHERE SOMETHING WAS STICKING OUT OF YOU KNOW WHERE.
But still, just showing a little of that ain't gonna fetch that kind of money.
WHAT? WHAT'S STICKING OUT?
NOTHING!! SHUT UP!
I FOUND IT.
klik
N CITY, CHIBA PRE-FECTURE.
WELCOME!
TO THE NATURE ISLAND HOME PAGE.
MINISTRY OF THE ENVIRON-MENT
NATURE ISLAND

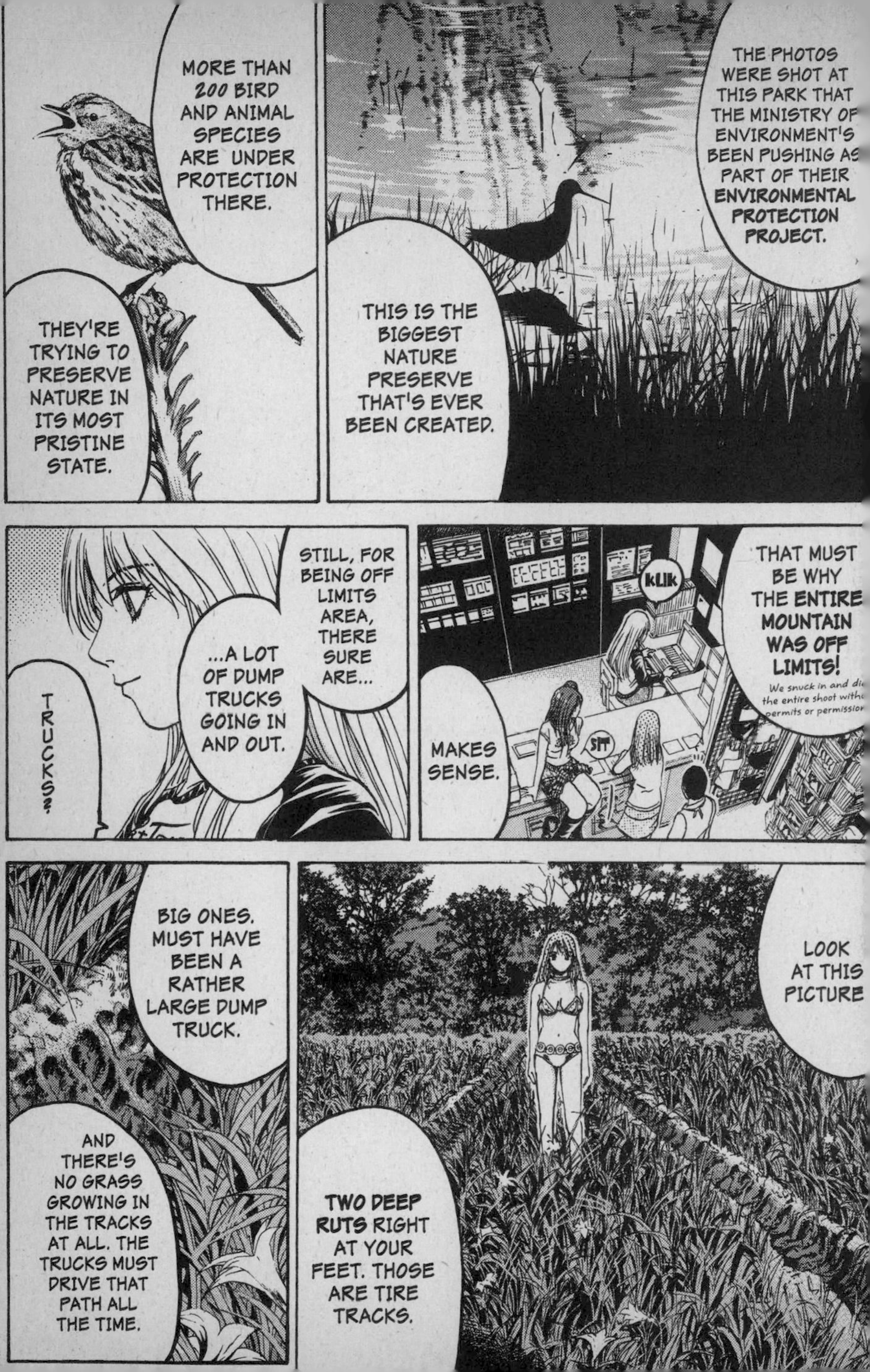
THE PHOTOS WERE SHOT AT THIS PARK THAT THE MINISTRY OF ENVIRONMENT'S BEEN PUSHING AS PART OF THEIR ENVIRONMENTAL PROTECTION PROJECT.
THIS IS THE BIGGEST NATURE PRESERVE THAT'S EVER BEEN CREATED.
MORE THAN 200 BIRD AND ANIMAL SPECIES ARE UNDER PROTECTION THERE.
THEY'RE TRYING TO PRESERVE NATURE IN ITS MOST PRISTINE STATE.
THAT MUST BE WHY THE ENTIRE MOUNTAIN WAS OFF LIMITS!
KLIK
SIT
MAKES SENSE.
STILL, FOR BEING OFF LIMITS AREA, THERE SURE ARE...
...A LOT OF DUMP TRUCKS GOING IN AND OUT.
TRUCKS?
LOOK AT THIS PICTURE
TWO DEEP RUTS RIGHT AT YOUR FEET. THOSE ARE TIRE TRACKS.
BIG ONES. MUST HAVE BEEN A RATHER LARGE DUMP TRUCK.
AND THERE'S NO GRASS GROWING IN THE TRACKS AT ALL. THE TRUCKS MUST DRIVE THAT PATH ALL THE TIME.

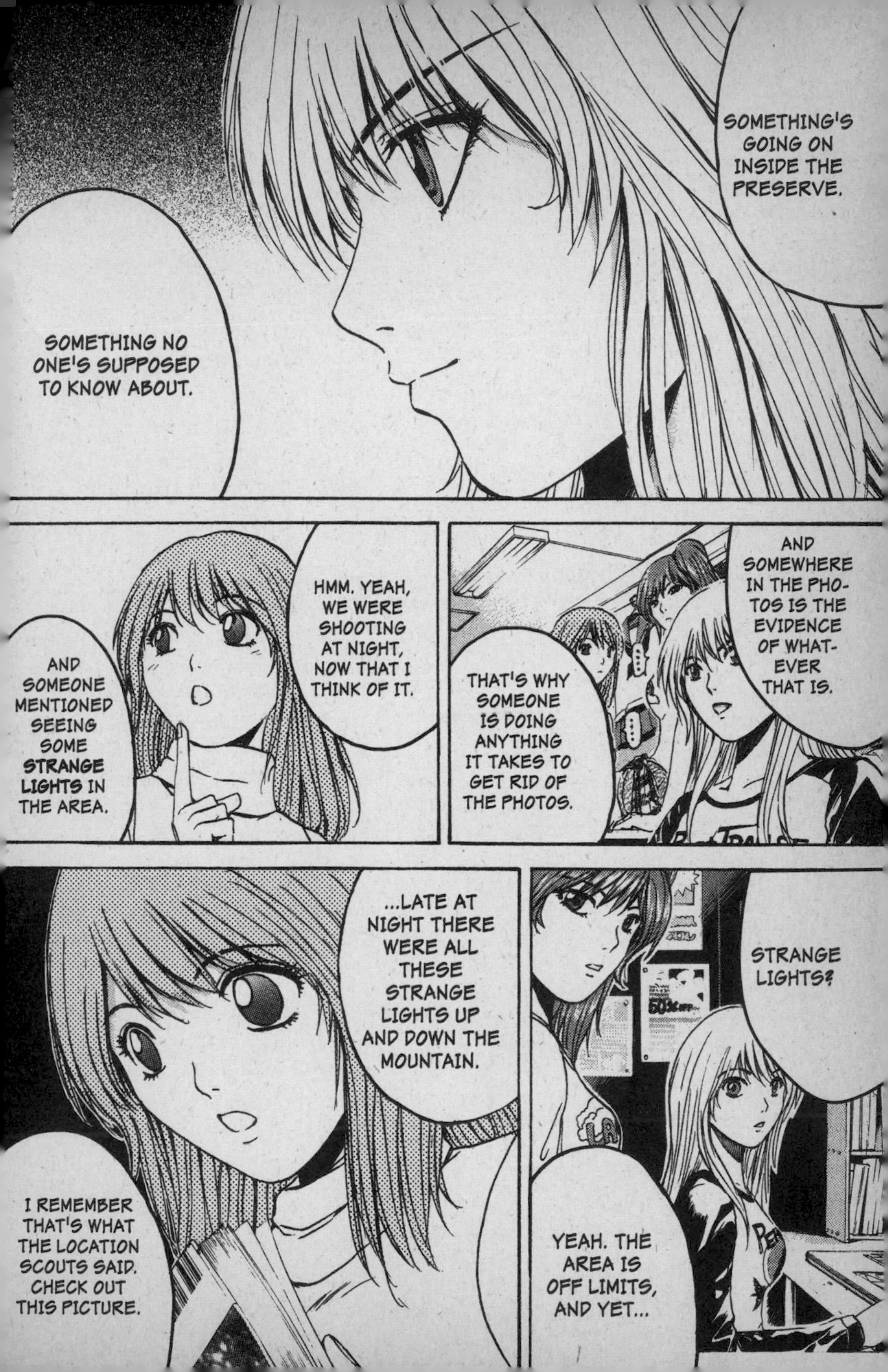
SOMETHING'S GOING ON INSIDE THE PRESERVE.
SOMETHING NO ONE'S SUPPOSED TO KNOW ABOUT.
AND SOMEWHERE IN THE PHOTOS IS THE EVIDENCE OF WHATEVER THAT IS.
THAT'S WHY SOMEONE IS DOING ANYTHING IT TAKES TO GET RID OF THE PHOTOS.
HMM. YEAH, WE WERE SHOOTING AT NIGHT, NOW THAT I THINK OF IT.
AND SOMEONE MENTIONED SEEING SOME **STRANGE LIGHTS** IN THE AREA.
STRANGE LIGHTS?
YEAH. THE AREA IS OFF LIMITS, AND YET...
...LATE AT NIGHT THERE WERE ALL THESE STRANGE LIGHTS UP AND DOWN THE MOUNTAIN.
I REMEMBER THAT'S WHAT THE LOCATION SCOUTS SAID. CHECK OUT THIS PICTURE.

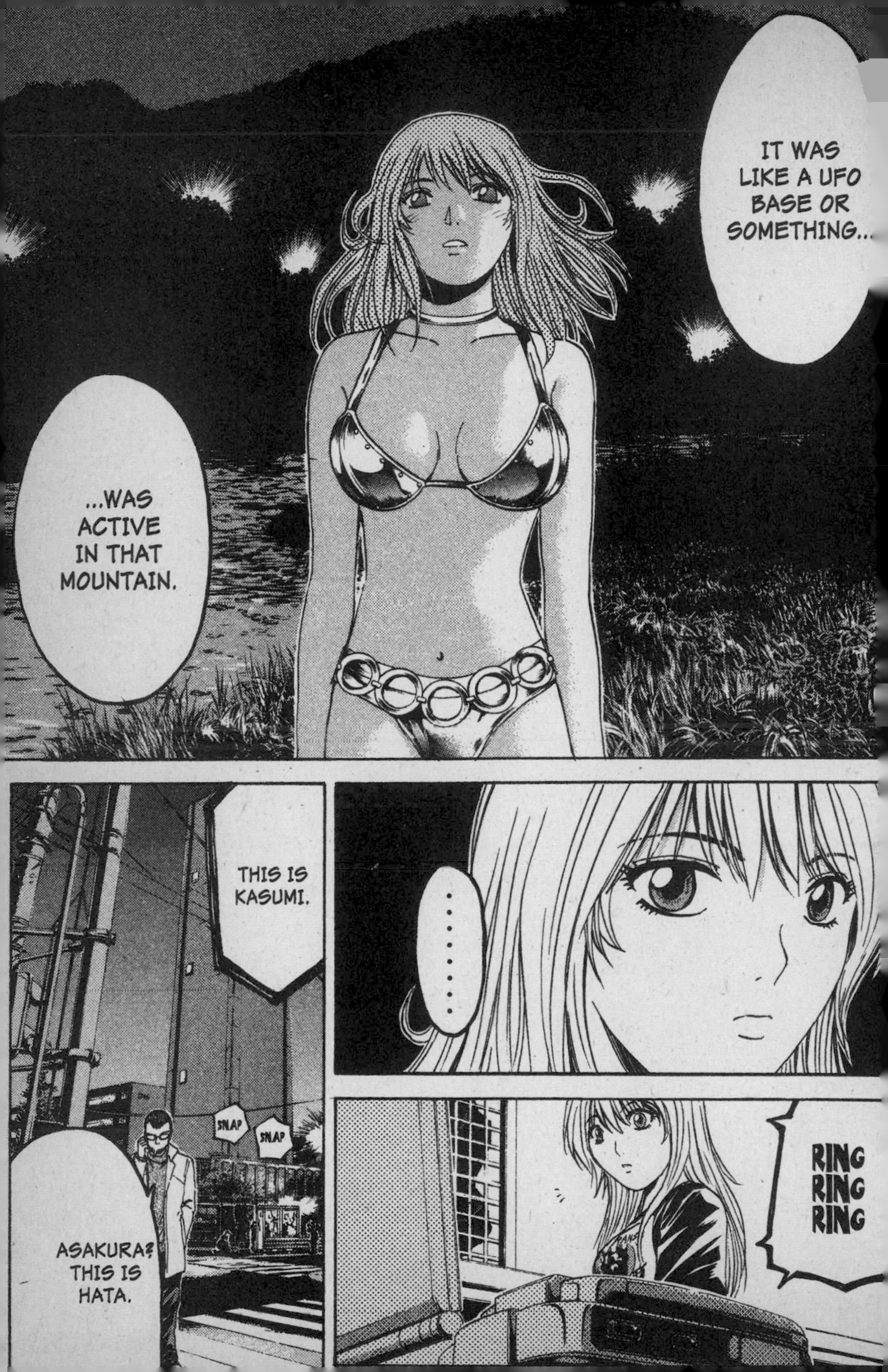
IT WAS LIKE A UFO BASE OR SOMETHING...
...WAS ACTIVE IN THAT MOUNTAIN.
......
RING RING RING
THIS IS KASUMI.
SNAP
SNAP
ASAKURA? THIS IS HATA.

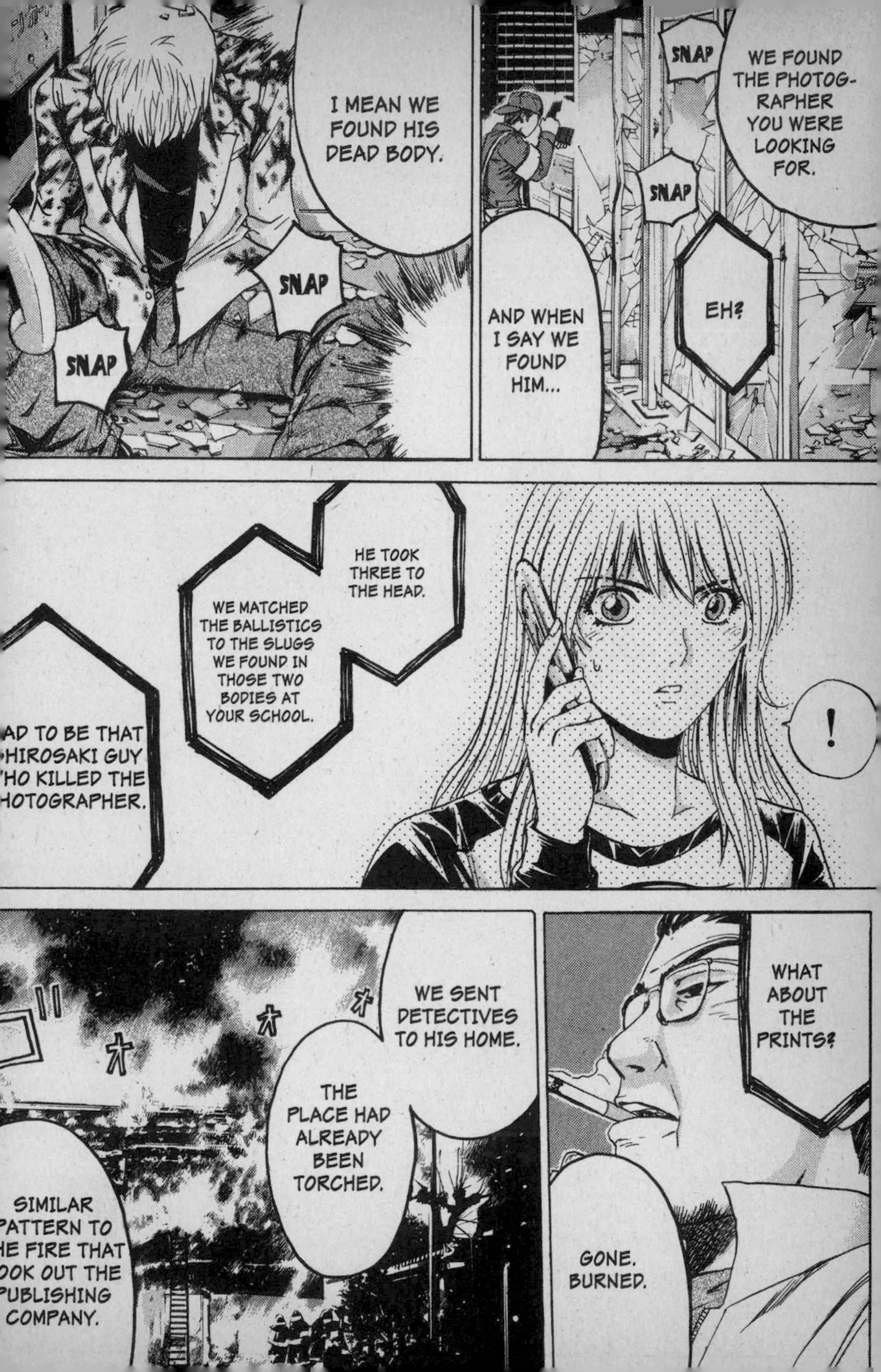
WE FOUND THE PHOTOG-RAPHER YOU WERE LOOKING FOR.
SNAP
SNAP
EH?
AND WHEN I SAY WE FOUND HIM...
I MEAN WE FOUND HIS DEAD BODY.
SNAP
SNAP
!
HE TOOK THREE TO THE HEAD.
WE MATCHED THE BALLISTICS TO THE SLUGS WE FOUND IN THOSE TWO BODIES AT YOUR SCHOOL.
AD TO BE THAT HIROSAKI GUY HO KILLED THE HOTOGRAPHER.
WHAT ABOUT THE PRINTS?
GONE. BURNED.
WE SENT DETECTIVES TO HIS HOME.
THE PLACE HAD ALREADY BEEN TORCHED.
SIMILAR PATTERN TO THE FIRE THAT OOK OUT THE PUBLISHING COMPANY.

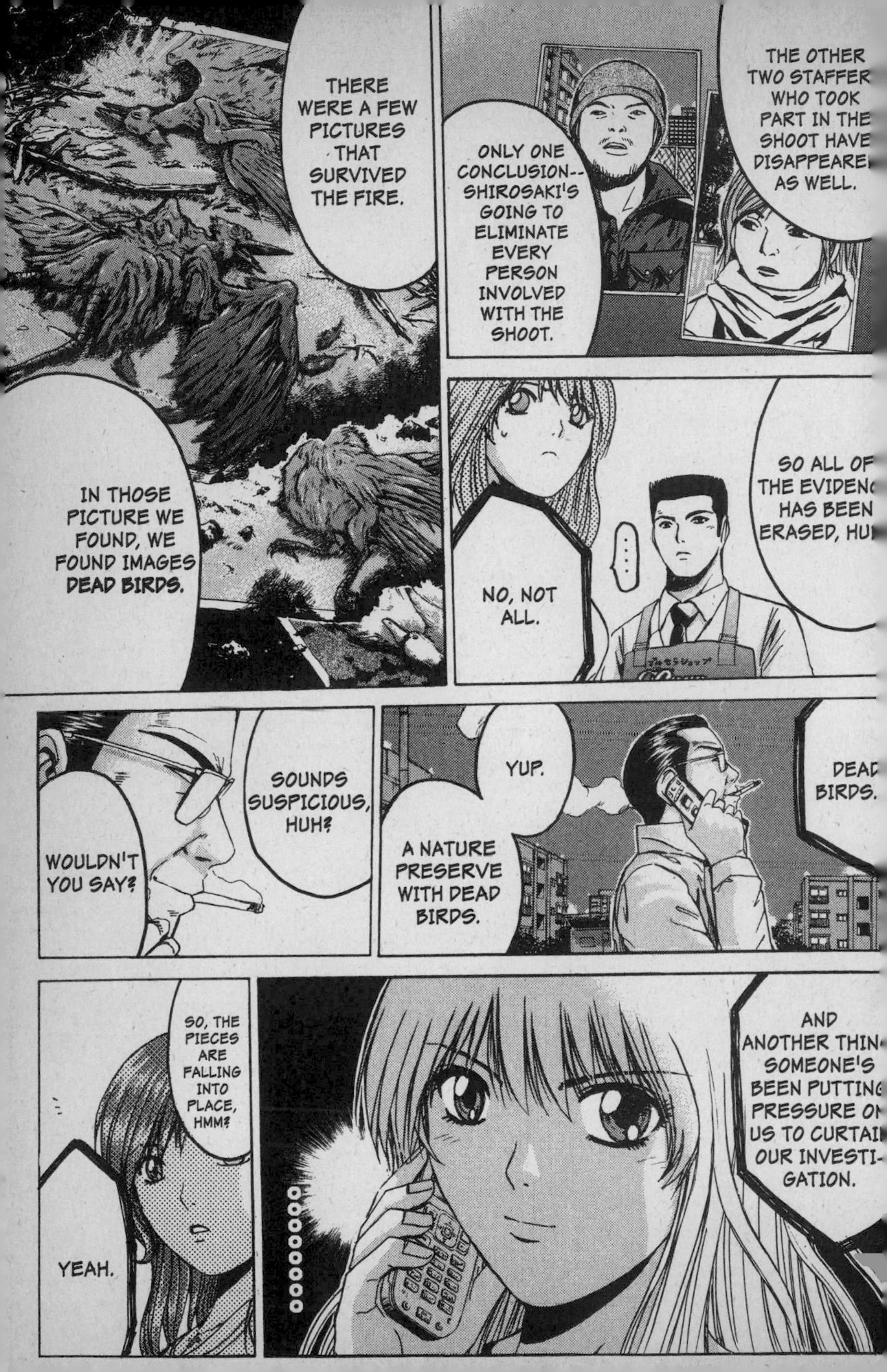
THE OTHER TWO STAFFER WHO TOOK PART IN THE SHOOT HAVE DISAPPEARE AS WELL.
ONLY ONE CONCLUSION-- SHIROSAKI'S GOING TO ELIMINATE EVERY PERSON INVOLVED WITH THE SHOOT.
SO ALL OF THE EVIDEN HAS BEEN ERASED, HU
...
NO, NOT ALL.
THERE WERE A FEW PICTURES THAT SURVIVED THE FIRE.
IN THOSE PICTURE WE FOUND, WE FOUND IMAGES DEAD BIRDS.
DEAD BIRDS.
YUP.
A NATURE PRESERVE WITH DEAD BIRDS.
SOUNDS SUSPICIOUS, HUH?
WOULDN'T YOU SAY?
AND ANOTHER THIN SOMEONE'S BEEN PUTTING PRESSURE O US TO CURTAI OUR INVESTI-GATION.
SO, THE PIECES ARE FALLING INTO PLACE, HMM?
YEAH.

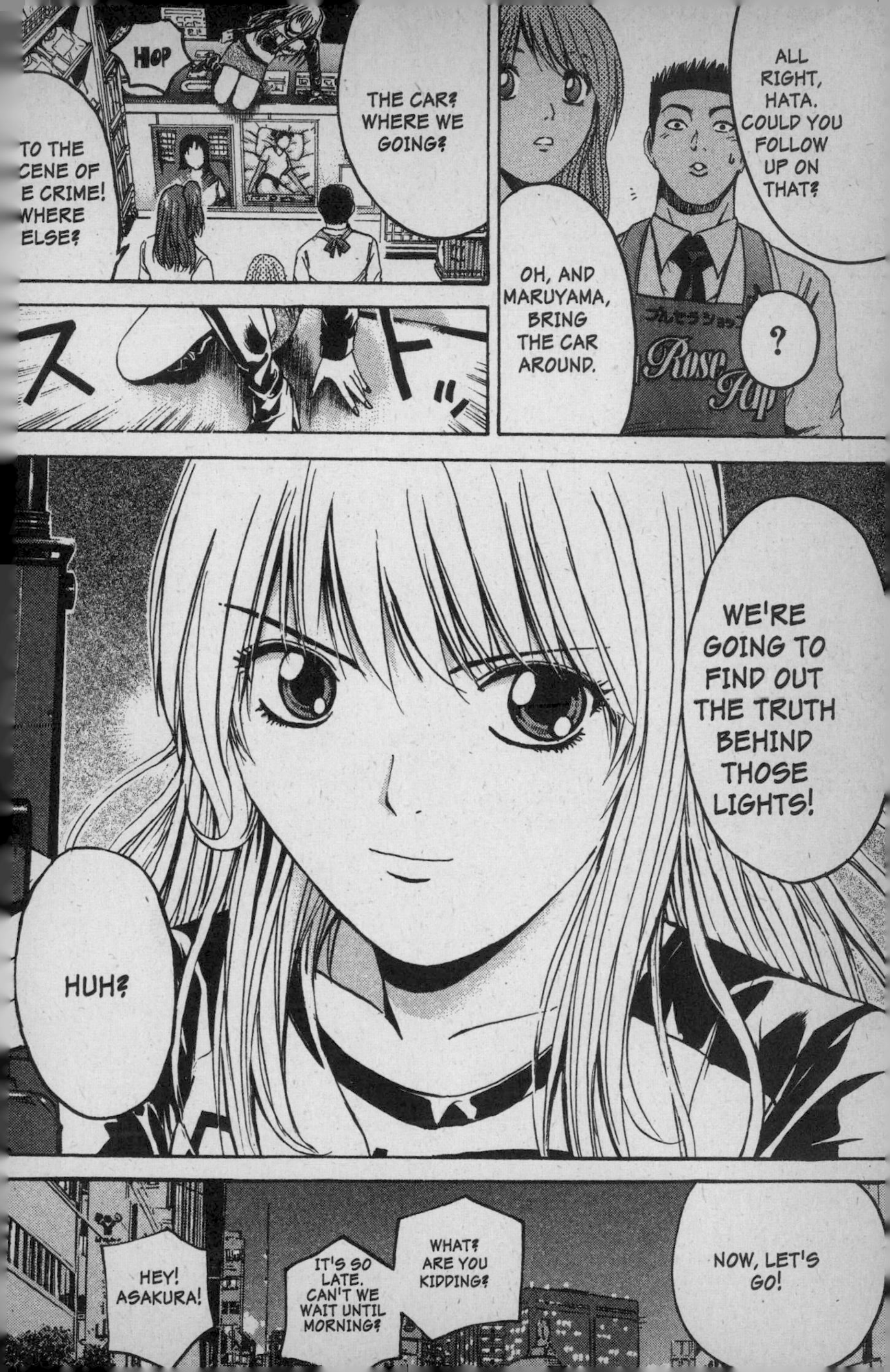
ALL RIGHT, HATA. COULD YOU FOLLOW UP ON THAT?
Rose Hip
?
OH, AND MARUYAMA, BRING THE CAR AROUND.
THE CAR? WHERE WE GOING?
HOP
TO THE CENE OF E CRIME! WHERE ELSE?
WE'RE GOING TO FIND OUT THE TRUTH BEHIND THOSE LIGHTS!
HUH?
NOW, LET'S GO!
WHAT? ARE YOU KIDDING?
IT'S SO LATE. CAN'T WE WAIT UNTIL MORNING?
HEY! ASAKURA!

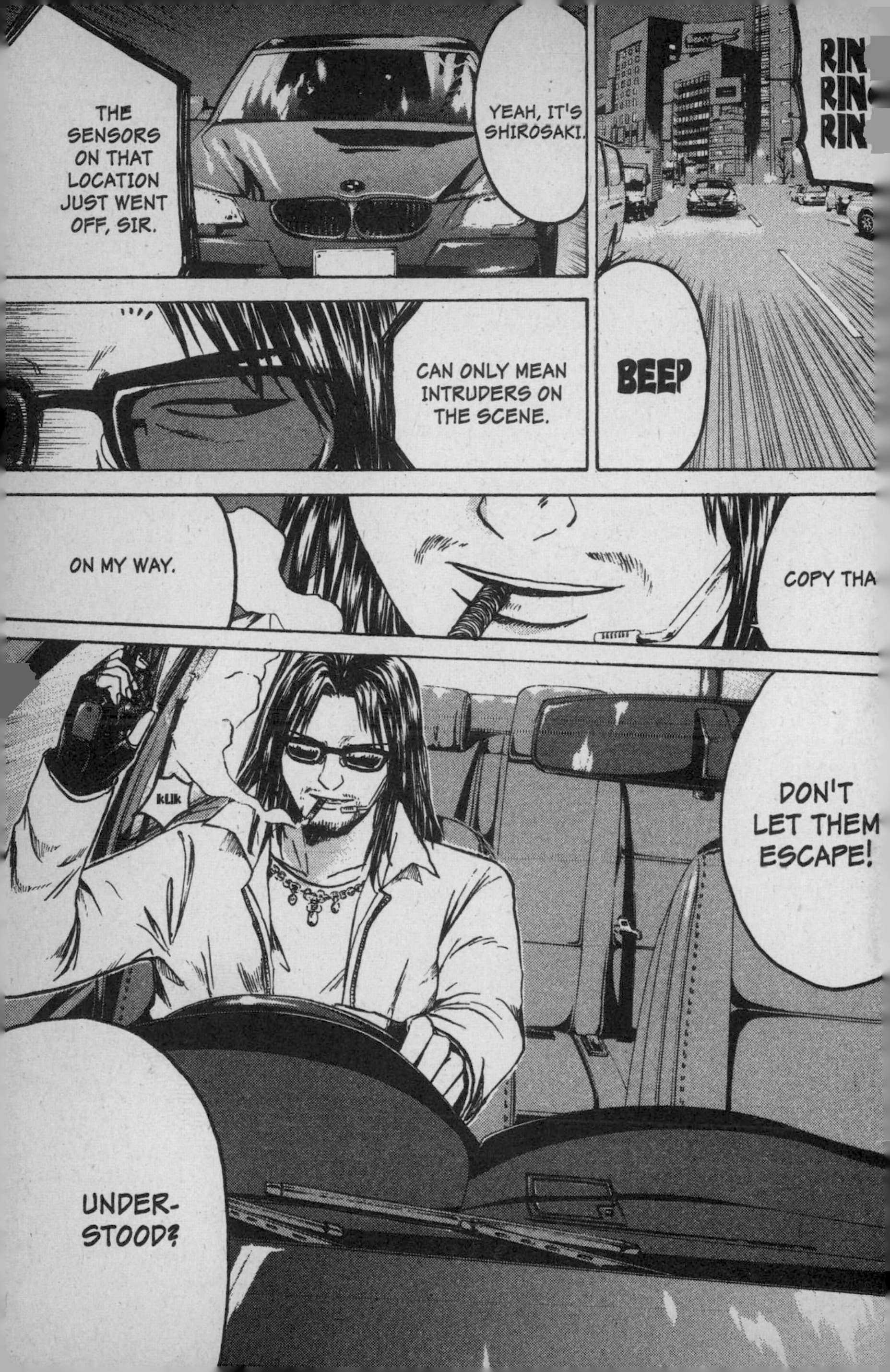
RIN
RIN
RIN
YEAH, IT'S SHIROSAKI.
THE SENSORS ON THAT LOCATION JUST WENT OFF, SIR.
BEEP
CAN ONLY MEAN INTRUDERS ON THE SCENE.
COPY THA
ON MY WAY.
DON'T LET THEM ESCAPE!
kLIk
UNDER-STOOD?

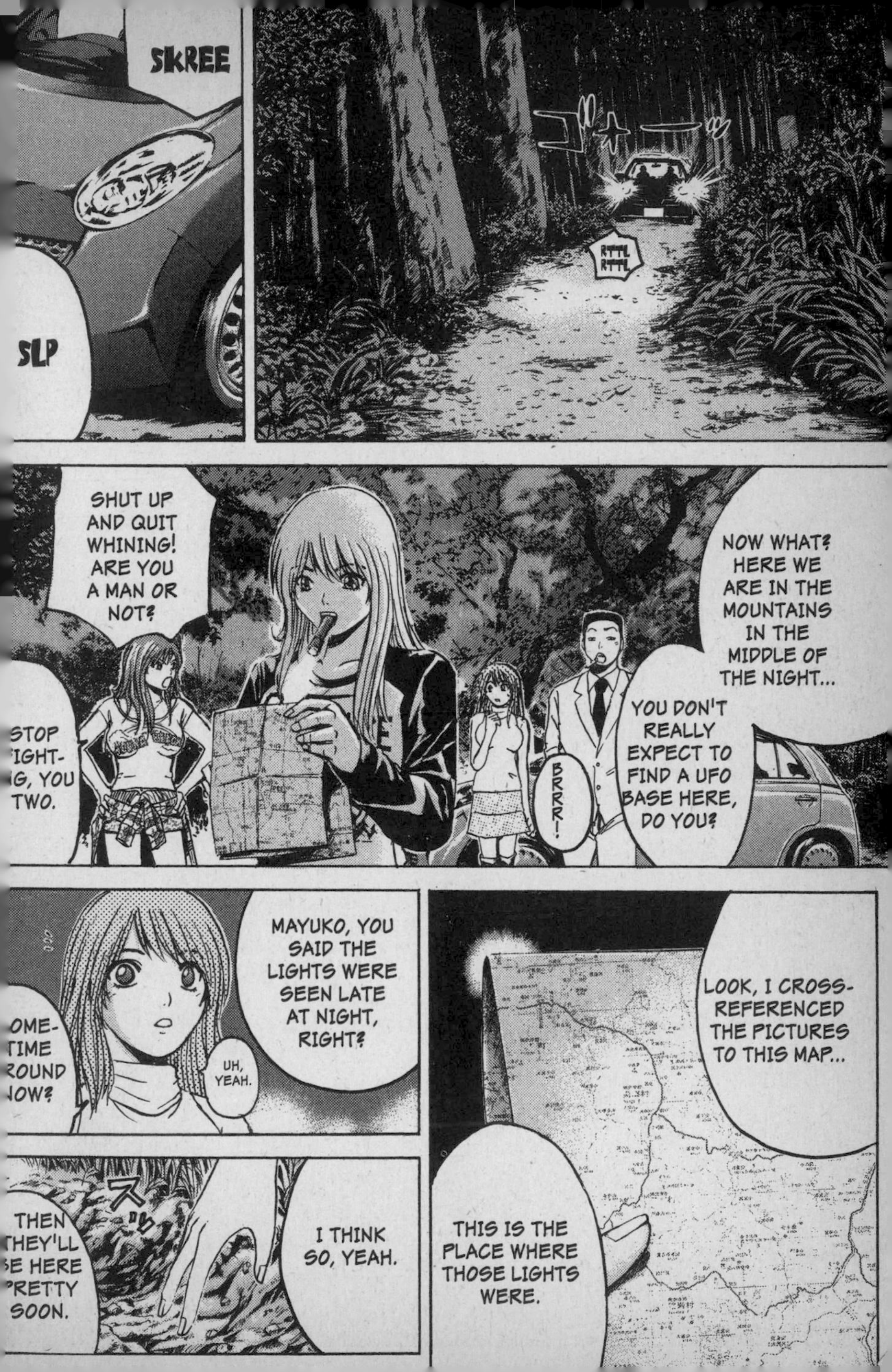
ゴォーーッ
RTTL RTTL
SKREE
SLP
NOW WHAT? HERE WE ARE IN THE MOUNTAINS IN THE MIDDLE OF THE NIGHT...
YOU DON'T REALLY EXPECT TO FIND A UFO BASE HERE, DO YOU?
BRRR!
SHUT UP AND QUIT WHINING! ARE YOU A MAN OR NOT?
STOP FIGHT- G, YOU TWO.
LOOK, I CROSS-REFERENCED THE PICTURES TO THIS MAP...
THIS IS THE PLACE WHERE THOSE LIGHTS WERE.
MAYUKO, YOU SAID THE LIGHTS WERE SEEN LATE AT NIGHT, RIGHT?
UH, YEAH.
OME-TIME ROUND NOW?
スッ
I THINK SO, YEAH.
THEN THEY'LL E HERE PRETTY SOON.

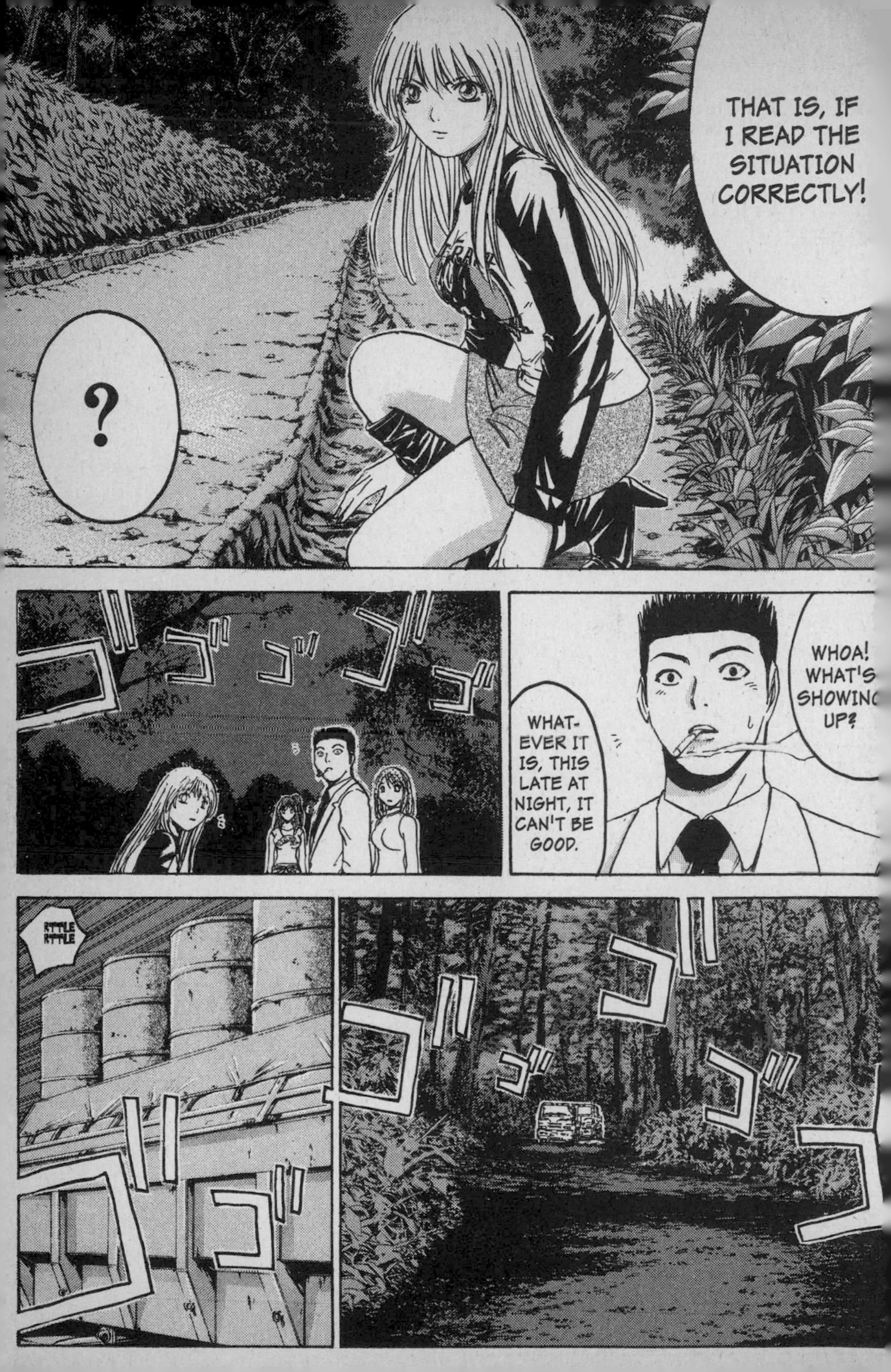
THAT IS, IF I READ THE SITUATION CORRECTLY!
?
WHOA! WHAT'S SHOWING UP?
WHAT-EVER IT IS, THIS LATE AT NIGHT, IT CAN'T BE GOOD.
RATTLE RATTLE

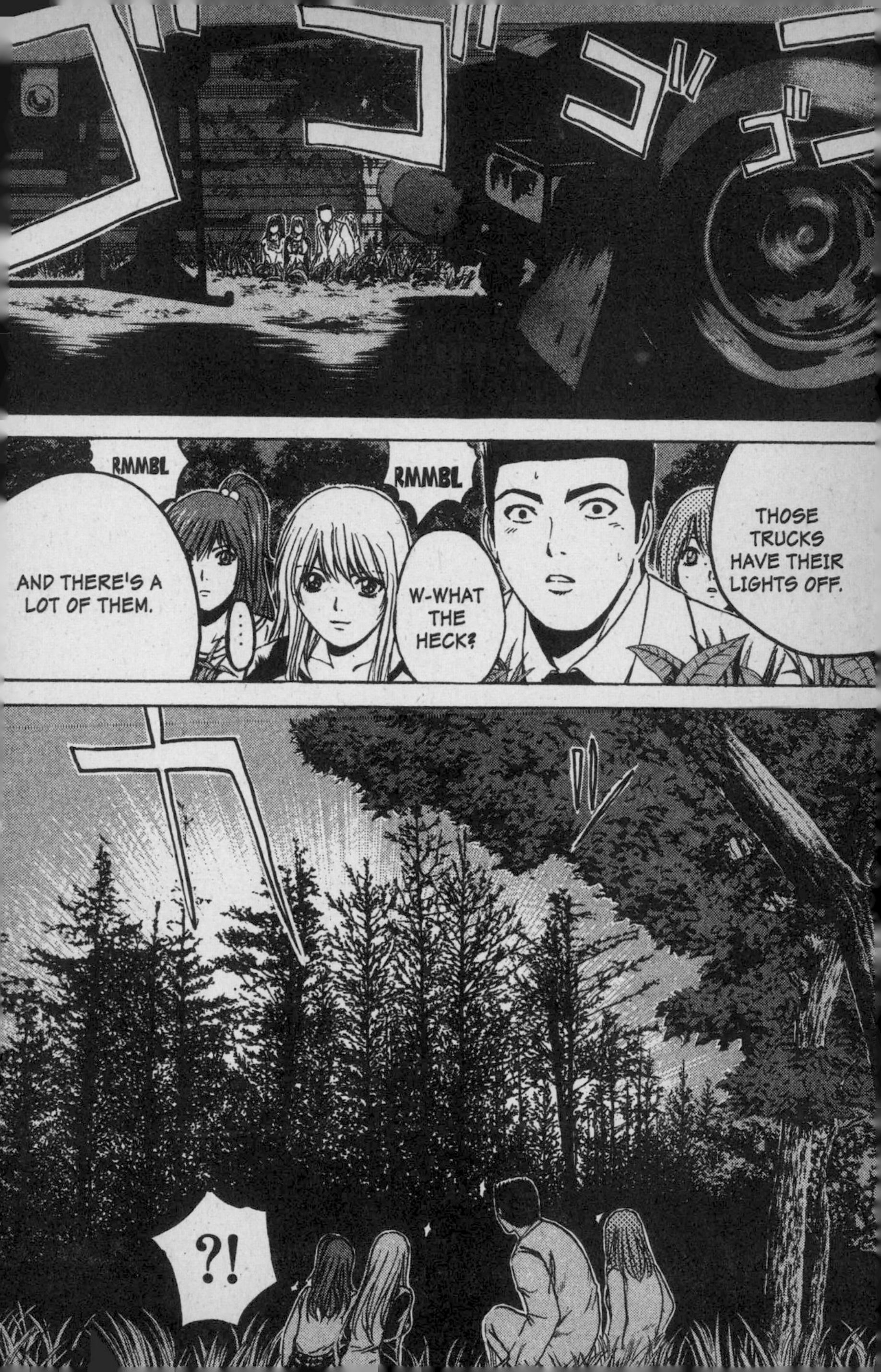
THOSE TRUCKS HAVE THEIR LIGHTS OFF.
RMMBL
W-WHAT THE HECK?
RMMBL
AND THERE'S A LOT OF THEM.
......
?!

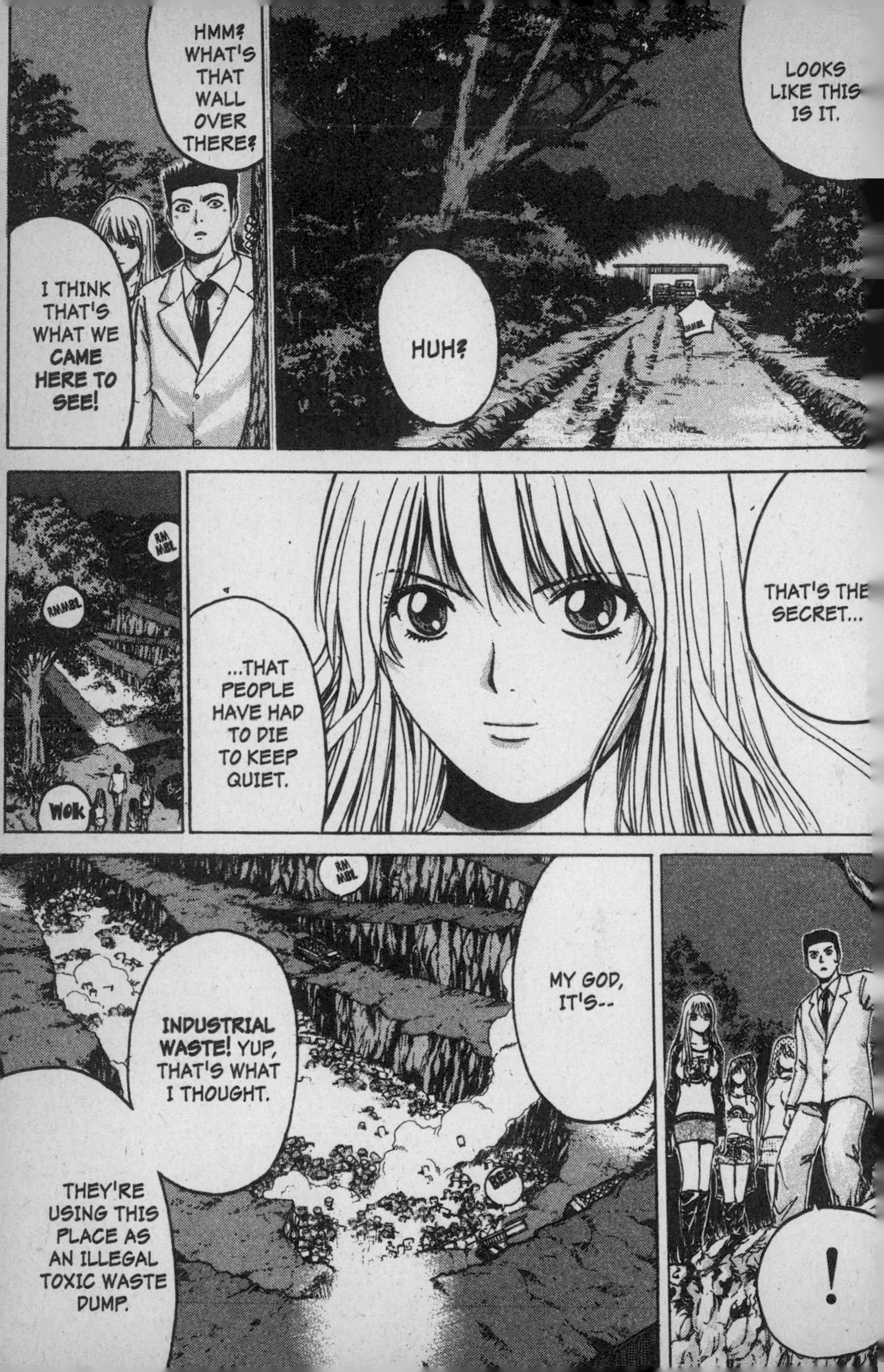
LOOKS LIKE THIS IS IT.
HUH?
RMMBL
HMM? WHAT'S THAT WALL OVER THERE?
I THINK THAT'S WHAT WE CAME HERE TO SEE!
THAT'S THE SECRET...
...THAT PEOPLE HAVE HAD TO DIE TO KEEP QUIET.
RM MBL
RMMBL
WOK
!
RM MBL
MY GOD, IT'S--
INDUSTRIAL WASTE! YUP, THAT'S WHAT I THOUGHT.
THEY'RE USING THIS PLACE AS AN ILLEGAL TOXIC WASTE DUMP.

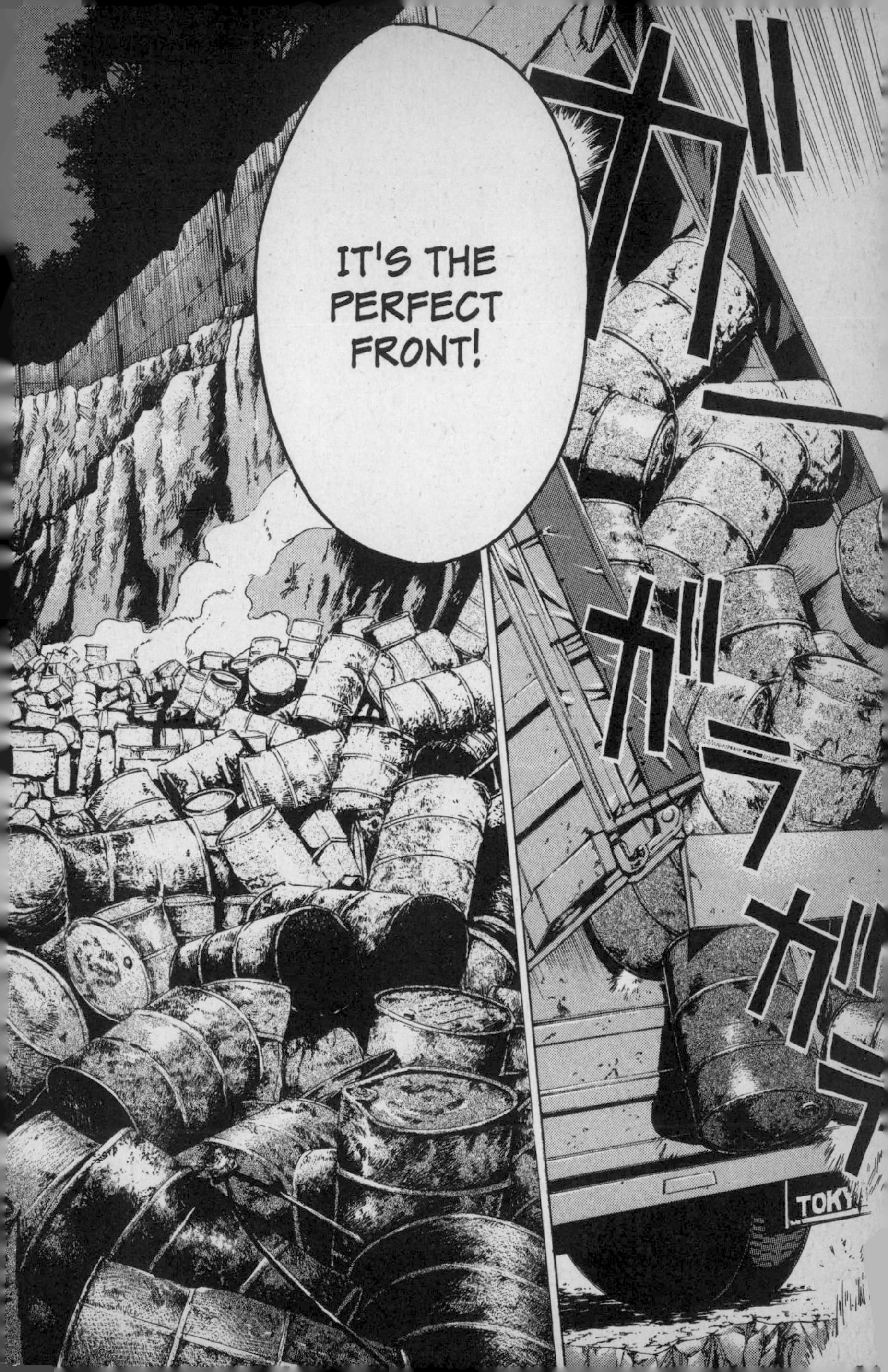
ガー
ガラ
ガラ
TOKY
IT'S THE PERFECT FRONT!

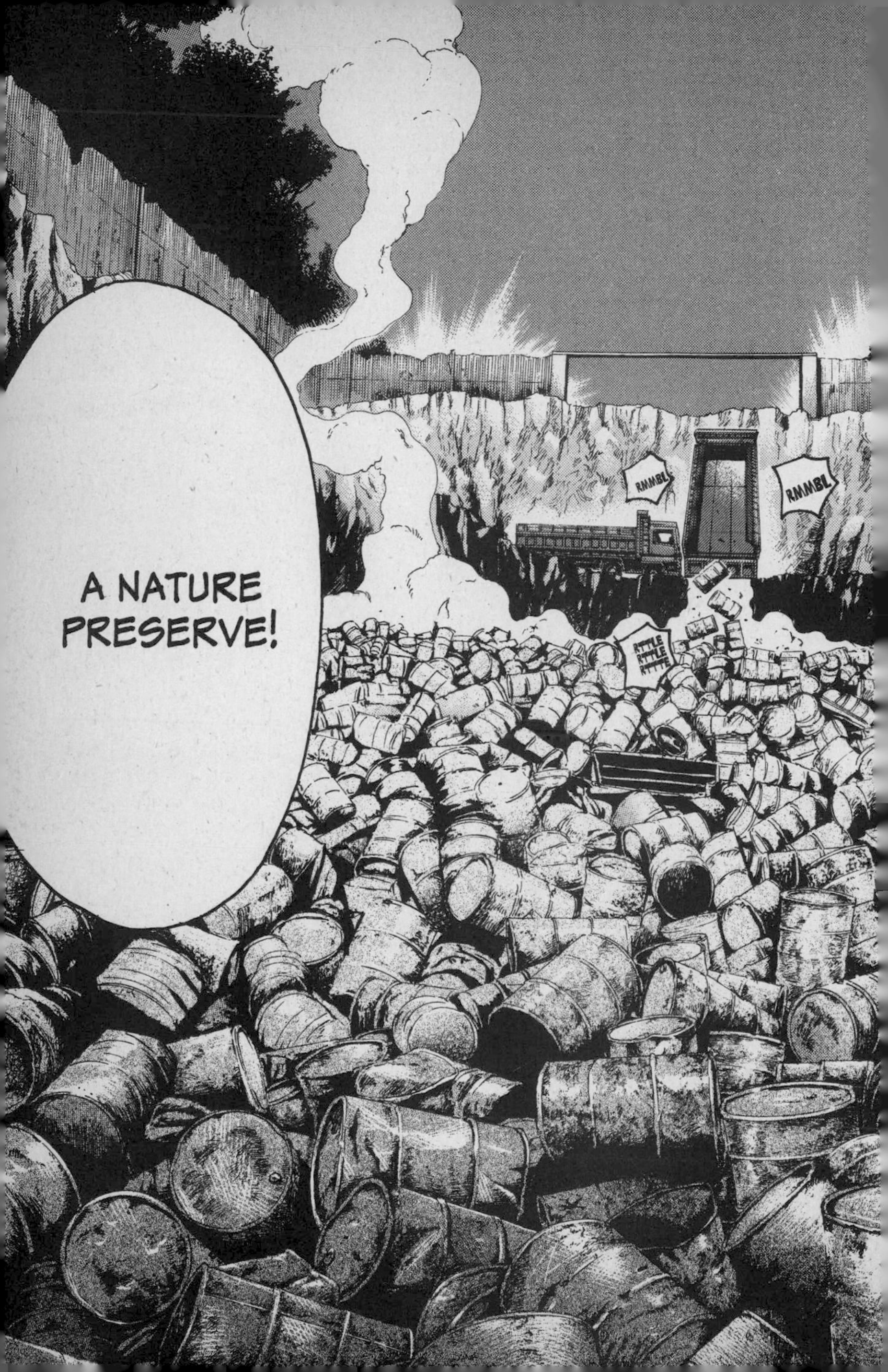
RMMBL
RMMBL
RTTTLE RTTTLE RTTTLE
A NATURE PRESERVE!

Rose Hip Rose

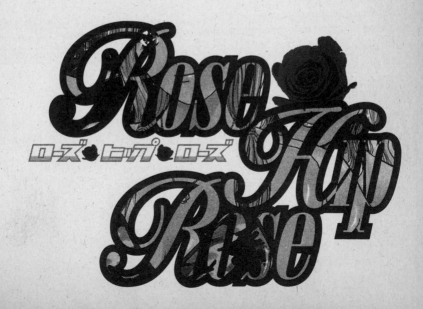

ローズ・ヒップ・ローズ

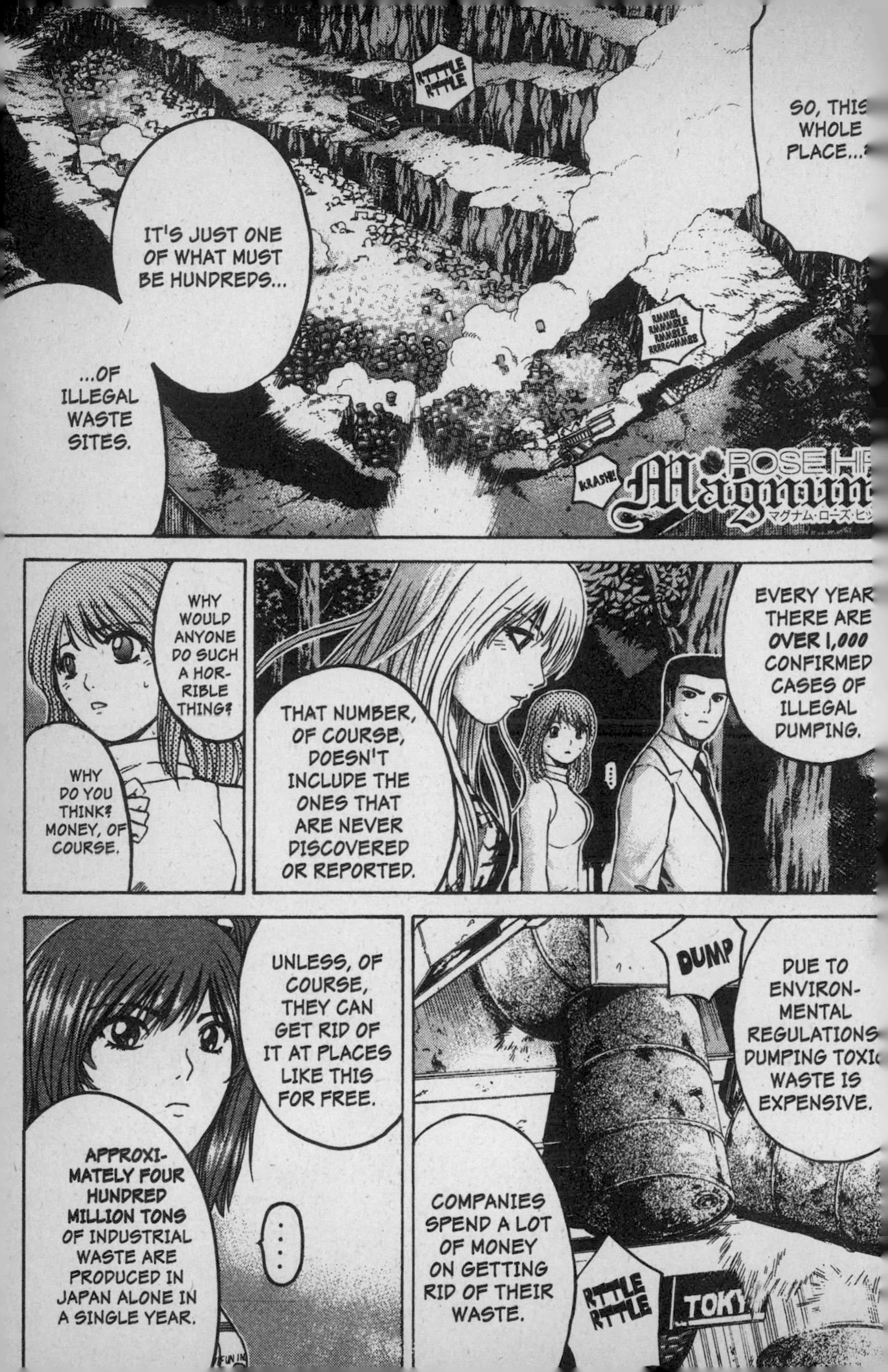
SO, THIS WHOLE PLACE...?
RTTTTLE RTTLE
IT'S JUST ONE OF WHAT MUST BE HUNDREDS...
...OF ILLEGAL WASTE SITES.
KRASH!
ROSE HIP Magnum
EVERY YEAR THERE ARE OVER 1,000 CONFIRMED CASES OF ILLEGAL DUMPING.
THAT NUMBER, OF COURSE, DOESN'T INCLUDE THE ONES THAT ARE NEVER DISCOVERED OR REPORTED.
...
WHY WOULD ANYONE DO SUCH A HORRIBLE THING?
WHY DO YOU THINK? MONEY, OF COURSE.
DUMP
DUE TO ENVIRONMENTAL REGULATIONS DUMPING TOXIC WASTE IS EXPENSIVE.
COMPANIES SPEND A LOT OF MONEY ON GETTING RID OF THEIR WASTE.
RTTLE RTTLE
TOKY
UNLESS, OF COURSE, THEY CAN GET RID OF IT AT PLACES LIKE THIS FOR FREE.
APPROXIMATELY FOUR HUNDRED MILLION TONS OF INDUSTRIAL WASTE ARE PRODUCED IN JAPAN ALONE IN A SINGLE YEAR.
....

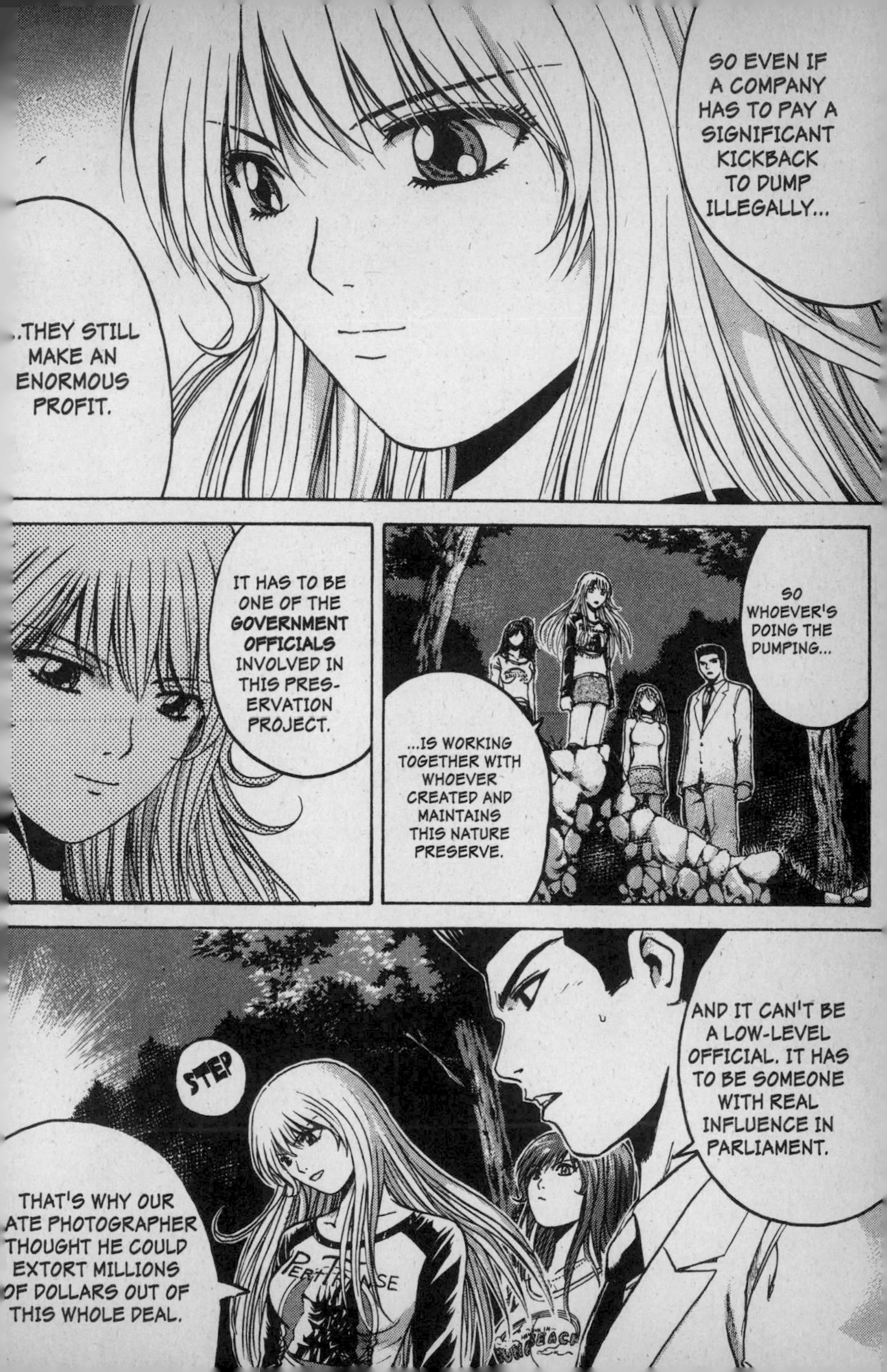
SO EVEN IF A COMPANY HAS TO PAY A SIGNIFICANT KICKBACK TO DUMP ILLEGALLY...
..THEY STILL MAKE AN ENORMOUS PROFIT.
SO WHOEVER'S DOING THE DUMPING...
...IS WORKING TOGETHER WITH WHOEVER CREATED AND MAINTAINS THIS NATURE PRESERVE.
IT HAS TO BE ONE OF THE GOVERNMENT OFFICIALS INVOLVED IN THIS PRES-ERVATION PROJECT.
AND IT CAN'T BE A LOW-LEVEL OFFICIAL. IT HAS TO BE SOMEONE WITH REAL INFLUENCE IN PARLIAMENT.
STEP
THAT'S WHY OUR ATE PHOTOGRAPHER THOUGHT HE COULD EXTORT MILLIONS OF DOLLARS OUT OF THIS WHOLE DEAL.

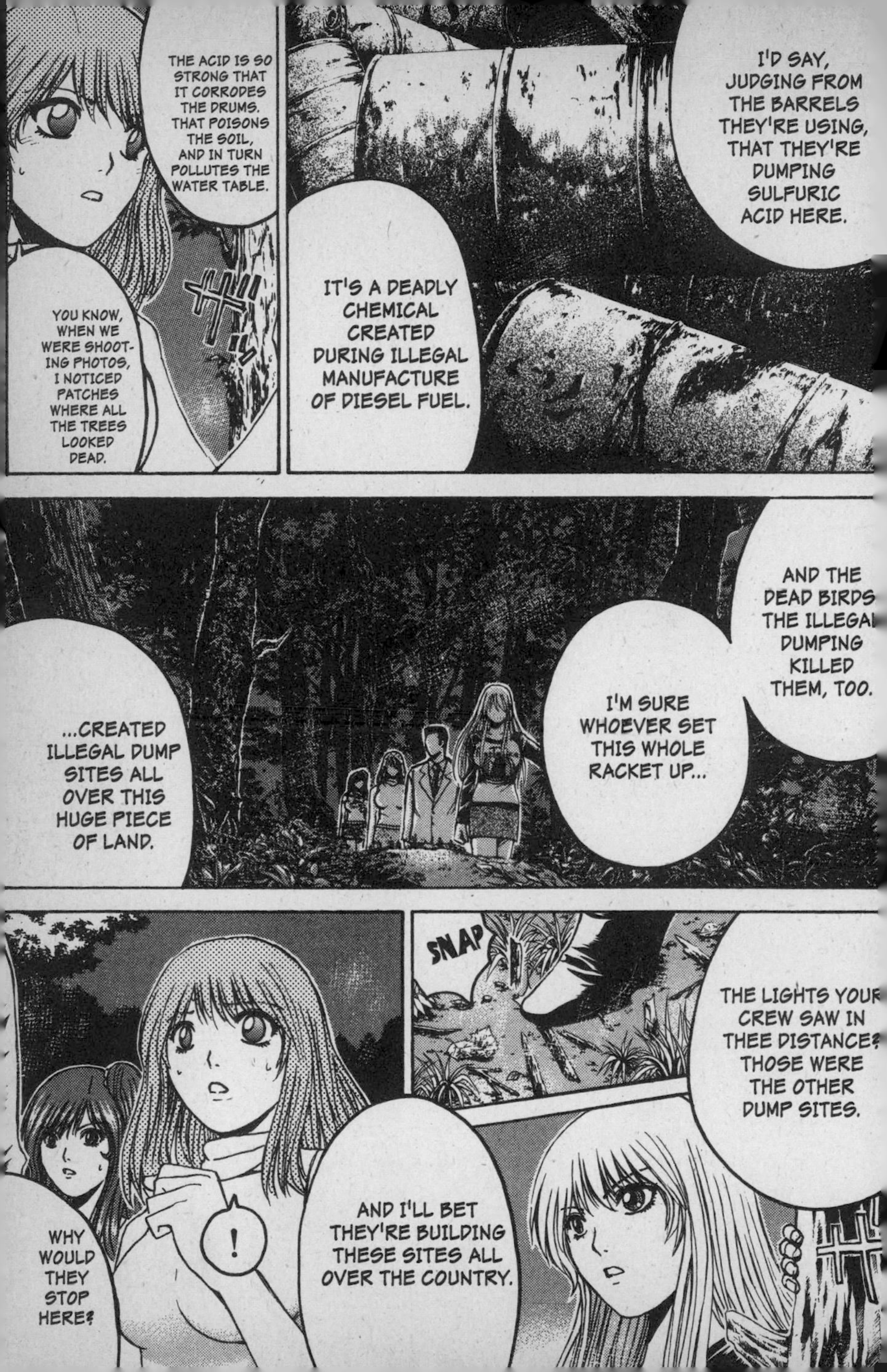
I'D SAY, JUDGING FROM THE BARRELS THEY'RE USING, THAT THEY'RE DUMPING SULFURIC ACID HERE.
IT'S A DEADLY CHEMICAL CREATED DURING ILLEGAL MANUFACTURE OF DIESEL FUEL.
THE ACID IS SO STRONG THAT IT CORRODES THE DRUMS. THAT POISONS THE SOIL, AND IN TURN POLLUTES THE WATER TABLE.
YOU KNOW, WHEN WE WERE SHOOT-ING PHOTOS, I NOTICED PATCHES WHERE ALL THE TREES LOOKED DEAD.
AND THE DEAD BIRDS THE ILLEGAL DUMPING KILLED THEM, TOO.
I'M SURE WHOEVER SET THIS WHOLE RACKET UP...
...CREATED ILLEGAL DUMP SITES ALL OVER THIS HUGE PIECE OF LAND.
SNAP
THE LIGHTS YOUR CREW SAW IN THEE DISTANCE? THOSE WERE THE OTHER DUMP SITES.
AND I'LL BET THEY'RE BUILDING THESE SITES ALL OVER THE COUNTRY.
!
WHY WOULD THEY STOP HERE?

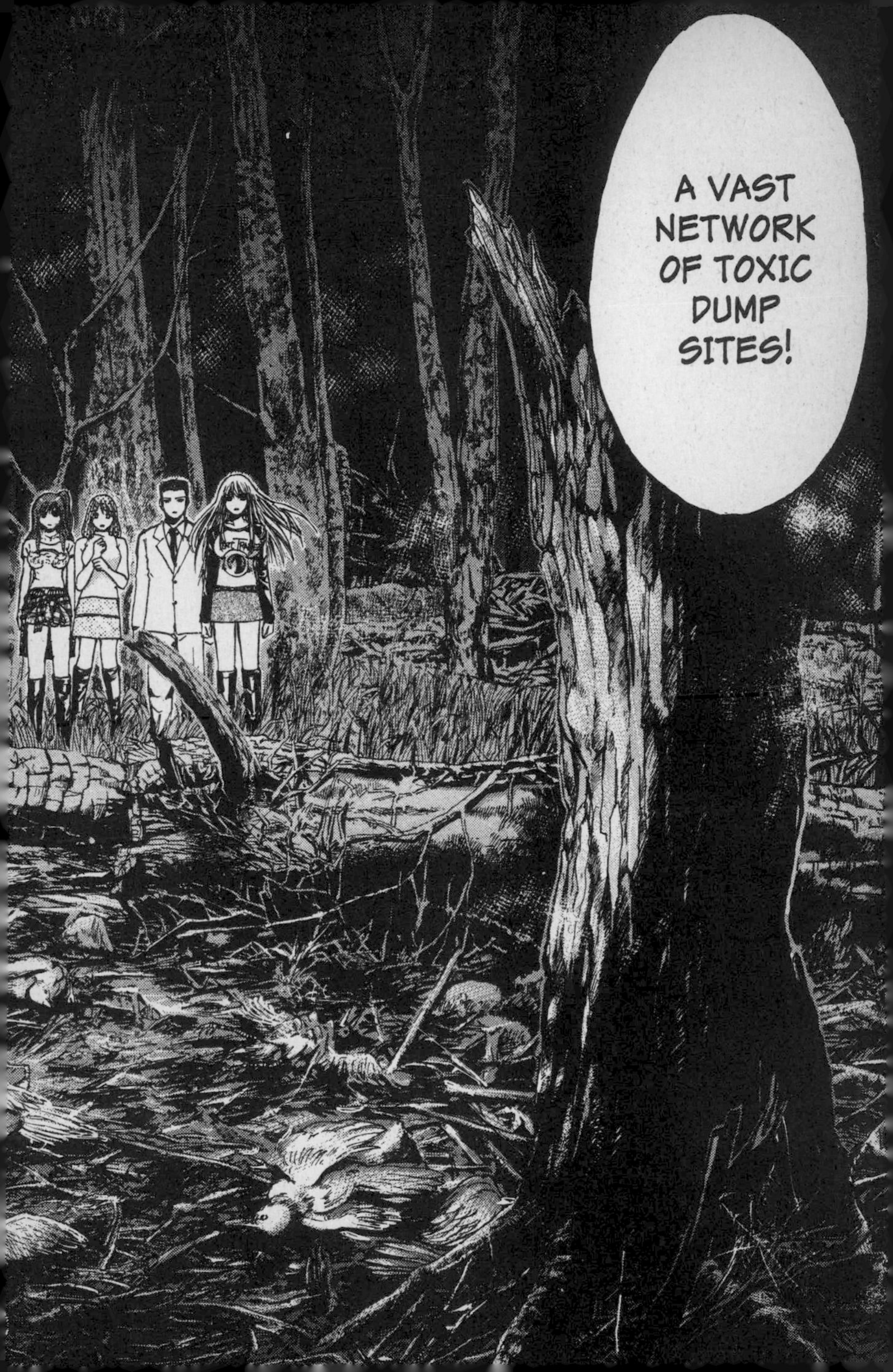
A VAST NETWORK OF TOXIC DUMP SITES!

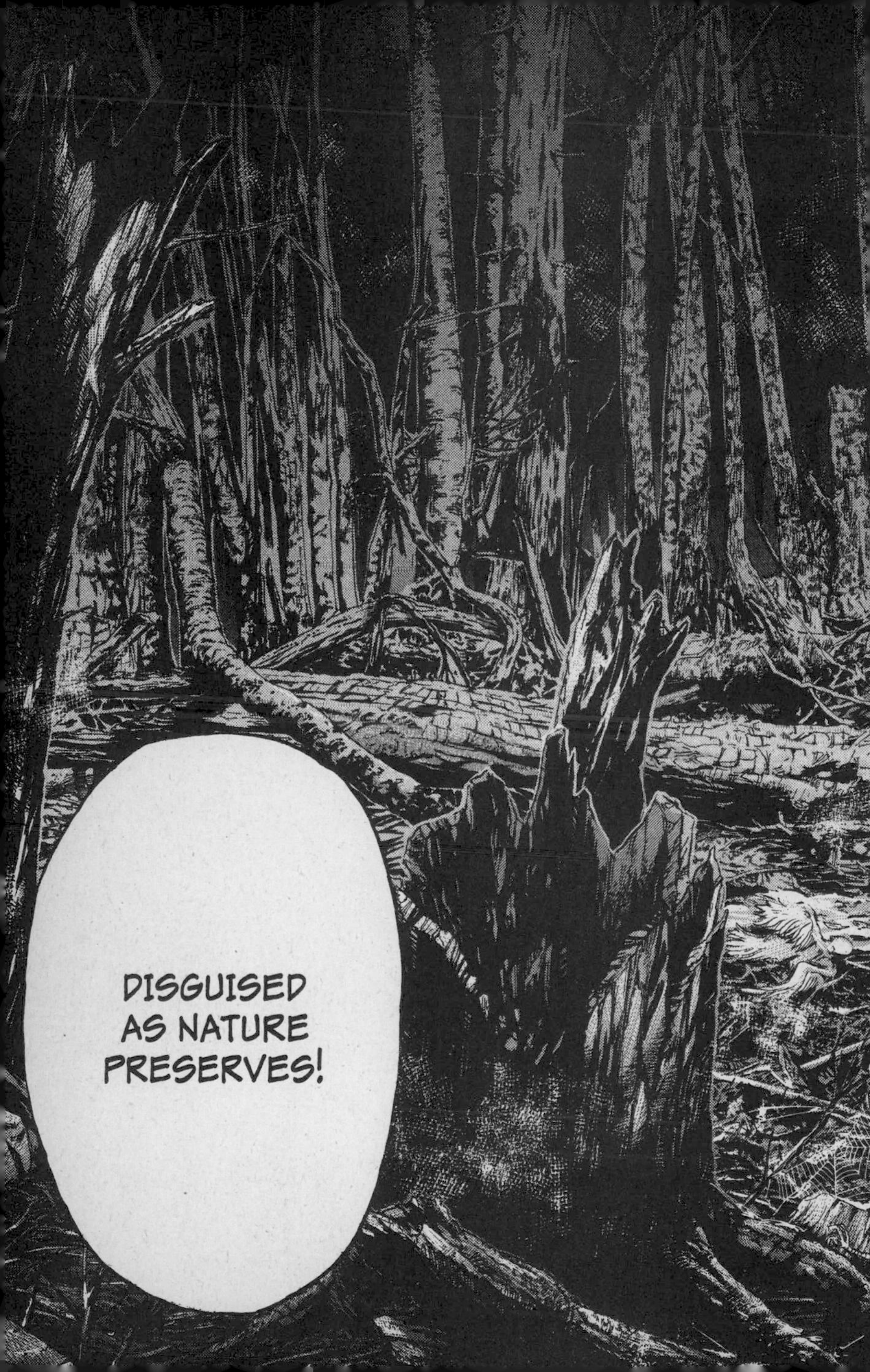
DISGUISED AS NATURE PRESERVES!

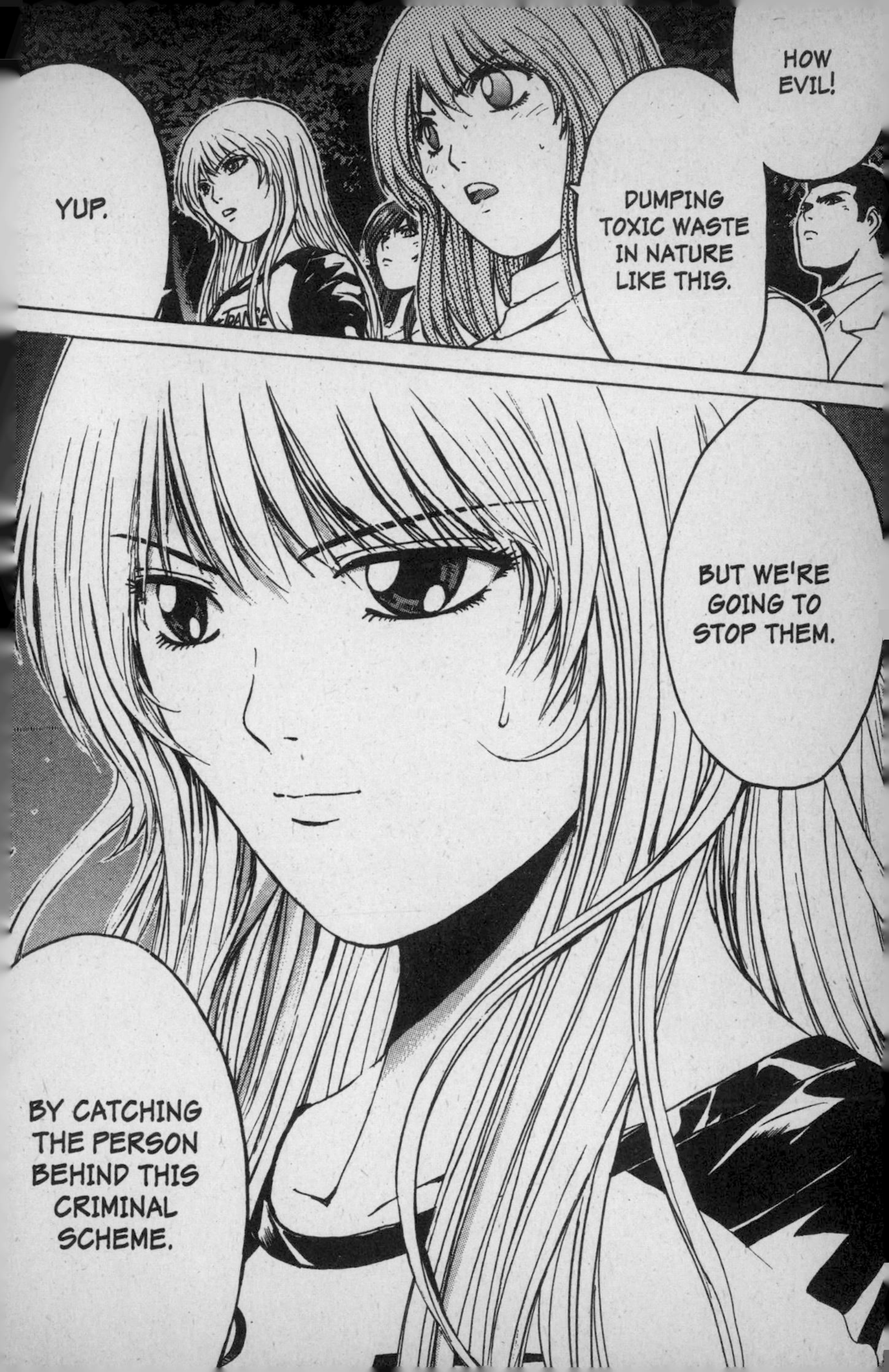
HOW EVIL!
DUMPING TOXIC WASTE IN NATURE LIKE THIS.
YUP.
BUT WE'RE GOING TO STOP THEM.
BY CATCHING THE PERSON BEHIND THIS CRIMINAL SCHEME.

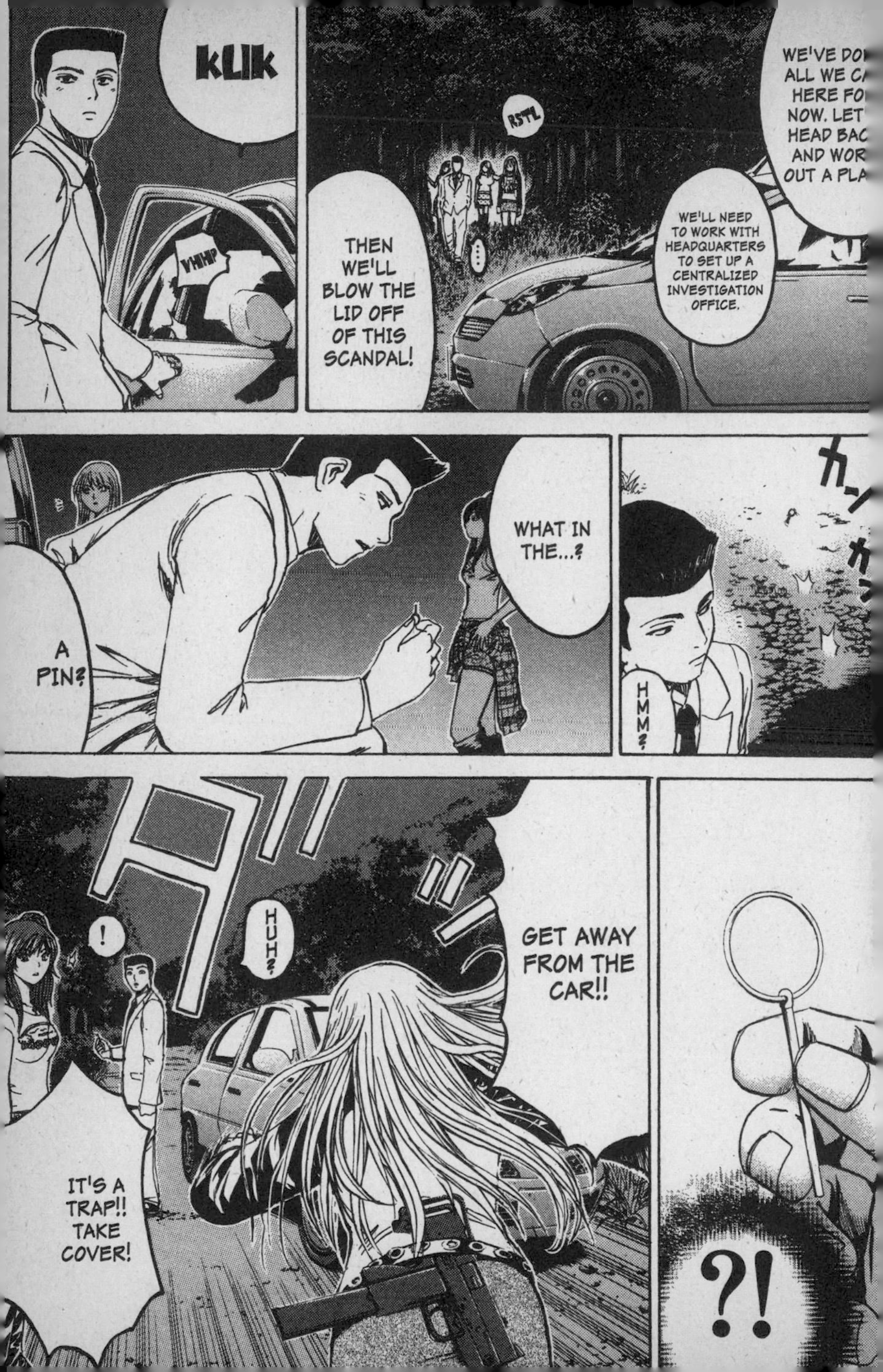
WE'VE DO
ALL WE C
HERE FO
NOW. LET
HEAD BAC
AND WOR
OUT A PLA
WE'LL NEED TO WORK WITH HEADQUARTERS TO SET UP A CENTRALIZED INVESTIGATION OFFICE.
RSTL
...
THEN WE'LL BLOW THE LID OFF OF THIS SCANDAL!
KLIK
VHHP
カッ
カッ
HMM?
WHAT IN THE...?
A PIN?
?!
GET AWAY FROM THE CAR!!
ダッ
HUH?
!
IT'S A TRAP!! TAKE COVER!

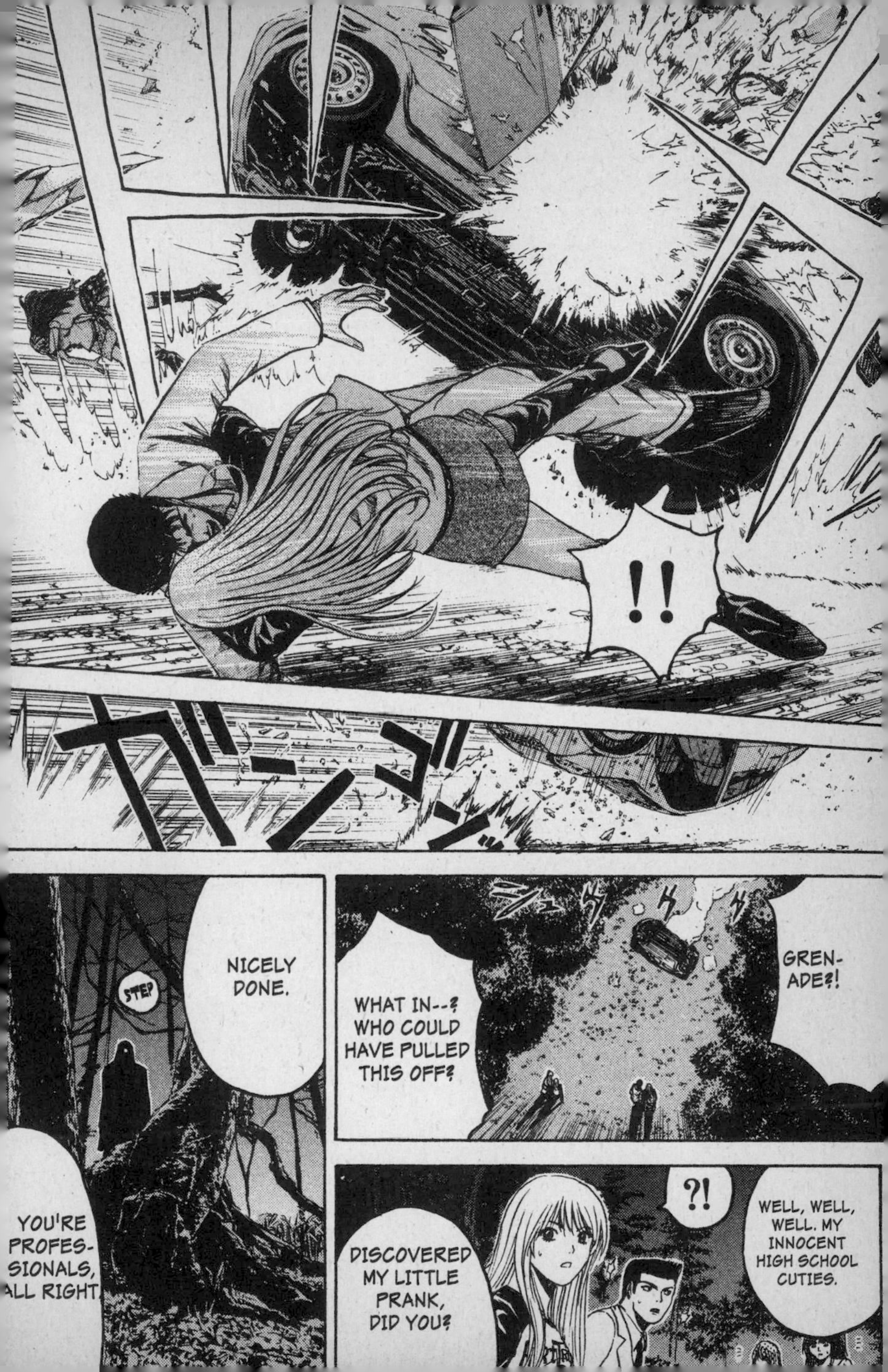
!!
GREN-ADE?!
WHAT IN--? WHO COULD HAVE PULLED THIS OFF?
WELL, WELL, WELL. MY INNOCENT HIGH SCHOOL CUTIES.
?!
DISCOVERED MY LITTLE PRANK, DID YOU?
NICELY DONE.
STEP
YOU'RE PROFES-SIONALS, ALL RIGHT.

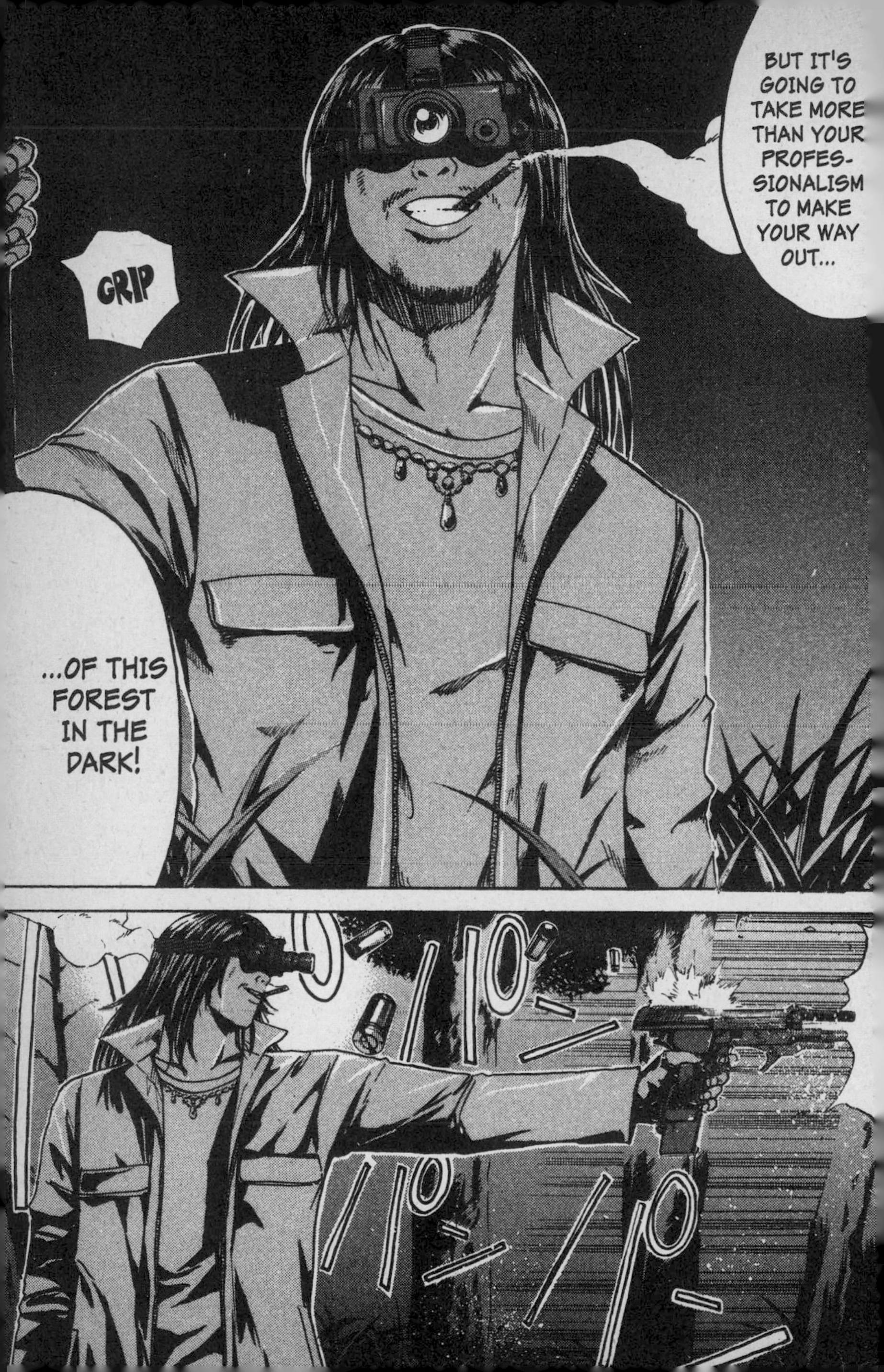
BUT IT'S GOING TO TAKE MORE THAN YOUR PROFES-SIONALISM TO MAKE YOUR WAY OUT...
GRIP
...OF THIS FOREST IN THE DARK!

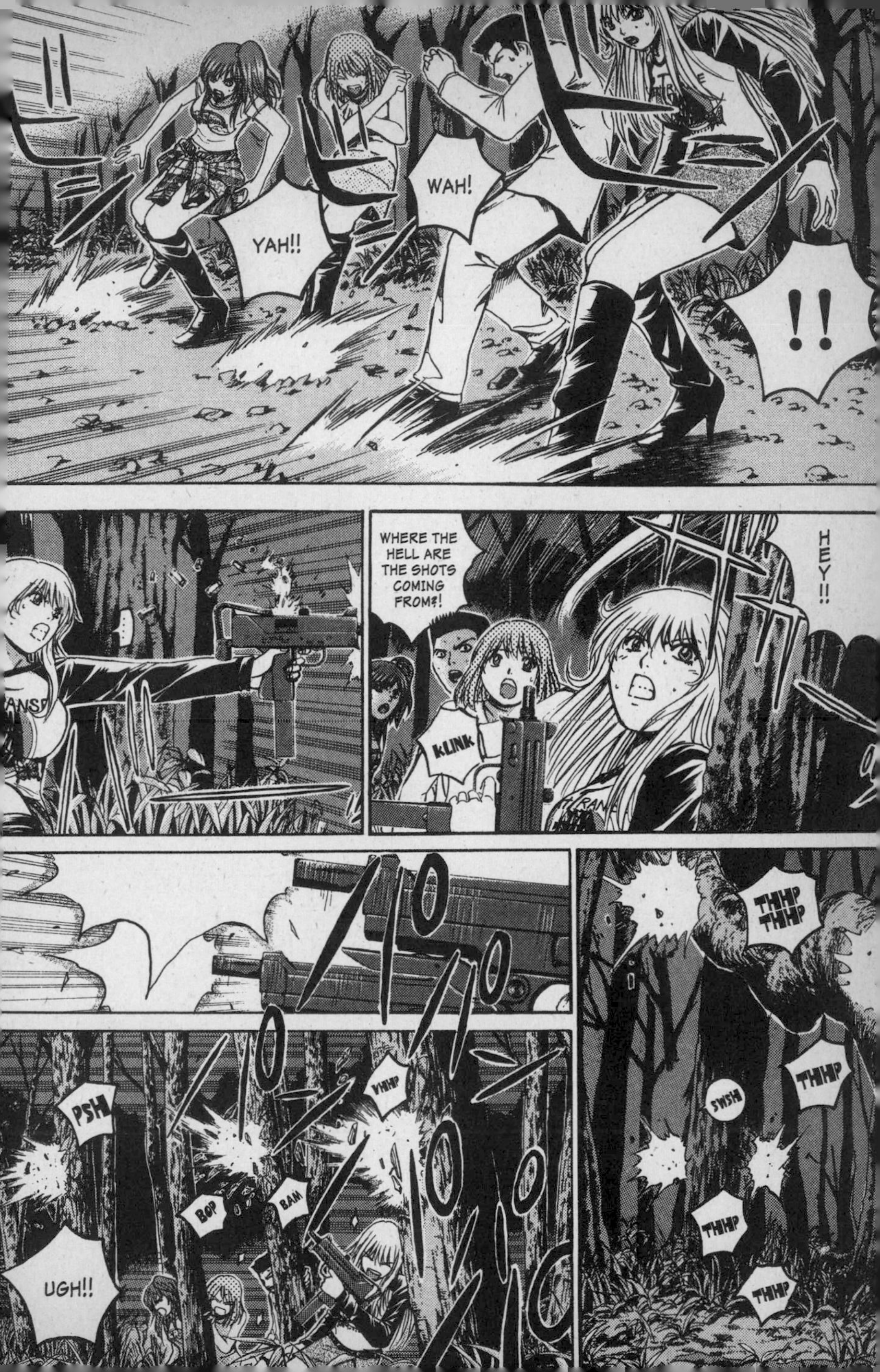
!!
WAH!
YAH!!
HEY!!
WHERE THE HELL ARE THE SHOTS COMING FROM?!
KLINK
THHP THHP
THHP
SWSH
THHP
THHP
VHHP
BAM
BOP
PSH
UGH!!

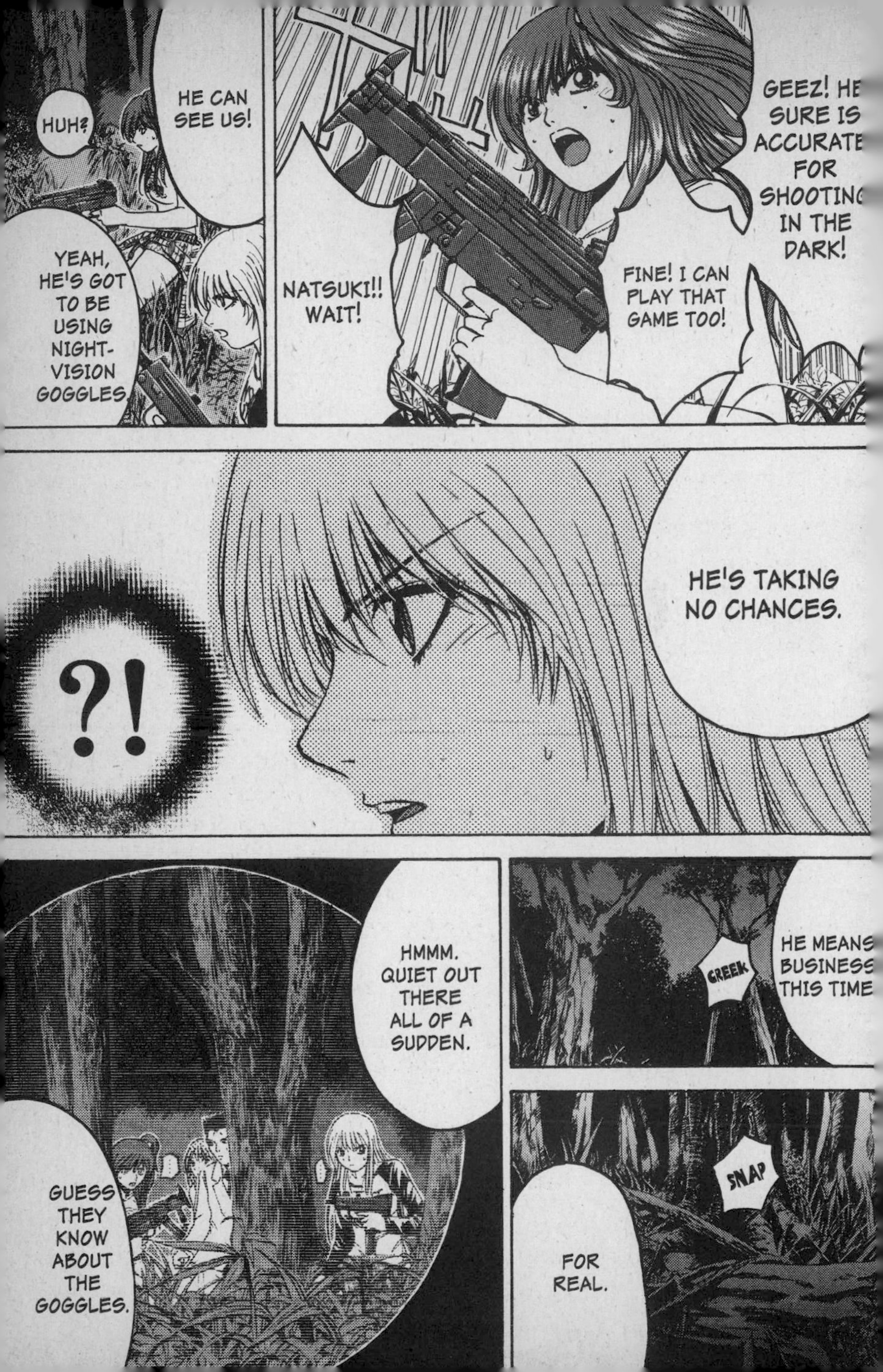
GEEZ! HE SURE IS ACCURATE FOR SHOOTING IN THE DARK!
FINE! I CAN PLAY THAT GAME TOO!
NATSUKI!! WAIT!
HE CAN SEE US!
HUH?
YEAH, HE'S GOT TO BE USING NIGHT-VISION GOGGLES.
HE'S TAKING NO CHANCES.
?!
HE MEANS BUSINESS THIS TIME
CREEK
SNAP
FOR REAL.
HMMM. QUIET OUT THERE ALL OF A SUDDEN.
GUESS THEY KNOW ABOUT THE GOGGLES.

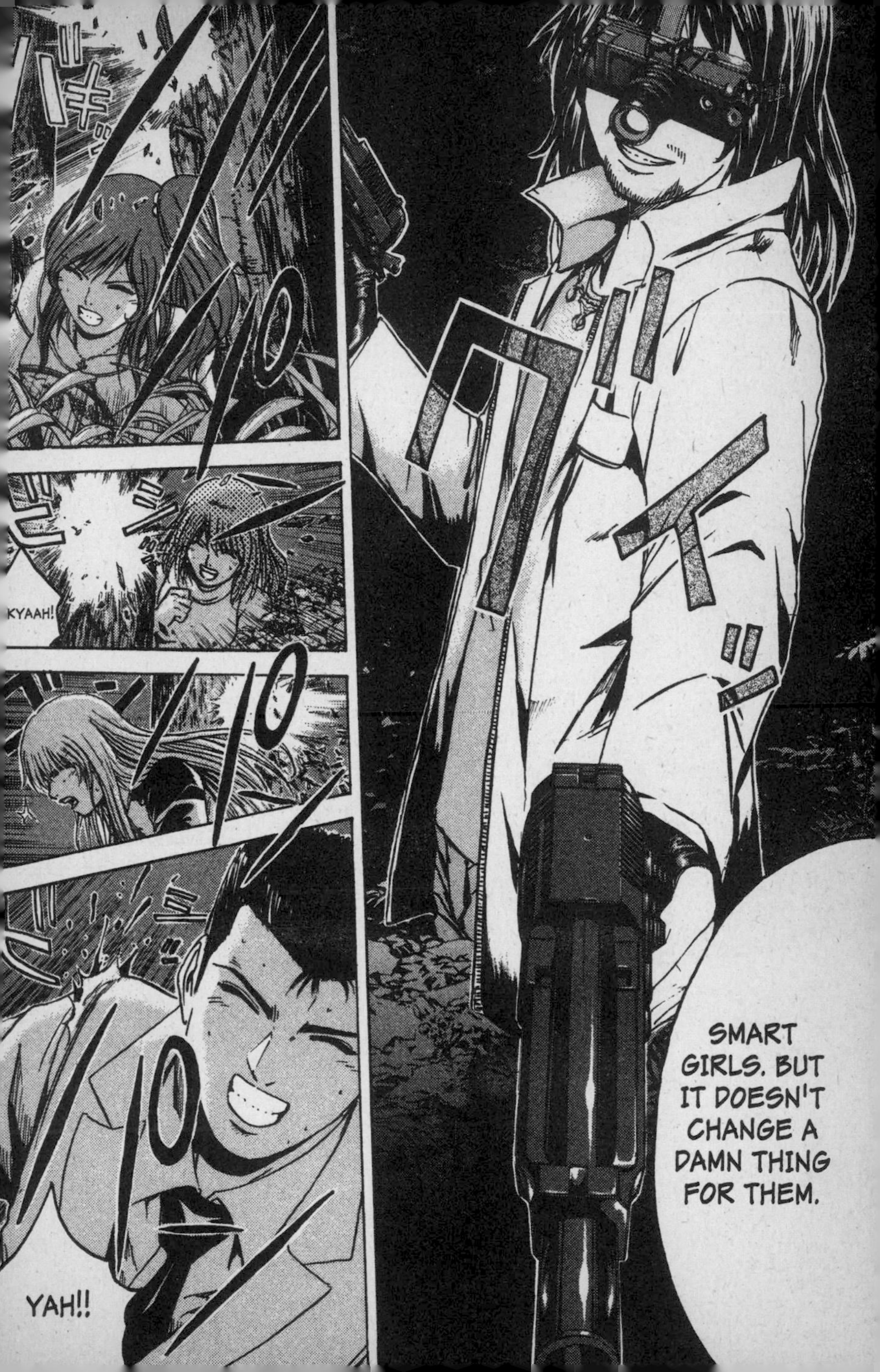
SMART GIRLS. BUT IT DOESN'T CHANGE A DAMN THING FOR THEM.
KYAAH!
YAH!!

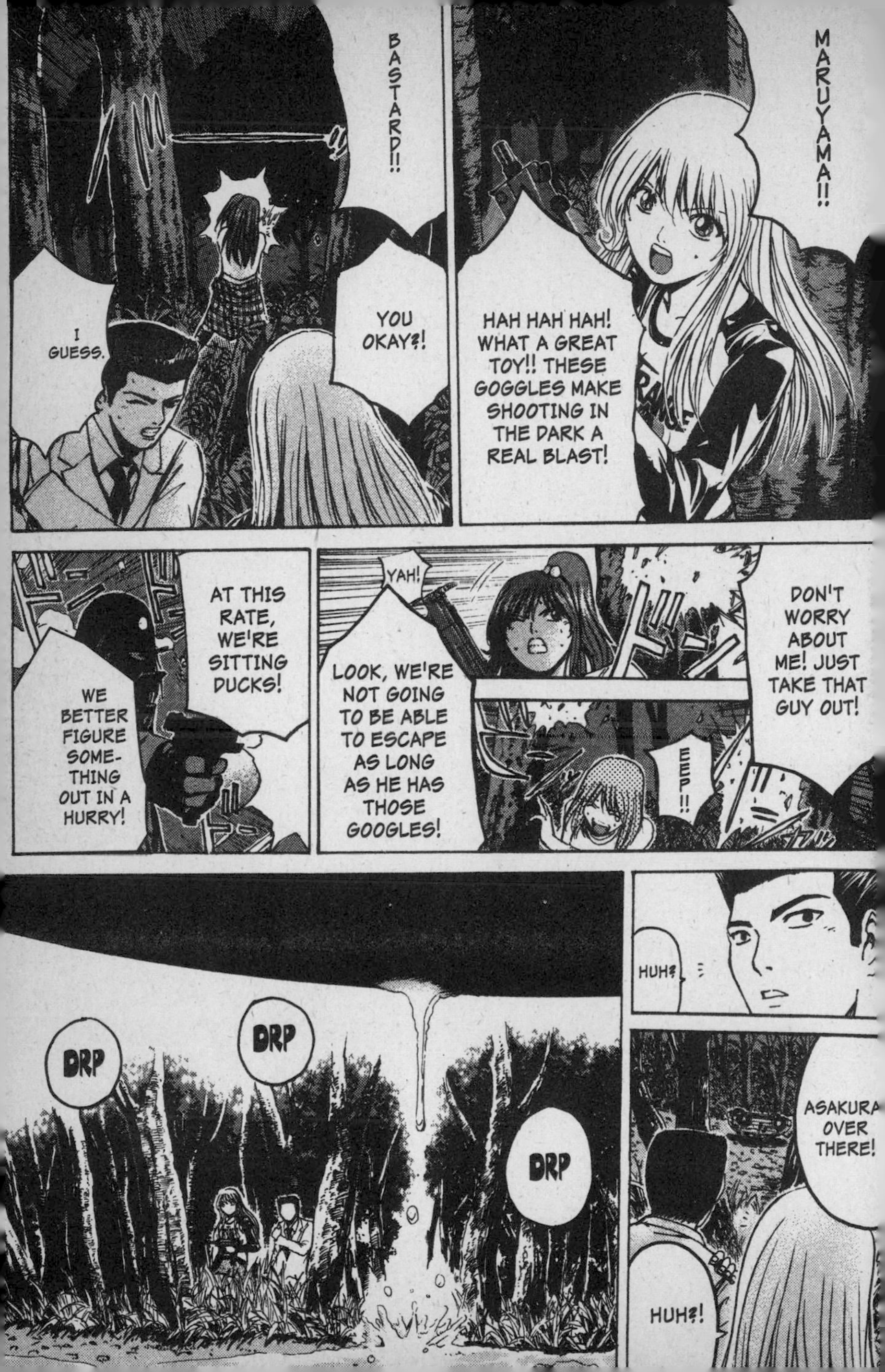
MARUYAMA!!
HAH HAH HAH! WHAT A GREAT TOY!! THESE GOGGLES MAKE SHOOTING IN THE DARK A REAL BLAST!
BASTARD!!
YOU OKAY?!
I GUESS.
DON'T WORRY ABOUT ME! JUST TAKE THAT GUY OUT!
YAH!
EEP!!
LOOK, WE'RE NOT GOING TO BE ABLE TO ESCAPE AS LONG AS HE HAS THOSE GOOGLES!
AT THIS RATE, WE'RE SITTING DUCKS!
WE BETTER FIGURE SOME-THING OUT IN A HURRY!
HUH?
ASAKURA OVER THERE!
HUH?!
DRP
DRP
DRP

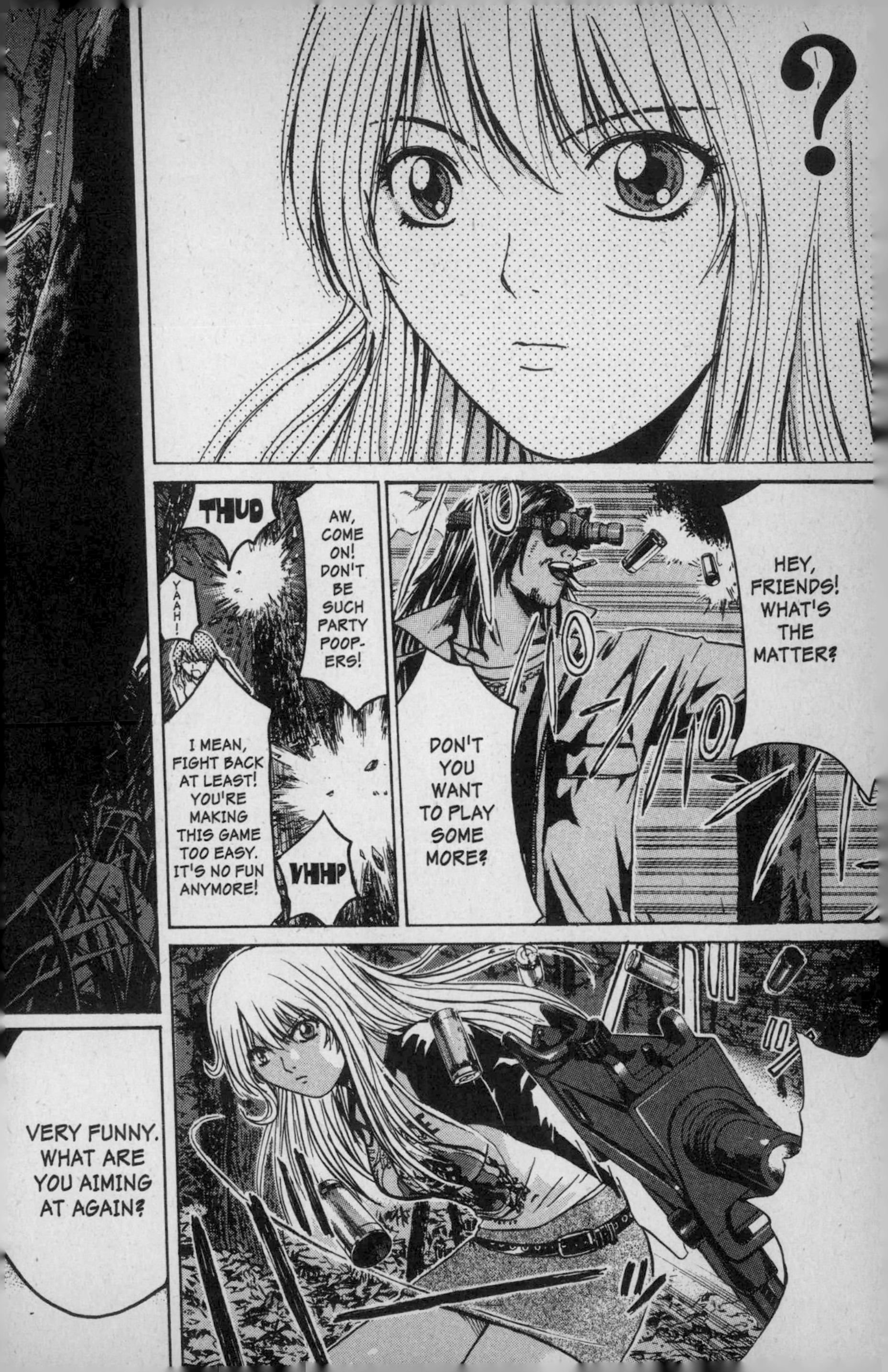
?
HEY, FRIENDS! WHAT'S THE MATTER?
DON'T YOU WANT TO PLAY SOME MORE?
AW, COME ON! DON'T BE SUCH PARTY POOPERS!
THUD
YAAH!
I MEAN, FIGHT BACK AT LEAST! YOU'RE MAKING THIS GAME TOO EASY. IT'S NO FUN ANYMORE!
VHHP
VERY FUNNY. WHAT ARE YOU AIMING AT AGAIN?

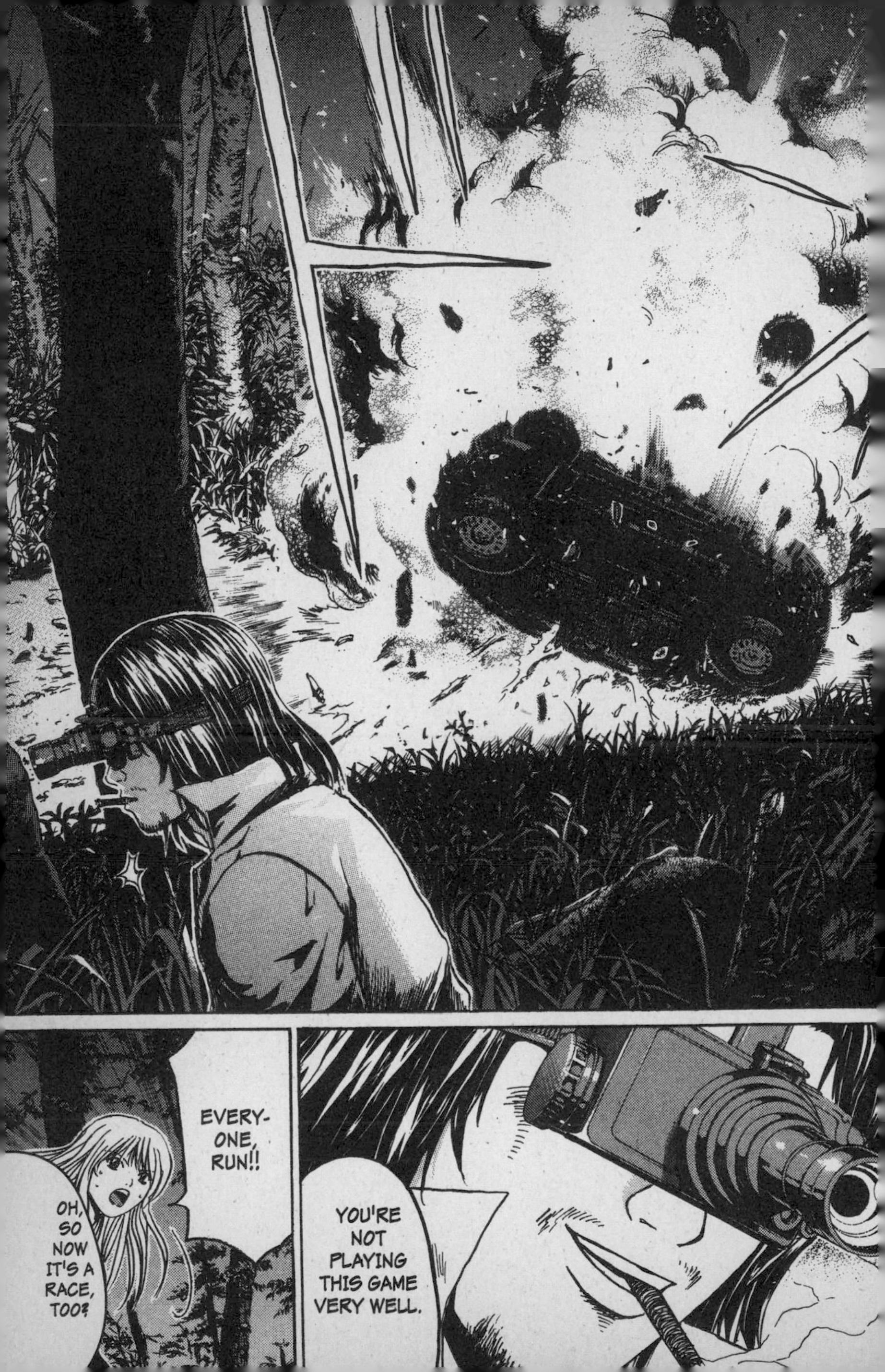
YOU'RE NOT PLAYING THIS GAME VERY WELL.
EVERY-ONE, RUN!!
OH, SO NOW IT'S A RACE, TOO?

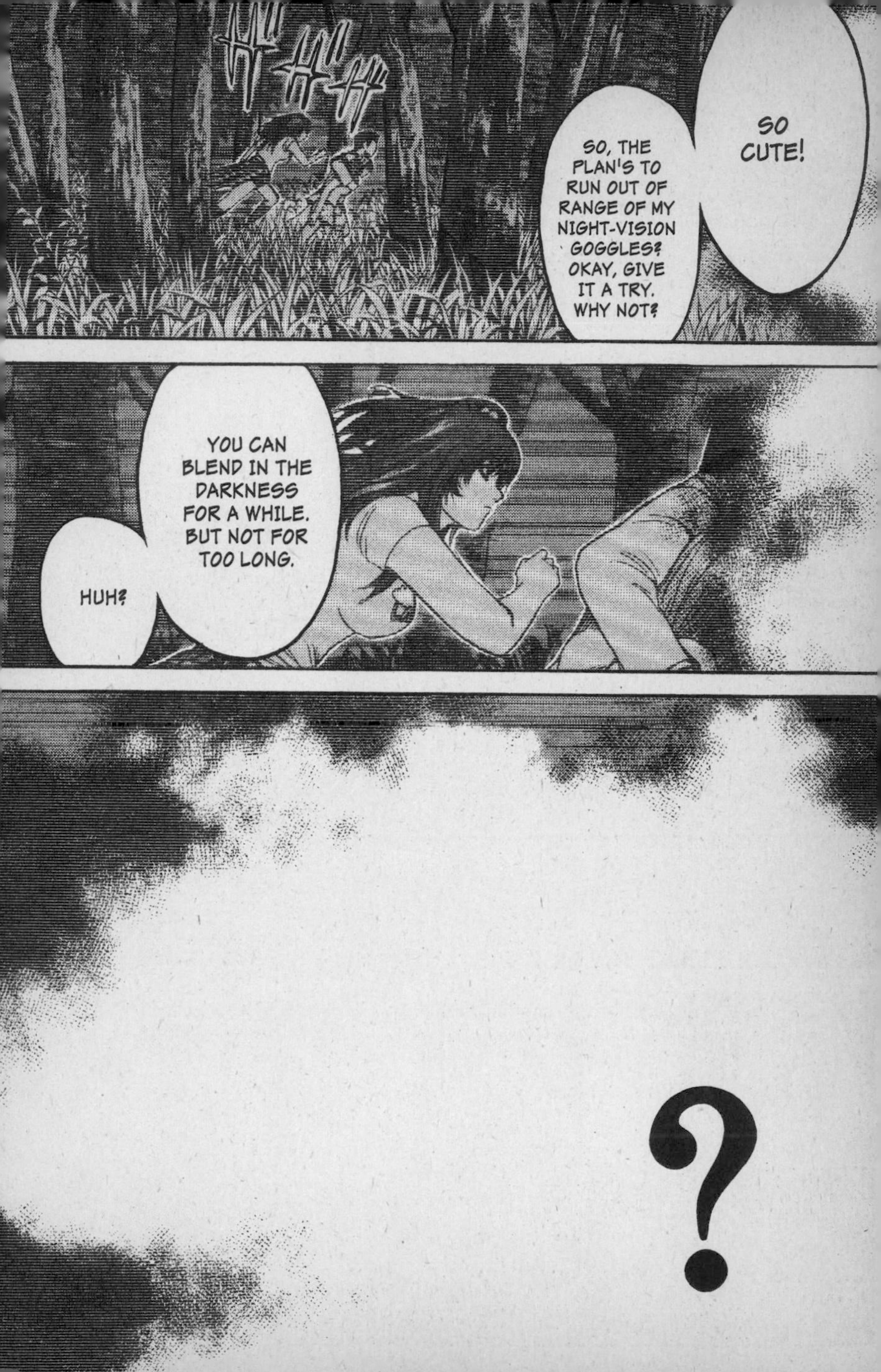
SO CUTE!
SO, THE PLAN'S TO RUN OUT OF RANGE OF MY NIGHT-VISION GOGGLES? OKAY, GIVE IT A TRY. WHY NOT?
YOU CAN BLEND IN THE DARKNESS FOR A WHILE. BUT NOT FOR TOO LONG.
HUH?
?

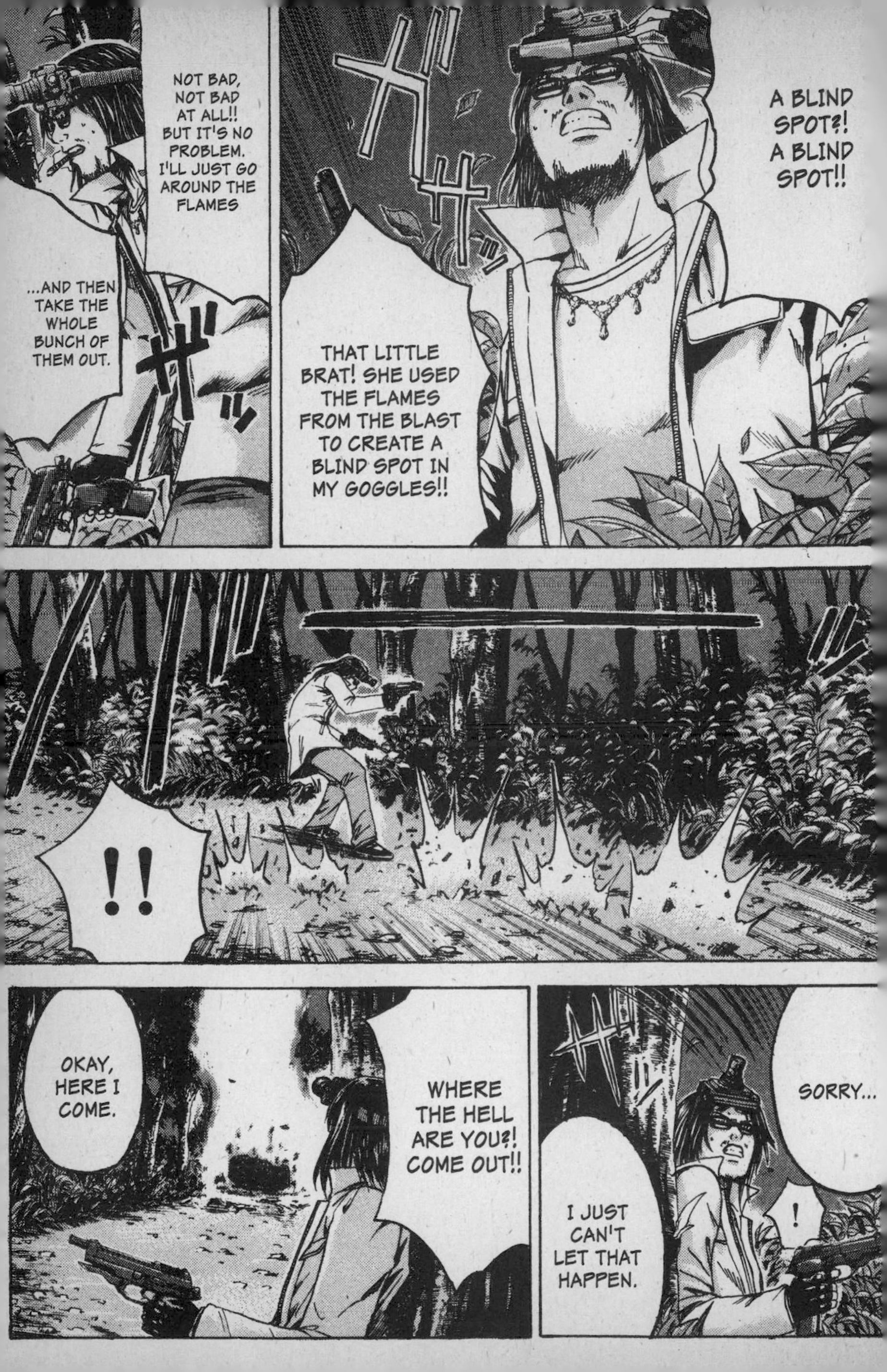
A BLIND SPOT?! A BLIND SPOT!!
THAT LITTLE BRAT! SHE USED THE FLAMES FROM THE BLAST TO CREATE A BLIND SPOT IN MY GOGGLES!!
NOT BAD, NOT BAD AT ALL!! BUT IT'S NO PROBLEM. I'LL JUST GO AROUND THE FLAMES
...AND THEN TAKE THE WHOLE BUNCH OF THEM OUT.
!!
SORRY...
!
I JUST CAN'T LET THAT HAPPEN.
WHERE THE HELL ARE YOU?! COME OUT!!
OKAY, HERE I COME.

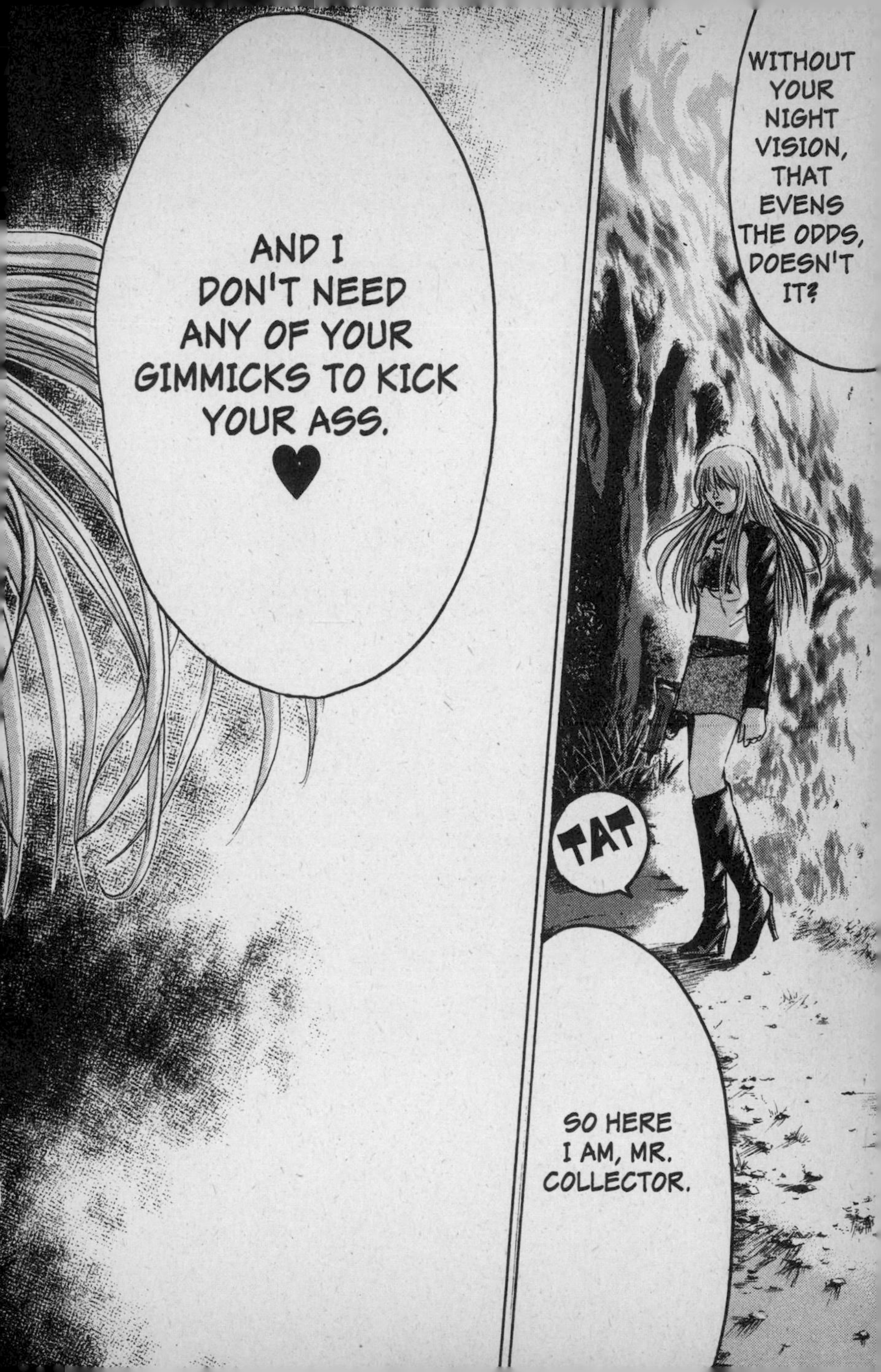
WITHOUT YOUR NIGHT VISION, THAT EVENS THE ODDS, DOESN'T IT?
TAT
SO HERE I AM, MR. COLLECTOR.
AND I DON'T NEED ANY OF YOUR GIMMICKS TO KICK YOUR ASS. ♥

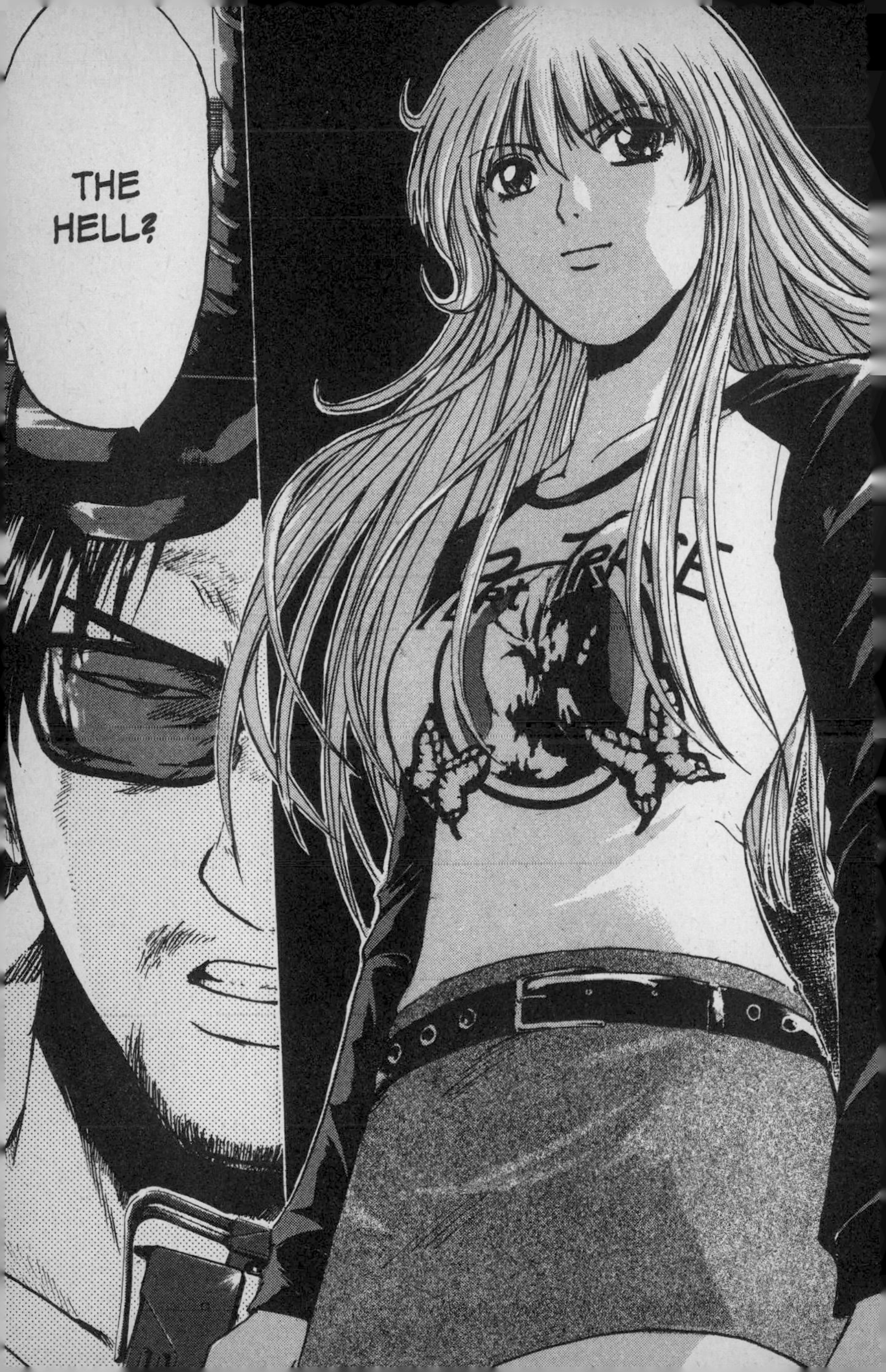
THE HELL?

Rose Hip Rose

ローズ・ヒップ・ローズ

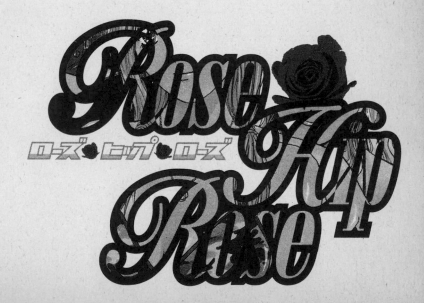

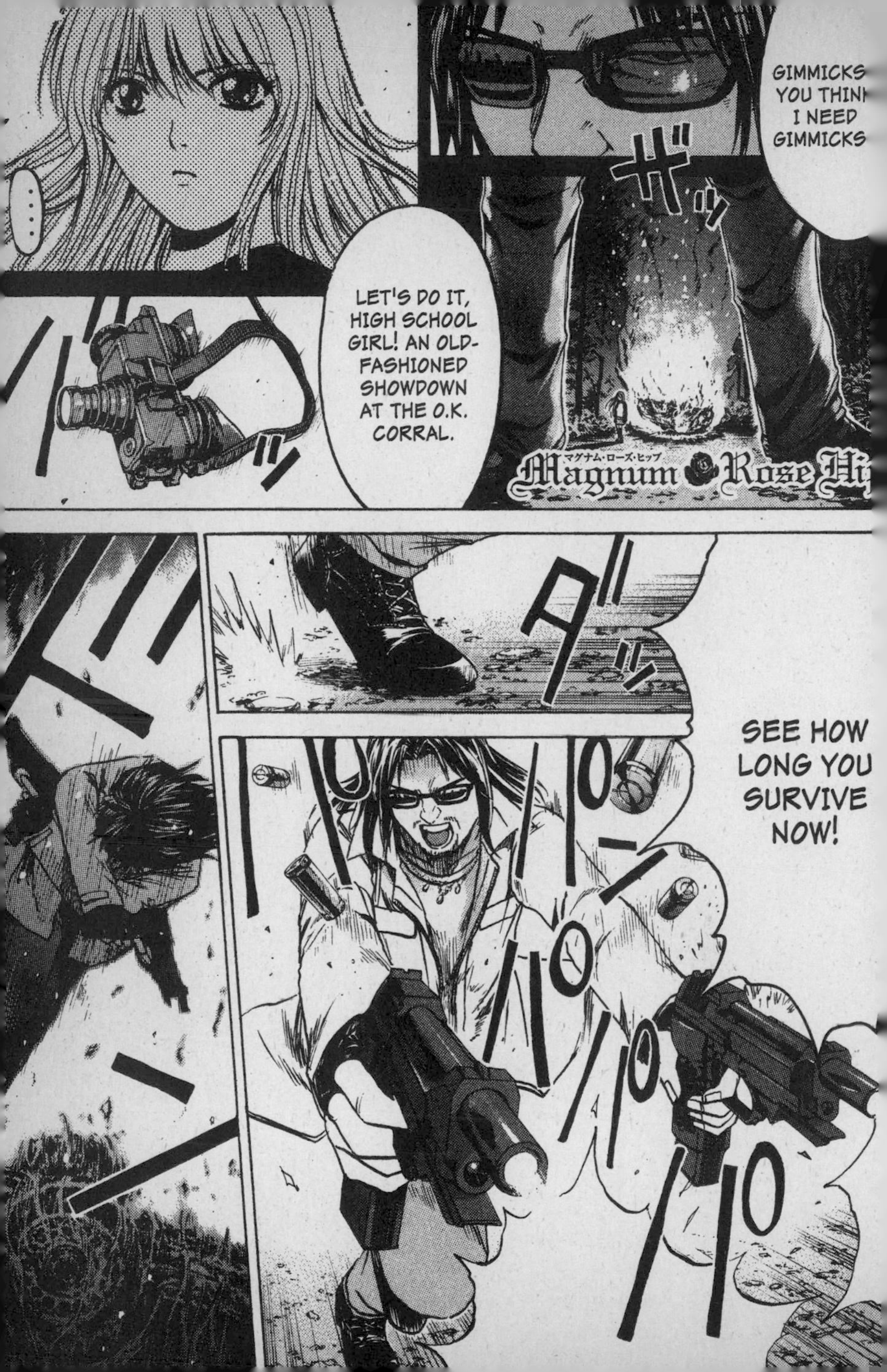
GIMMICKS YOU THINK I NEED GIMMICKS
ザッ
…
LET'S DO IT, HIGH SCHOOL GIRL! AN OLD-FASHIONED SHOWDOWN AT THE O.K. CORRAL.
マグナム・ローズ・ヒップ
Magnum Rose Hi
ダッ
SEE HOW LONG YOU SURVIVE NOW!

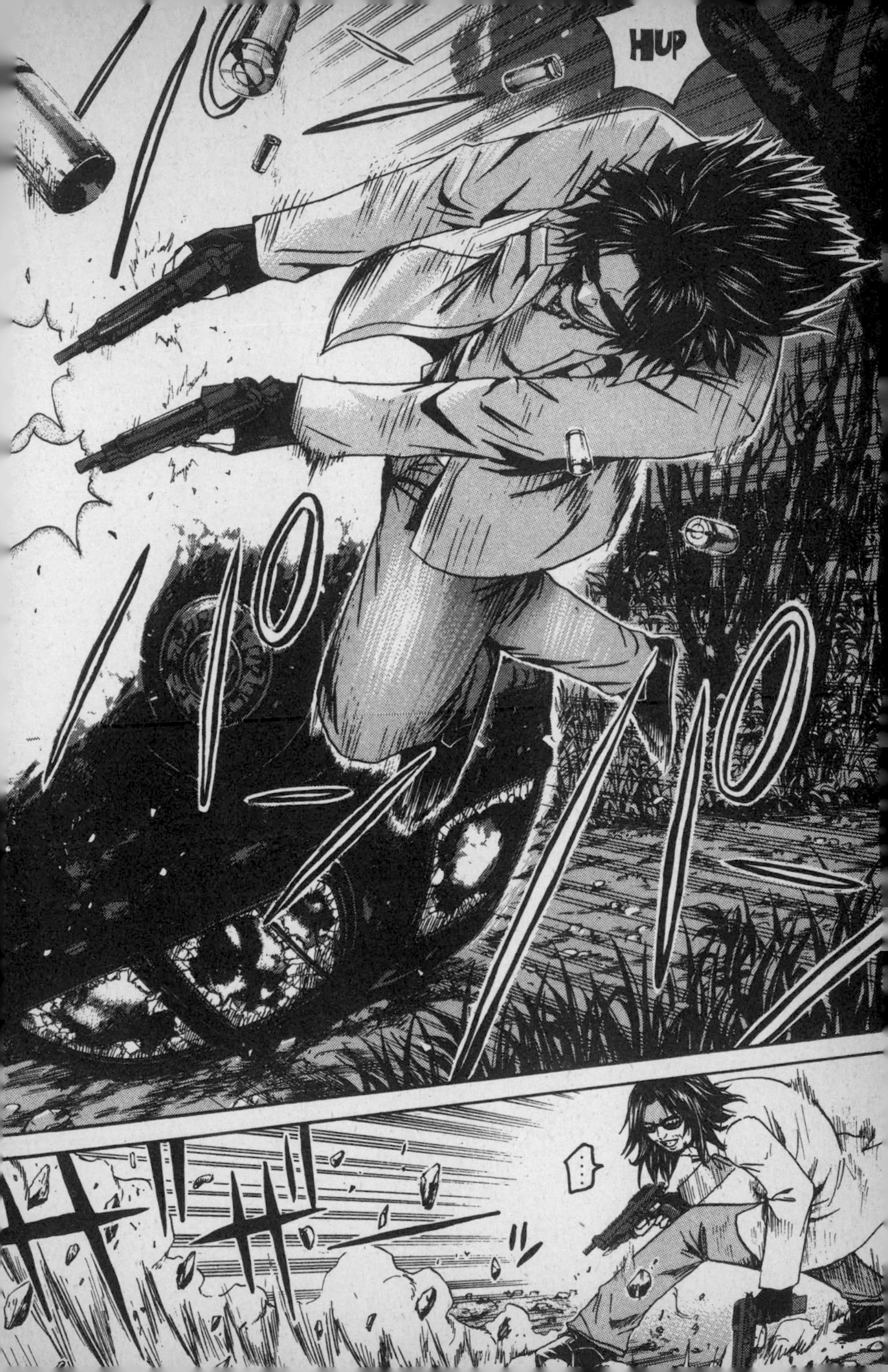
HUP
...

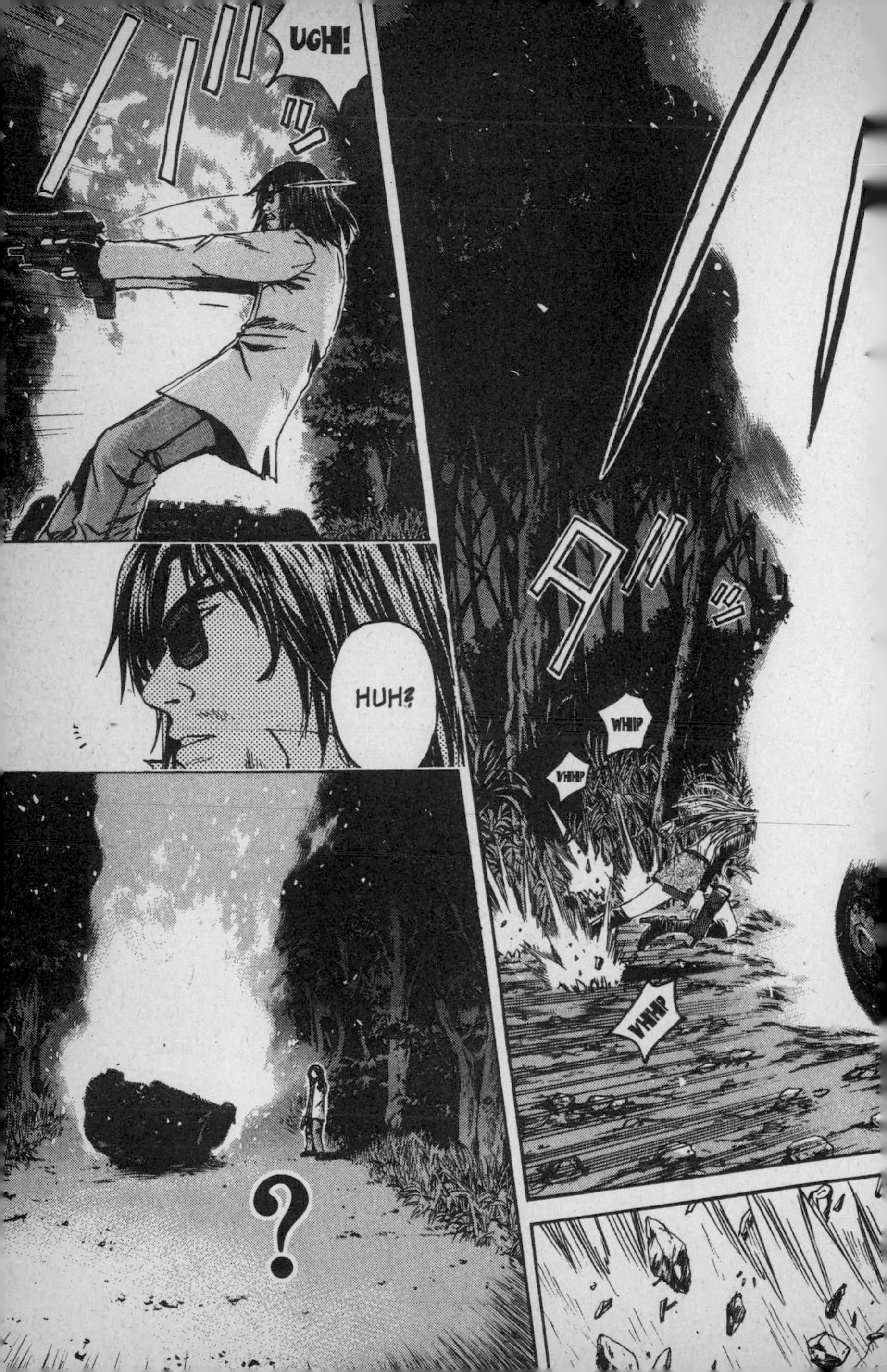
WHIP
WHIP
WHIP
UGH!
HUH?
?

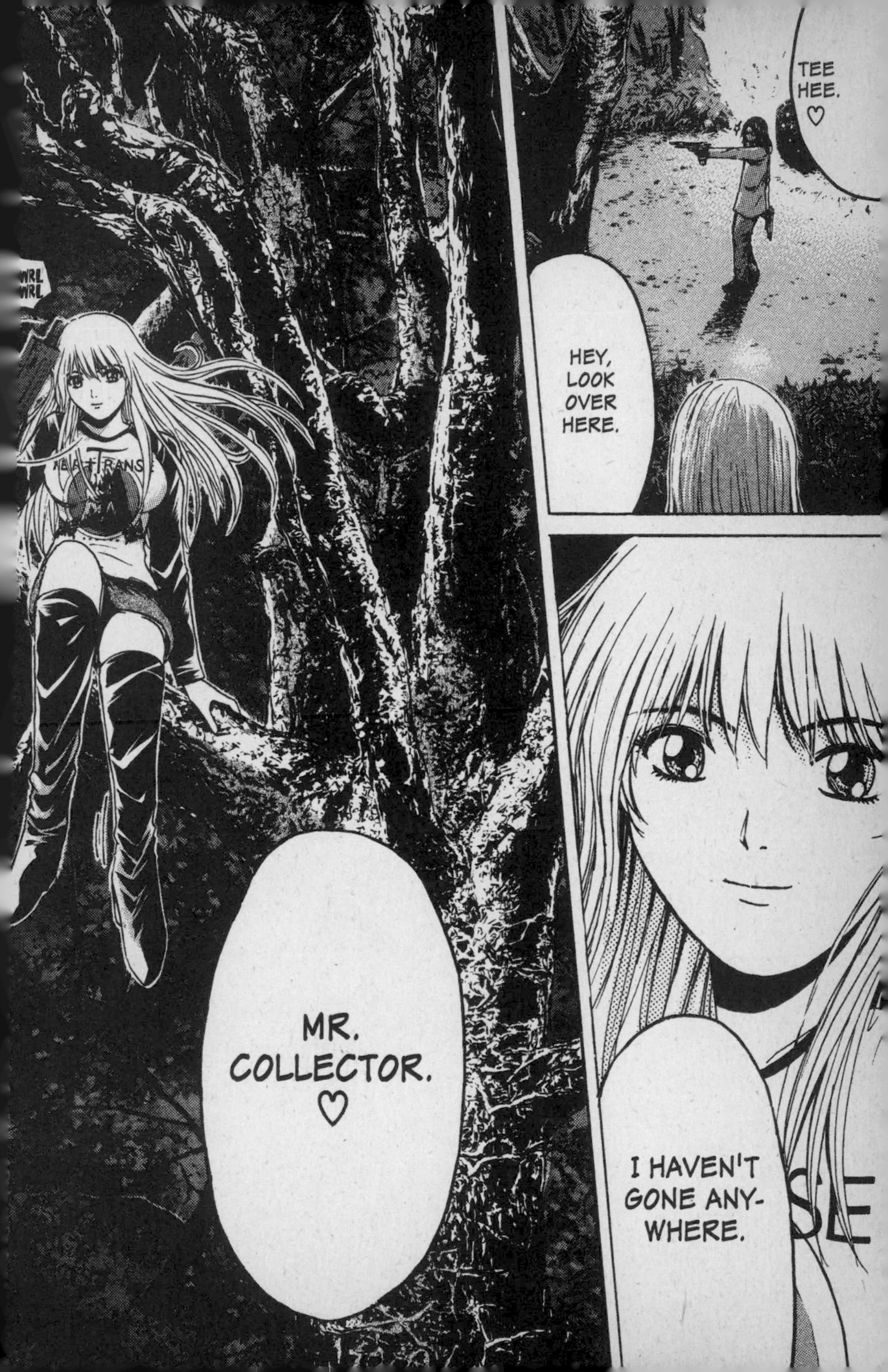
TEE HEE. ♡
HEY, LOOK OVER HERE.
I HAVEN'T GONE ANY-WHERE.
MR. COLLECTOR. ♡

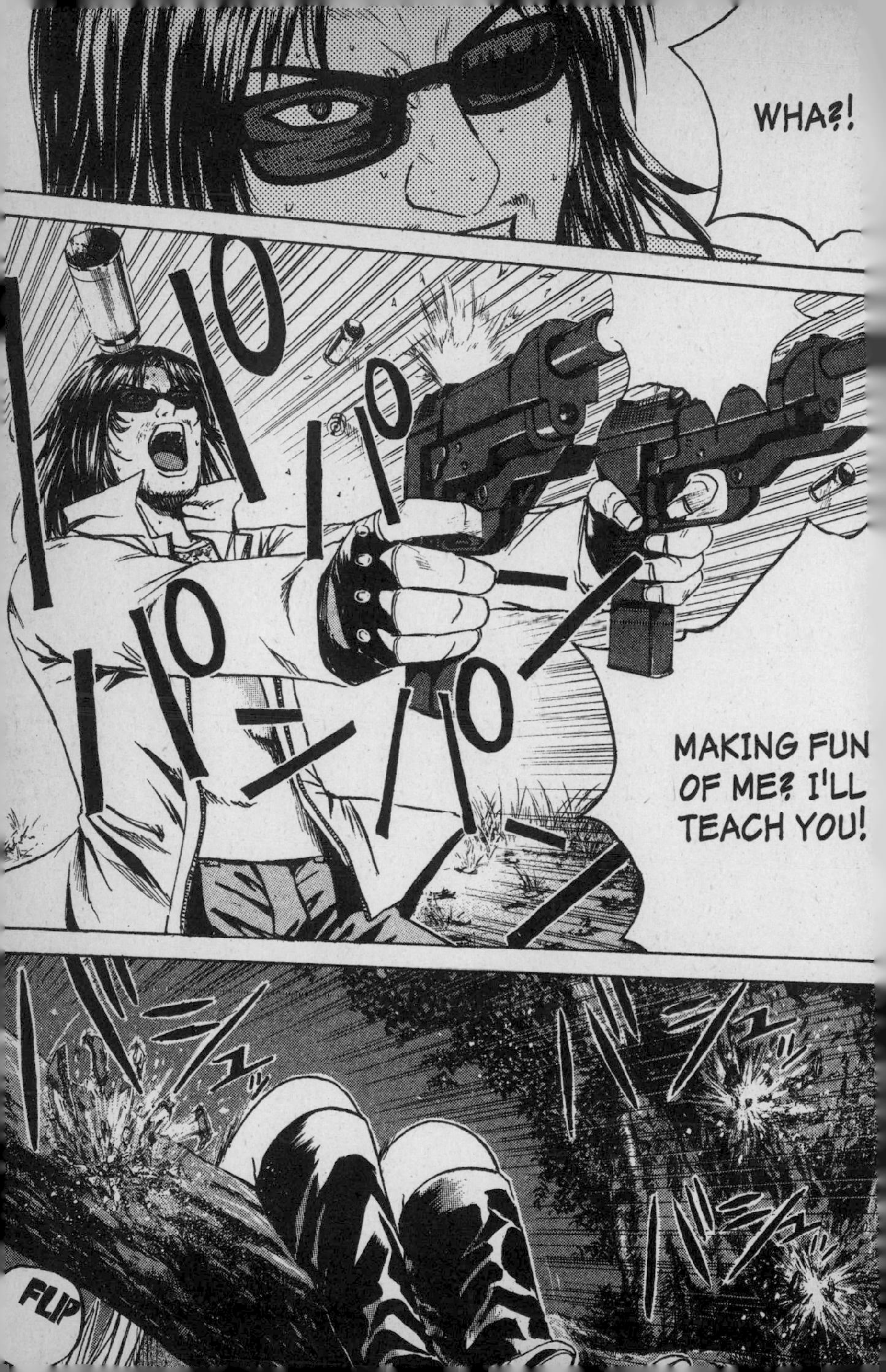
WHA?!
MAKING FUN OF ME? I'LL TEACH YOU!
FLIP

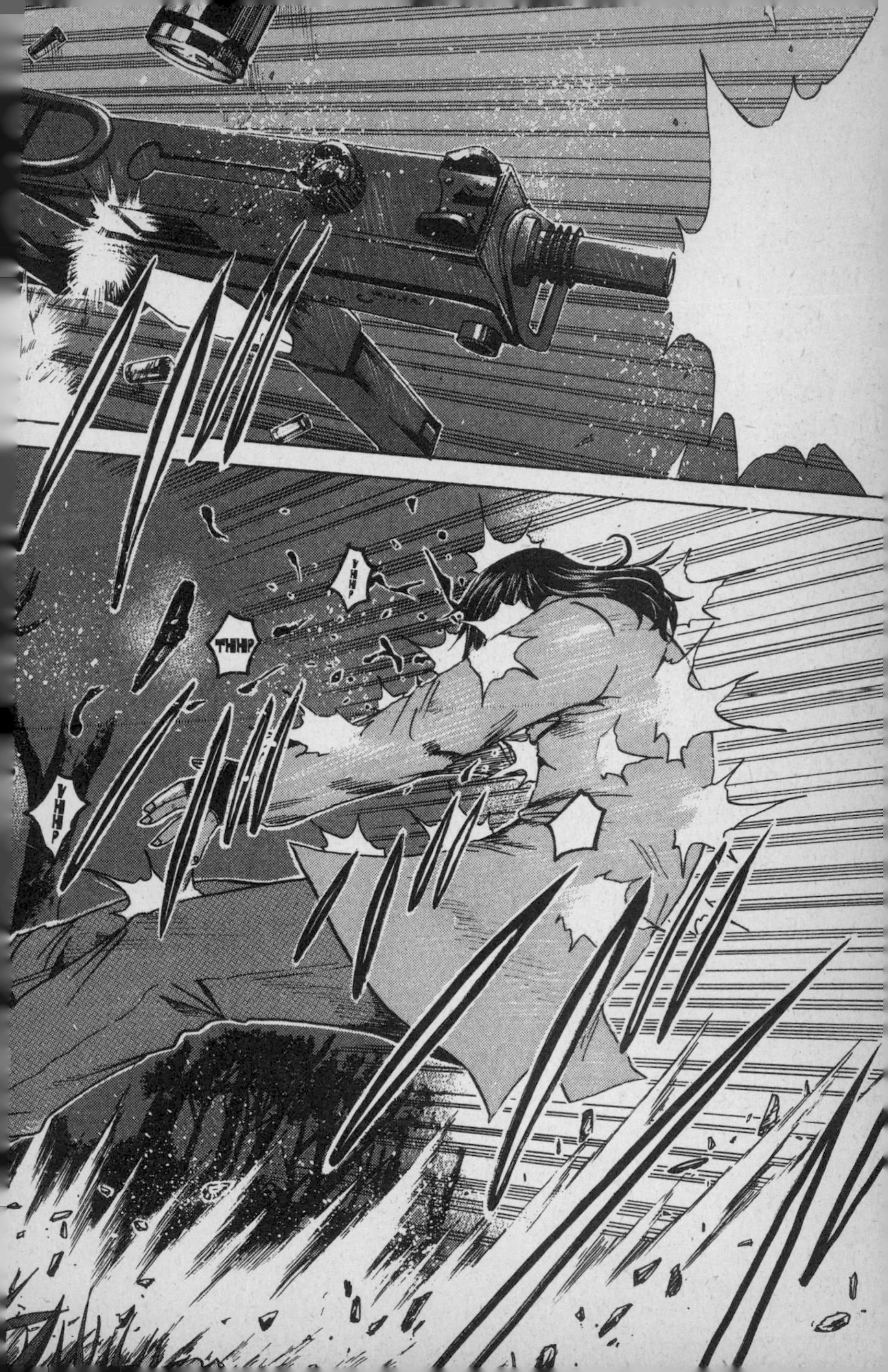
VHHP
THHP
VHHP

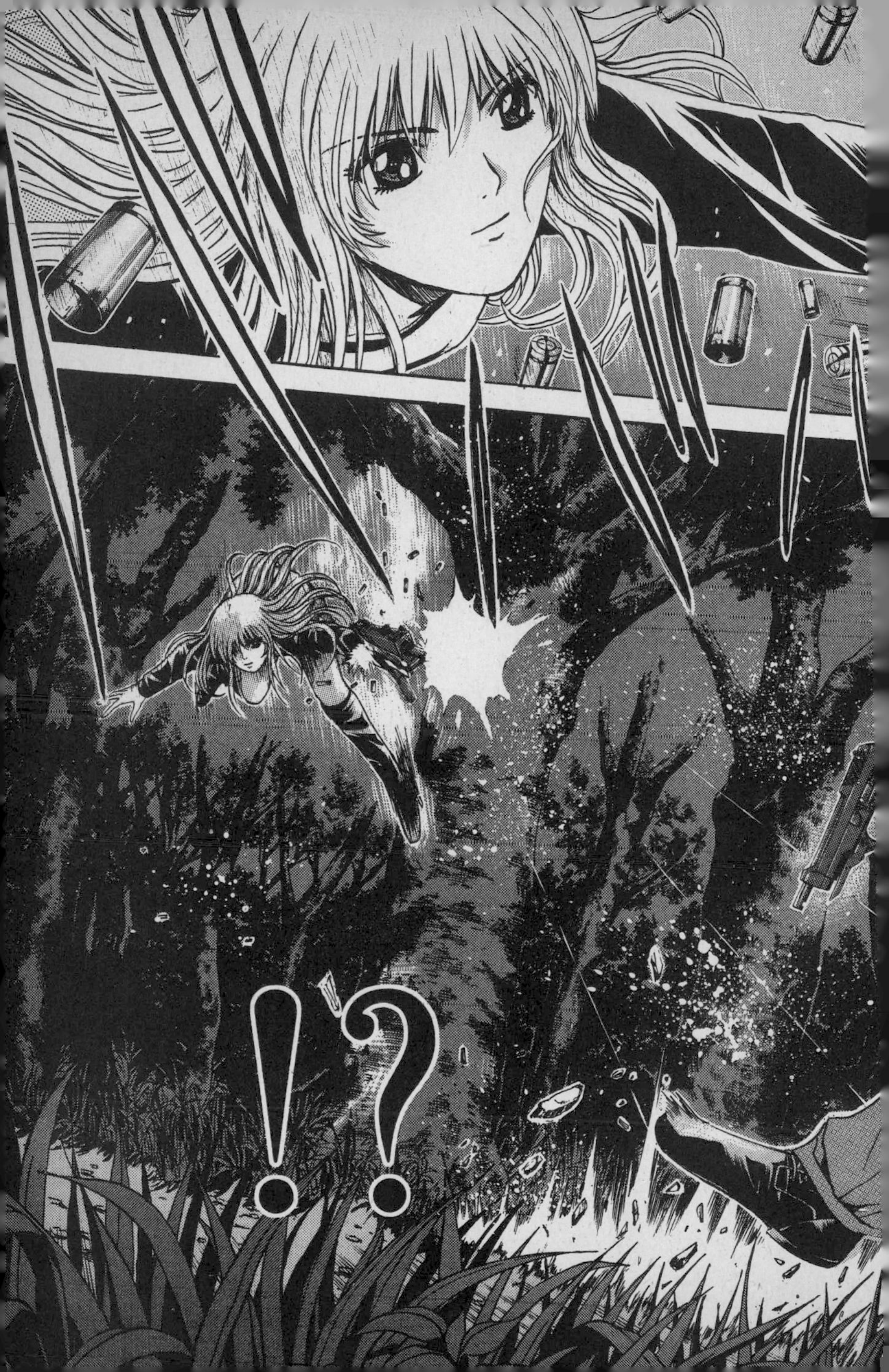
!?

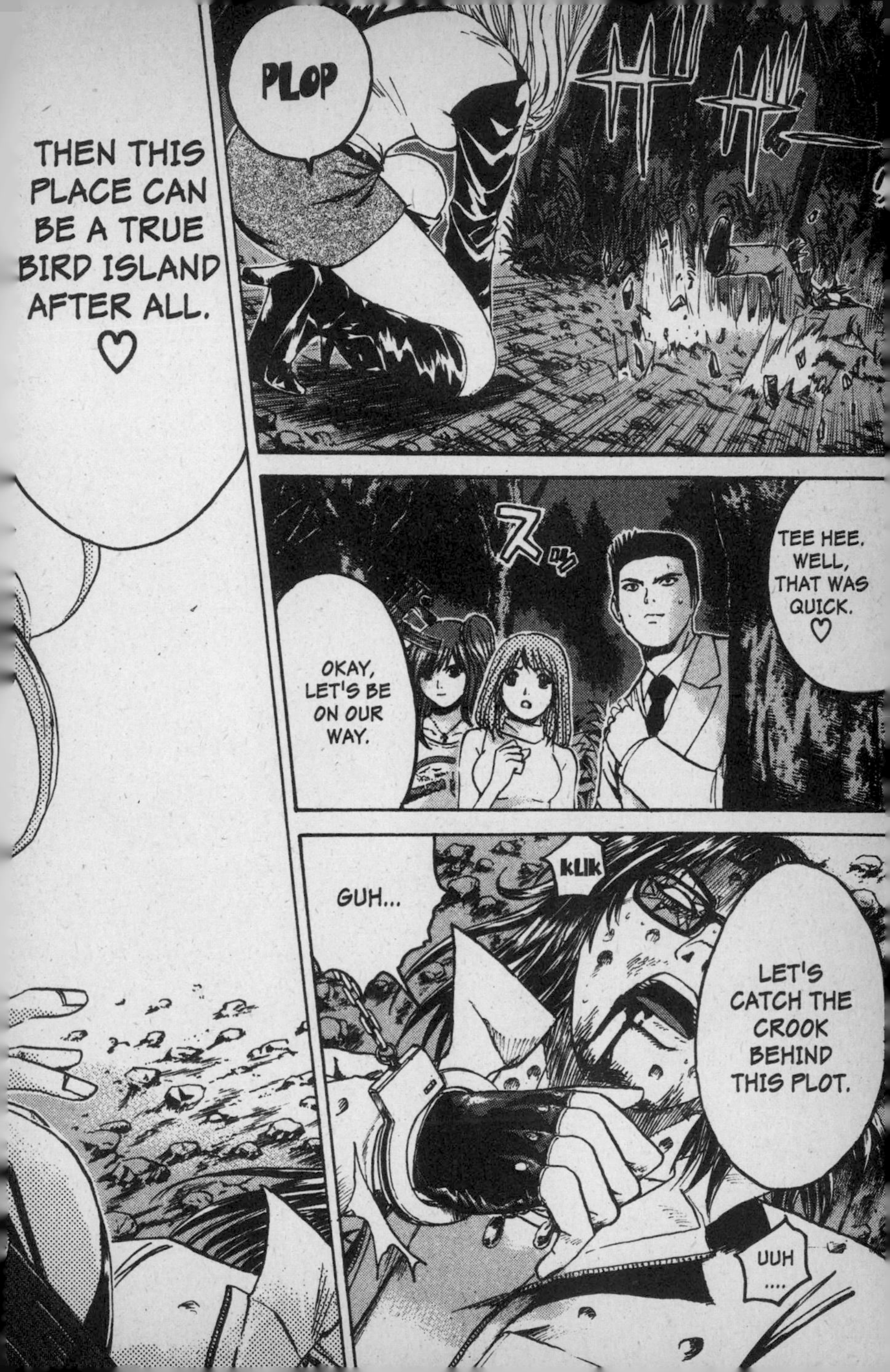
PLOP
TEE HEE. WELL, THAT WAS QUICK. ♡
スッ
OKAY, LET'S BE ON OUR WAY.
KLIK
LET'S CATCH THE CROOK BEHIND THIS PLOT.
GUH...
UUH ....
THEN THIS PLACE CAN BE A TRUE BIRD ISLAND AFTER ALL. ♡

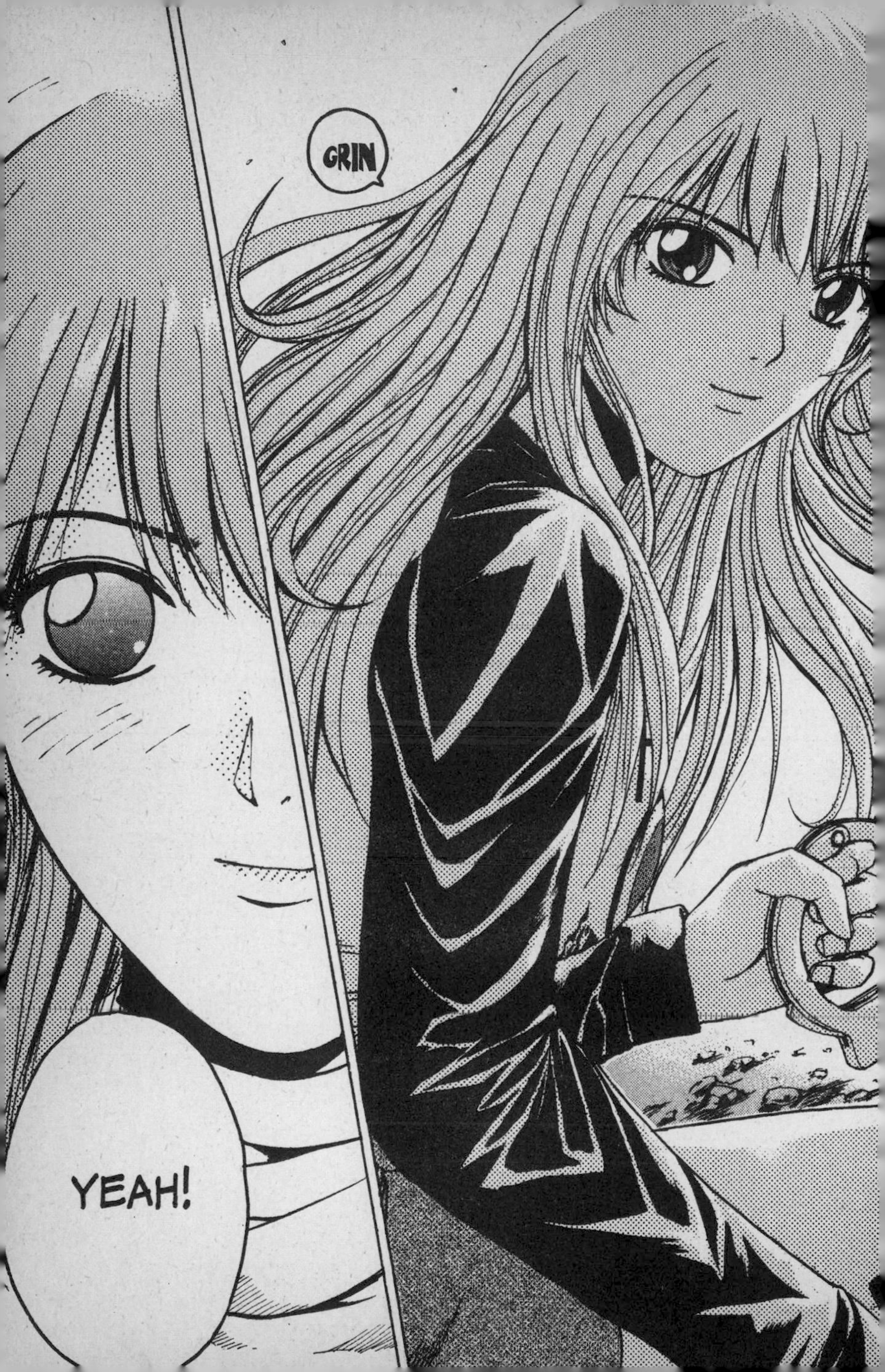
GRIN
YEAH!

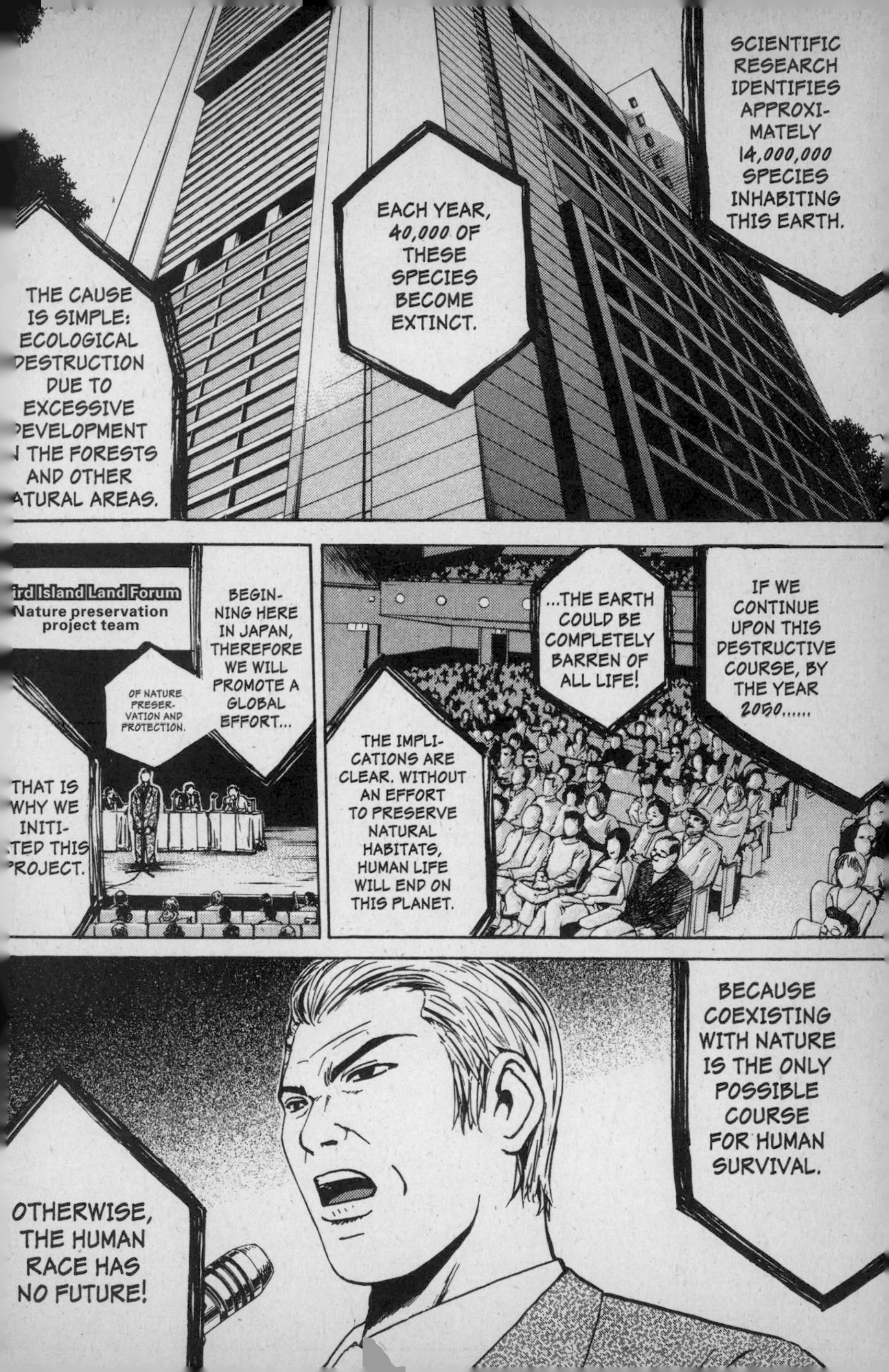
SCIENTIFIC RESEARCH IDENTIFIES APPROXIMATELY 14,000,000 SPECIES INHABITING THIS EARTH.
EACH YEAR, 40,000 OF THESE SPECIES BECOME EXTINCT.
THE CAUSE IS SIMPLE: ECOLOGICAL DESTRUCTION DUE TO EXCESSIVE DEVELOPMENT IN THE FORESTS AND OTHER NATURAL AREAS.
IF WE CONTINUE UPON THIS DESTRUCTIVE COURSE, BY THE YEAR 2050......
...THE EARTH COULD BE COMPLETELY BARREN OF ALL LIFE!
THE IMPLICATIONS ARE CLEAR. WITHOUT AN EFFORT TO PRESERVE NATURAL HABITATS, HUMAN LIFE WILL END ON THIS PLANET.
ird Island Land Forum
Nature preservation project team
BEGINNING HERE IN JAPAN, THEREFORE WE WILL PROMOTE A GLOBAL EFFORT...
OF NATURE PRESERVATION AND PROTECTION.
THAT IS WHY WE INITIATED THIS PROJECT.
BECAUSE COEXISTING WITH NATURE IS THE ONLY POSSIBLE COURSE FOR HUMAN SURVIVAL.
OTHERWISE, THE HUMAN RACE HAS NO FUTURE!

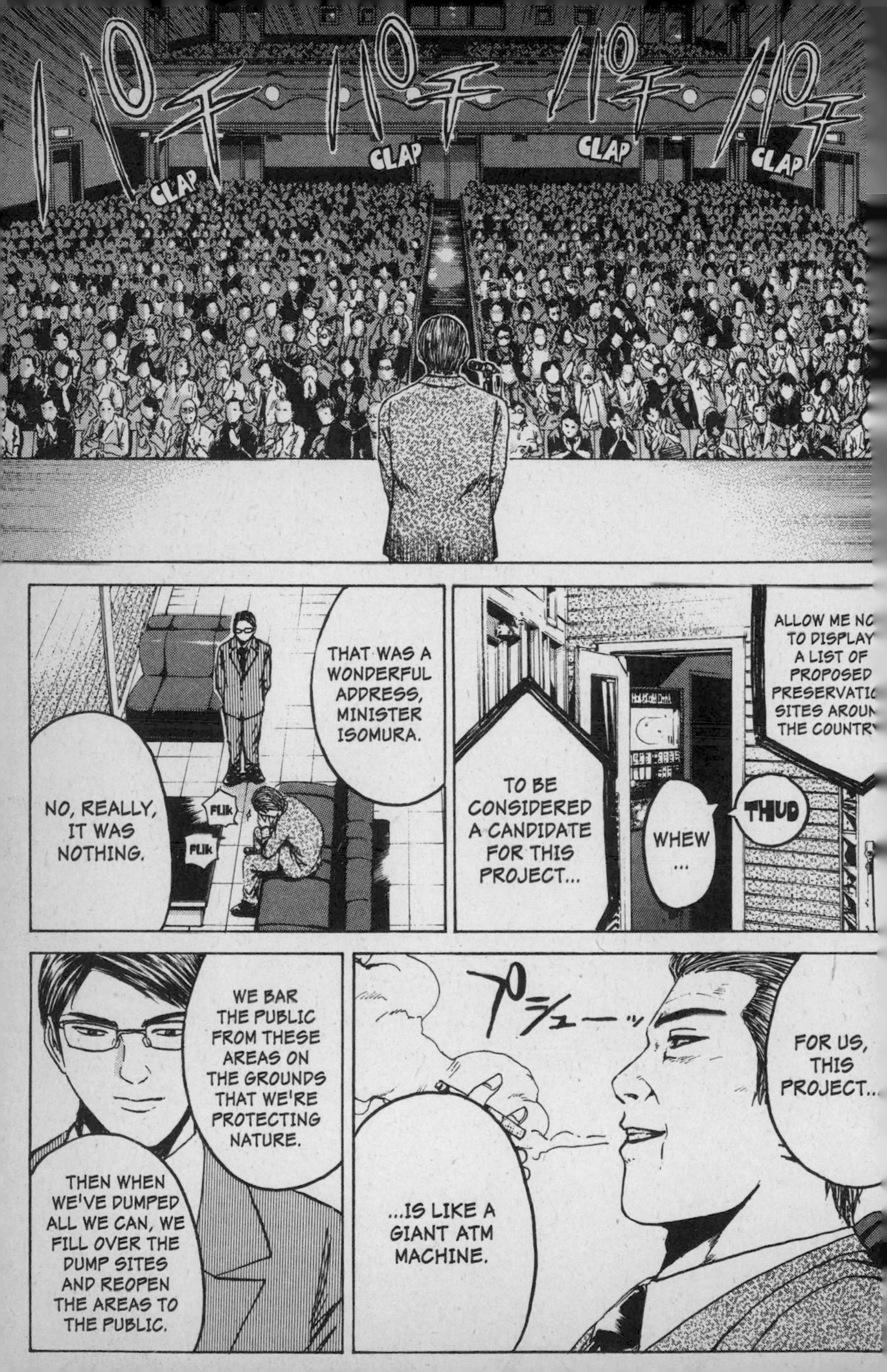
パチ
CLAP
パチ
CLAP
パチ
CLAP
パチ
CLAP
ALLOW ME NO TO DISPLAY A LIST OF PROPOSED PRESERVATIO SITES AROUN THE COUNTRY
THUD
WHEW ...
TO BE CONSIDERED A CANDIDATE FOR THIS PROJECT...
THAT WAS A WONDERFUL ADDRESS, MINISTER ISOMURA.
FLIK
FLIK
NO, REALLY, IT WAS NOTHING.
プシューッ
FOR US, THIS PROJECT...
...IS LIKE A GIANT ATM MACHINE.
WE BAR THE PUBLIC FROM THESE AREAS ON THE GROUNDS THAT WE'RE PROTECTING NATURE.
THEN WHEN WE'VE DUMPED ALL WE CAN, WE FILL OVER THE DUMP SITES AND REOPEN THE AREAS TO THE PUBLIC.

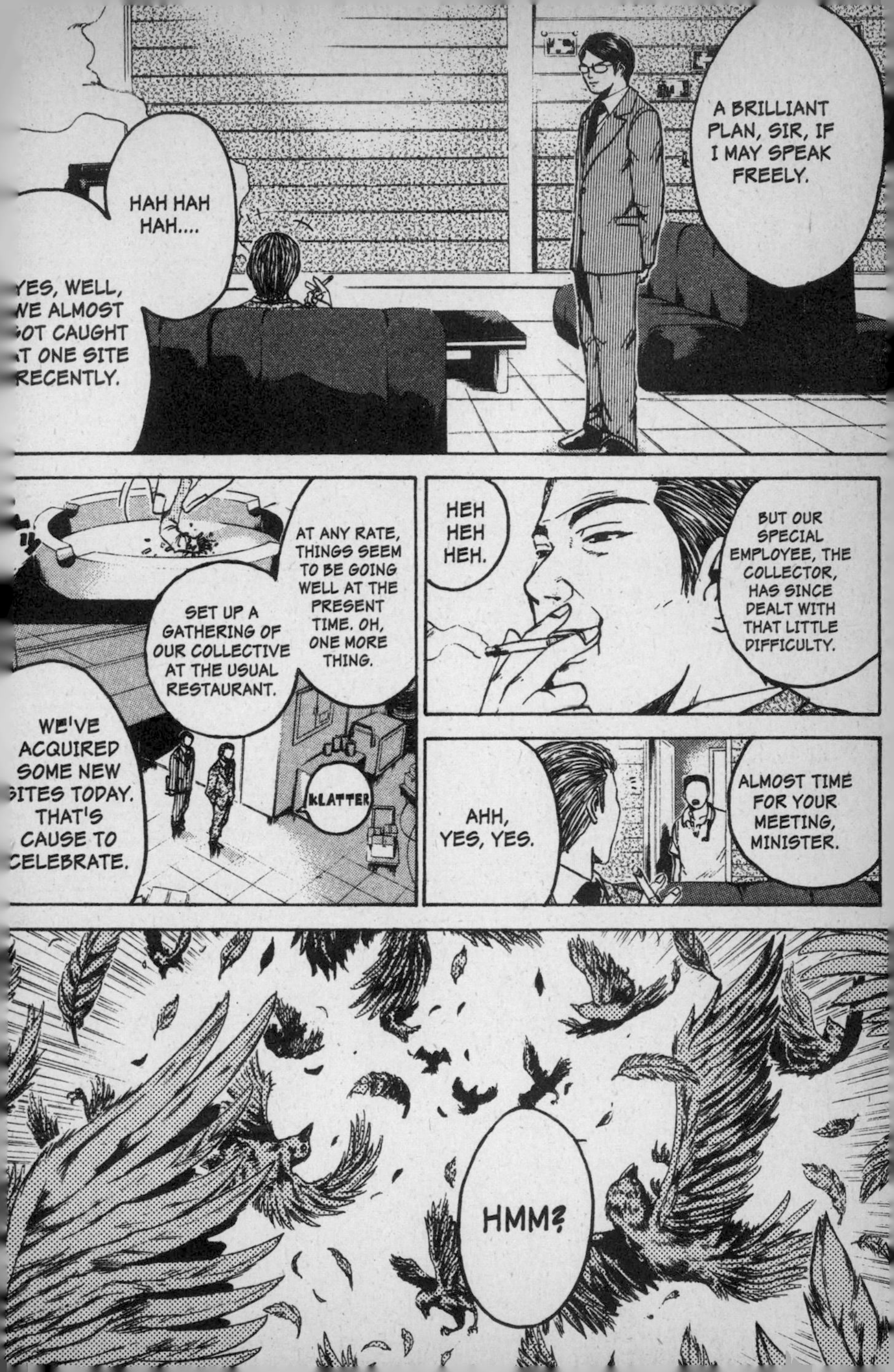
A BRILLIANT PLAN, SIR, IF I MAY SPEAK FREELY.
HAH HAH HAH....
YES, WELL, WE ALMOST GOT CAUGHT AT ONE SITE RECENTLY.
BUT OUR SPECIAL EMPLOYEE, THE COLLECTOR, HAS SINCE DEALT WITH THAT LITTLE DIFFICULTY.
HEH HEH HEH.
ALMOST TIME FOR YOUR MEETING, MINISTER.
AHH, YES, YES.
AT ANY RATE, THINGS SEEM TO BE GOING WELL AT THE PRESENT TIME. OH, ONE MORE THING.
SET UP A GATHERING OF OUR COLLECTIVE AT THE USUAL RESTAURANT.
KLATTER
WE'VE ACQUIRED SOME NEW SITES TODAY. THAT'S CAUSE TO CELEBRATE.
HMM?

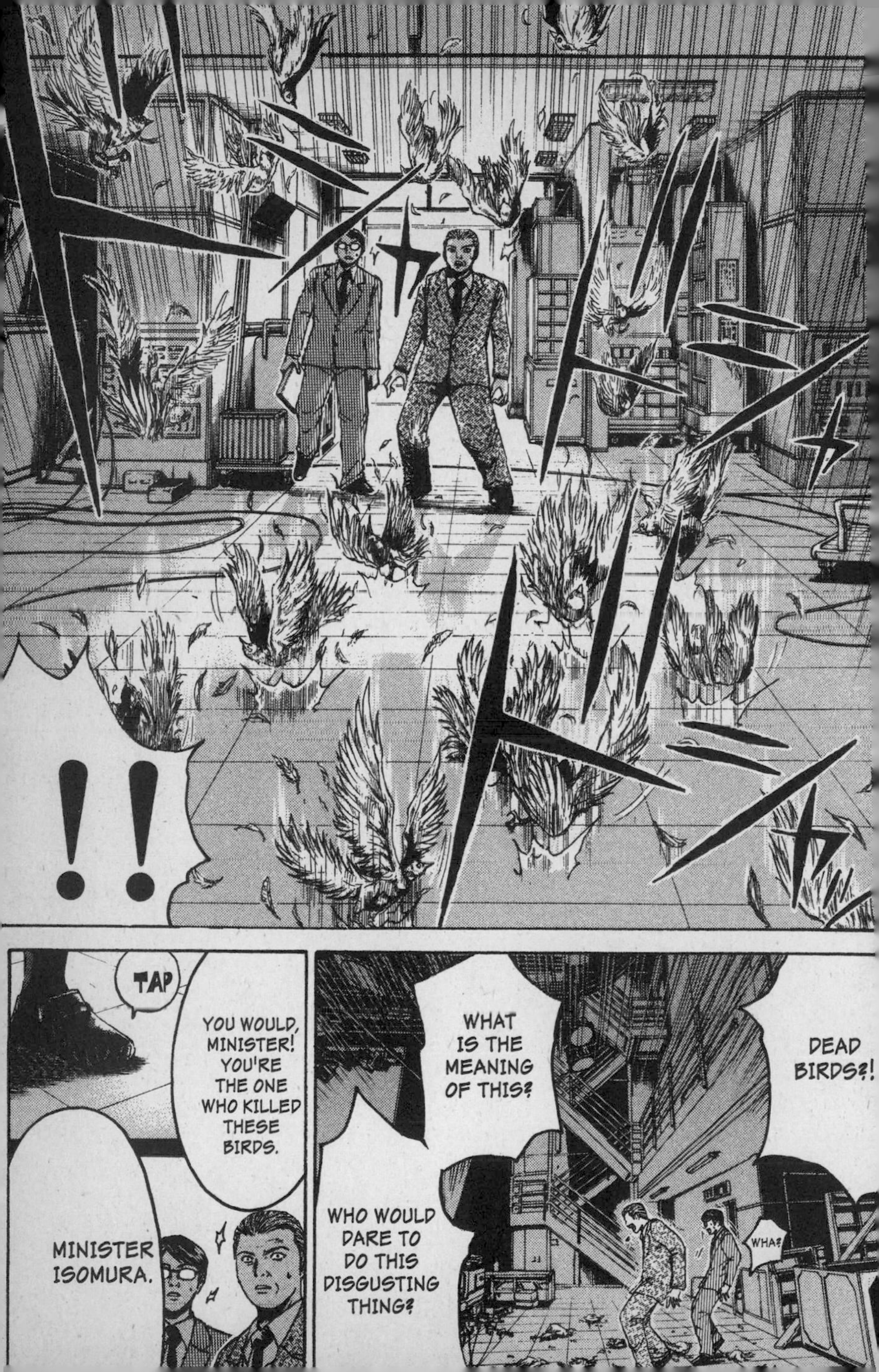
!!
DEAD BIRDS?!
WHAT IS THE MEANING OF THIS?
WHA?
WHO WOULD DARE TO DO THIS DISGUSTING THING?
TAP
YOU WOULD, MINISTER! YOU'RE THE ONE WHO KILLED THESE BIRDS.
MINISTER ISOMURA.

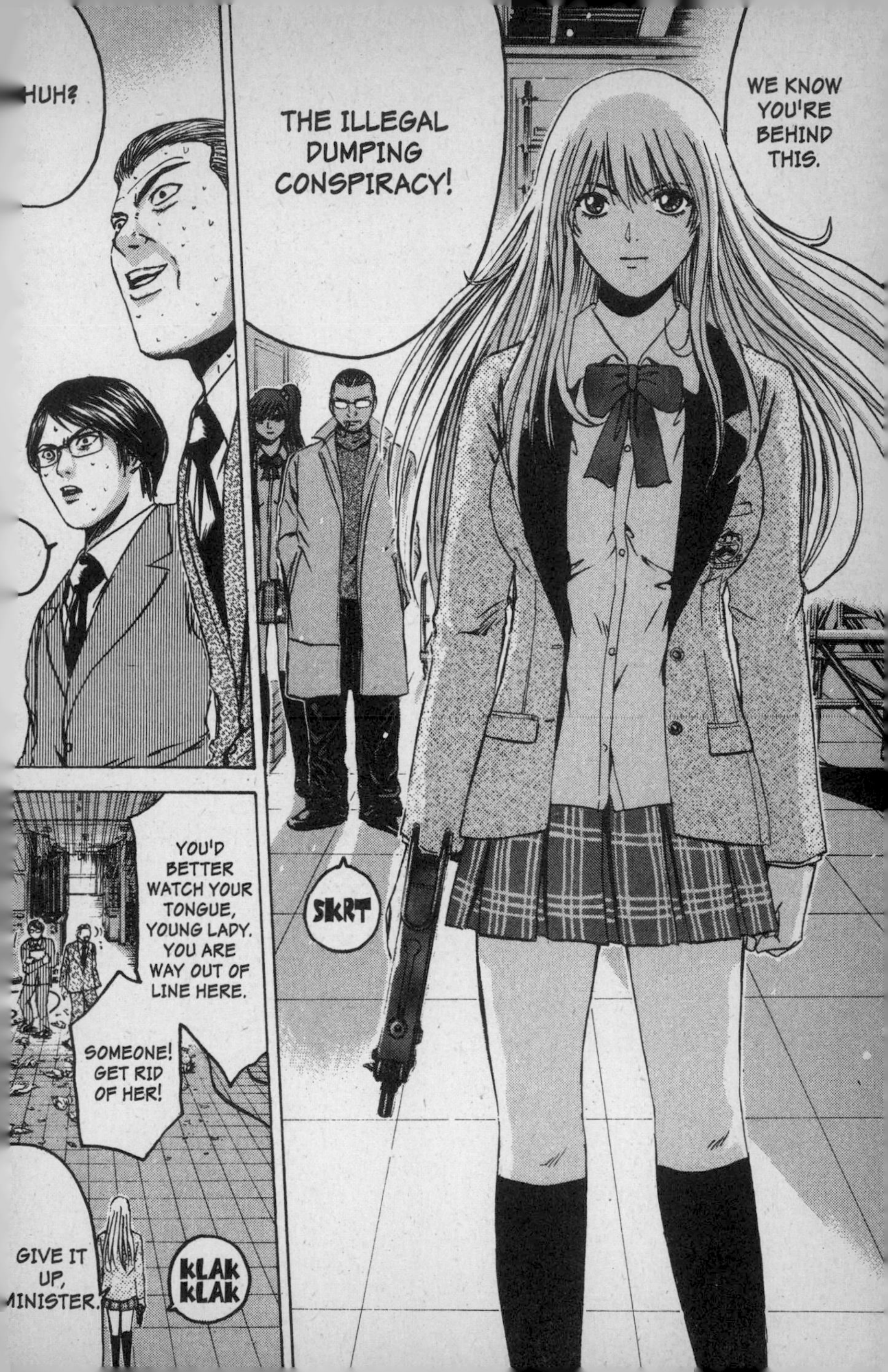
WE KNOW YOU'RE BEHIND THIS.
THE ILLEGAL DUMPING CONSPIRACY!
SKRT
HUH?
YOU'D BETTER WATCH YOUR TONGUE, YOUNG LADY. YOU ARE WAY OUT OF LINE HERE.
SOMEONE! GET RID OF HER!
KLAK KLAK
GIVE IT UP, MINISTER.

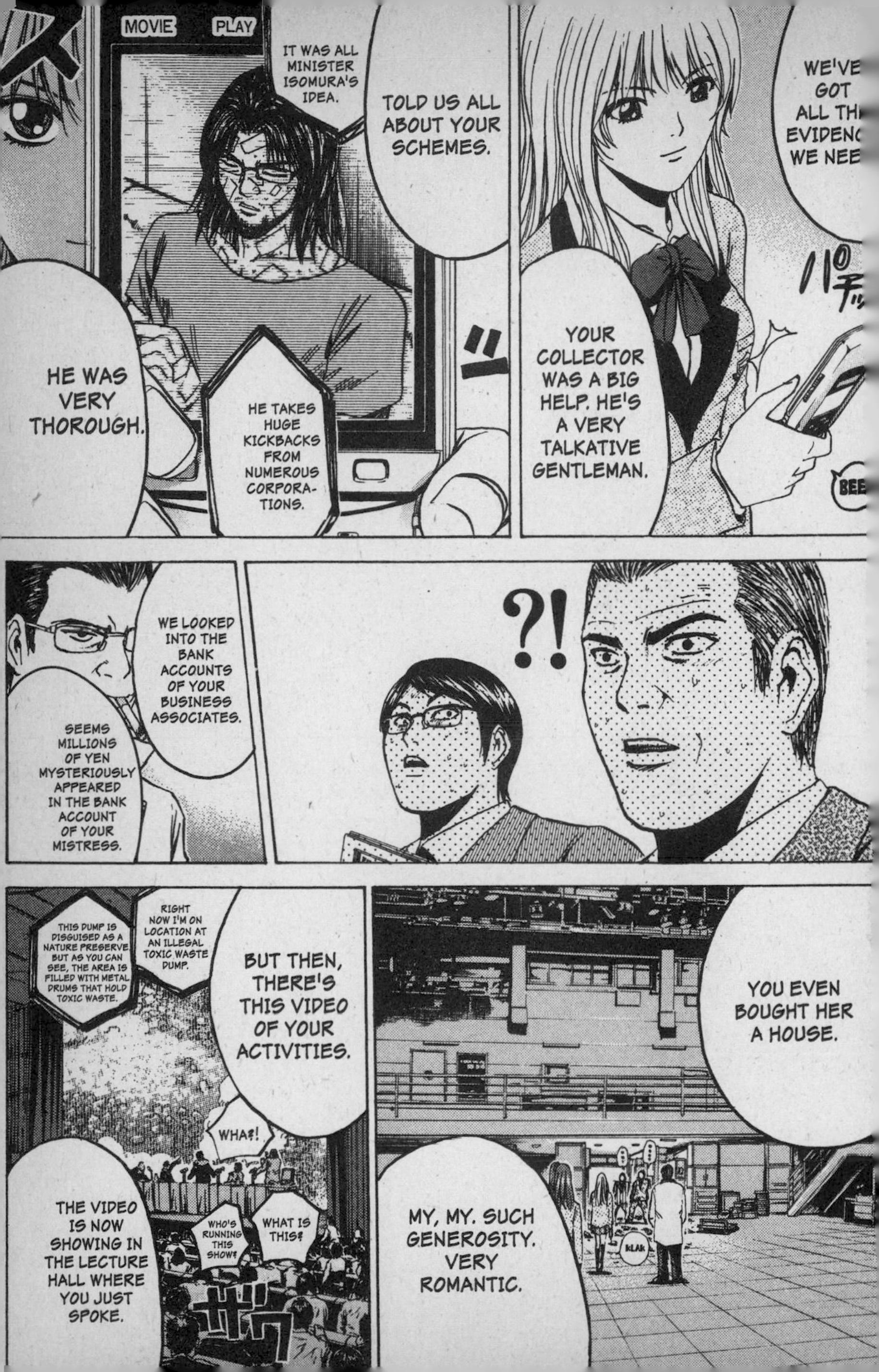
WE'VE GOT ALL TH EVIDENC WE NEE
YOUR COLLECTOR WAS A BIG HELP. HE'S A VERY TALKATIVE GENTLEMAN.
BEE
TOLD US ALL ABOUT YOUR SCHEMES.
IT WAS ALL MINISTER ISOMURA'S IDEA.
MOVIE
PLAY
HE TAKES HUGE KICKBACKS FROM NUMEROUS CORPORATIONS.
HE WAS VERY THOROUGH.
?!
WE LOOKED INTO THE BANK ACCOUNTS OF YOUR BUSINESS ASSOCIATES.
SEEMS MILLIONS OF YEN MYSTERIOUSLY APPEARED IN THE BANK ACCOUNT OF YOUR MISTRESS.
YOU EVEN BOUGHT HER A HOUSE.
MY, MY. SUCH GENEROSITY. VERY ROMANTIC.
KLAK
BUT THEN, THERE'S THIS VIDEO OF YOUR ACTIVITIES.
RIGHT NOW I'M ON LOCATION AT AN ILLEGAL TOXIC WASTE DUMP.
THIS DUMP IS DISGUISED AS A NATURE PRESERVE BUT AS YOU CAN SEE, THE AREA IS FILLED WITH METAL DRUMS THAT HOLD TOXIC WASTE.
WHA?!
WHAT IS THIS?
WHO'S RUNNING THIS SHOW?
THE VIDEO IS NOW SHOWING IN THE LECTURE HALL WHERE YOU JUST SPOKE.

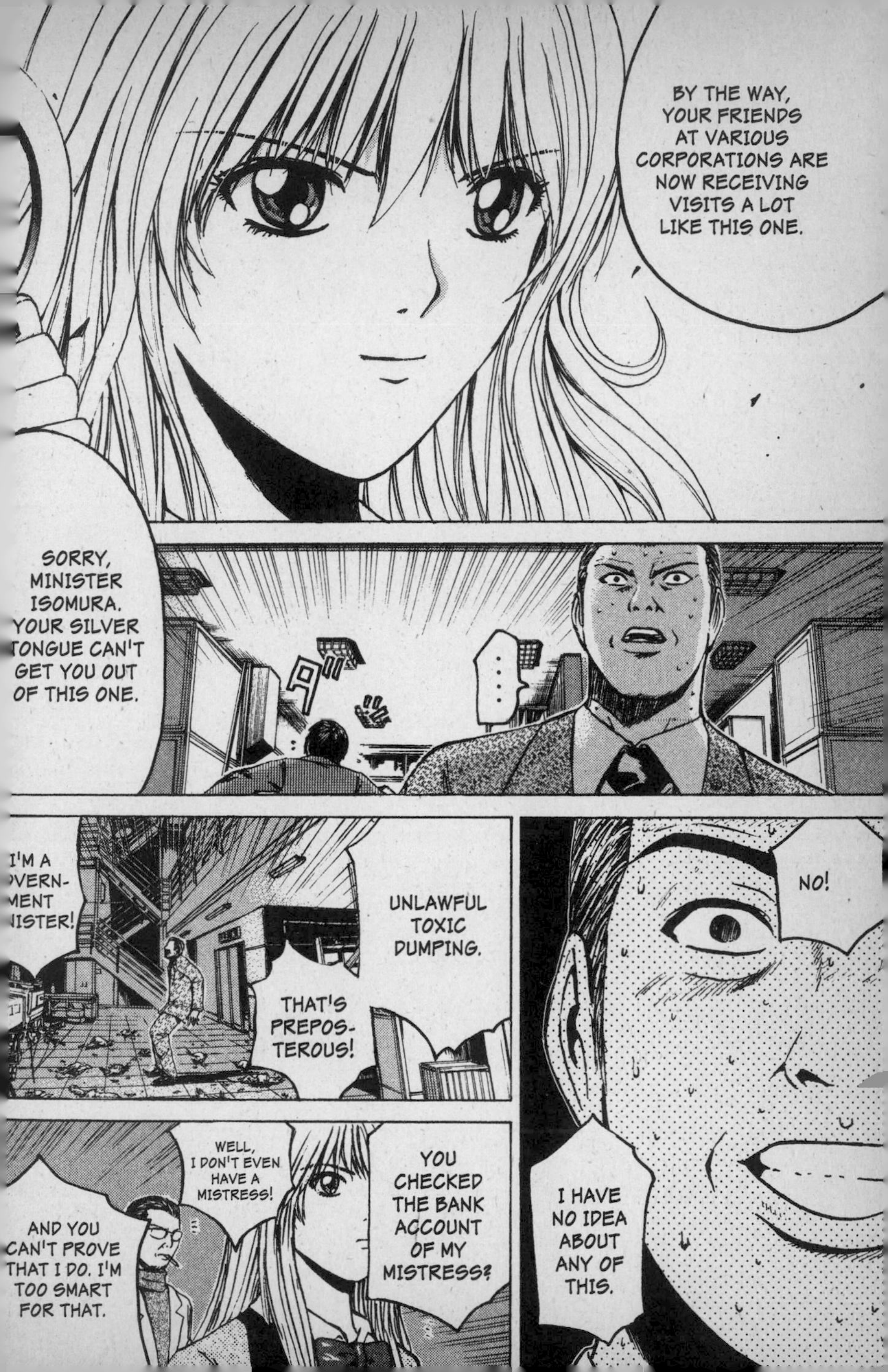
BY THE WAY, YOUR FRIENDS AT VARIOUS CORPORATIONS ARE NOW RECEIVING VISITS A LOT LIKE THIS ONE.
SORRY, MINISTER ISOMURA. YOUR SILVER TONGUE CAN'T GET YOU OUT OF THIS ONE.
...
NO!
I HAVE NO IDEA ABOUT ANY OF THIS.
UNLAWFUL TOXIC DUMPING.
I'M A OVERN-MENT NISTER!
THAT'S PREPOS-TEROUS!
YOU CHECKED THE BANK ACCOUNT OF MY MISTRESS?
WELL, I DON'T EVEN HAVE A MISTRESS!
AND YOU CAN'T PROVE THAT I DO. I'M TOO SMART FOR THAT.

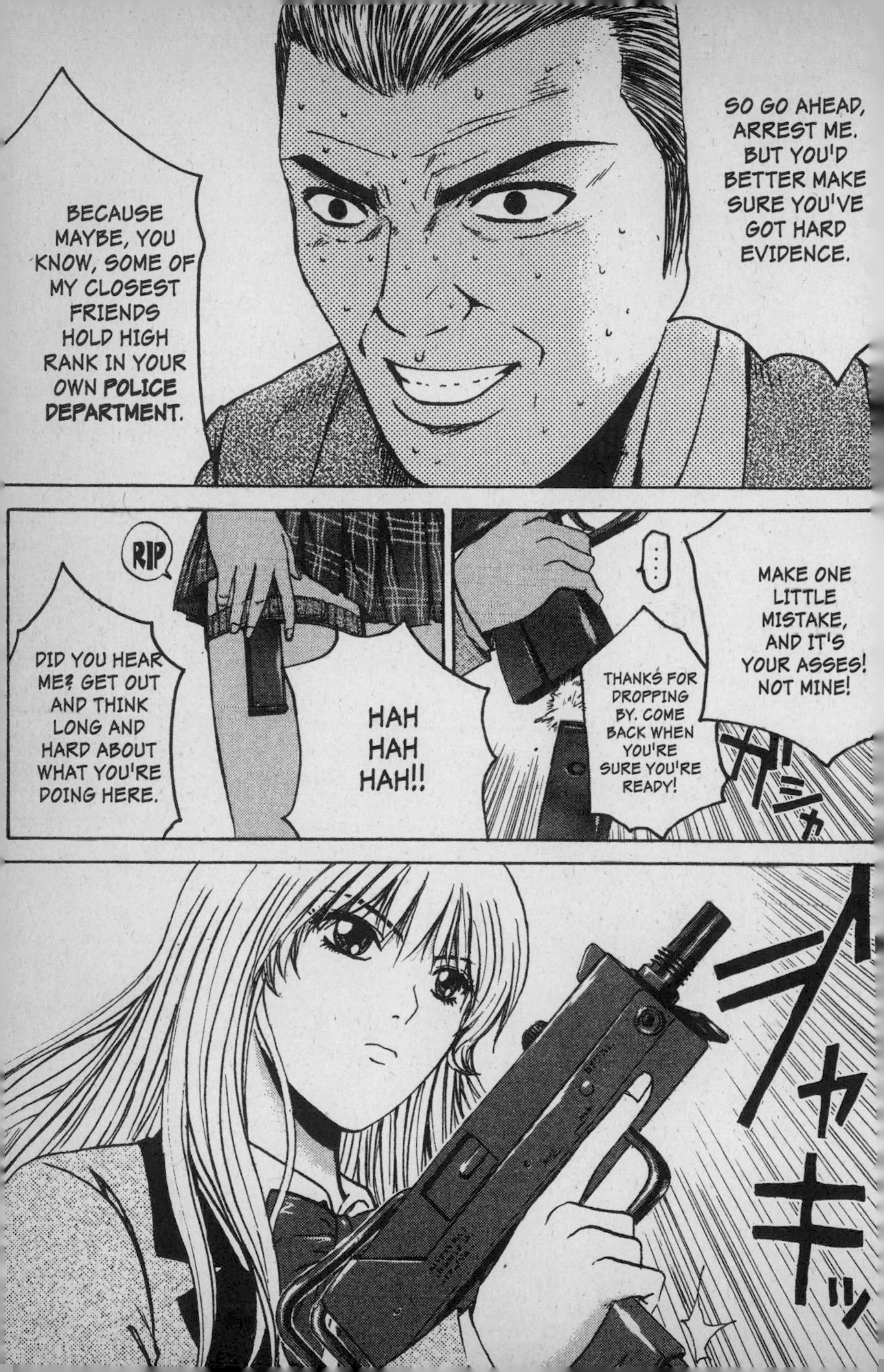
SO GO AHEAD, ARREST ME. BUT YOU'D BETTER MAKE SURE YOU'VE GOT HARD EVIDENCE.
BECAUSE MAYBE, YOU KNOW, SOME OF MY CLOSEST FRIENDS HOLD HIGH RANK IN YOUR OWN POLICE DEPARTMENT.
MAKE ONE LITTLE MISTAKE, AND IT'S YOUR ASSES! NOT MINE!
...
THANKS FOR DROPPING BY. COME BACK WHEN YOU'RE SURE YOU'RE READY!
ガシャ
RIP
HAH HAH HAH!!
DID YOU HEAR ME? GET OUT AND THINK LONG AND HARD ABOUT WHAT YOU'RE DOING HERE.
ジャキッ

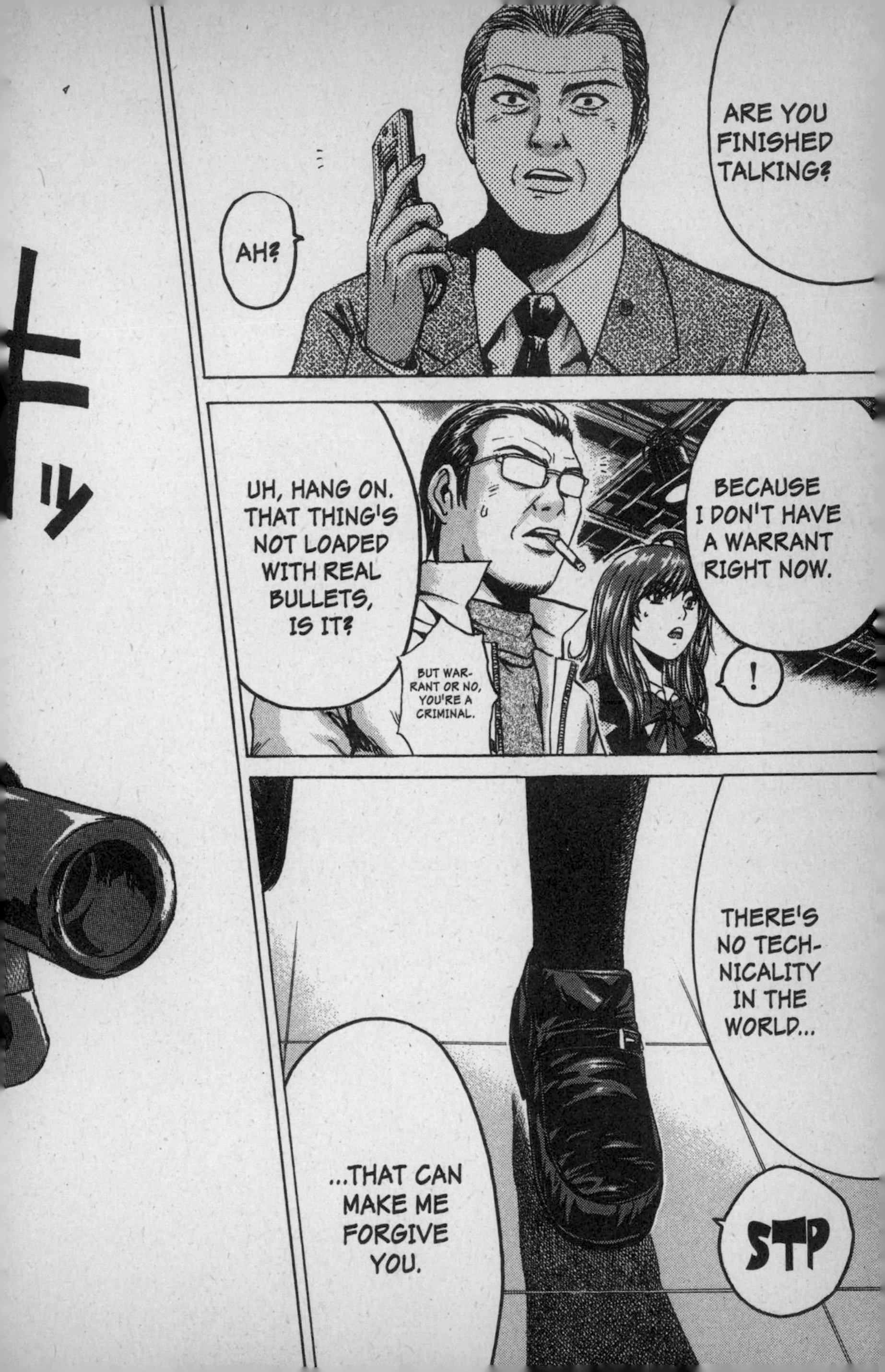
ARE YOU FINISHED TALKING?
AH?
BECAUSE I DON'T HAVE A WARRANT RIGHT NOW.
UH, HANG ON. THAT THING'S NOT LOADED WITH REAL BULLETS, IS IT?
!
BUT WAR-RANT OR NO, YOU'RE A CRIMINAL.
THERE'S NO TECH-NICALITY IN THE WORLD...
STP
...THAT CAN MAKE ME FORGIVE YOU.

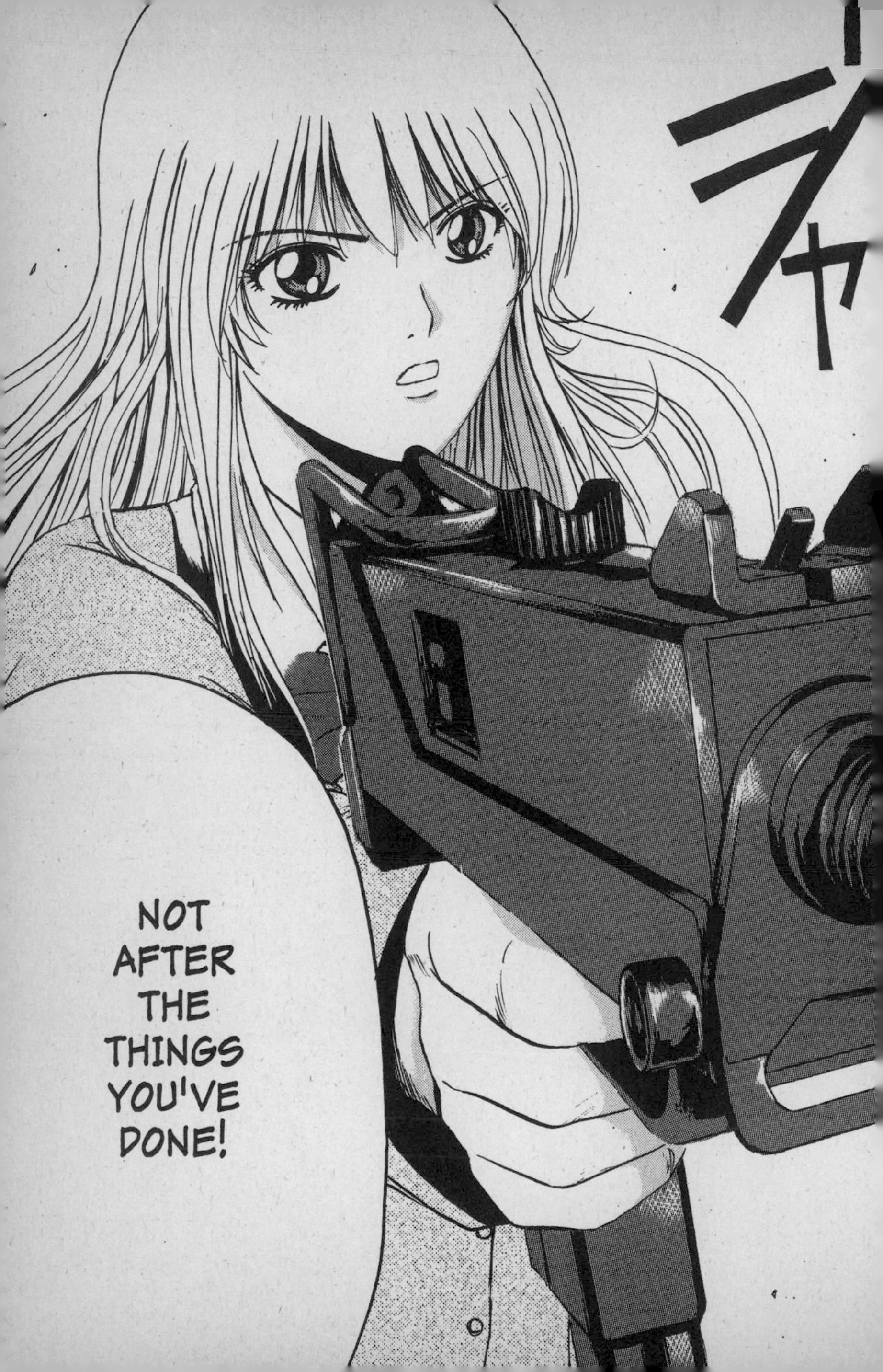
NOT AFTER THE THINGS YOU'VE DONE!

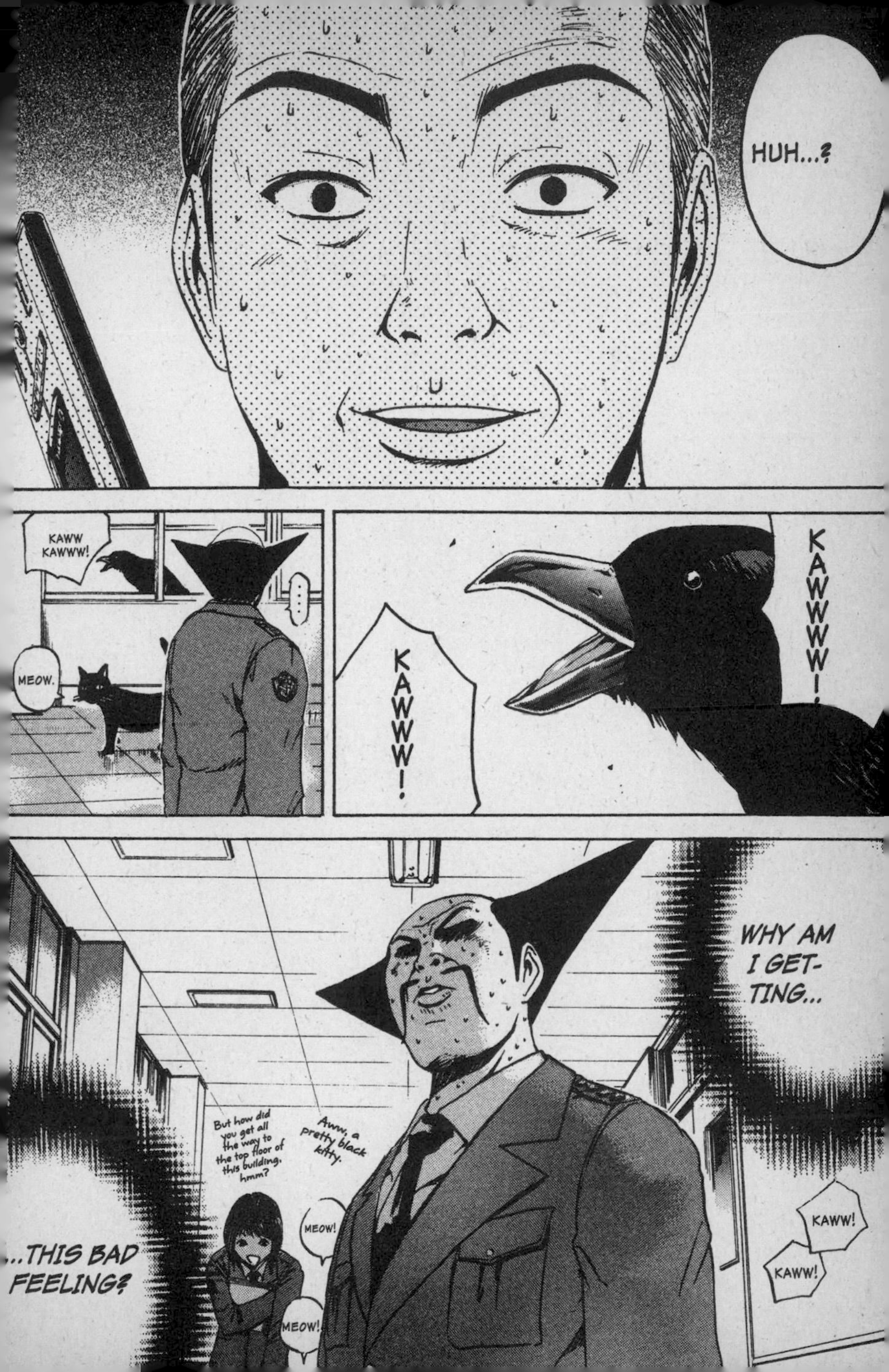
HUH...?
KAWWWWWW!
KAWWW!
KAWW KAWWW!
...
MEOW.
WHY AM I GETTING...
KAWW!
KAWW!
Aww, a pretty black kitty.
But how did you get all the way to the top floor of this building, hmm?
MEOW!
MEOW!
...THIS BAD FEELING?

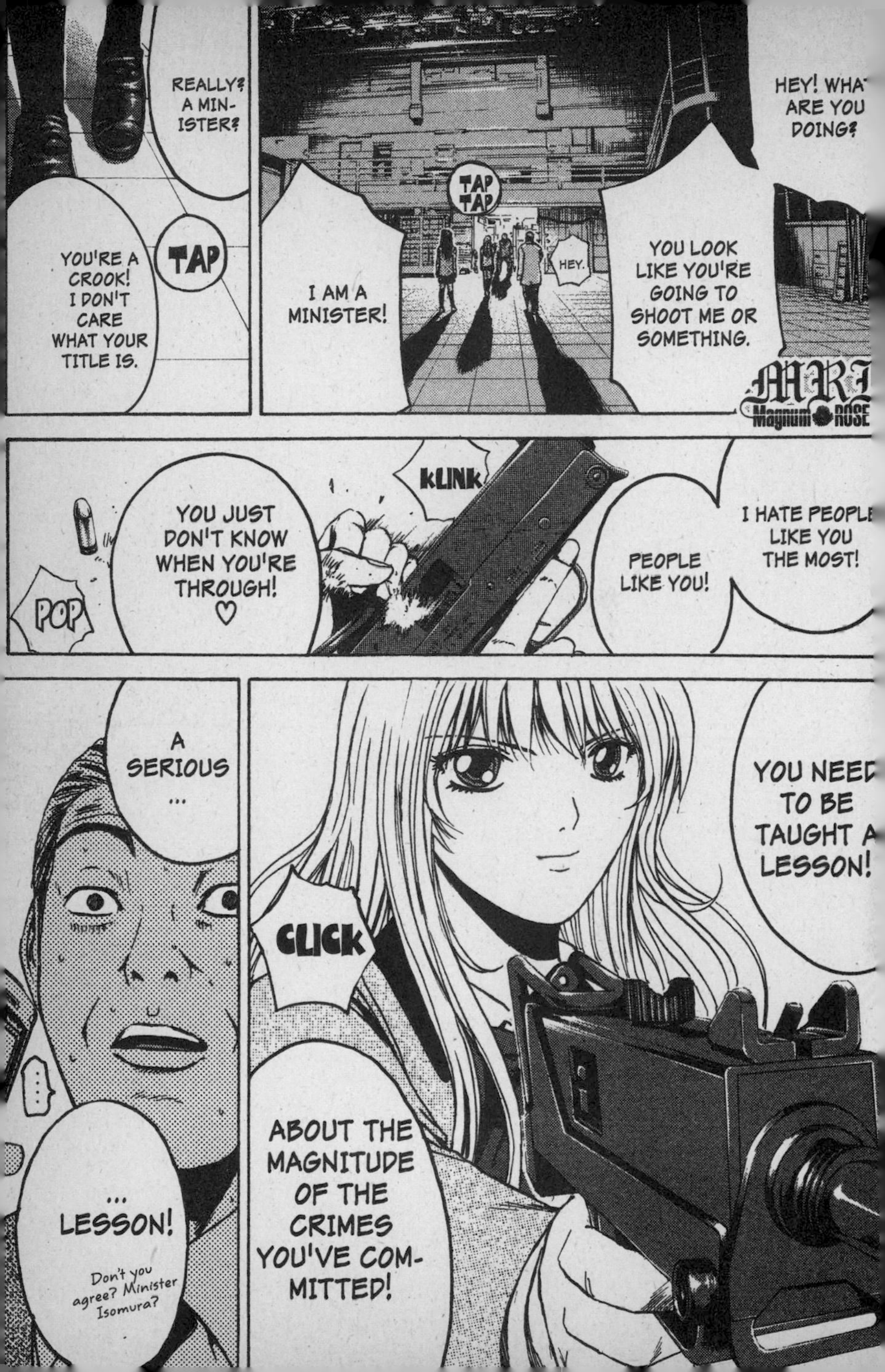
HEY! WHAT ARE YOU DOING?
YOU LOOK LIKE YOU'RE GOING TO SHOOT ME OR SOMETHING.
HEY.
TAP TAP
I AM A MINISTER!
REALLY? A MIN-ISTER?
TAP
YOU'RE A CROOK! I DON'T CARE WHAT YOUR TITLE IS.
I HATE PEOPLE LIKE YOU THE MOST!
PEOPLE LIKE YOU!
kLINK
YOU JUST DON'T KNOW WHEN YOU'RE THROUGH! ♡
POP
YOU NEED TO BE TAUGHT A LESSON!
CLICK
ABOUT THE MAGNITUDE OF THE CRIMES YOU'VE COM-MITTED!
A SERIOUS ...
...
... LESSON!
Don't you agree? Minister Isomura?

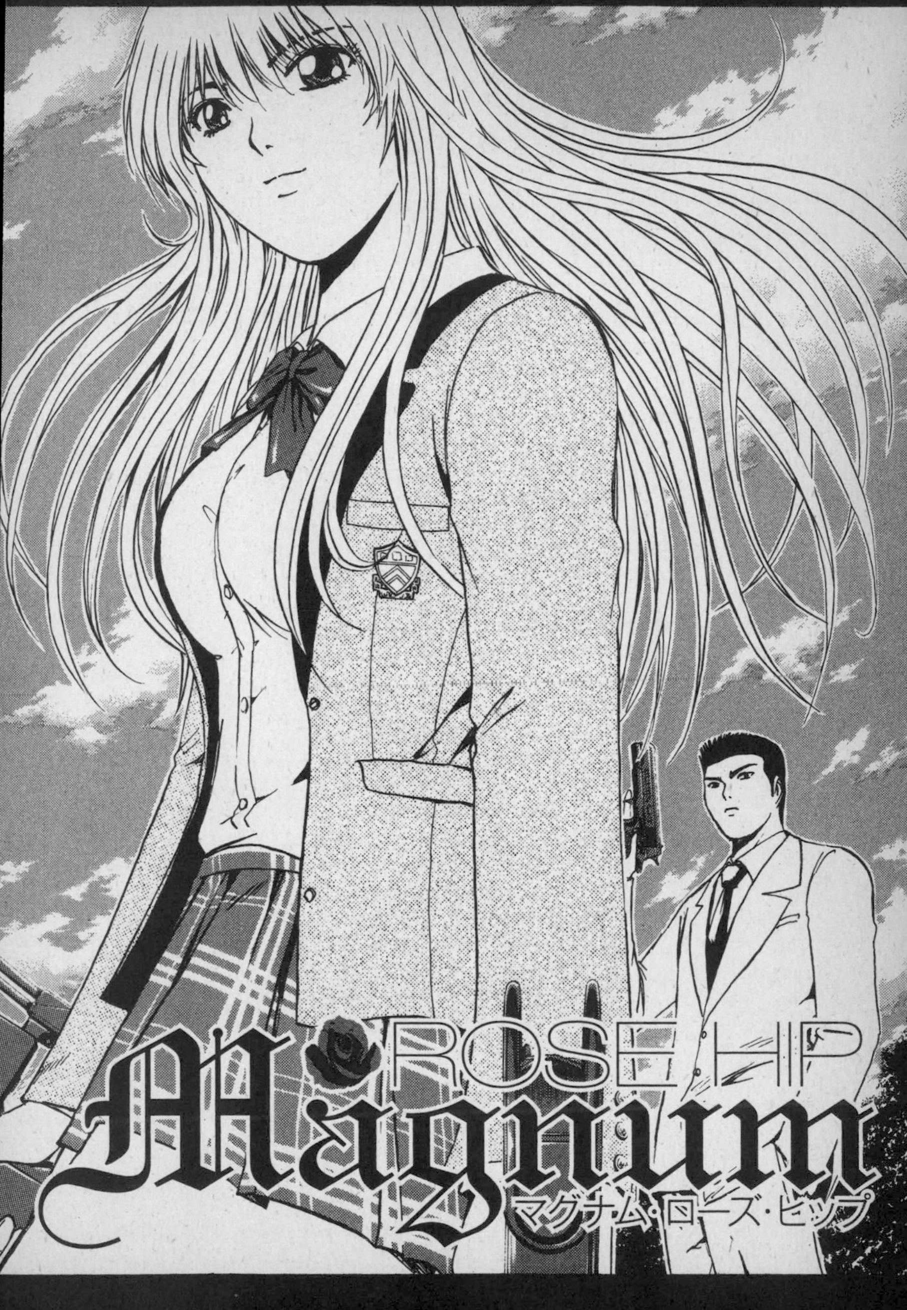
ROSE HIP
Magnum
マグナム・ローズ・ヒップ

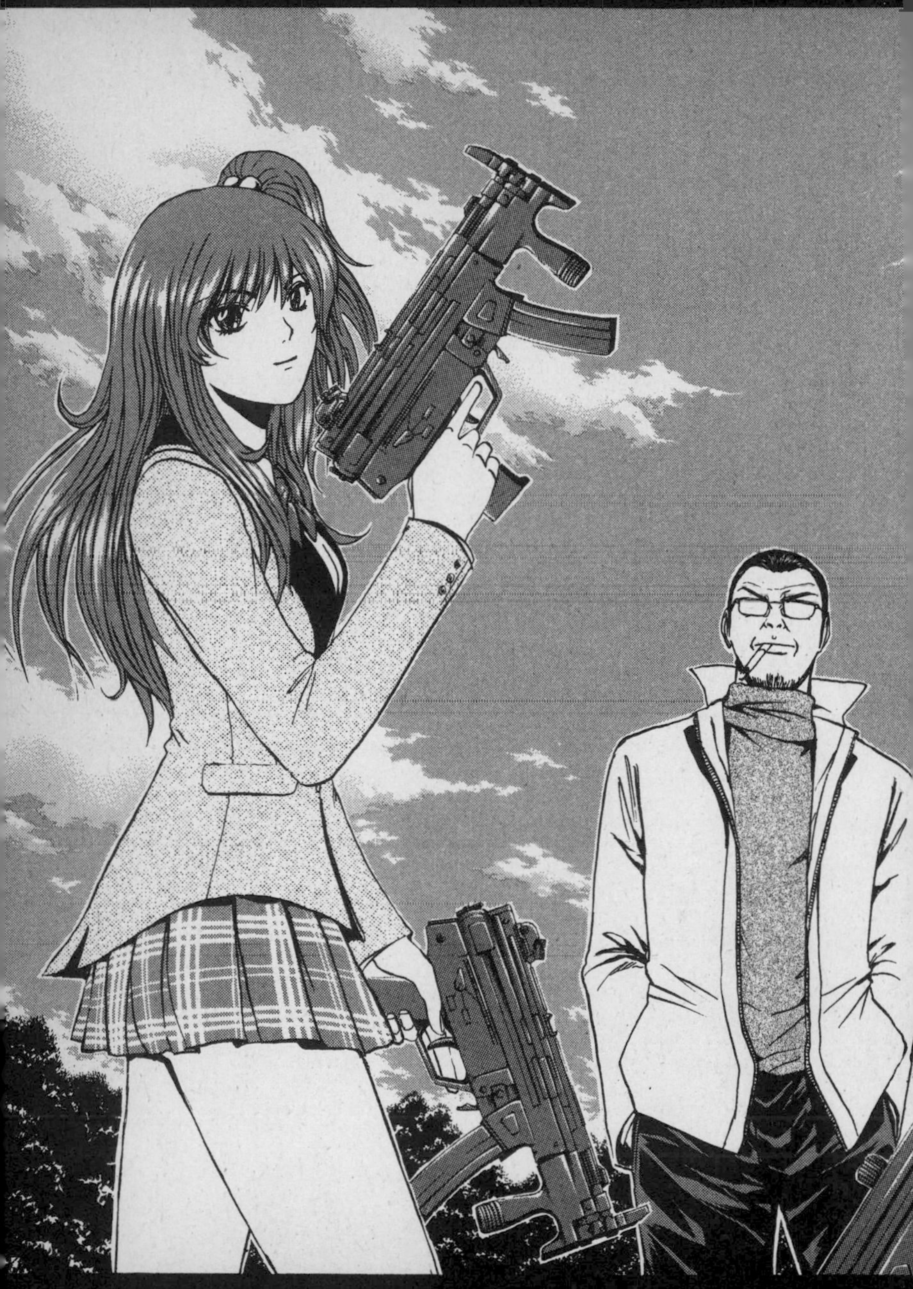

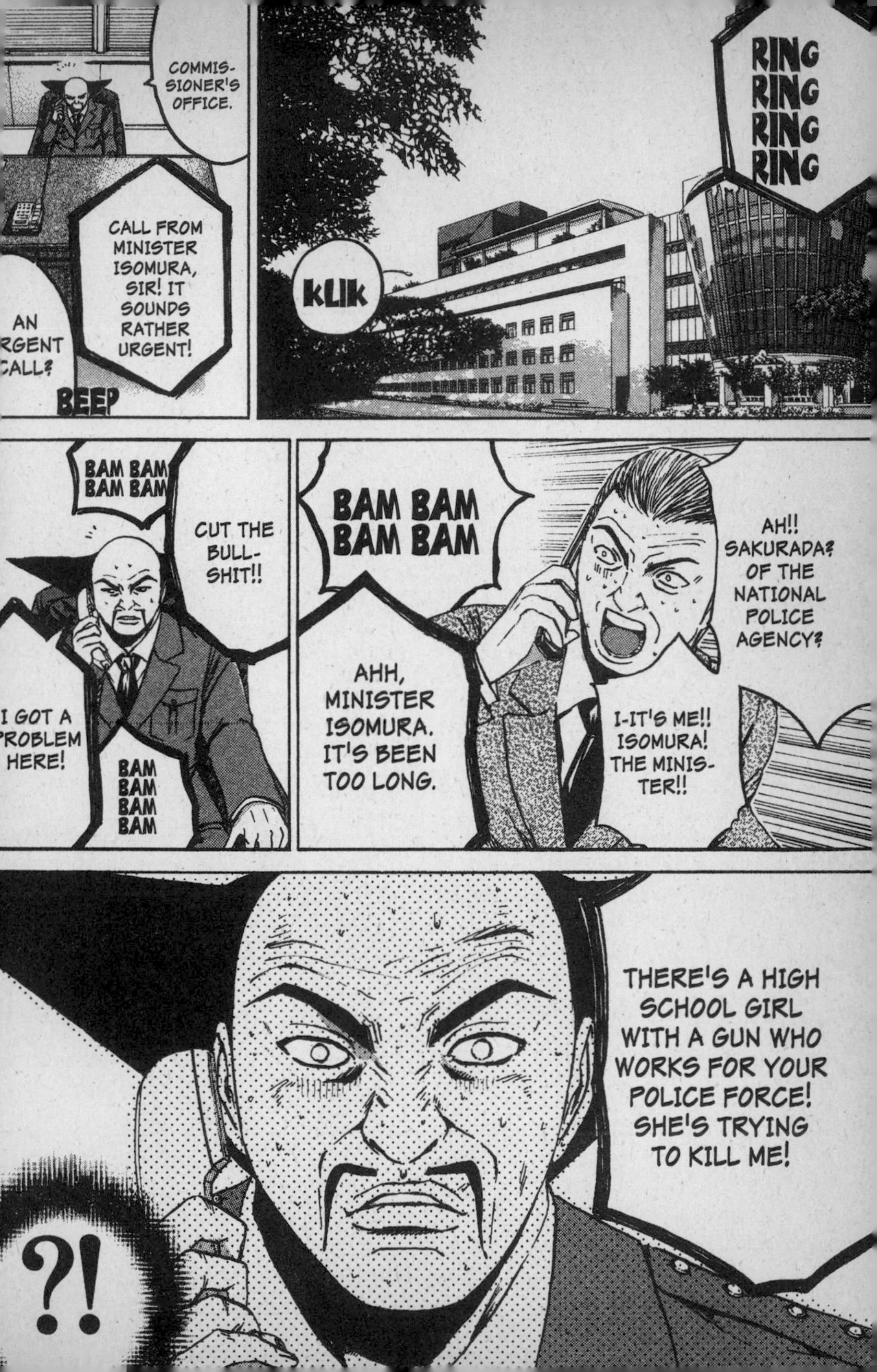
RING RING RING RING
KLIK
COMMIS-SIONER'S OFFICE.
CALL FROM MINISTER ISOMURA, SIR! IT SOUNDS RATHER URGENT!
AN RGENT CALL?
BEEP
AH!! SAKURADA? OF THE NATIONAL POLICE AGENCY?
I-IT'S ME!! ISOMURA! THE MINIS-TER!!
BAM BAM BAM BAM
AHH, MINISTER ISOMURA. IT'S BEEN TOO LONG.
BAM BAM BAM BAM
CUT THE BULL-SHIT!!
I GOT A ROBLEM HERE!
BAM BAM BAM BAM
THERE'S A HIGH SCHOOL GIRL WITH A GUN WHO WORKS FOR YOUR POLICE FORCE! SHE'S TRYING TO KILL ME!
?!

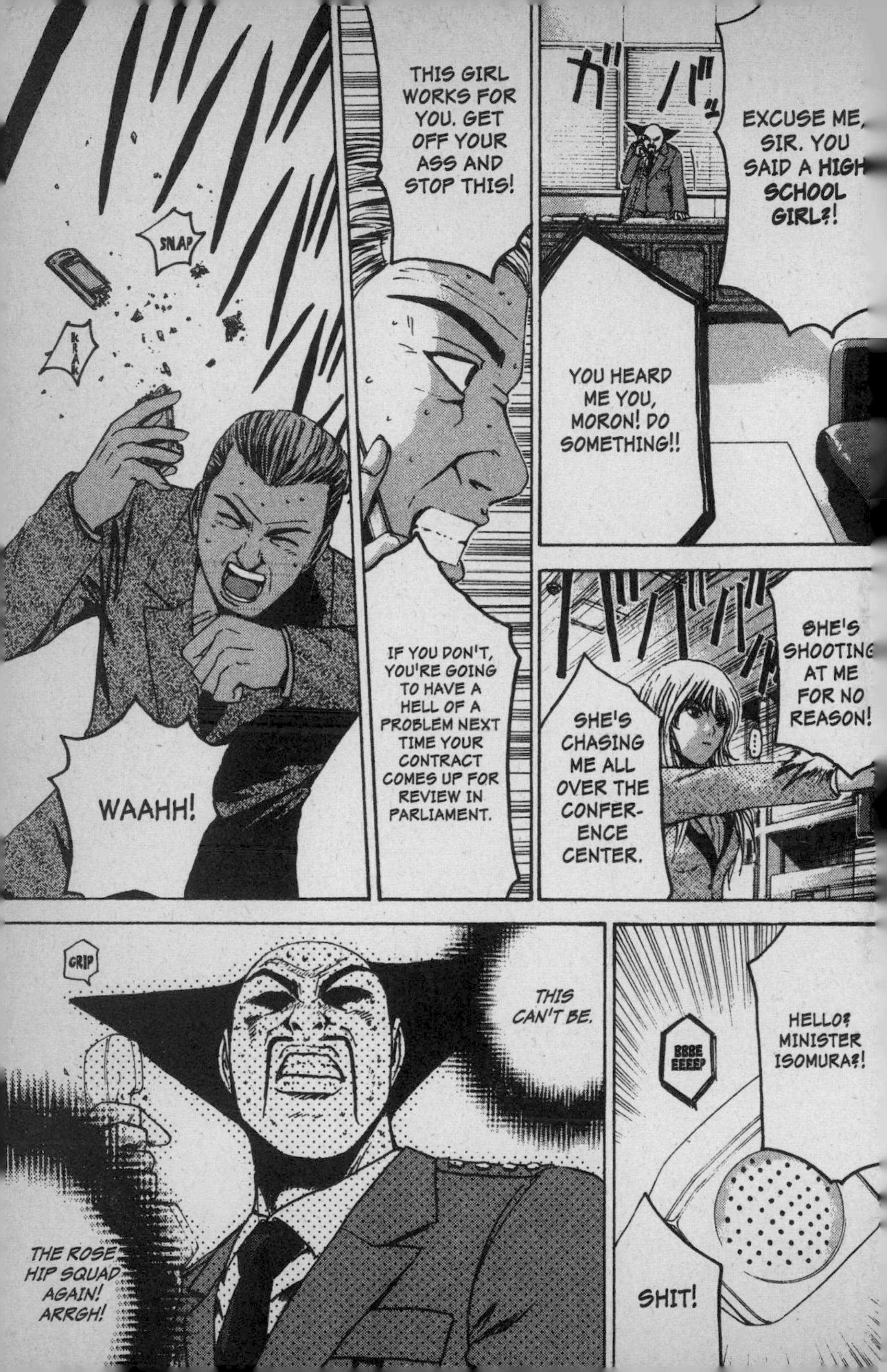
ガバッ
EXCUSE ME, SIR. YOU SAID A HIGH SCHOOL GIRL?!
YOU HEARD ME YOU, MORON! DO SOMETHING!!
SHE'S SHOOTING AT ME FOR NO REASON!
SHE'S CHASING ME ALL OVER THE CONFER-ENCE CENTER.
THIS GIRL WORKS FOR YOU. GET OFF YOUR ASS AND STOP THIS!
IF YOU DON'T, YOU'RE GOING TO HAVE A HELL OF A PROBLEM NEXT TIME YOUR CONTRACT COMES UP FOR REVIEW IN PARLIAMENT.
SNAP
KRAK
WAAHH!
BBBEEEEP
HELLO? MINISTER ISOMURA?!
SHIT!
GRIP
THIS CAN'T BE.
THE ROSE HIP SQUAD AGAIN! ARRGH!

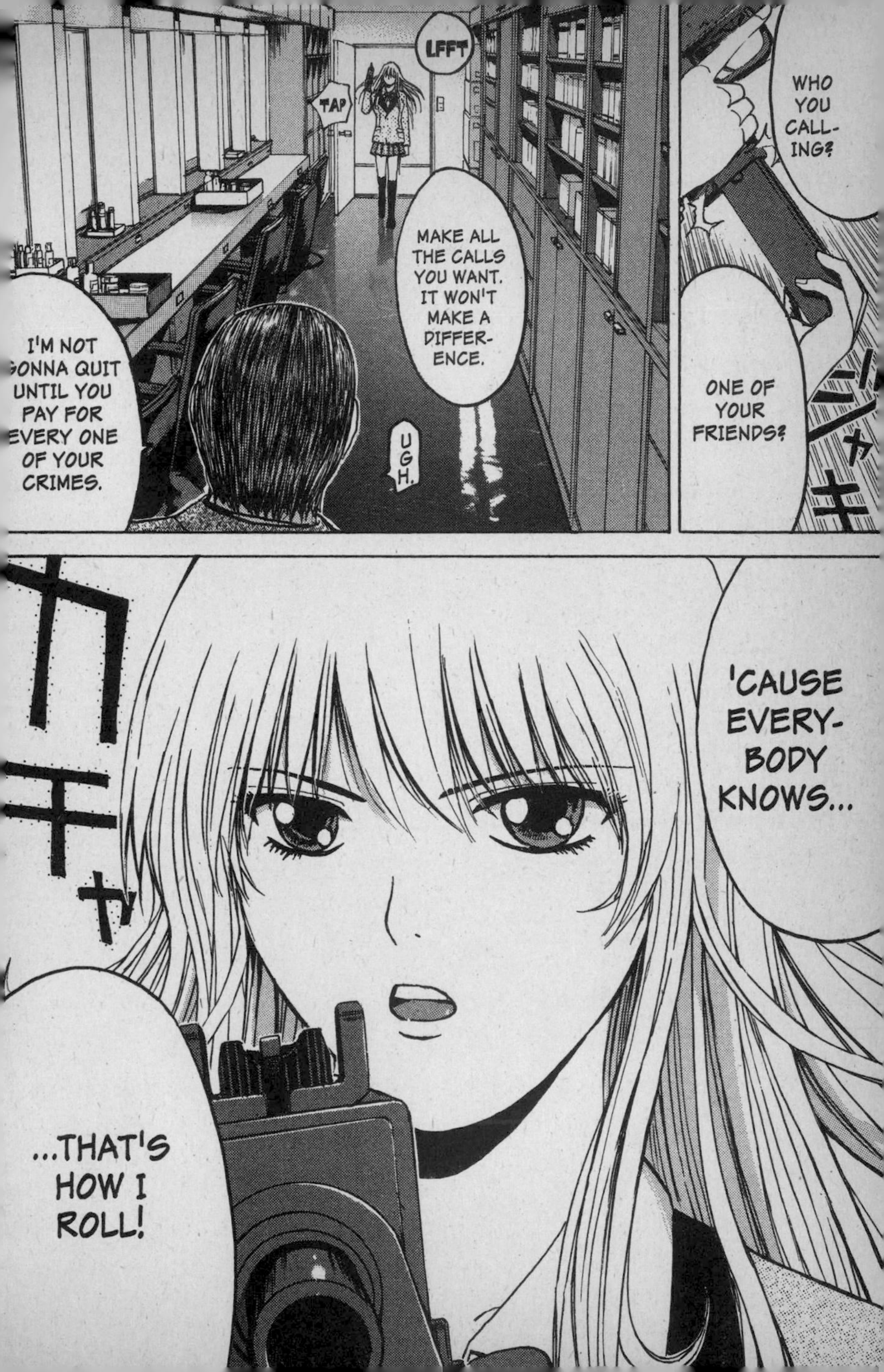

WHO YOU CALLING?
ONE OF YOUR FRIENDS?
ジャキ
LFFT
TAP
MAKE ALL THE CALLS YOU WANT. IT WON'T MAKE A DIFFERENCE.
UGH.
I'M NOT GONNA QUIT UNTIL YOU PAY FOR EVERY ONE OF YOUR CRIMES.
'CAUSE EVERYBODY KNOWS...
カチャ
...THAT'S HOW I ROLL!

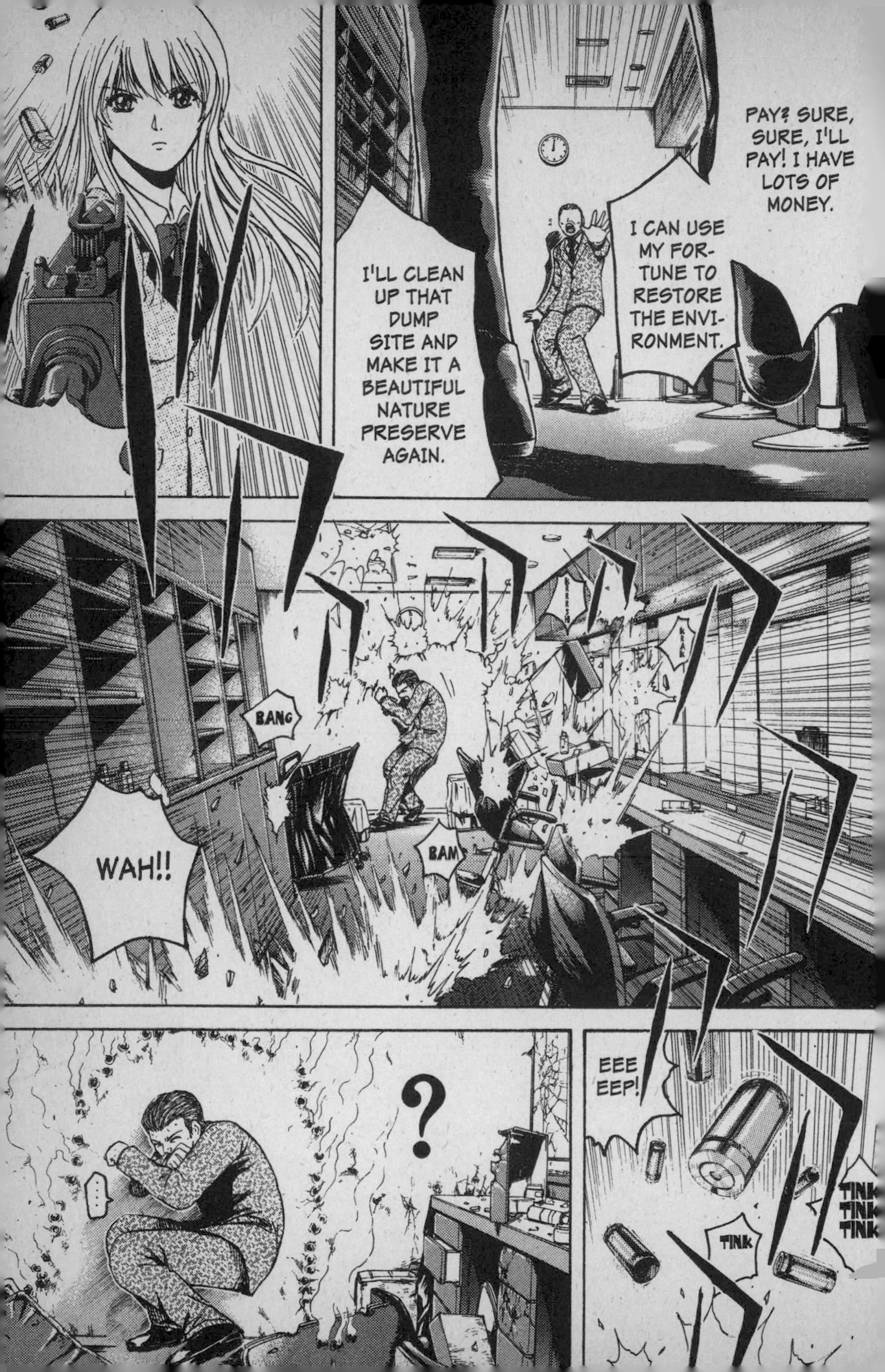
PAY? SURE, SURE, I'LL PAY! I HAVE LOTS OF MONEY.
I CAN USE MY FOR-TUNE TO RESTORE THE ENVI-RONMENT.
I'LL CLEAN UP THAT DUMP SITE AND MAKE IT A BEAUTIFUL NATURE PRESERVE AGAIN.
KRAK
BANG
BAM
WAH!!
EEE EEP!
TINK TINK TINK
TINK
?
...

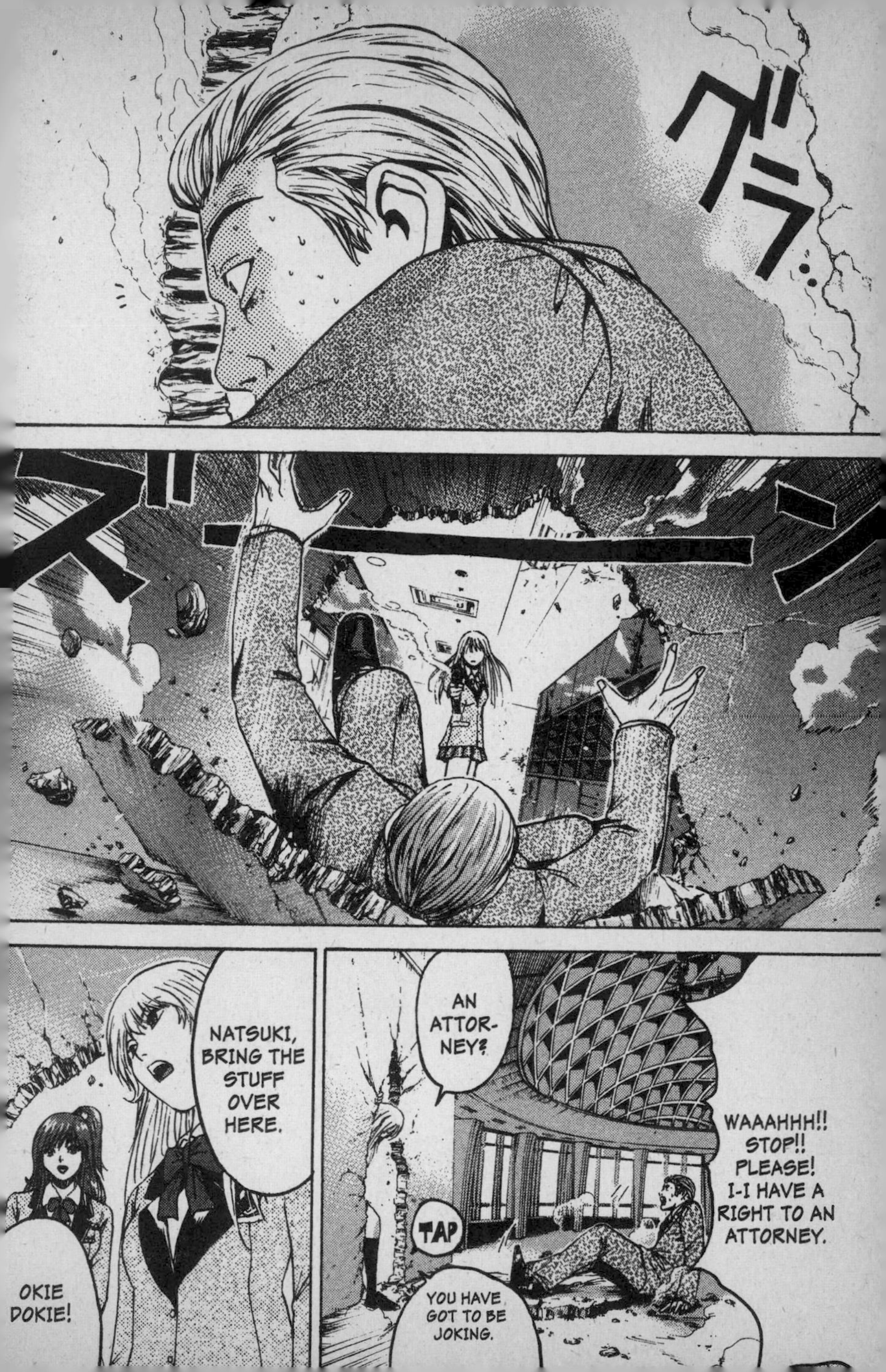
グラ
ズーン
WAAAHHH!! STOP!! PLEASE! I-I HAVE A RIGHT TO AN ATTORNEY.
AN ATTORNEY?
TAP
YOU HAVE GOT TO BE JOKING.
NATSUKI, BRING THE STUFF OVER HERE.
OKIE DOKIE!

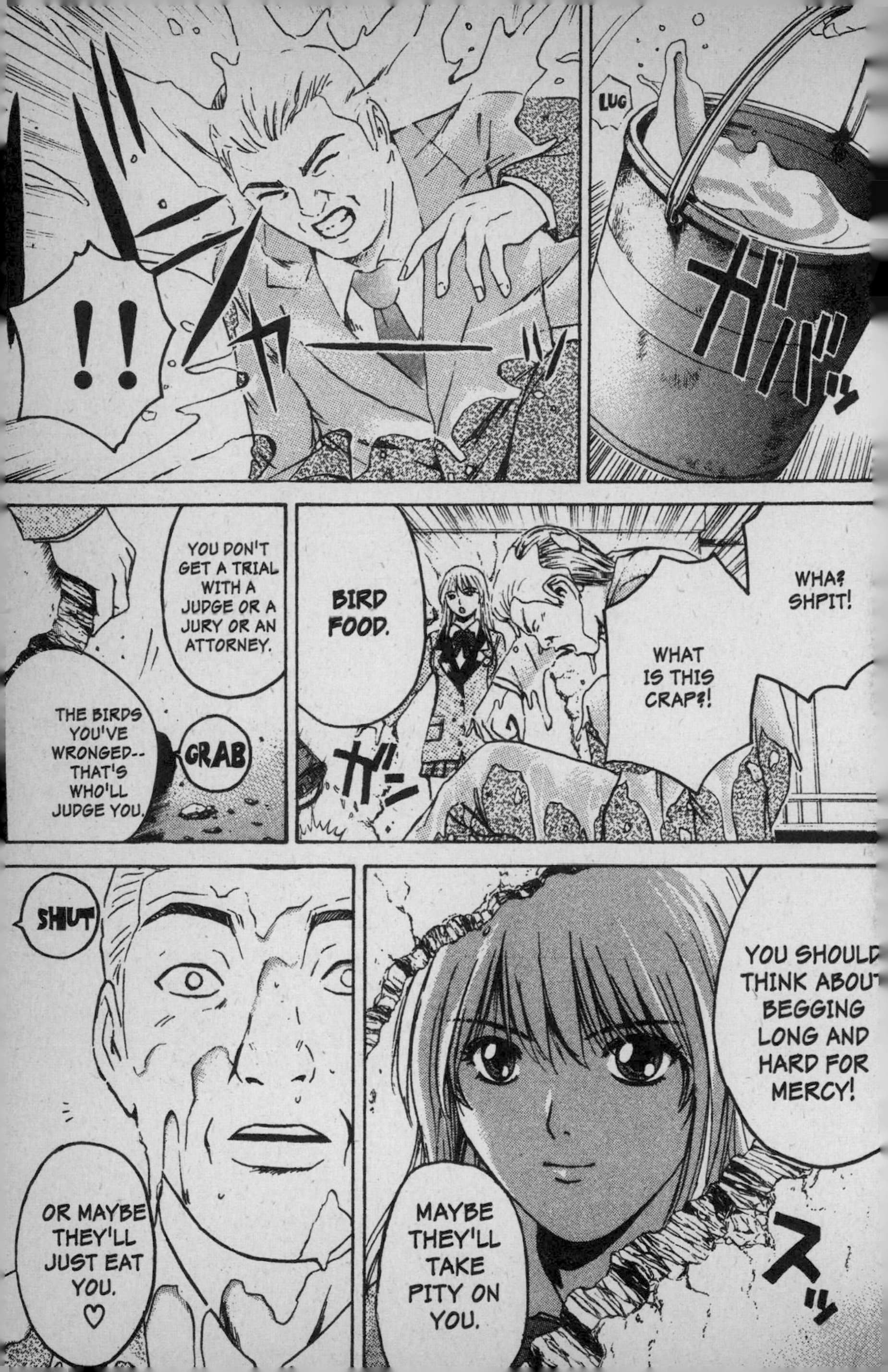
LUG
!!
WHA? SHPIT!
WHAT IS THIS CRAP?!
BIRD FOOD.
YOU DON'T GET A TRIAL WITH A JUDGE OR A JURY OR AN ATTORNEY.
GRAB
THE BIRDS YOU'VE WRONGED-- THAT'S WHO'LL JUDGE YOU.
YOU SHOULD THINK ABOUT BEGGING LONG AND HARD FOR MERCY!
MAYBE THEY'LL TAKE PITY ON YOU.
SHUT
OR MAYBE THEY'LL JUST EAT YOU. ♡

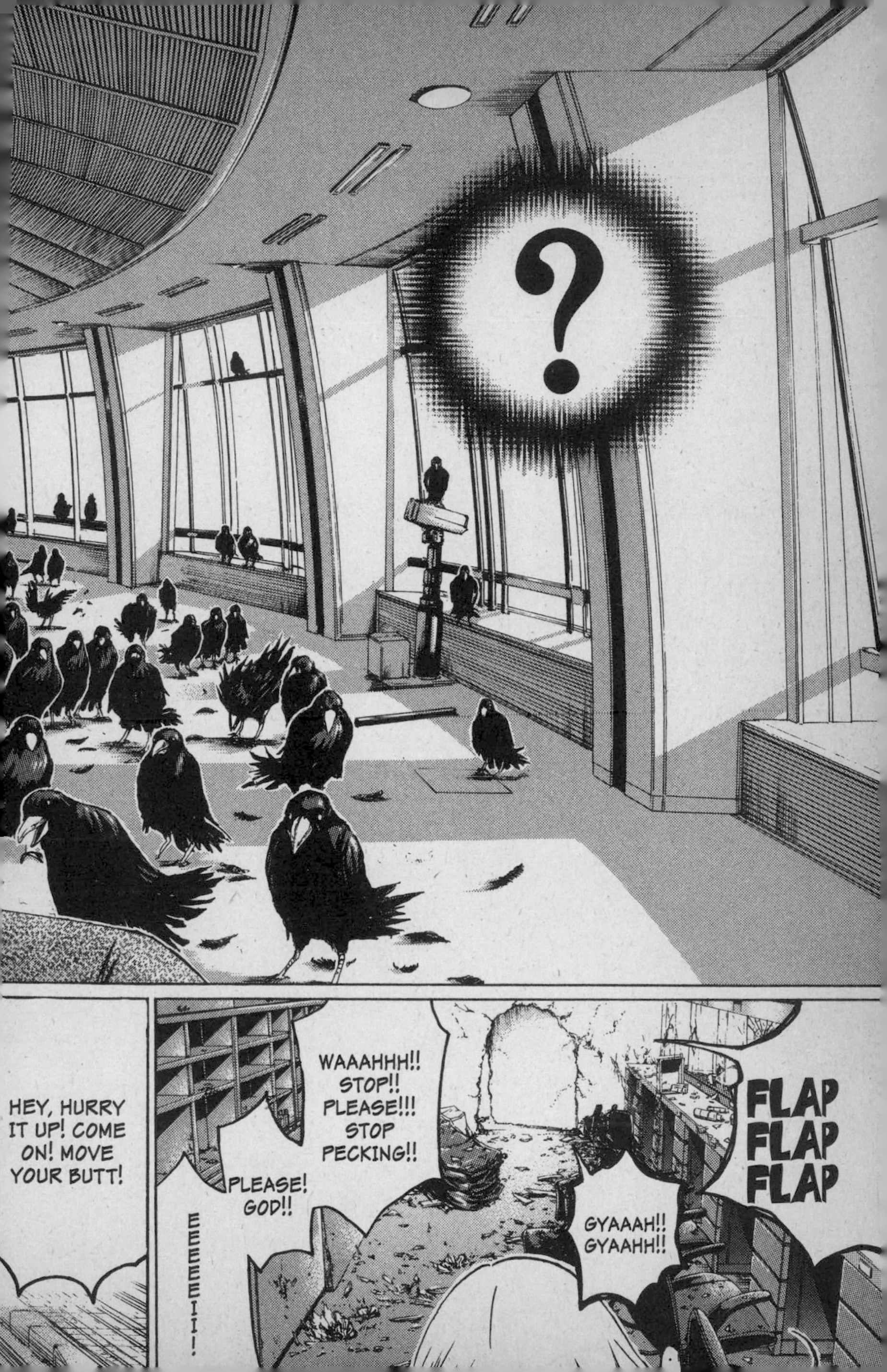
?
FLAP FLAP FLAP
WAAAHHH!! STOP!! PLEASE!!! STOP PECKING!!
GYAAAH!! GYAAHH!!
PLEASE! GOD!!
EEEEEIII!
HEY, HURRY IT UP! COME ON! MOVE YOUR BUTT!

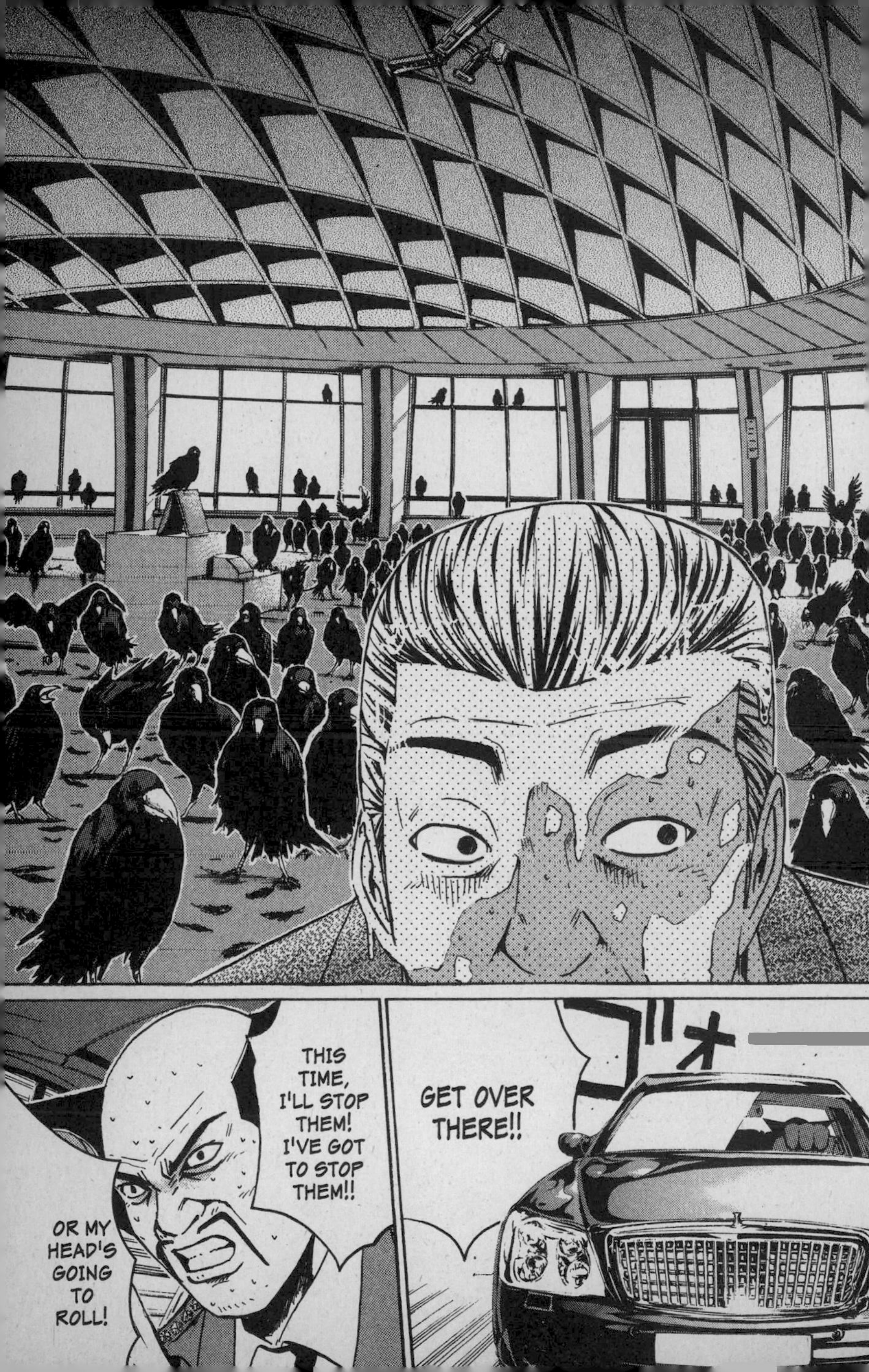
ゴオ
GET OVER THERE!!
THIS TIME, I'LL STOP THEM! I'VE GOT TO STOP THEM!!
OR MY HEAD'S GOING TO ROLL!

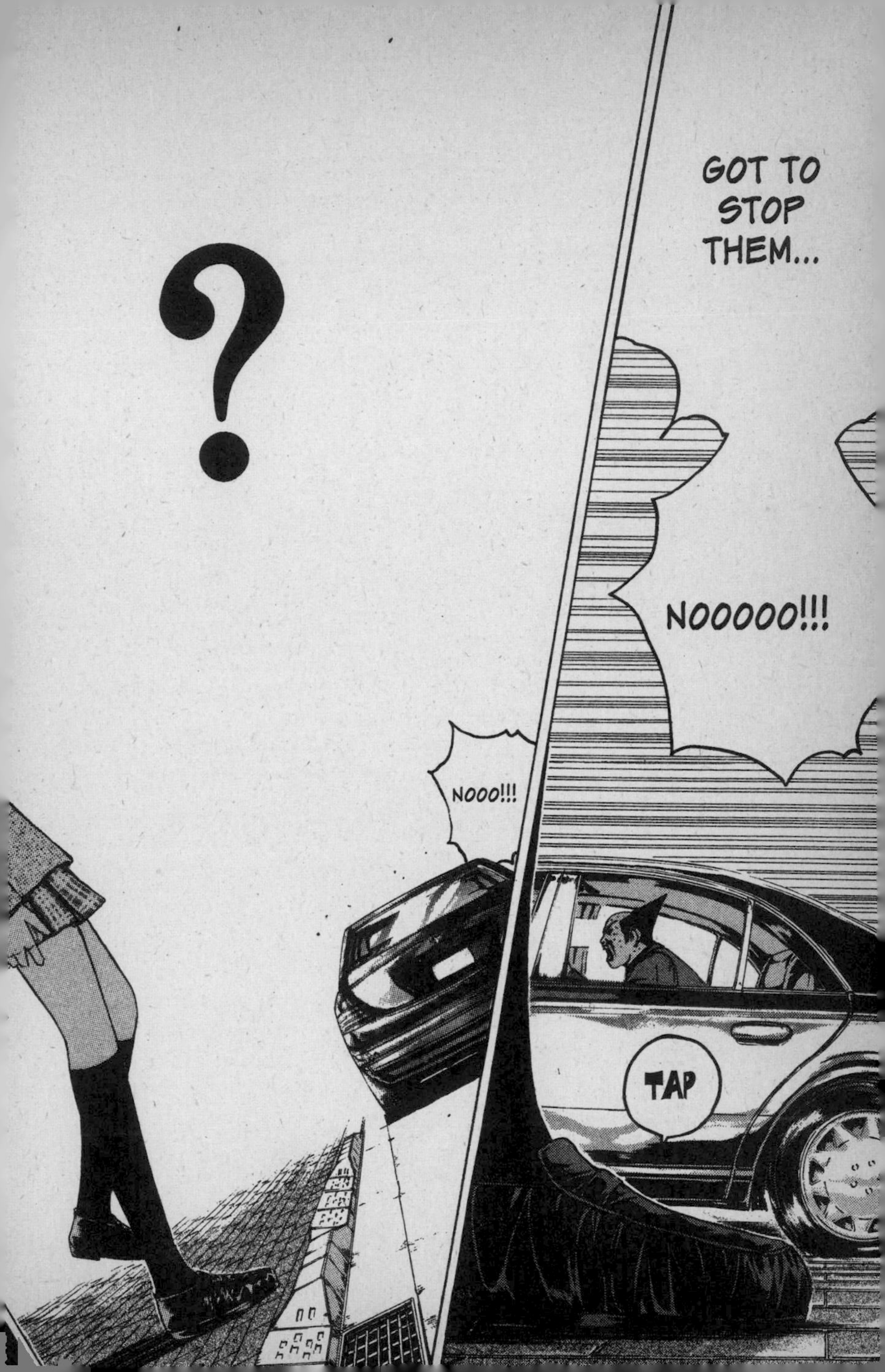
GOT TO STOP THEM...
NOOOOO!!!
TAP
NOOO!!!
?

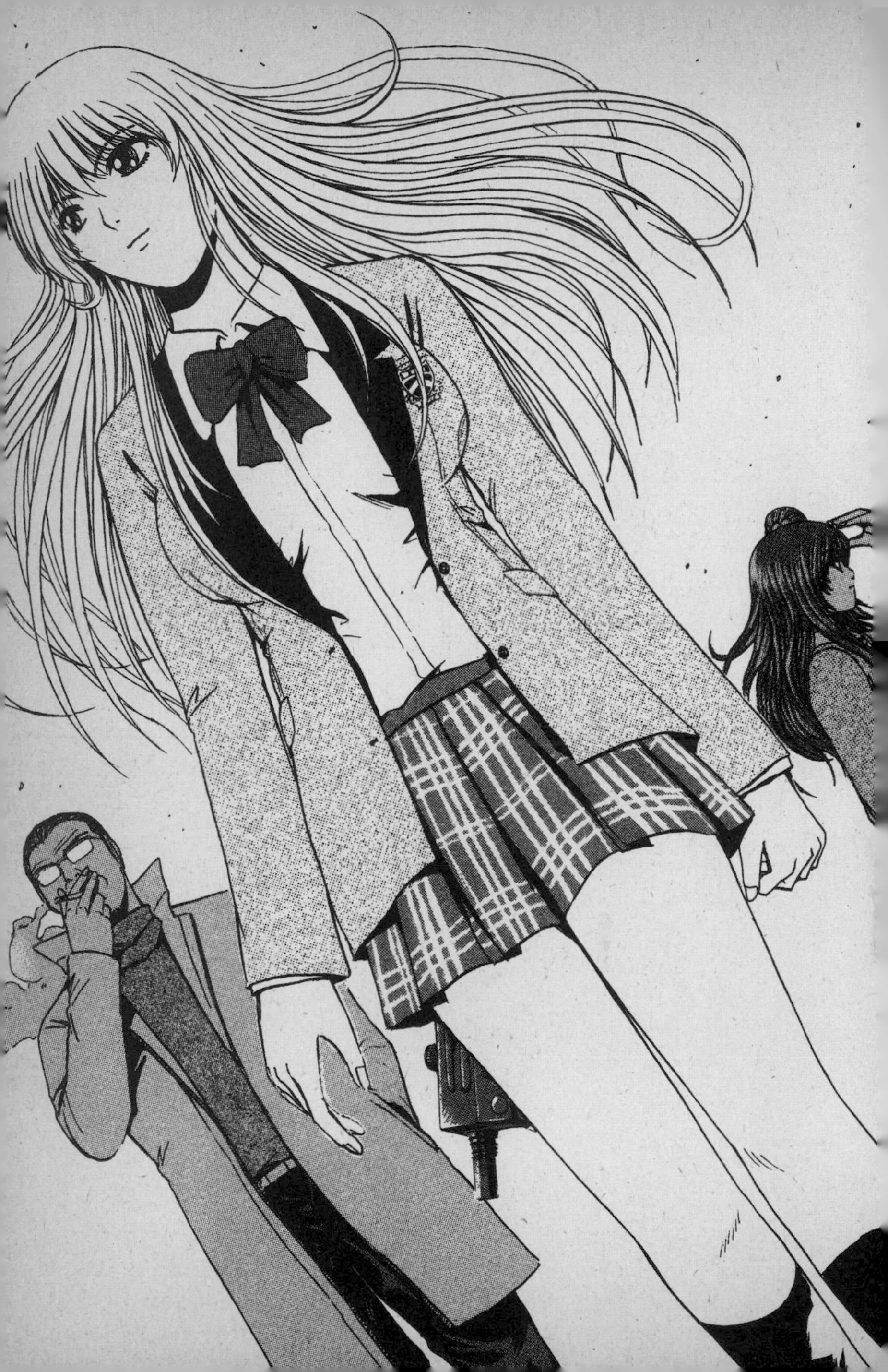

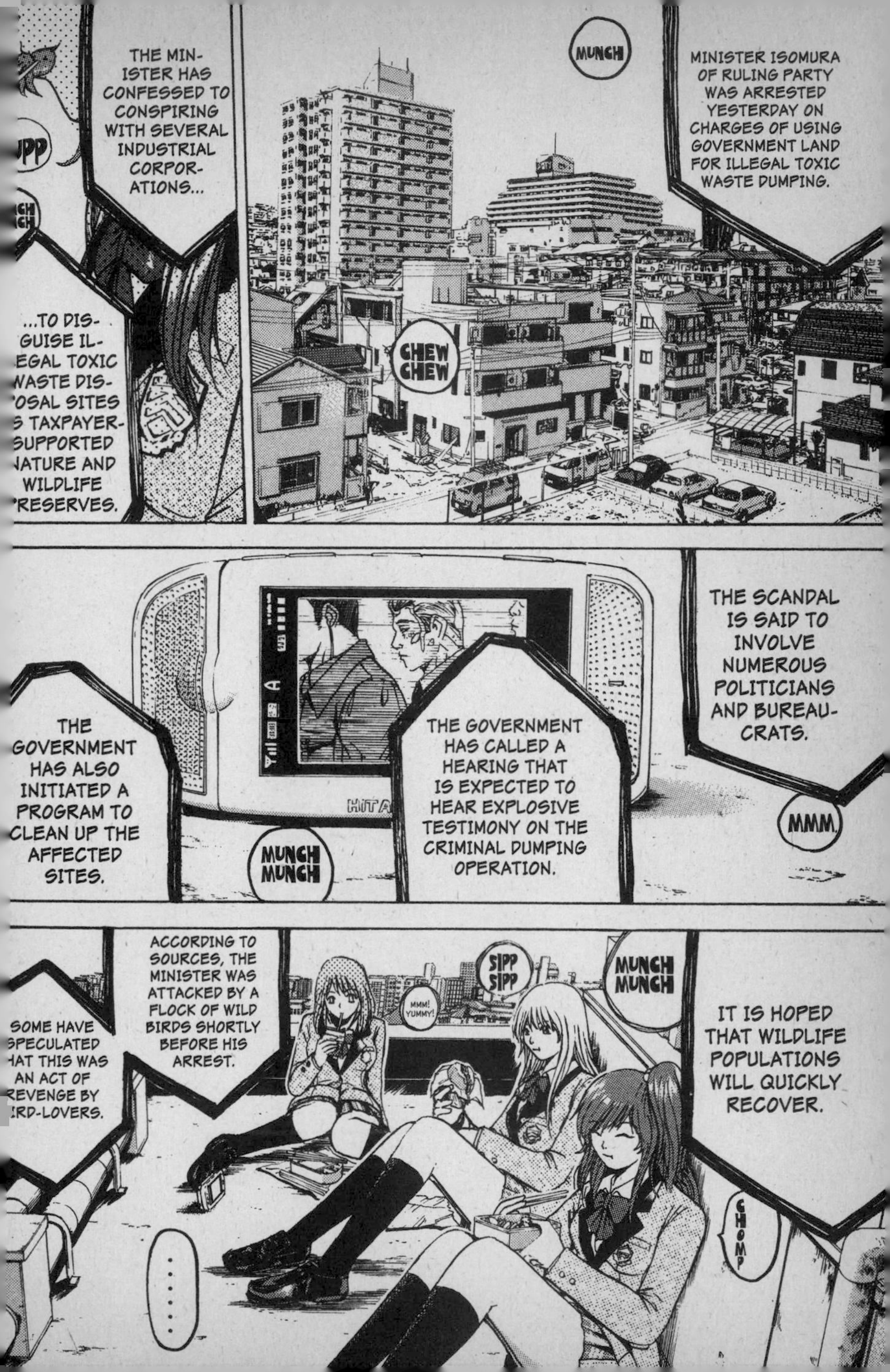
MINISTER ISOMURA OF RULING PARTY WAS ARRESTED YESTERDAY ON CHARGES OF USING GOVERNMENT LAND FOR ILLEGAL TOXIC WASTE DUMPING.
MUNCH
CHEW CHEW
THE MIN- ISTER HAS CONFESSED TO CONSPIRING WITH SEVERAL INDUSTRIAL CORPOR- ATIONS...
...TO DIS- GUISE IL- EGAL TOXIC VASTE DIS- OSAL SITES S TAXPAYER- SUPPORTED NATURE AND WILDLIFE RESERVES.
THE SCANDAL IS SAID TO INVOLVE NUMEROUS POLITICIANS AND BUREAU- CRATS.
MMM.
THE GOVERNMENT HAS CALLED A HEARING THAT IS EXPECTED TO HEAR EXPLOSIVE TESTIMONY ON THE CRIMINAL DUMPING OPERATION.
MUNCH MUNCH
THE GOVERNMENT HAS ALSO INITIATED A PROGRAM TO CLEAN UP THE AFFECTED SITES.
IT IS HOPED THAT WILDLIFE POPULATIONS WILL QUICKLY RECOVER.
CHOMP
MUNCH MUNCH
SIPP SIPP
MMM! YUMMY!
ACCORDING TO SOURCES, THE MINISTER WAS ATTACKED BY A FLOCK OF WILD BIRDS SHORTLY BEFORE HIS ARREST.
SOME HAVE SPECULATED HAT THIS WAS AN ACT OF REVENGE BY IRD-LOVERS.
......

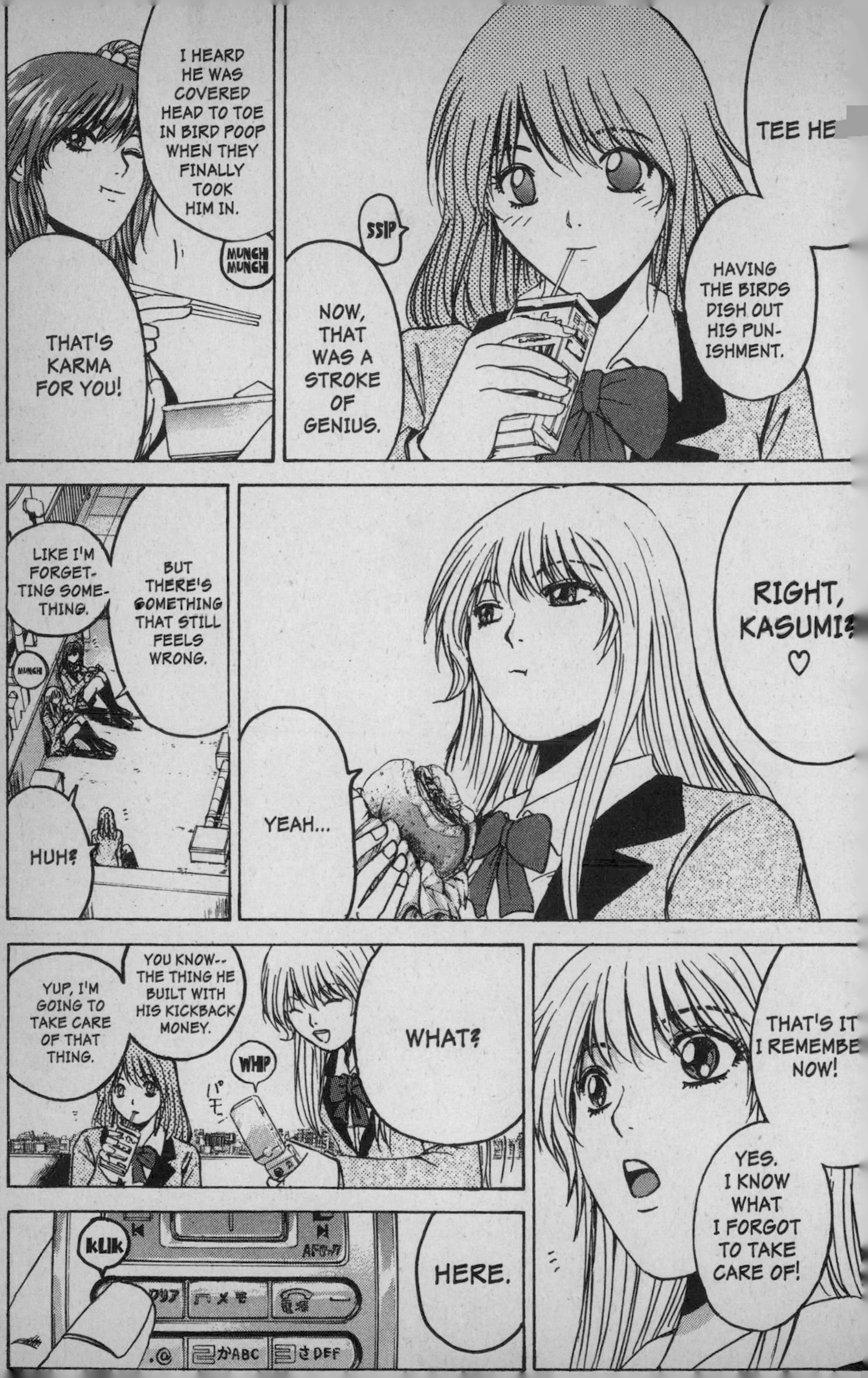
TEE HE
HAVING THE BIRDS DISH OUT HIS PUN-ISHMENT.
SSIP
NOW, THAT WAS A STROKE OF GENIUS.
I HEARD HE WAS COVERED HEAD TO TOE IN BIRD POOP WHEN THEY FINALLY TOOK HIM IN.
MUNCH MUNCH
THAT'S KARMA FOR YOU!
RIGHT, KASUMI? ♡
YEAH...
BUT THERE'S SOMETHING THAT STILL FEELS WRONG.
LIKE I'M FORGET-TING SOME-THING.
MUNCH
HUH?
THAT'S IT
I REMEMBE
NOW!
YES. I KNOW WHAT I FORGOT TO TAKE CARE OF!
WHAT?
YOU KNOW-- THE THING HE BUILT WITH HIS KICKBACK MONEY.
YUP, I'M GOING TO TAKE CARE OF THAT THING.
WHP
HERE.
KLIK
かABC
さDEF

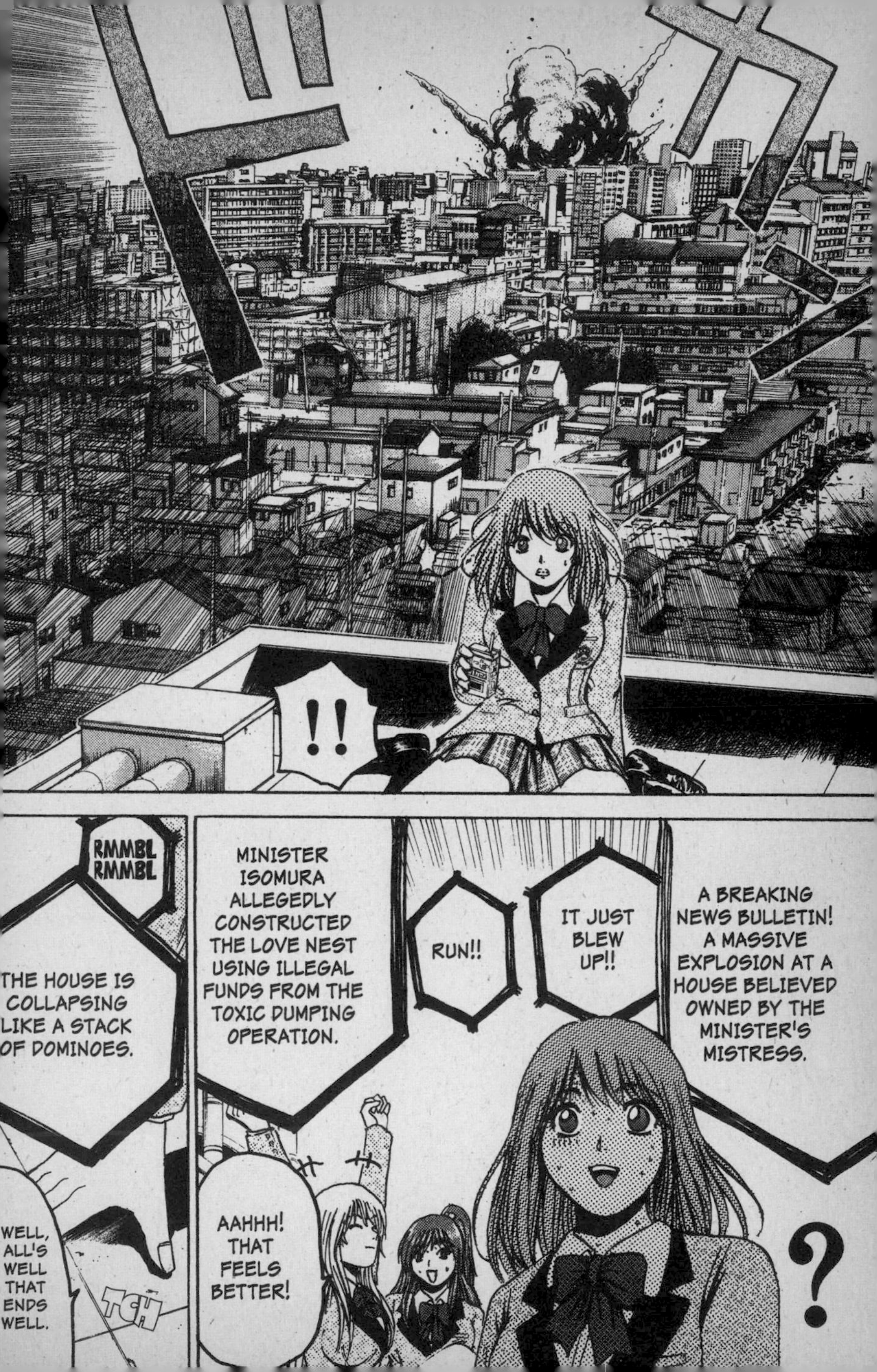
!!
A BREAKING NEWS BULLETIN! A MASSIVE EXPLOSION AT A HOUSE BELIEVED OWNED BY THE MINISTER'S MISTRESS.
IT JUST BLEW UP!!
RUN!!
MINISTER ISOMURA ALLEGEDLY CONSTRUCTED THE LOVE NEST USING ILLEGAL FUNDS FROM THE TOXIC DUMPING OPERATION.
RMMBL RMMBL
THE HOUSE IS COLLAPSING LIKE A STACK OF DOMINOES.
?
AAHHH! THAT FEELS BETTER!
WELL, ALL'S WELL THAT ENDS WELL.
TCH

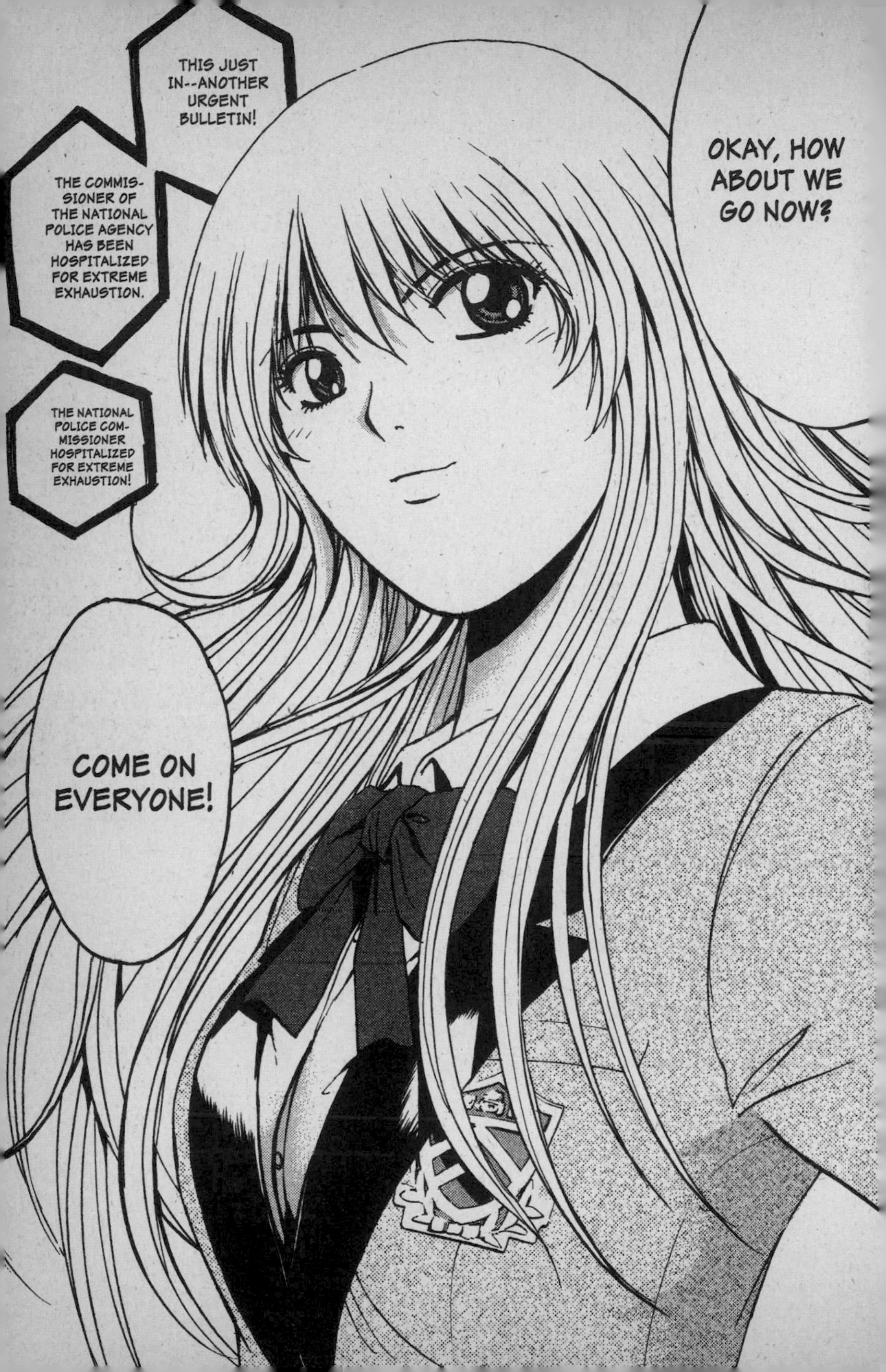
OKAY, HOW ABOUT WE GO NOW?
THIS JUST IN--ANOTHER URGENT BULLETIN!
THE COMMISSIONER OF THE NATIONAL POLICE AGENCY HAS BEEN HOSPITALIZED FOR EXTREME EXHAUSTION.
THE NATIONAL POLICE COMMISSIONER HOSPITALIZED FOR EXTREME EXHAUSTION!
COME ON EVERYONE!

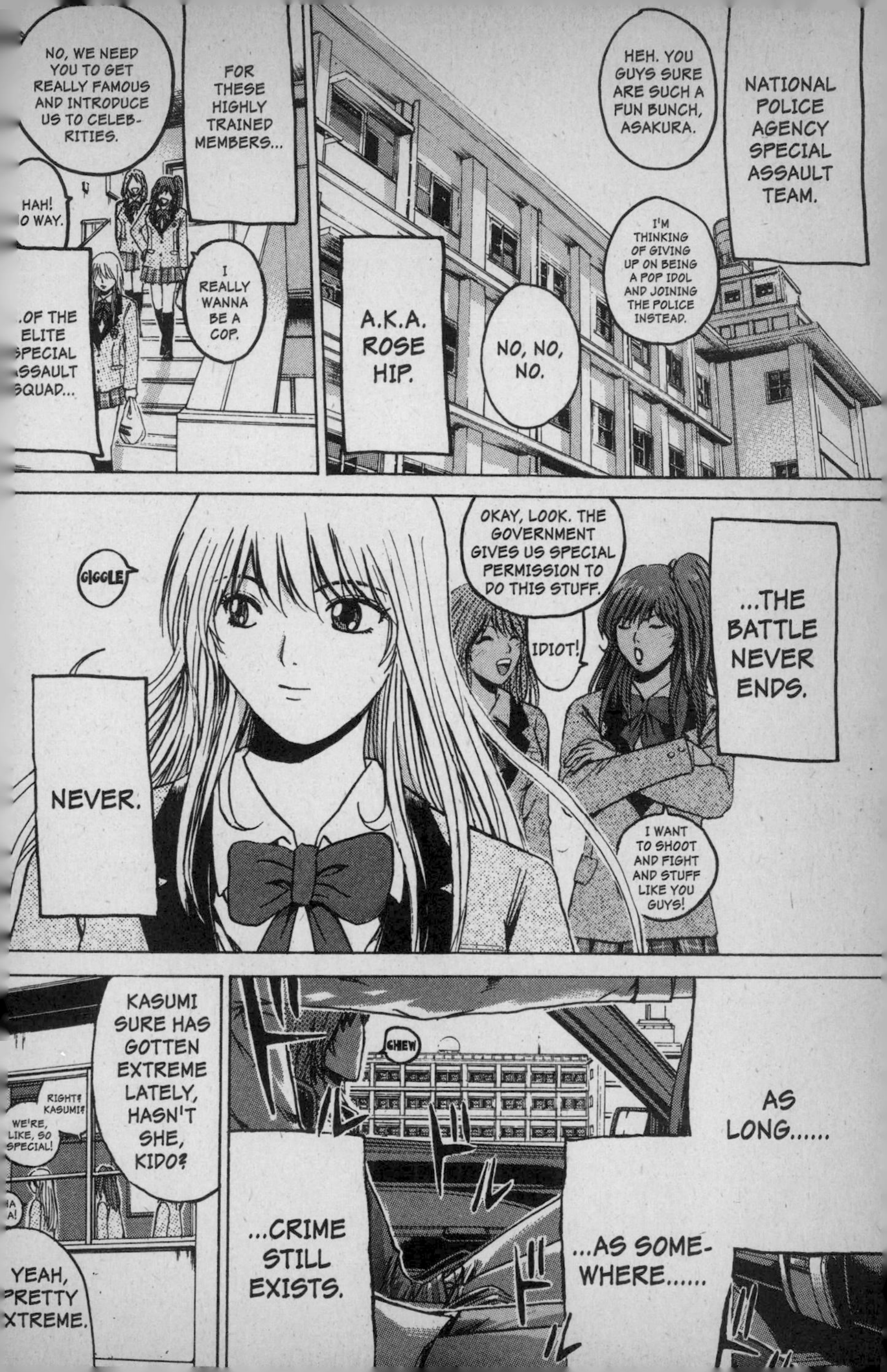

NATIONAL POLICE AGENCY SPECIAL ASSAULT TEAM.
HEH. YOU GUYS SURE ARE SUCH A FUN BUNCH, ASAKURA.
I'M THINKING OF GIVING UP ON BEING A POP IDOL AND JOINING THE POLICE INSTEAD.
NO, NO, NO.
A.K.A. ROSE HIP.
FOR THESE HIGHLY TRAINED MEMBERS...
NO, WE NEED YOU TO GET REALLY FAMOUS AND INTRODUCE US TO CELEB-RITIES.
I REALLY WANNA BE A COP.
HAH! O WAY.
.OF THE ELITE PECIAL SSAULT SQUAD...
...THE BATTLE NEVER ENDS.
OKAY, LOOK. THE GOVERNMENT GIVES US SPECIAL PERMISSION TO DO THIS STUFF.
IDIOT!
I WANT TO SHOOT AND FIGHT AND STUFF LIKE YOU GUYS!
GIGGLE
NEVER.
AS LONG......
...AS SOME-WHERE......
CHEW
...CRIME STILL EXISTS.
KASUMI SURE HAS GOTTEN EXTREME LATELY, HASN'T SHE, KIDO?
RIGHT? KASUMI?
WE'RE, LIKE, SO SPECIAL!
YEAH, PRETTY EXTREME.

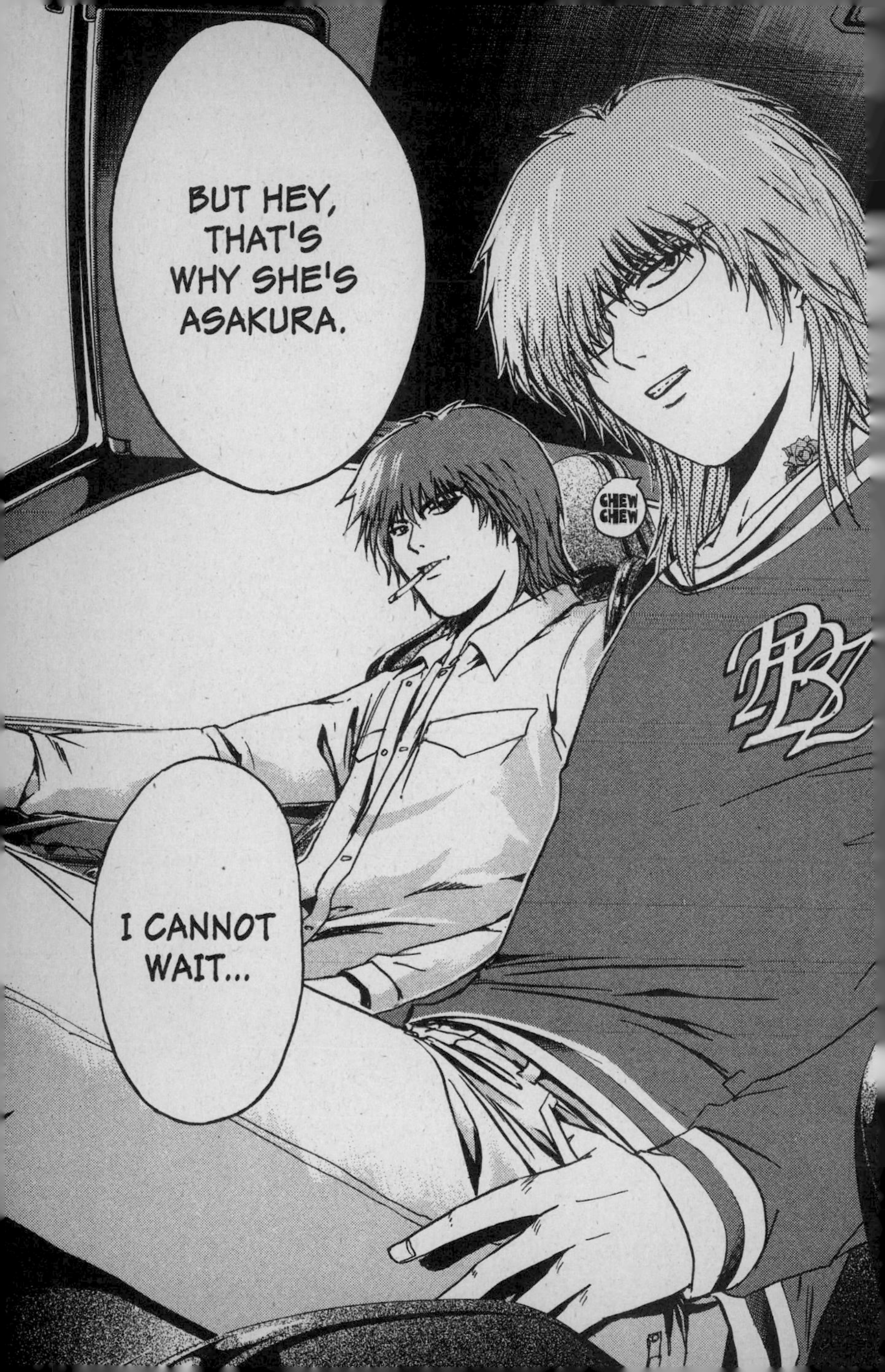
BUT HEY, THAT'S WHY SHE'S ASAKURA.
CHEW CHEW
I CANNOT WAIT...

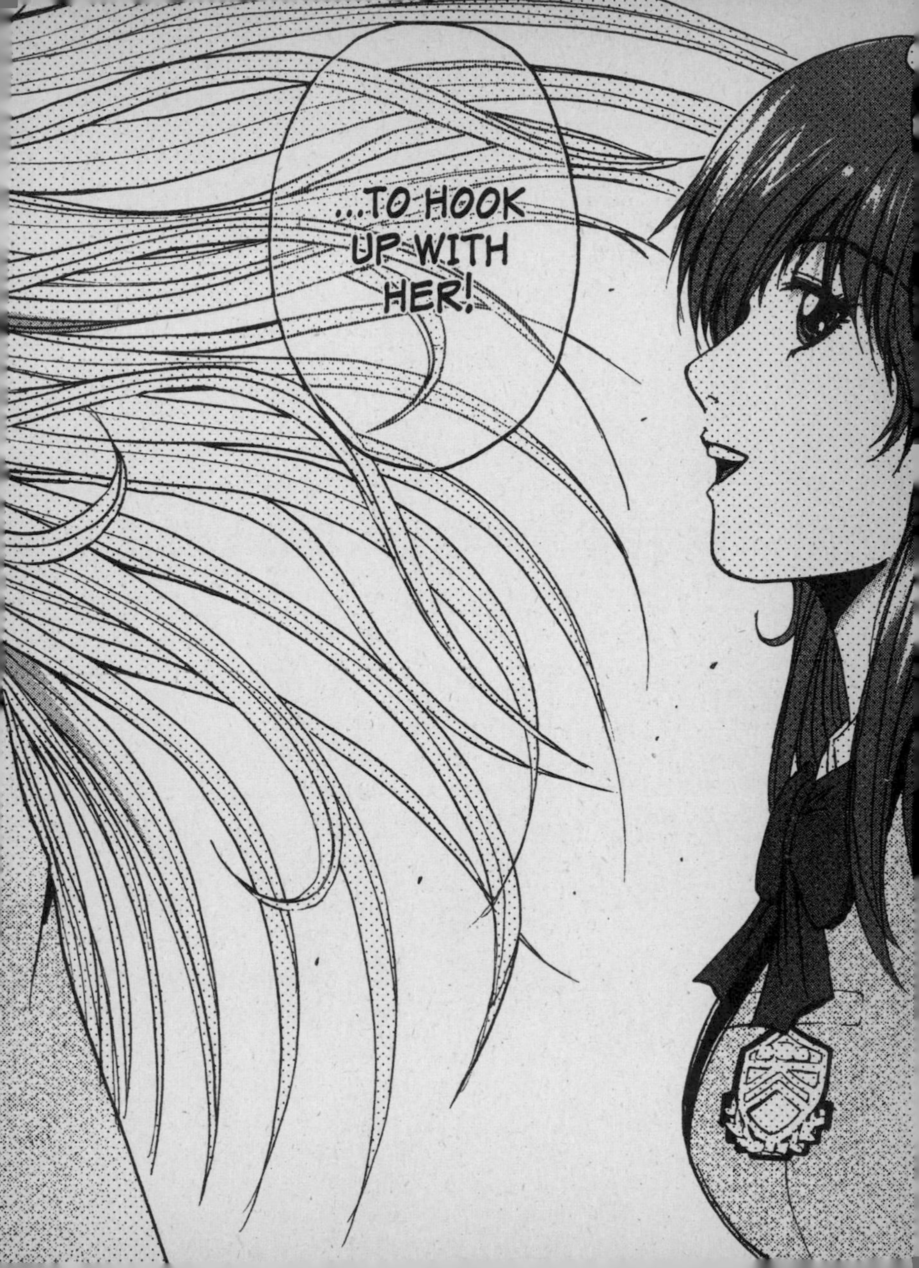
...TO HOOK UP WITH HER!

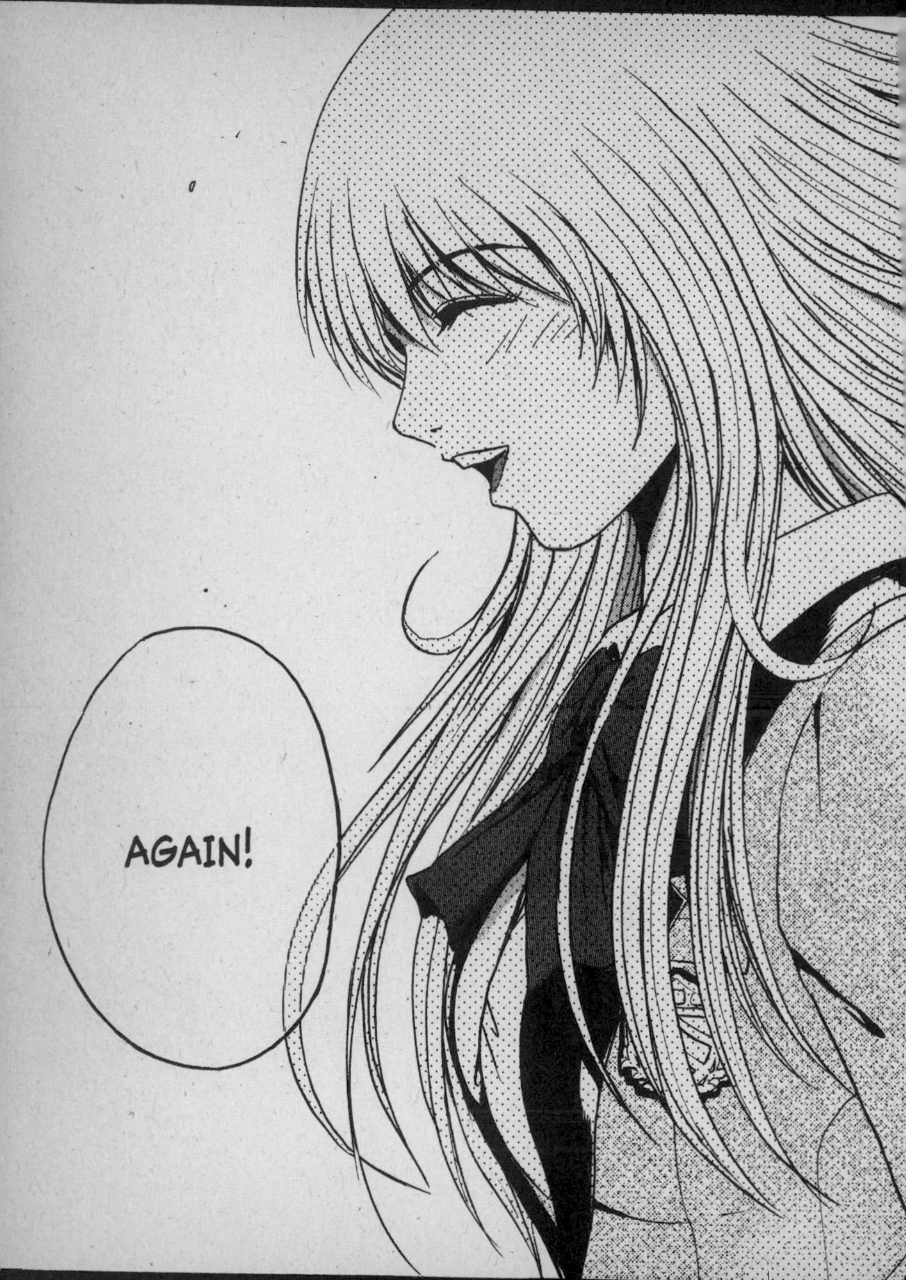
AGAIN!

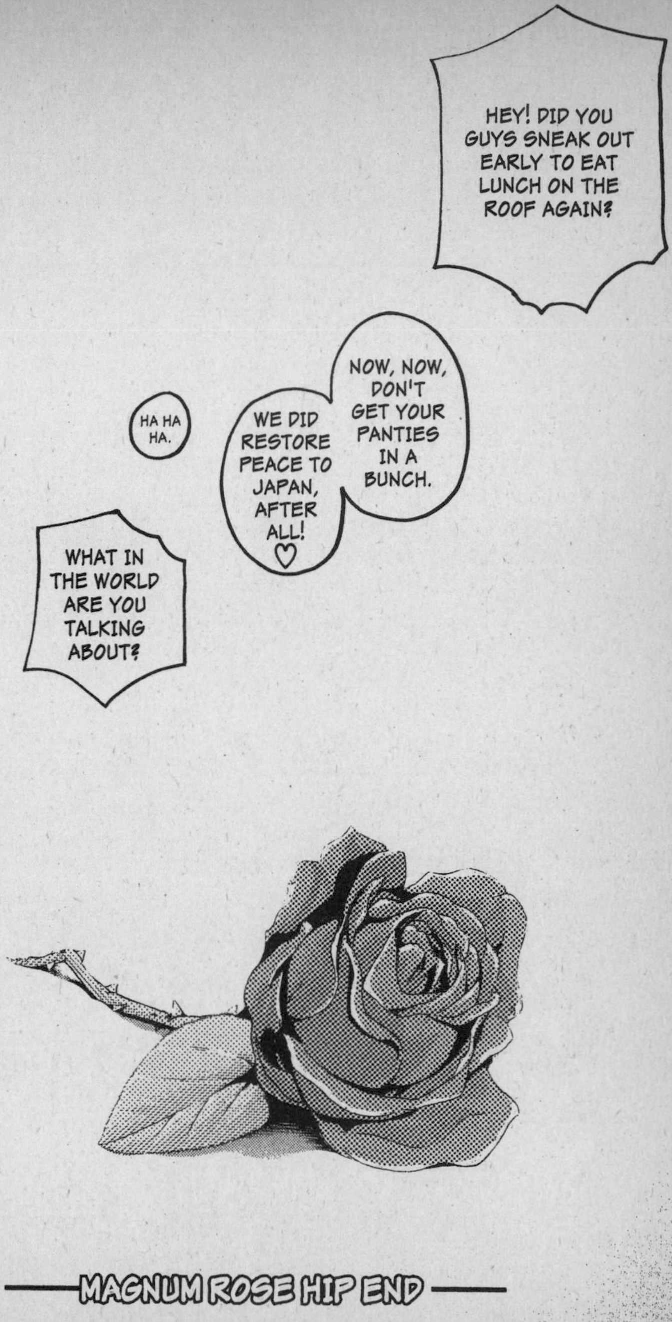
HEY! DID YOU GUYS SNEAK OUT EARLY TO EAT LUNCH ON THE ROOF AGAIN?
NOW, NOW, DON'T GET YOUR PANTIES IN A BUNCH.
WE DID RESTORE PEACE TO JAPAN, AFTER ALL! ♡
HA HA HA.
WHAT IN THE WORLD ARE YOU TALKING ABOUT?
—MAGNUM ROSE HIP END—

Rose Hip Rose

ローズ・ヒップ・ローズ

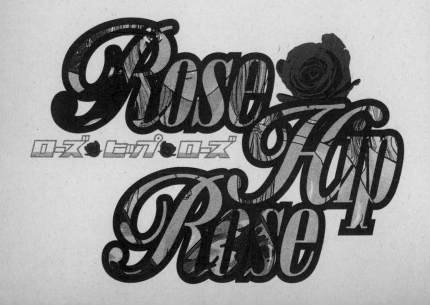

Special Extra Chapter.
"Rose Hip Rose" (May, 2002.)

This chapter was first published in the May, 2002 edition of Young Magazine Uppers, as part of the Guns and Action Series.

Because the story proved very popular, I changed the story and settings a little and Rose Hip Rose was born. ROSE HIP ZERO is now considered the stories of Kasumi's past.

This story was also included in KC's ROSE HIP ZERO, as I wanted to created a complete record of the Rose Hip series. I now include it in this book as well. I hope you enjoy the antics of a slightly different Kasumi!

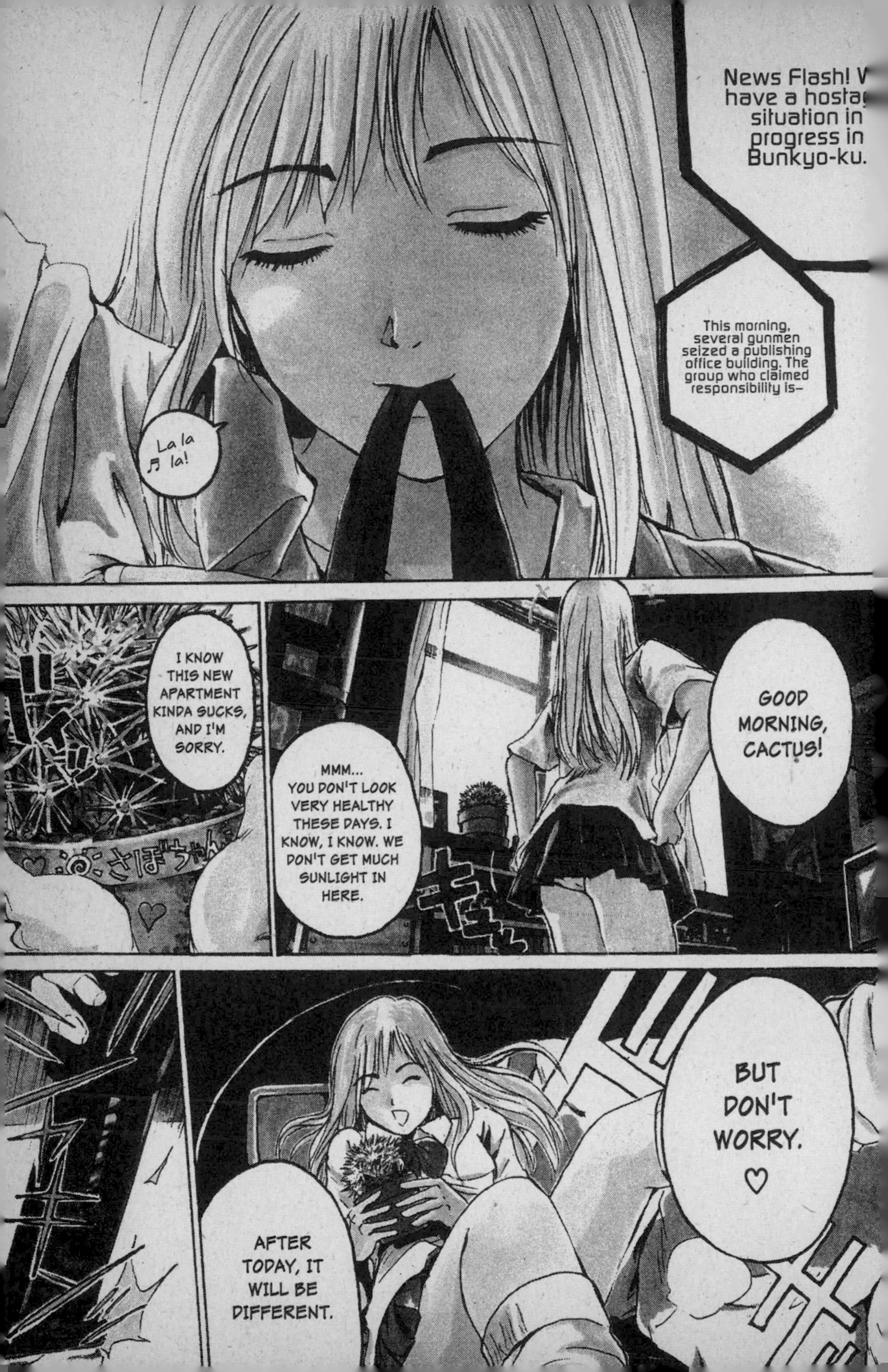
News Flash! W
have a hostag
situation in
progress in
Bunkyo-ku.
This morning, several gunmen seized a publishing office building. The group who claimed responsibility is–
La la ♬ la!
GOOD MORNING, CACTUS!
MMM... YOU DON'T LOOK VERY HEALTHY THESE DAYS. I KNOW, I KNOW. WE DON'T GET MUCH SUNLIGHT IN HERE.
I KNOW THIS NEW APARTMENT KINDA SUCKS, AND I'M SORRY.
さぼちゃん
BUT DON'T WORRY. ♡
AFTER TODAY, IT WILL BE DIFFERENT.

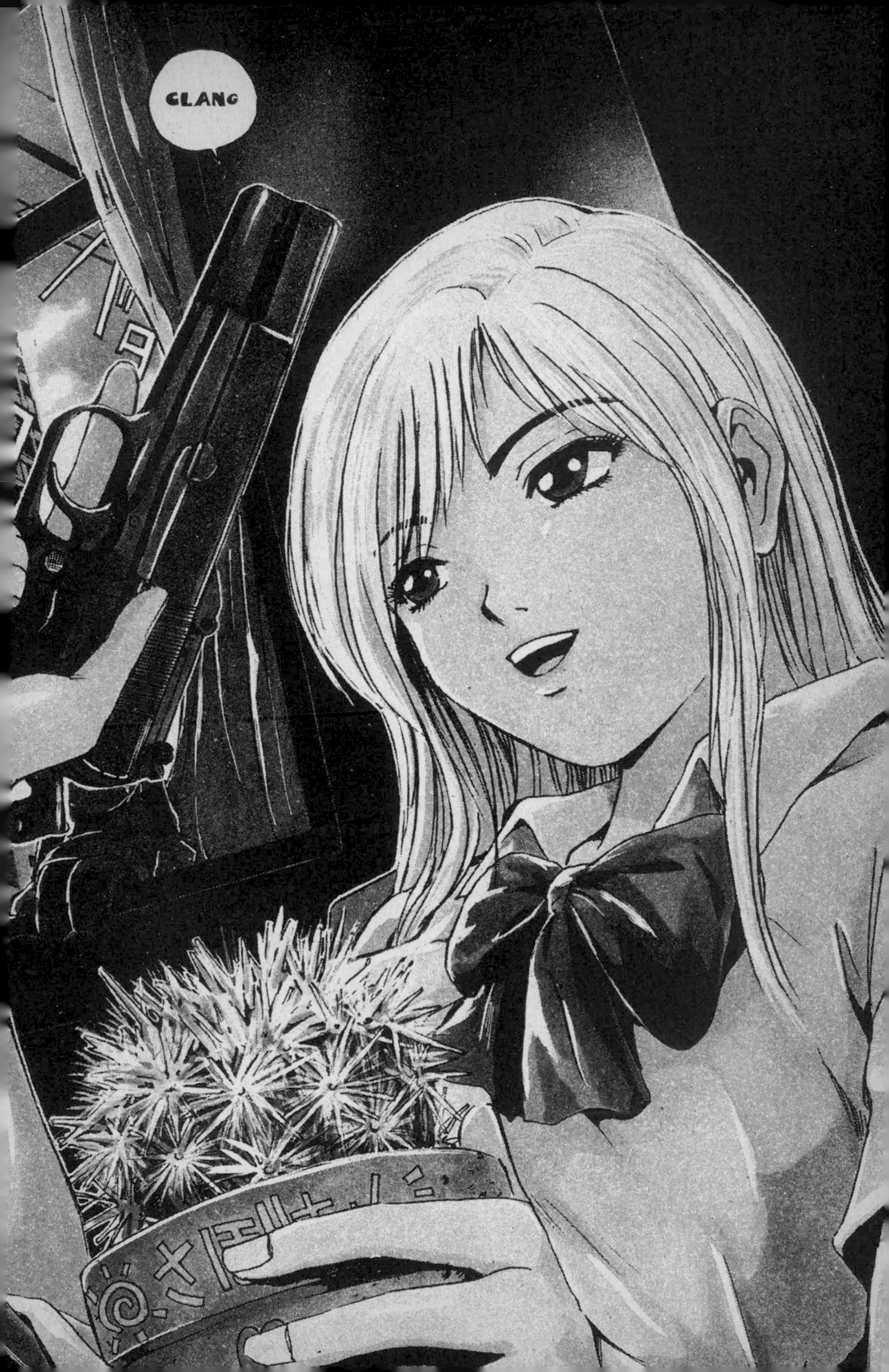
CLANG

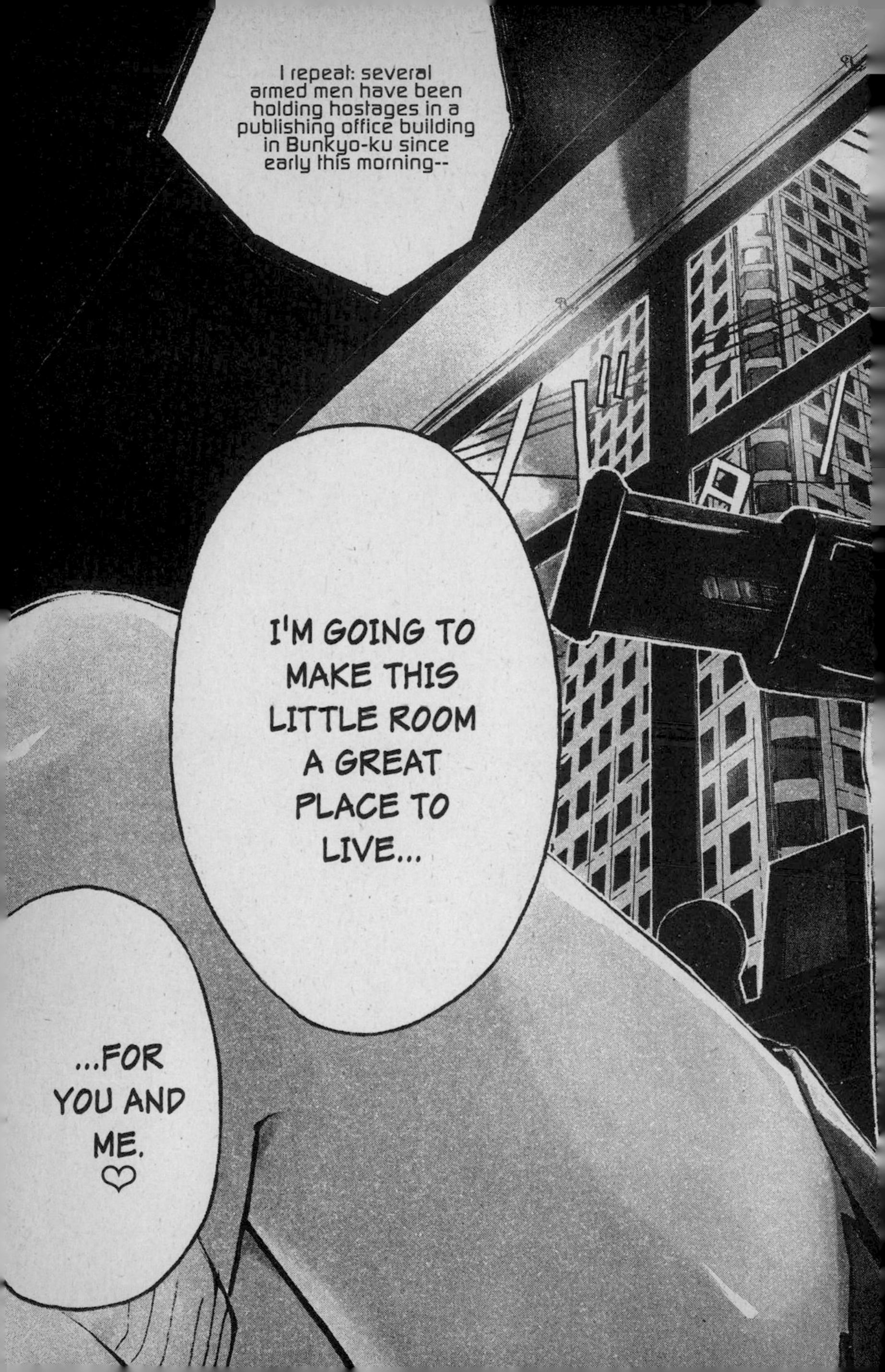
I repeat: several armed men have been holding hostages in a publishing office building in Bunkyo-ku since early this morning--
I'M GOING TO MAKE THIS LITTLE ROOM A GREAT PLACE TO LIVE...
...FOR YOU AND ME. ♡

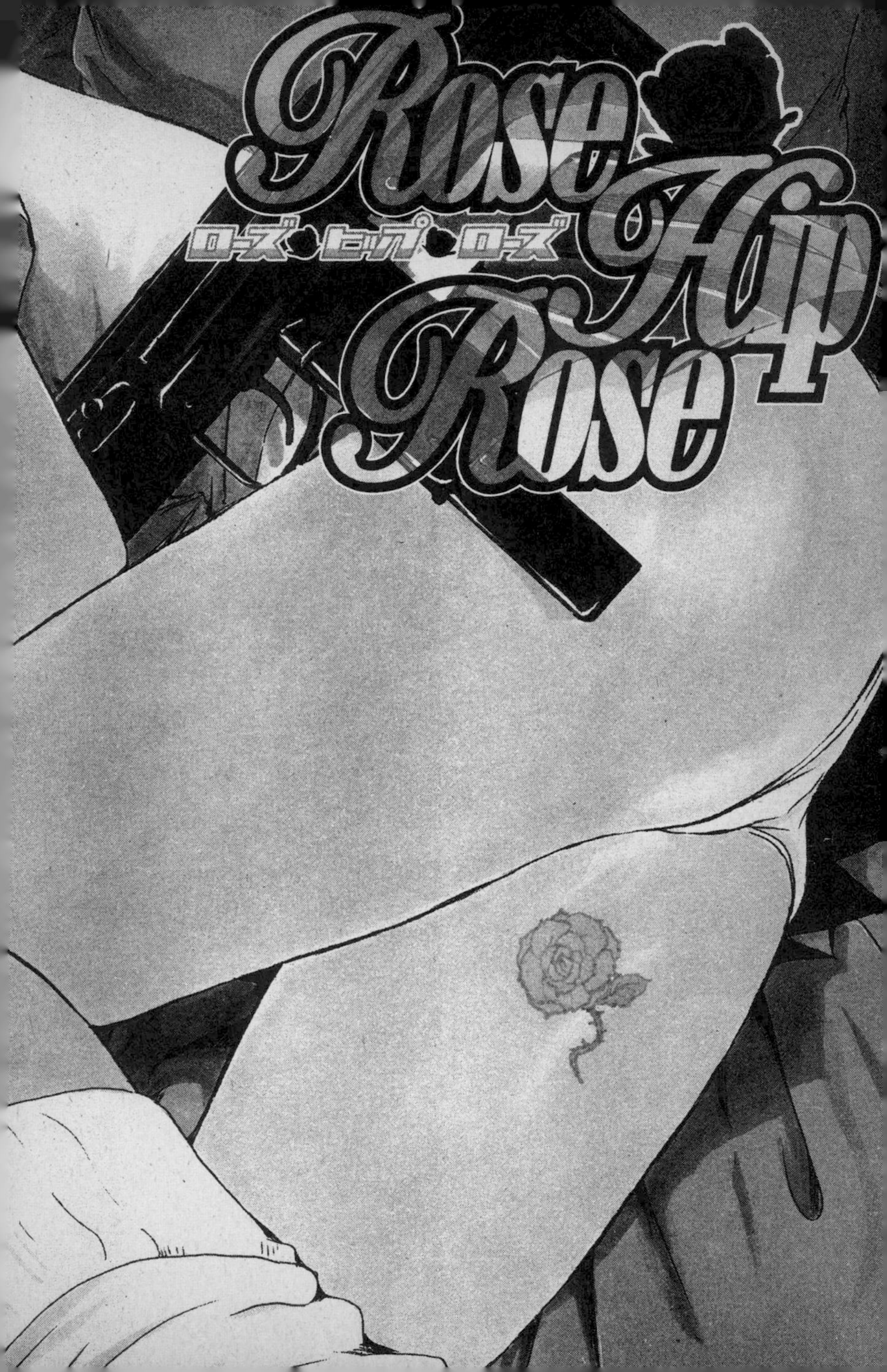
Rose Hip Rose
ローズ・ヒップ・ローズ
4

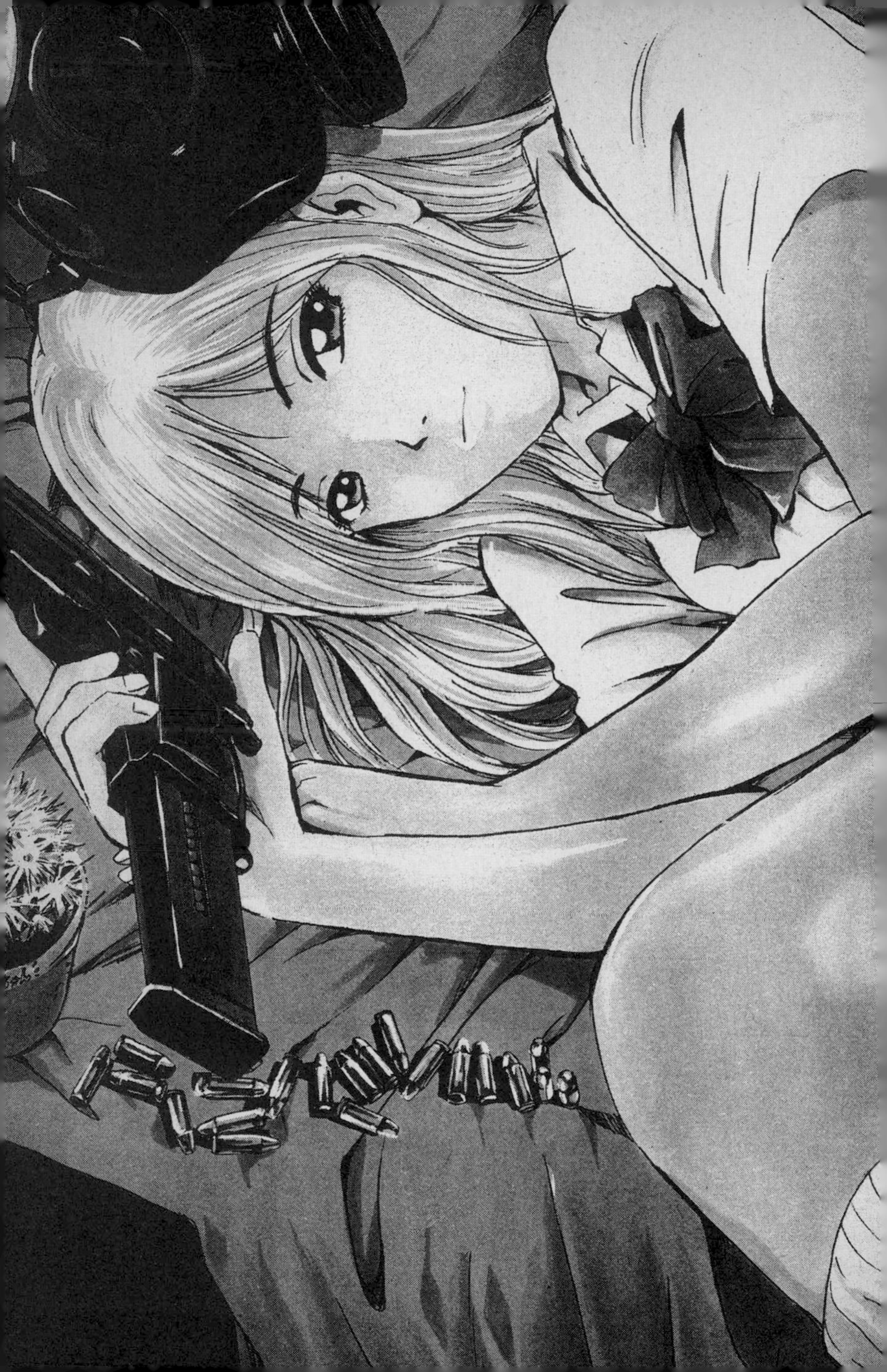

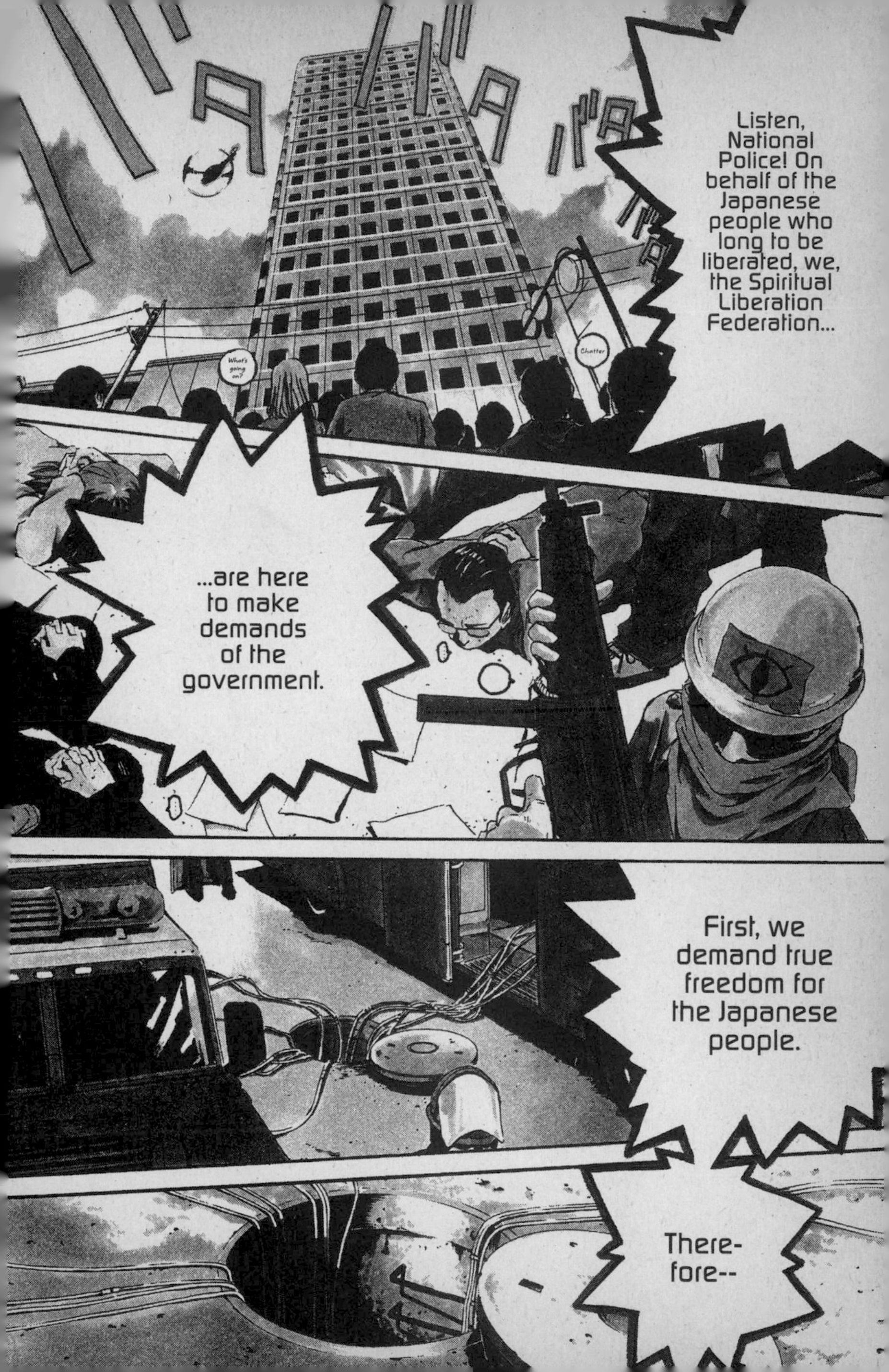

Listen, National Police! On behalf of the Japanese people who long to be liberated, we, the Spiritual Liberation Federation...
Chatter
What's going on?
...are here to make demands of the government.
First, we demand true freedom for the Japanese people.
There-fore--

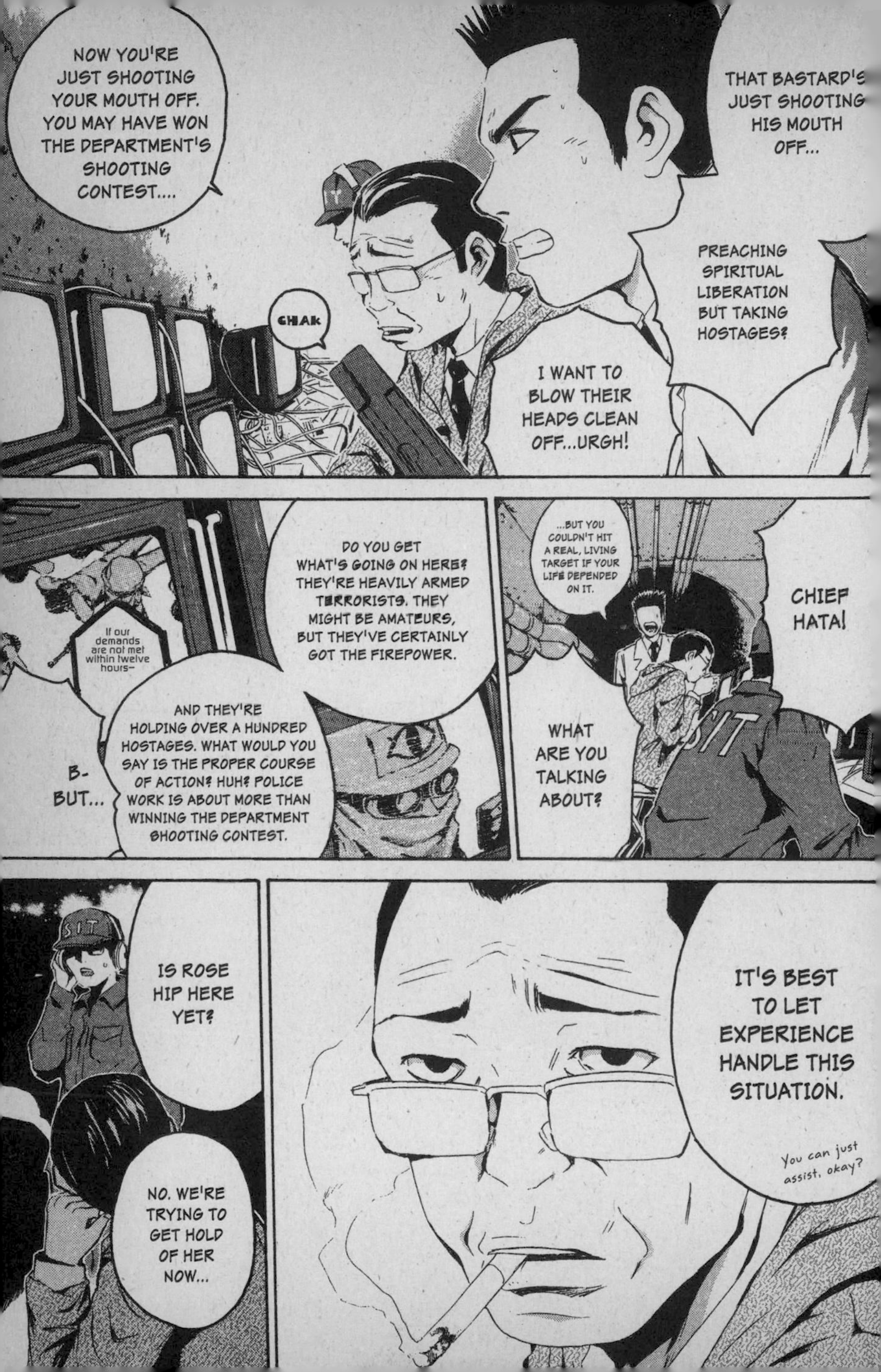
THAT BASTARD'S JUST SHOOTING HIS MOUTH OFF...
PREACHING SPIRITUAL LIBERATION BUT TAKING HOSTAGES?
I WANT TO BLOW THEIR HEADS CLEAN OFF...URGH!
NOW YOU'RE JUST SHOOTING YOUR MOUTH OFF. YOU MAY HAVE WON THE DEPARTMENT'S SHOOTING CONTEST....
CHAK
CHIEF HATA!
...BUT YOU COULDN'T HIT A REAL, LIVING TARGET IF YOUR LIFE DEPENDED ON IT.
WHAT ARE YOU TALKING ABOUT?
DO YOU GET WHAT'S GOING ON HERE? THEY'RE HEAVILY ARMED TERRORISTS. THEY MIGHT BE AMATEURS, BUT THEY'VE CERTAINLY GOT THE FIREPOWER.
If our demands are not met within twelve hours–
AND THEY'RE HOLDING OVER A HUNDRED HOSTAGES. WHAT WOULD YOU SAY IS THE PROPER COURSE OF ACTION? HUH? POLICE WORK IS ABOUT MORE THAN WINNING THE DEPARTMENT SHOOTING CONTEST.
B-BUT...
IT'S BEST TO LET EXPERIENCE HANDLE THIS SITUATION.
You can just assist, okay?
IS ROSE HIP HERE YET?
NO. WE'RE TRYING TO GET HOLD OF HER NOW...

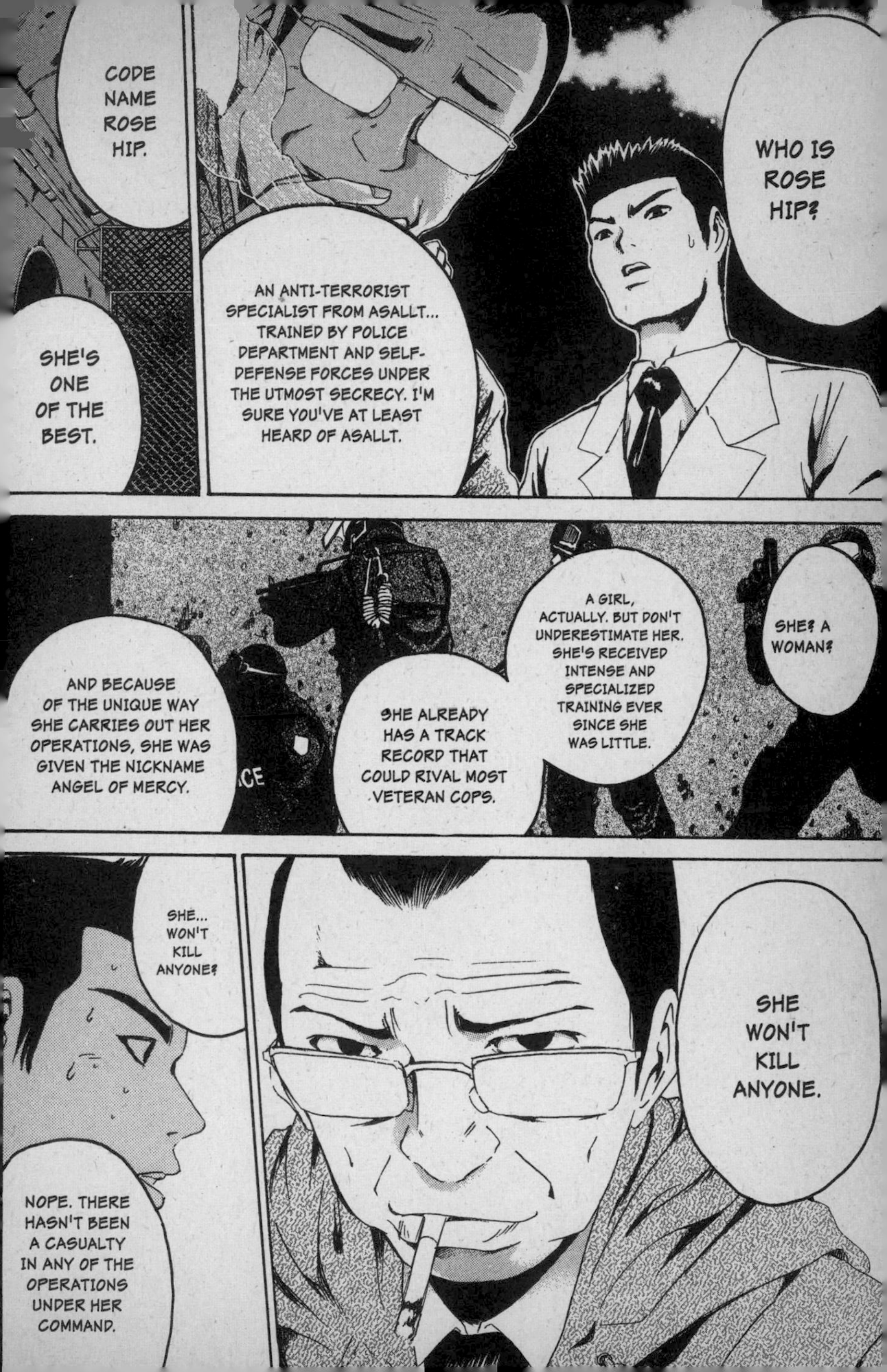
WHO IS ROSE HIP?
AN ANTI-TERRORIST SPECIALIST FROM ASALLT... TRAINED BY POLICE DEPARTMENT AND SELF-DEFENSE FORCES UNDER THE UTMOST SECRECY. I'M SURE YOU'VE AT LEAST HEARD OF ASALLT.
CODE NAME ROSE HIP.
SHE'S ONE OF THE BEST.
SHE? A WOMAN?
A GIRL, ACTUALLY. BUT DON'T UNDERESTIMATE HER. SHE'S RECEIVED INTENSE AND SPECIALIZED TRAINING EVER SINCE SHE WAS LITTLE.
SHE ALREADY HAS A TRACK RECORD THAT COULD RIVAL MOST VETERAN COPS.
AND BECAUSE OF THE UNIQUE WAY SHE CARRIES OUT HER OPERATIONS, SHE WAS GIVEN THE NICKNAME ANGEL OF MERCY.
SHE WON'T KILL ANYONE.
SHE... WON'T KILL ANYONE?
NOPE. THERE HASN'T BEEN A CASUALTY IN ANY OF THE OPERATIONS UNDER HER COMMAND.

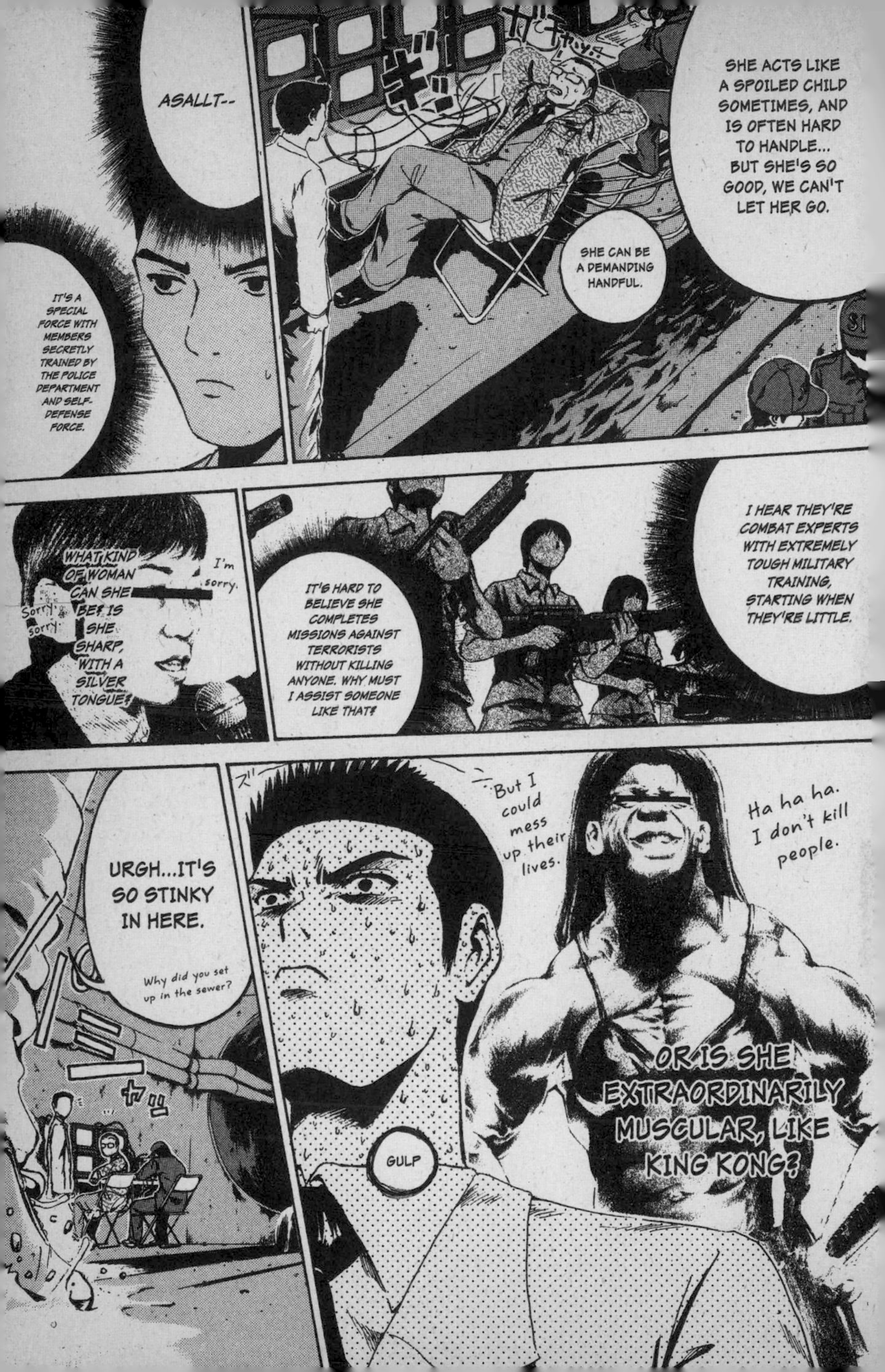
SHE ACTS LIKE A SPOILED CHILD SOMETIMES, AND IS OFTEN HARD TO HANDLE... BUT SHE'S SO GOOD, WE CAN'T LET HER GO.
SHE CAN BE A DEMANDING HANDFUL.
ASALLT--
IT'S A SPECIAL FORCE WITH MEMBERS SECRETLY TRAINED BY THE POLICE DEPARTMENT AND SELF-DEFENSE FORCE.
I HEAR THEY'RE COMBAT EXPERTS WITH EXTREMELY TOUGH MILITARY TRAINING, STARTING WHEN THEY'RE LITTLE.
IT'S HARD TO BELIEVE SHE COMPLETES MISSIONS AGAINST TERRORISTS WITHOUT KILLING ANYONE. WHY MUST I ASSIST SOMEONE LIKE THAT?
WHAT KIND OF WOMAN CAN SHE BE? IS SHE SHARP, WITH A SILVER TONGUE?
I'm sorry.
Sorry sorry
Ha ha ha. I don't kill people.
But I could mess up their lives.
OR IS SHE EXTRAORDINARILY MUSCULAR, LIKE KING KONG?
GULP
URGH...IT'S SO STINKY IN HERE.
Why did you set up in the sewer?

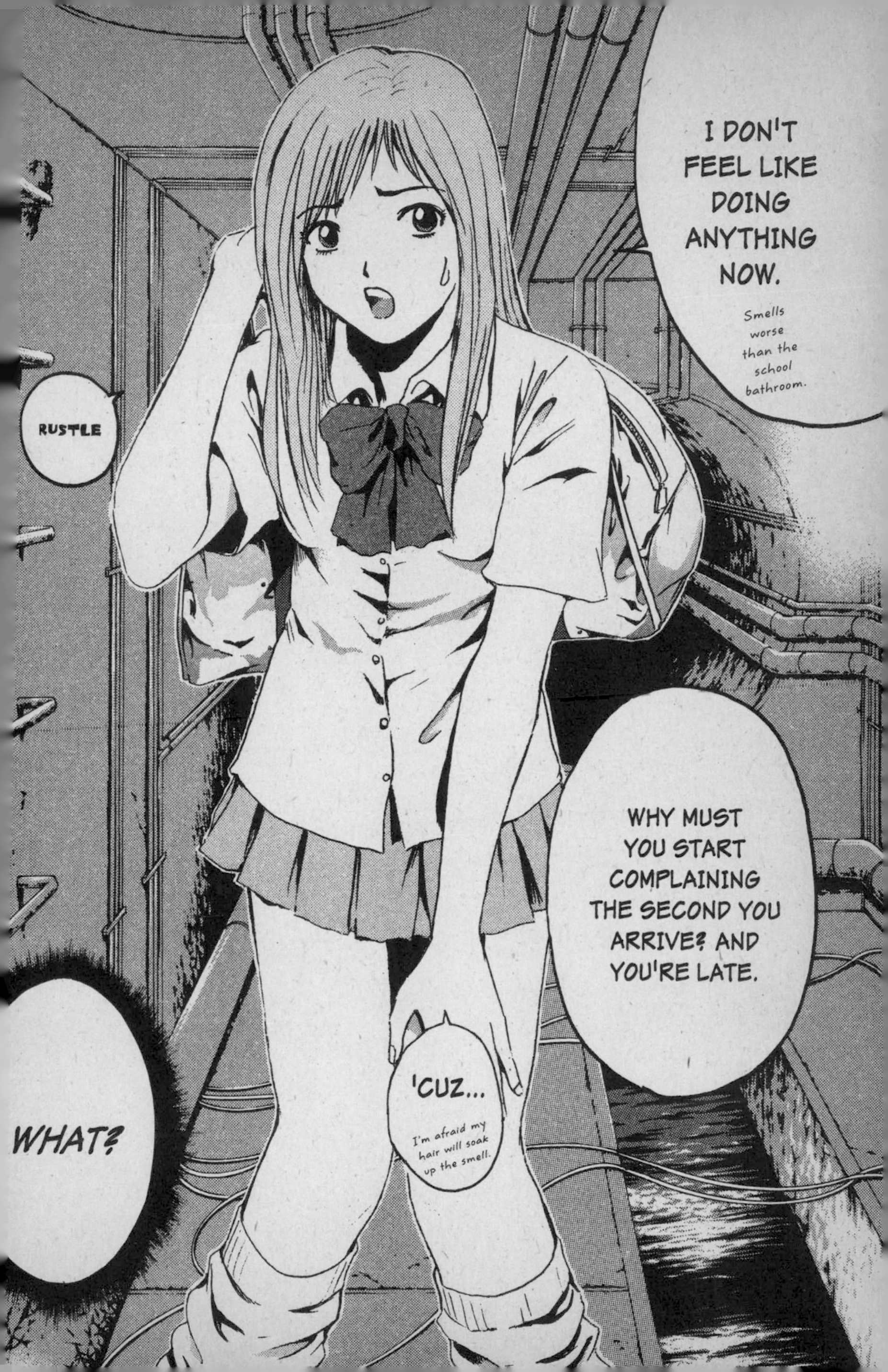
I DON'T FEEL LIKE DOING ANYTHING NOW.
Smells worse than the school bathroom.
RUSTLE
WHY MUST YOU START COMPLAINING THE SECOND YOU ARRIVE? AND YOU'RE LATE.
'CUZ...
I'm afraid my hair will soak up the smell.
WHAT?

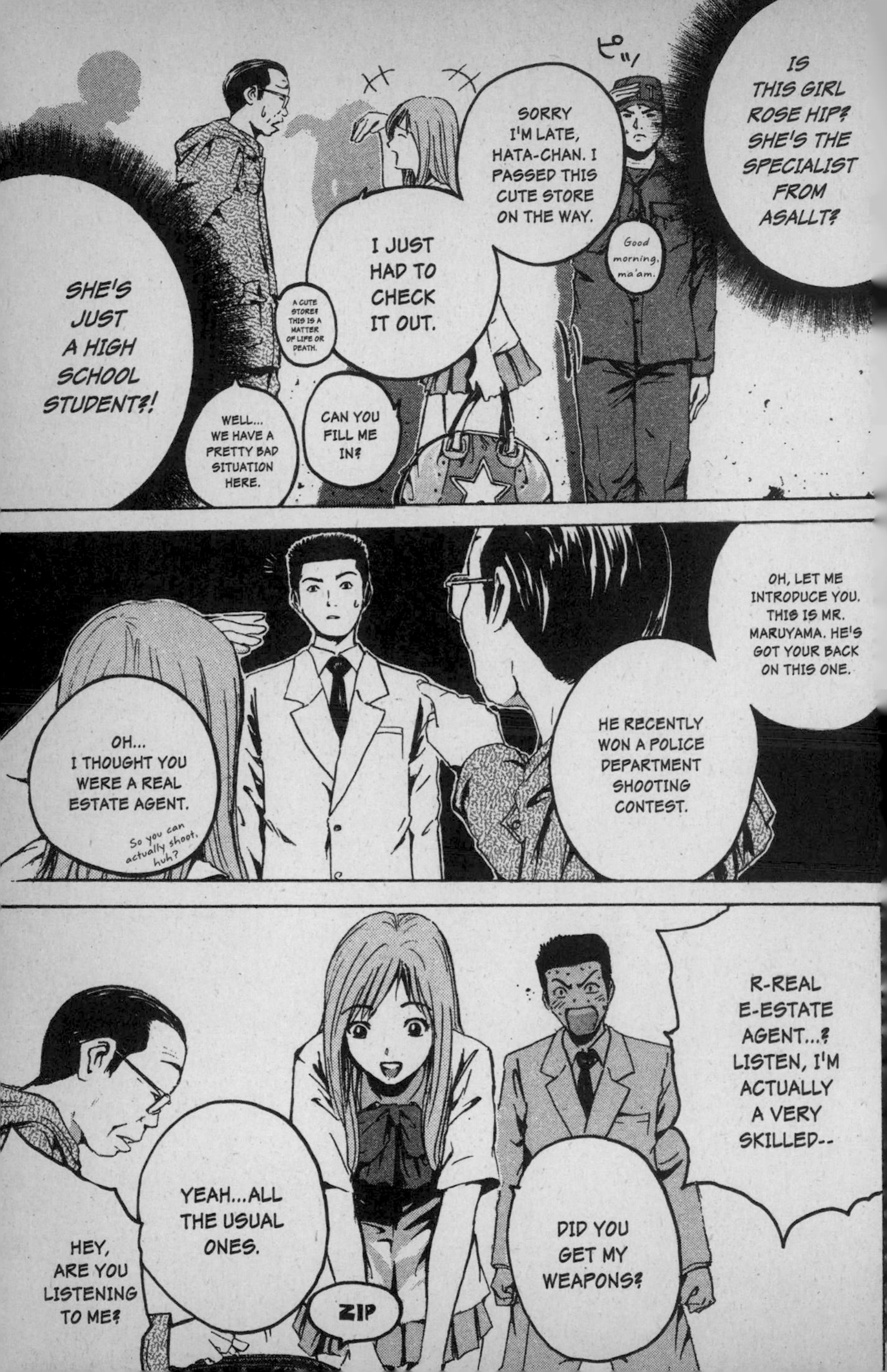
IS THIS GIRL ROSE HIP? SHE'S THE SPECIALIST FROM ASALLT?
Good morning, ma'am.
SORRY I'M LATE, HATA-CHAN. I PASSED THIS CUTE STORE ON THE WAY.
I JUST HAD TO CHECK IT OUT.
A CUTE STORE? THIS IS A MATTER OF LIFE OR DEATH.
CAN YOU FILL ME IN?
WELL... WE HAVE A PRETTY BAD SITUATION HERE.
SHE'S JUST A HIGH SCHOOL STUDENT?!
OH, LET ME INTRODUCE YOU. THIS IS MR. MARUYAMA. HE'S GOT YOUR BACK ON THIS ONE.
HE RECENTLY WON A POLICE DEPARTMENT SHOOTING CONTEST.
OH... I THOUGHT YOU WERE A REAL ESTATE AGENT.
So you can actually shoot, huh?
R-REAL E-ESTATE AGENT...? LISTEN, I'M ACTUALLY A VERY SKILLED--
DID YOU GET MY WEAPONS?
YEAH...ALL THE USUAL ONES.
ZIP
HEY, ARE YOU LISTENING TO ME?

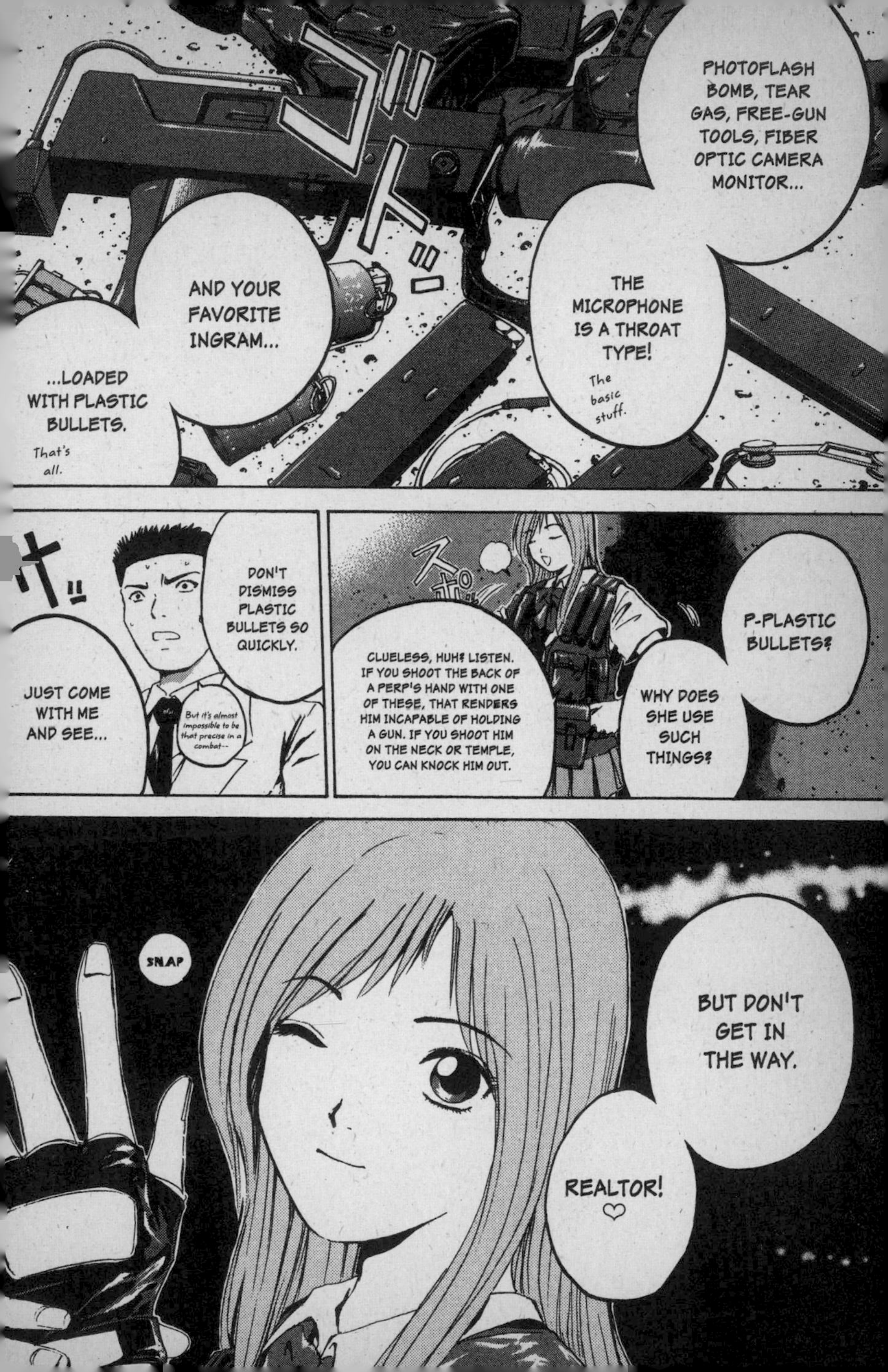
PHOTOFLASH BOMB, TEAR GAS, FREE-GUN TOOLS, FIBER OPTIC CAMERA MONITOR...
THE MICROPHONE IS A THROAT TYPE!
The basic stuff.
AND YOUR FAVORITE INGRAM...
...LOADED WITH PLASTIC BULLETS.
That's all.
P-PLASTIC BULLETS?
WHY DOES SHE USE SUCH THINGS?
CLUELESS, HUH? LISTEN. IF YOU SHOOT THE BACK OF A PERP'S HAND WITH ONE OF THESE, THAT RENDERS HIM INCAPABLE OF HOLDING A GUN. IF YOU SHOOT HIM ON THE NECK OR TEMPLE, YOU CAN KNOCK HIM OUT.
DON'T DISMISS PLASTIC BULLETS SO QUICKLY.
But it's almost impossible to be that precise in a combat--
JUST COME WITH ME AND SEE...
BUT DON'T GET IN THE WAY.
REALTOR! ♡
SNAP

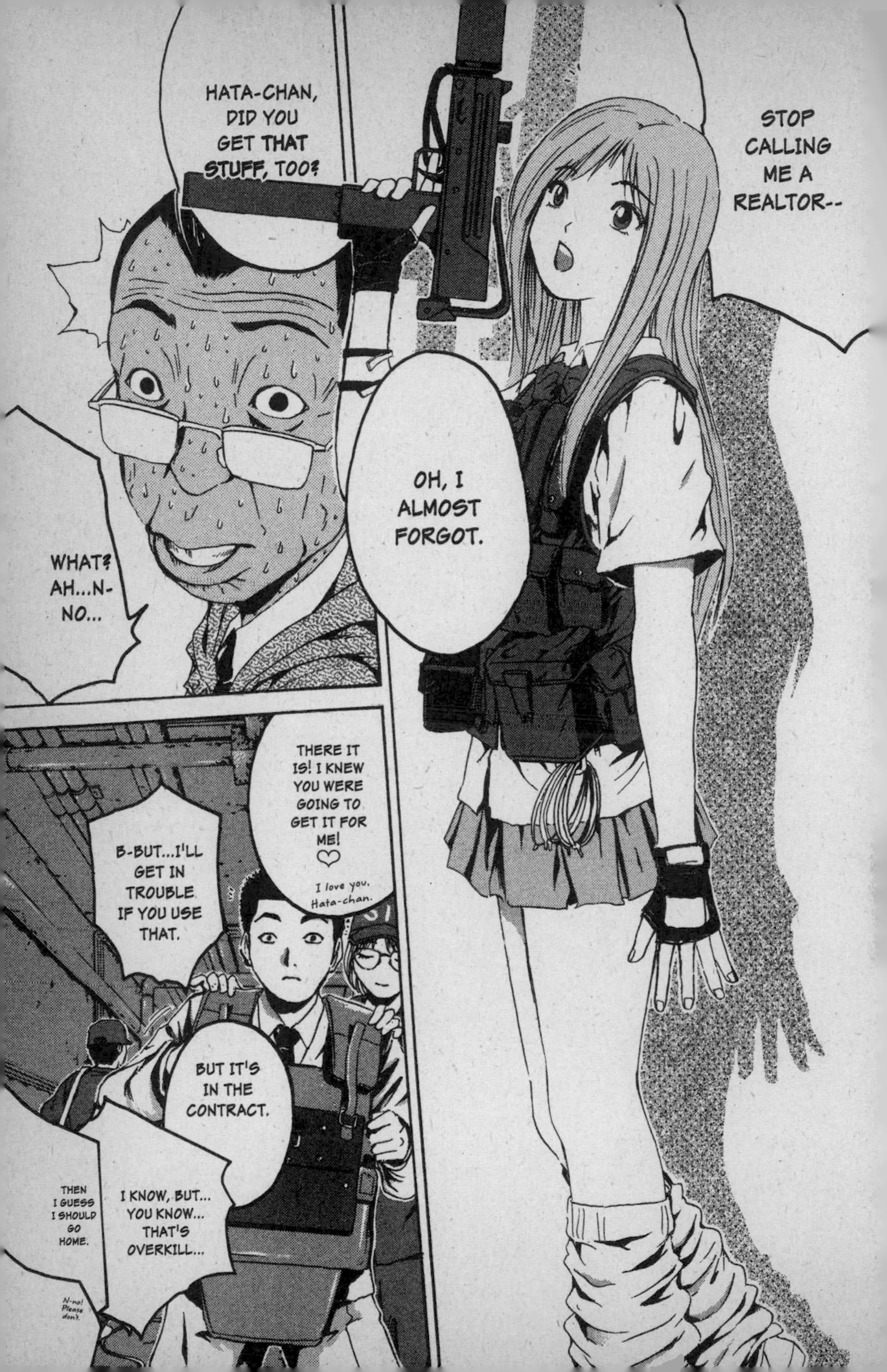
STOP CALLING ME A REALTOR--
OH, I ALMOST FORGOT.
HATA-CHAN, DID YOU GET THAT STUFF, TOO?
WHAT? AH...N-NO...
THERE IT IS! I KNEW YOU WERE GOING TO GET IT FOR ME! ♡
I love you, Hata-chan.
B-BUT...I'LL GET IN TROUBLE IF YOU USE THAT.
BUT IT'S IN THE CONTRACT.
I KNOW, BUT... YOU KNOW... THAT'S OVERKILL...
THEN I GUESS I SHOULD GO HOME.
N-no! Please don't.

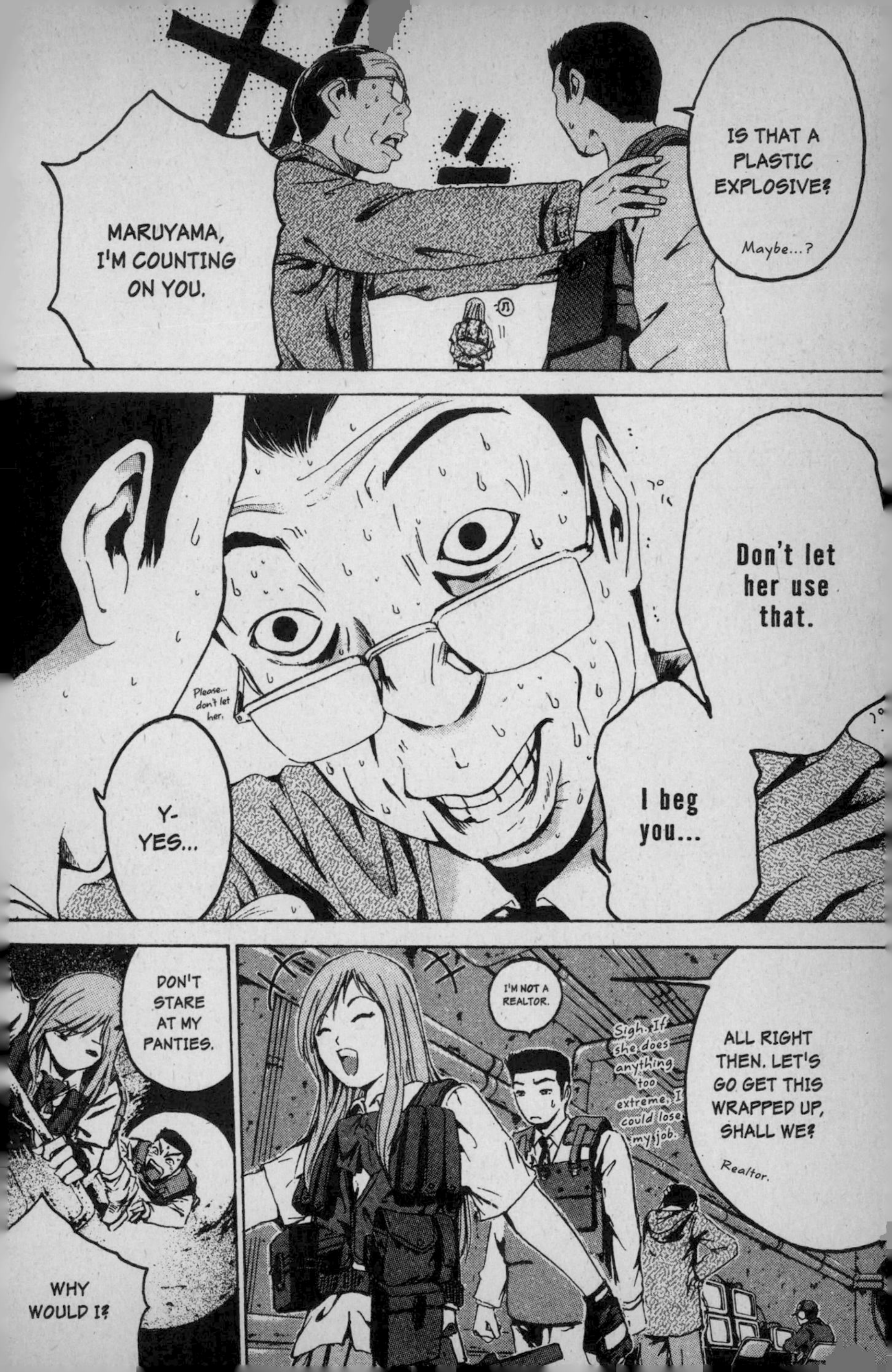
IS THAT A PLASTIC EXPLOSIVE?
Maybe...?
MARUYAMA, I'M COUNTING ON YOU.
Don't let her use that.
I beg you...
Please... don't let her.
Y- YES...
ALL RIGHT THEN. LET'S GO GET THIS WRAPPED UP, SHALL WE?
Realtor.
I'M NOT A REALTOR.
Sigh. If she does anything too extreme, I could lose my job.
DON'T STARE AT MY PANTIES.
WHY WOULD I?

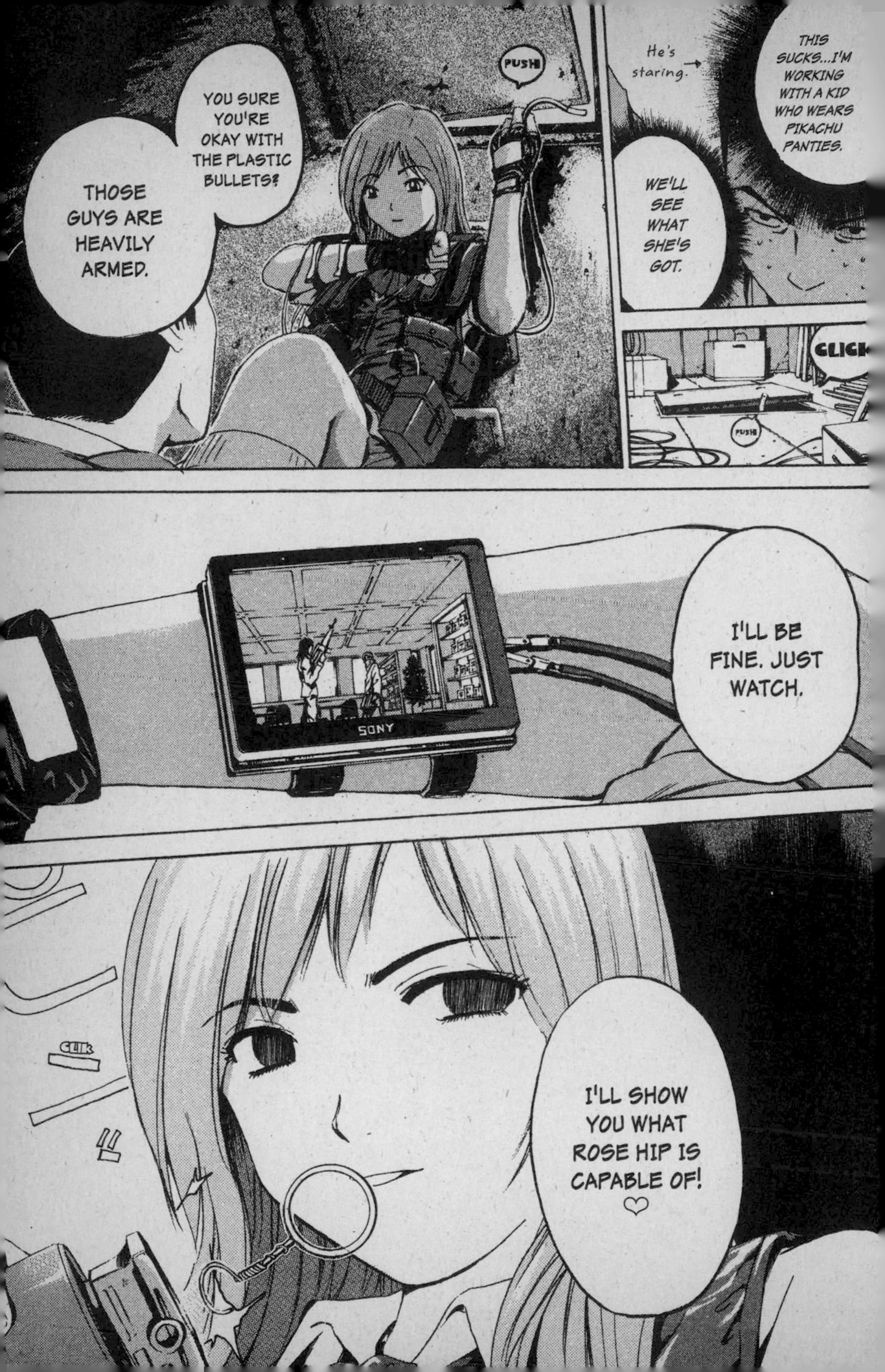
THIS SUCKS...I'M WORKING WITH A KID WHO WEARS PIKACHU PANTIES.
He's staring.
WE'LL SEE WHAT SHE'S GOT.
CLICK
PUSH
PUSH
YOU SURE YOU'RE OKAY WITH THE PLASTIC BULLETS?
THOSE GUYS ARE HEAVILY ARMED.
I'LL BE FINE. JUST WATCH.
SONY
I'LL SHOW YOU WHAT ROSE HIP IS CAPABLE OF! ♡
CLIK

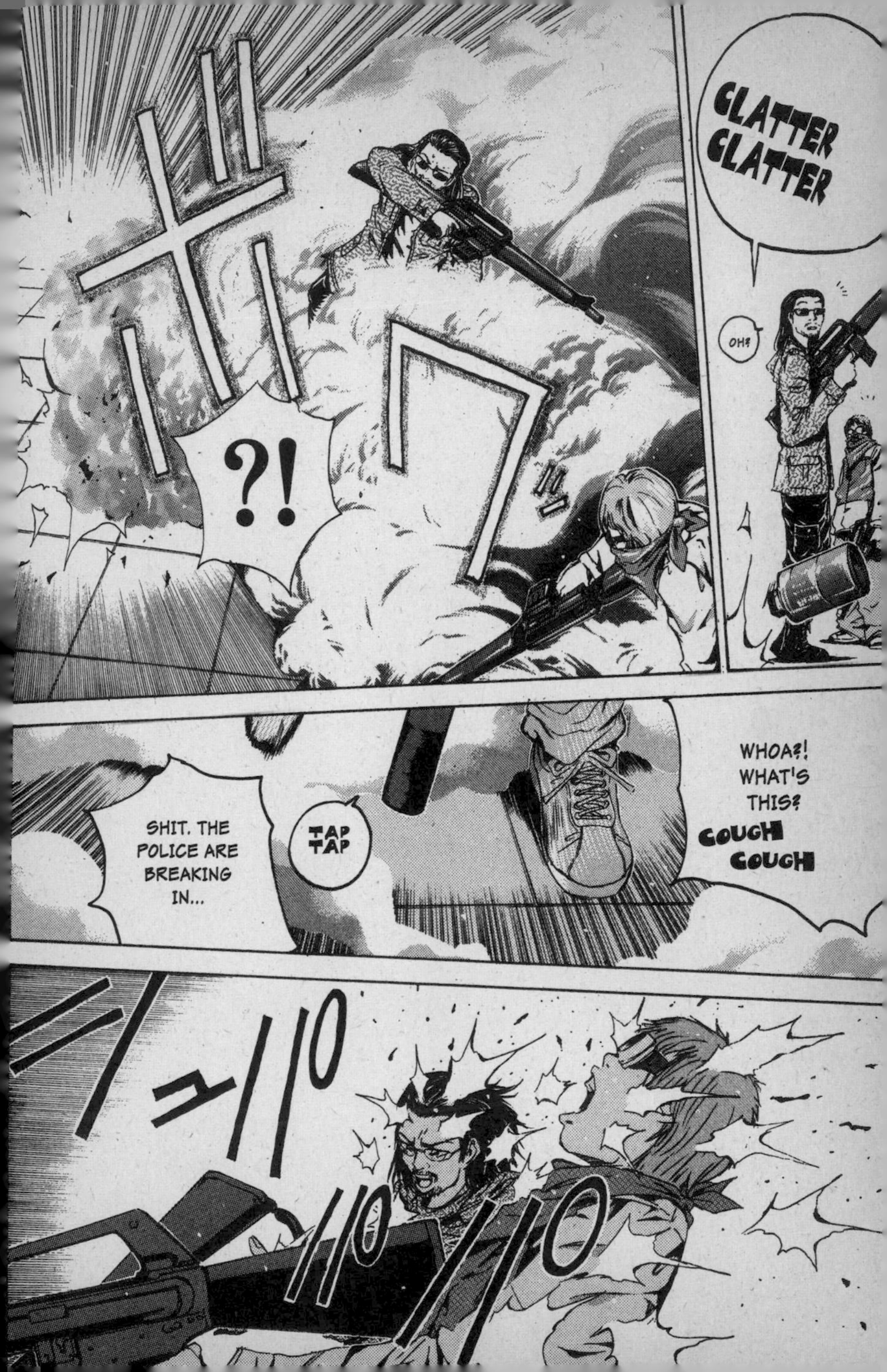
CLATTER CLATTER
OH?
?!
WHOA?! WHAT'S THIS?
COUGH COUGH
TAP TAP
SHIT. THE POLICE ARE BREAKING IN...

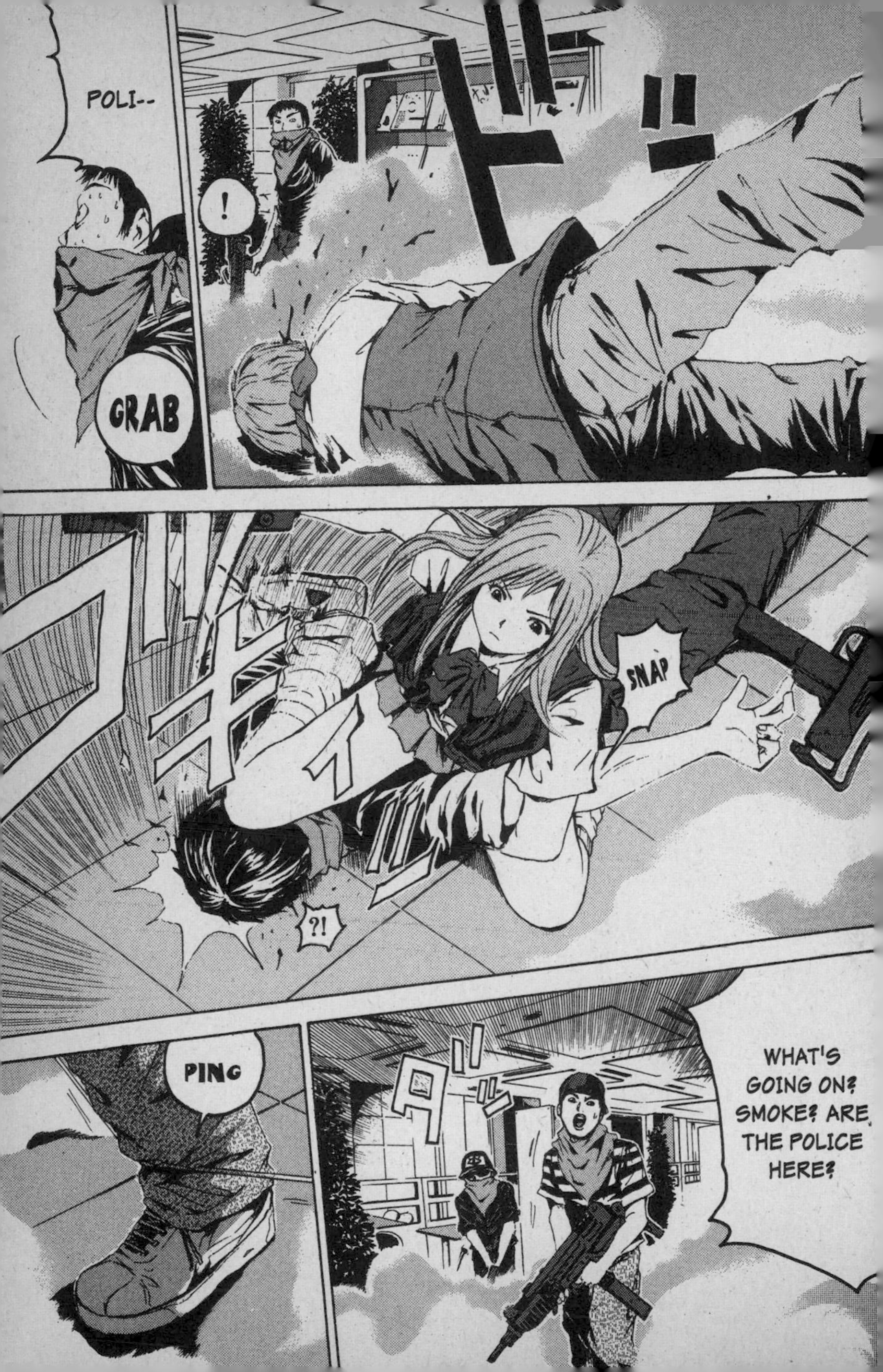
!
POLI--
GRAB
SNAP
?!
WHAT'S GOING ON? SMOKE? ARE THE POLICE HERE?
PING

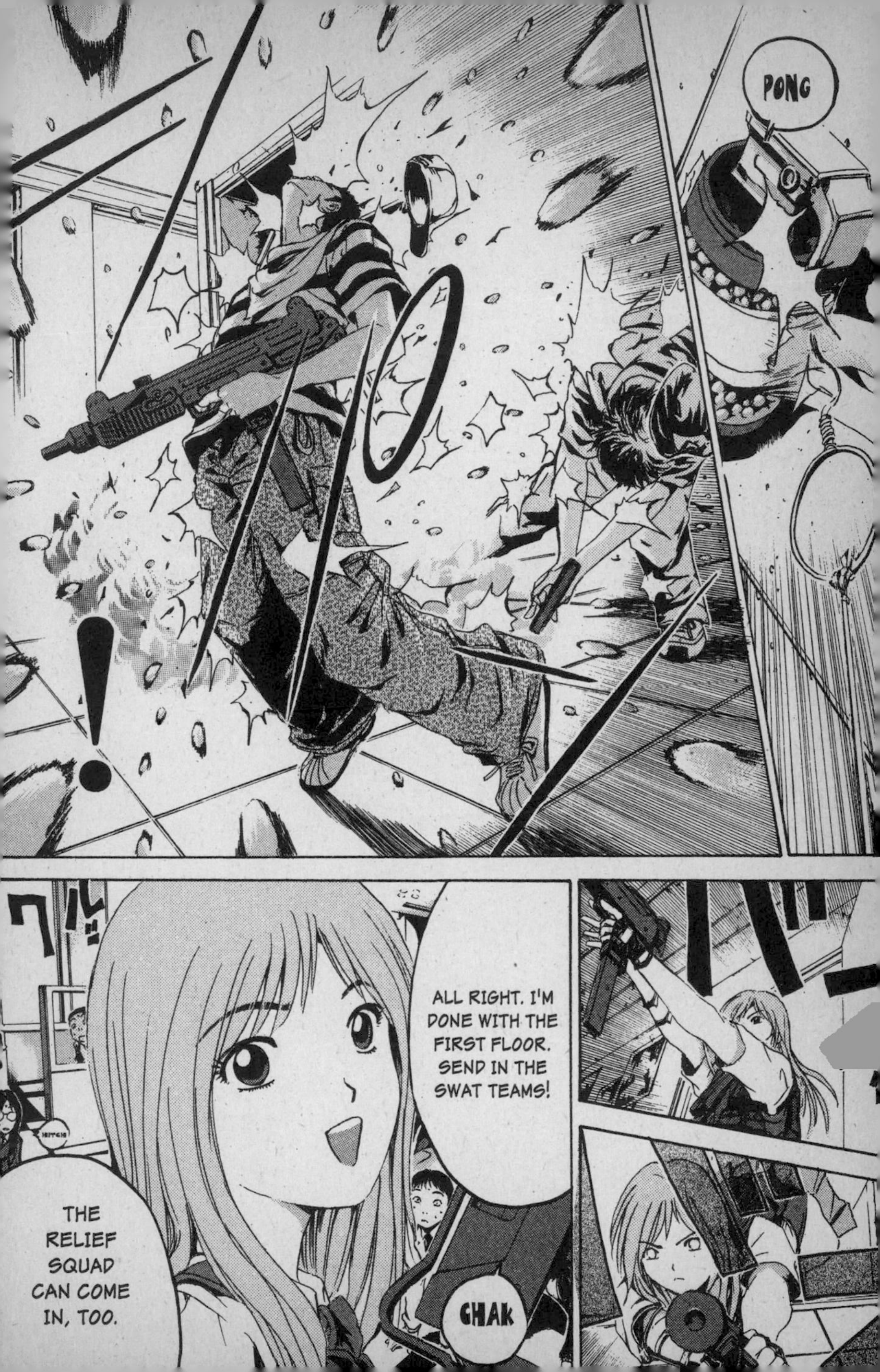
PONG
ALL RIGHT. I'M DONE WITH THE FIRST FLOOR. SEND IN THE SWAT TEAMS!
GHAK
THE RELIEF SQUAD CAN COME IN, TOO.

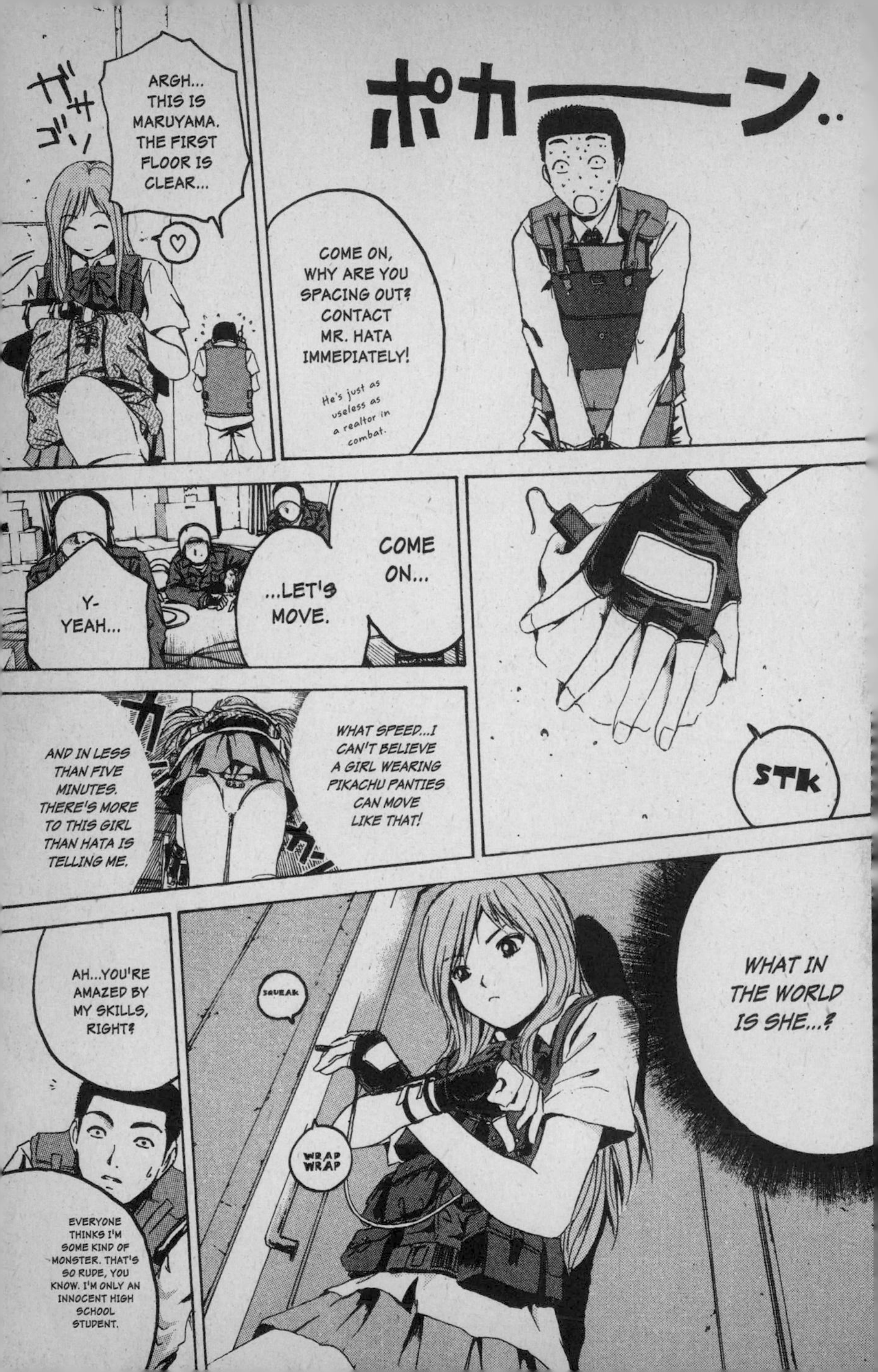
ポカーン
COME ON, WHY ARE YOU SPACING OUT? CONTACT MR. HATA IMMEDIATELY!
He's just as useless as a realtor in combat.
ガサゴソ
ARGH... THIS IS MARUYAMA. THE FIRST FLOOR IS CLEAR...
♡
STK
COME ON...
...LET'S MOVE.
Y- YEAH...
WHAT SPEED...I CAN'T BELIEVE A GIRL WEARING PIKACHU PANTIES CAN MOVE LIKE THAT!
AND IN LESS THAN FIVE MINUTES. THERE'S MORE TO THIS GIRL THAN HATA IS TELLING ME.
WHAT IN THE WORLD IS SHE...?
SQUEAK
WRAP WRAP
AH...YOU'RE AMAZED BY MY SKILLS, RIGHT?
EVERYONE THINKS I'M SOME KIND OF MONSTER. THAT'S SO RUDE, YOU KNOW. I'M ONLY AN INNOCENT HIGH SCHOOL STUDENT.

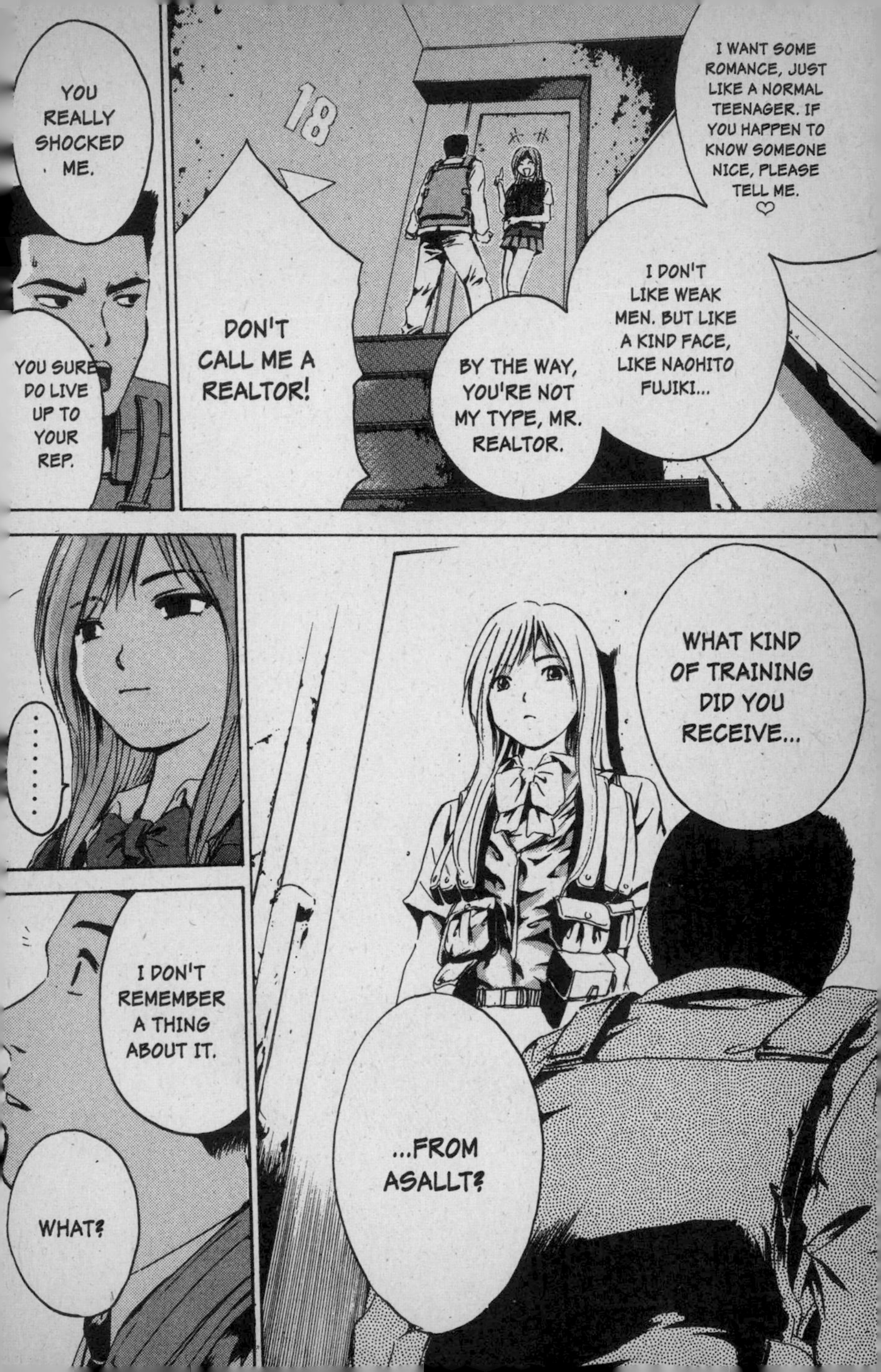
18
I WANT SOME ROMANCE, JUST LIKE A NORMAL TEENAGER. IF YOU HAPPEN TO KNOW SOMEONE NICE, PLEASE TELL ME. ♡
I DON'T LIKE WEAK MEN. BUT LIKE A KIND FACE, LIKE NAOHITO FUJIKI...
BY THE WAY, YOU'RE NOT MY TYPE, MR. REALTOR.
DON'T CALL ME A REALTOR!
YOU REALLY SHOCKED ME.
YOU SURE DO LIVE UP TO YOUR REP.
WHAT KIND OF TRAINING DID YOU RECEIVE...
...FROM ASALLT?
....
I DON'T REMEMBER A THING ABOUT IT.
WHAT?

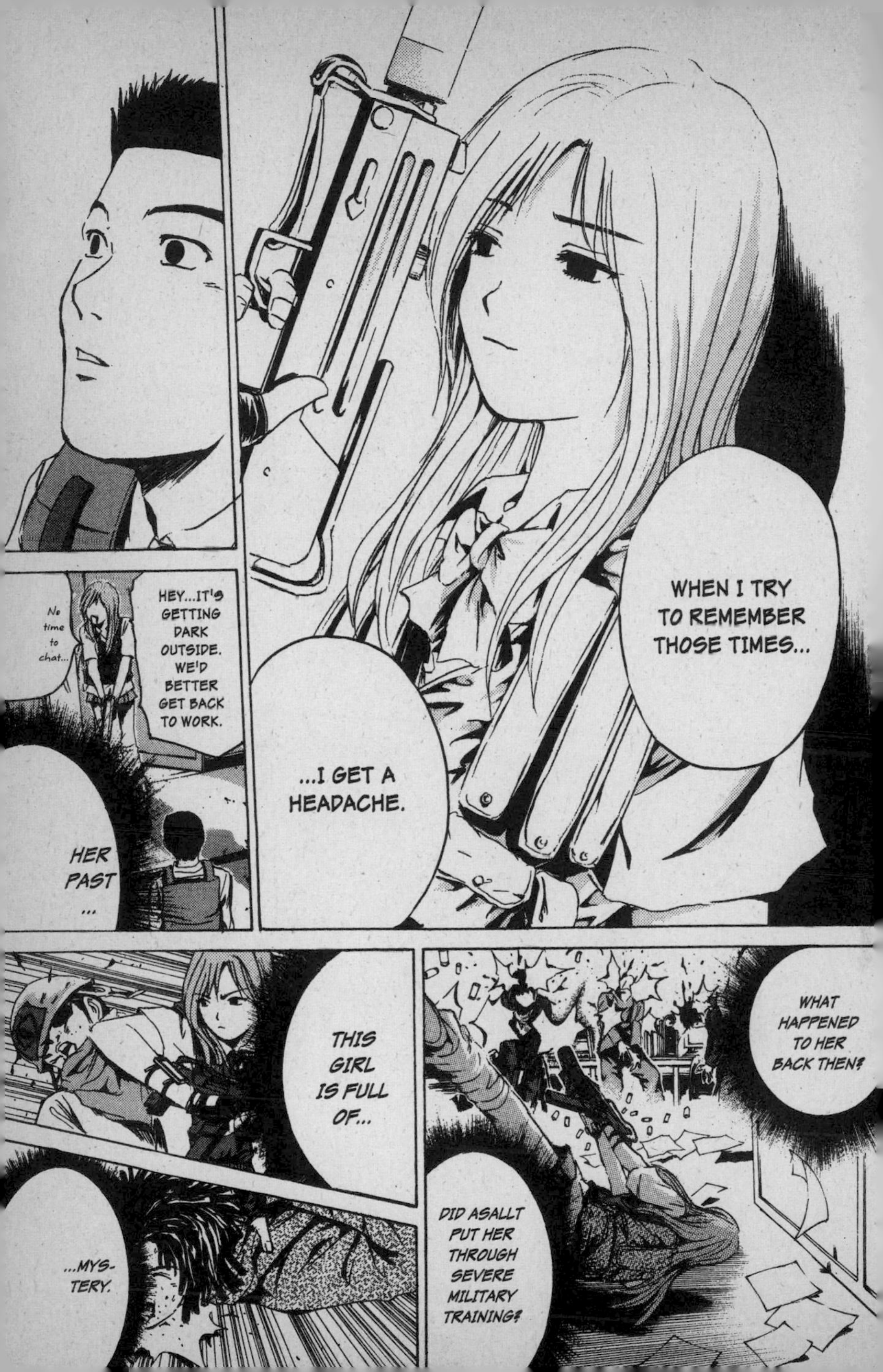
WHEN I TRY TO REMEMBER THOSE TIMES...
...I GET A HEADACHE.
HEY...IT'S GETTING DARK OUTSIDE. WE'D BETTER GET BACK TO WORK.
No time to chat...
HER PAST ...
WHAT HAPPENED TO HER BACK THEN?
DID ASALLT PUT HER THROUGH SEVERE MILITARY TRAINING?
THIS GIRL IS FULL OF...
...MYS-TERY.

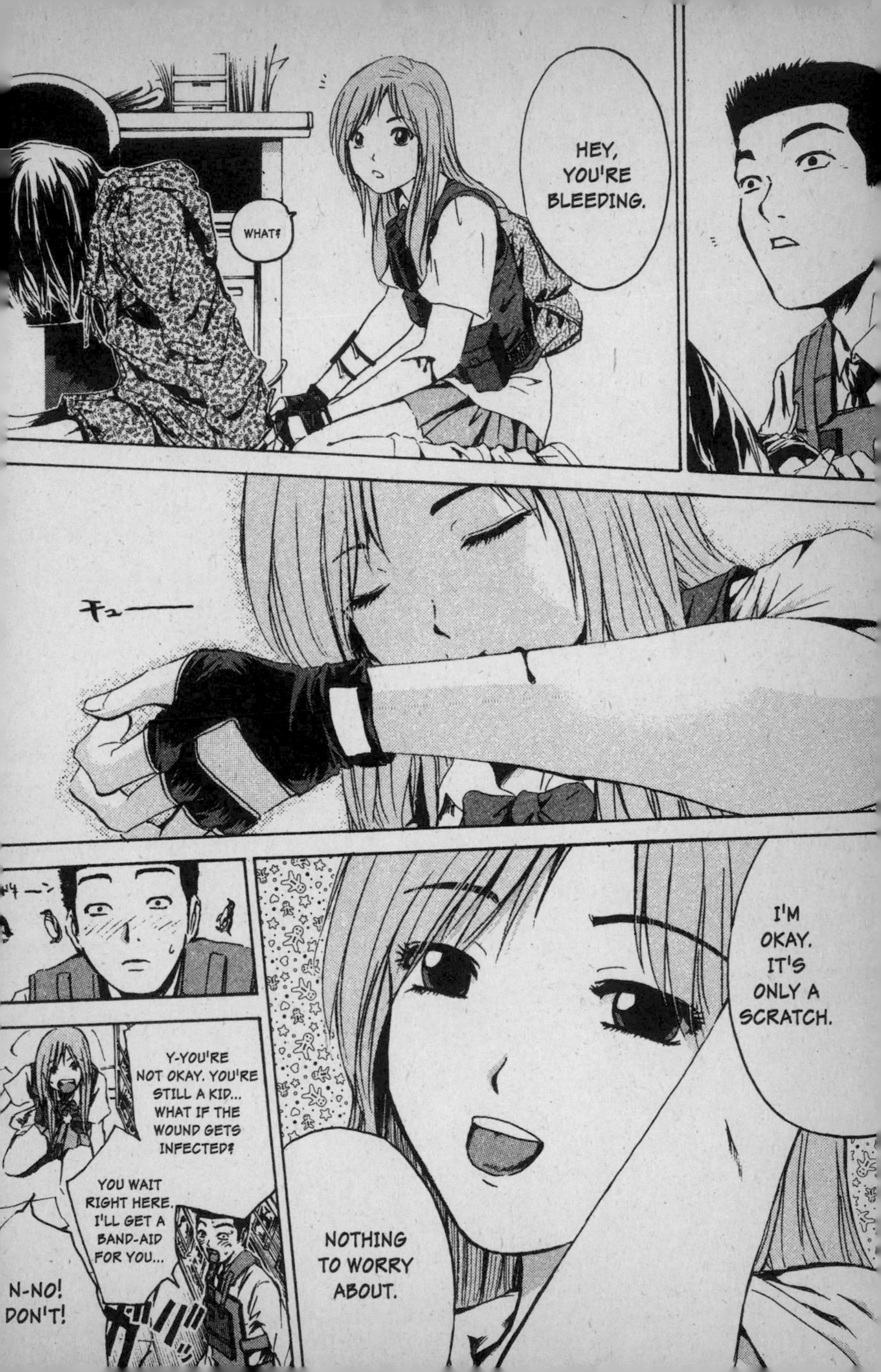
HEY, YOU'RE BLEEDING.
WHAT?
チュー
I'M OKAY. IT'S ONLY A SCRATCH.
NOTHING TO WORRY ABOUT.
Y-YOU'RE NOT OKAY. YOU'RE STILL A KID... WHAT IF THE WOUND GETS INFECTED?
YOU WAIT RIGHT HERE. I'LL GET A BAND-AID FOR YOU...
N-NO! DON'T!

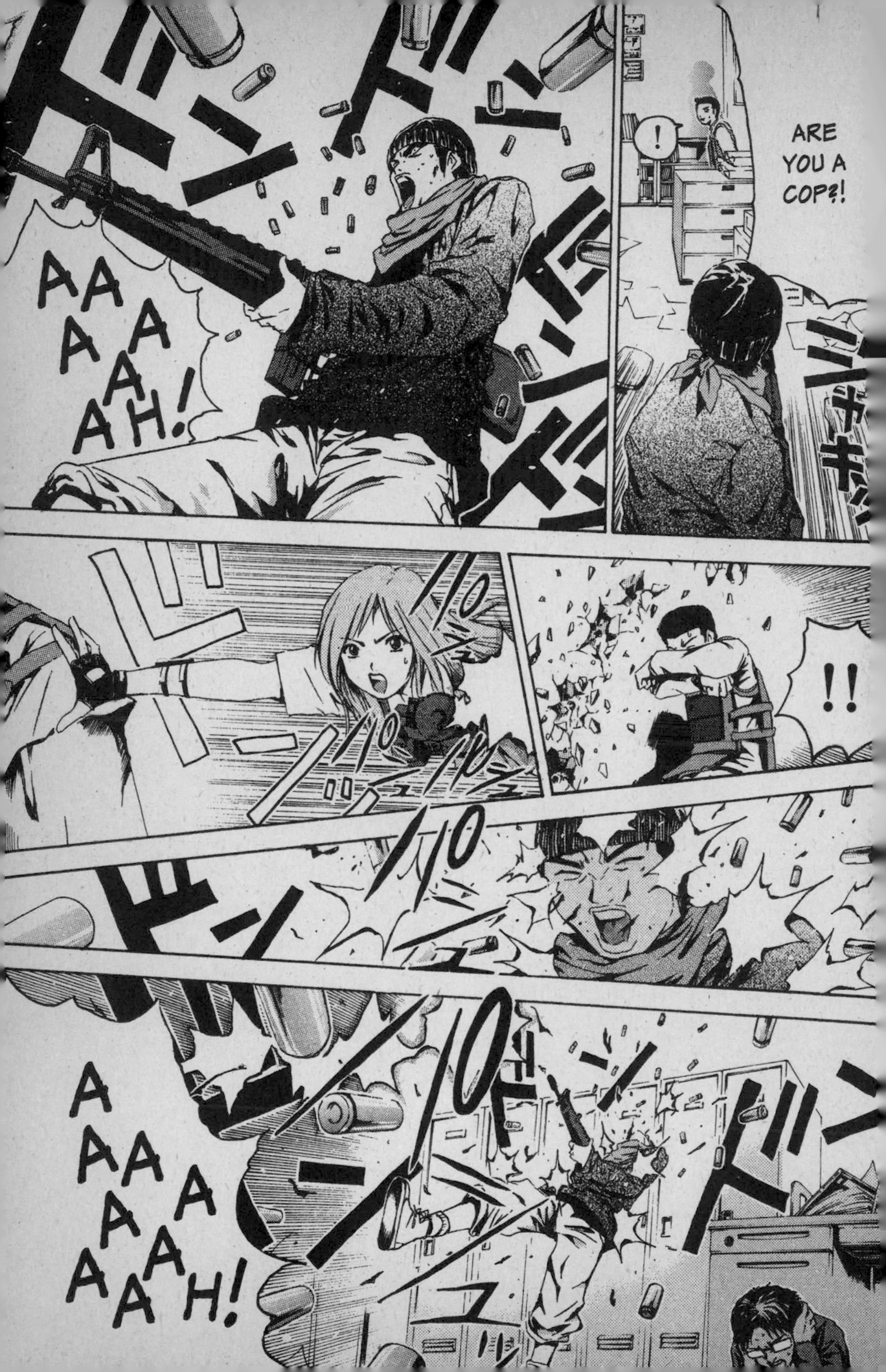

ARE YOU A COP?!
!
AAAAAAH!
!!
AAAAAAAAAH!

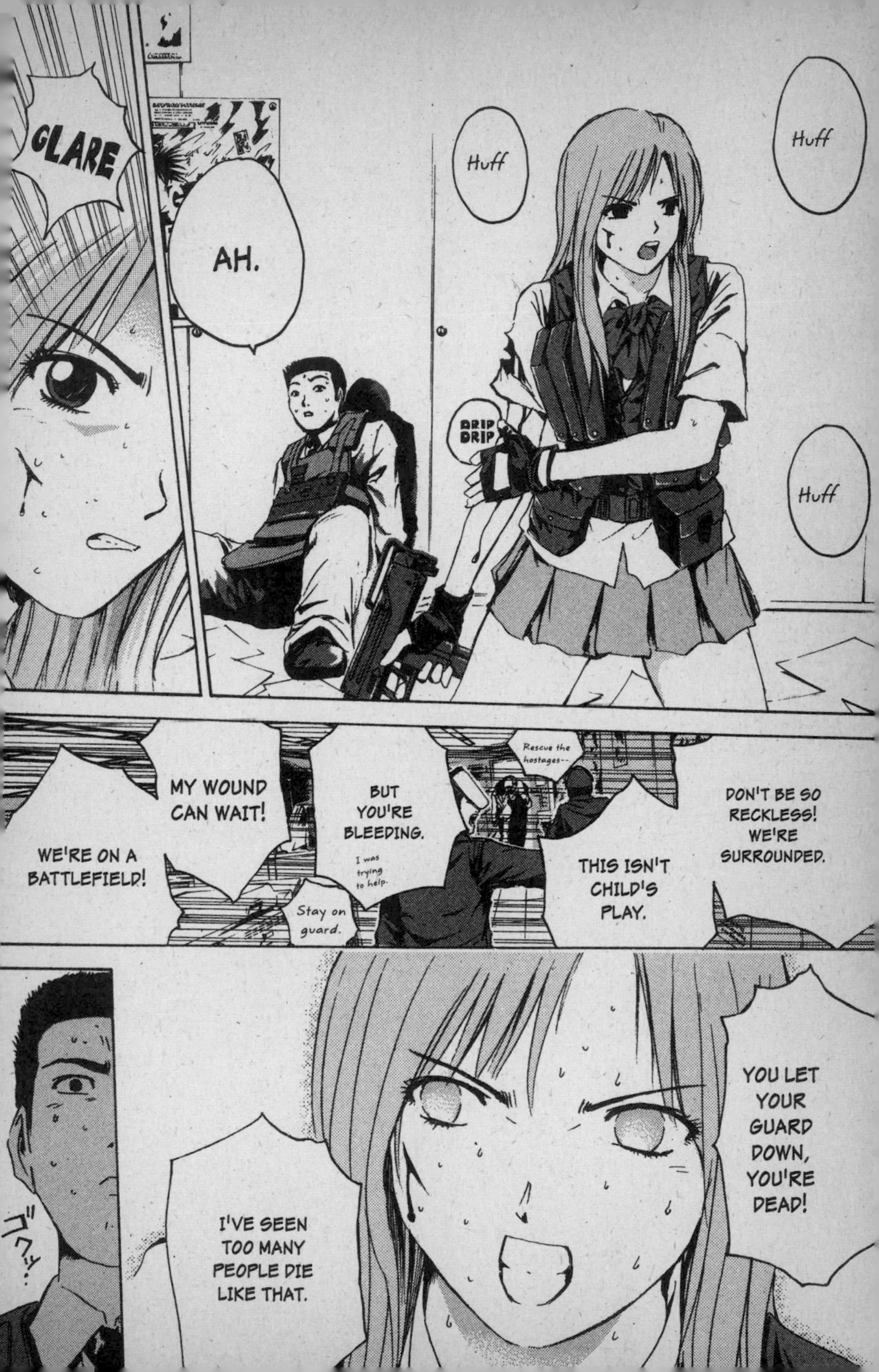

Huff
Huff
Huff
DRIP DRIP
AH.
GLARE
DON'T BE SO RECKLESS! WE'RE SURROUNDED.
THIS ISN'T CHILD'S PLAY.
Rescue the hostages--
BUT YOU'RE BLEEDING.
I was trying to help.
Stay on guard.
MY WOUND CAN WAIT!
WE'RE ON A BATTLEFIELD!
YOU LET YOUR GUARD DOWN, YOU'RE DEAD!
I'VE SEEN TOO MANY PEOPLE DIE LIKE THAT.

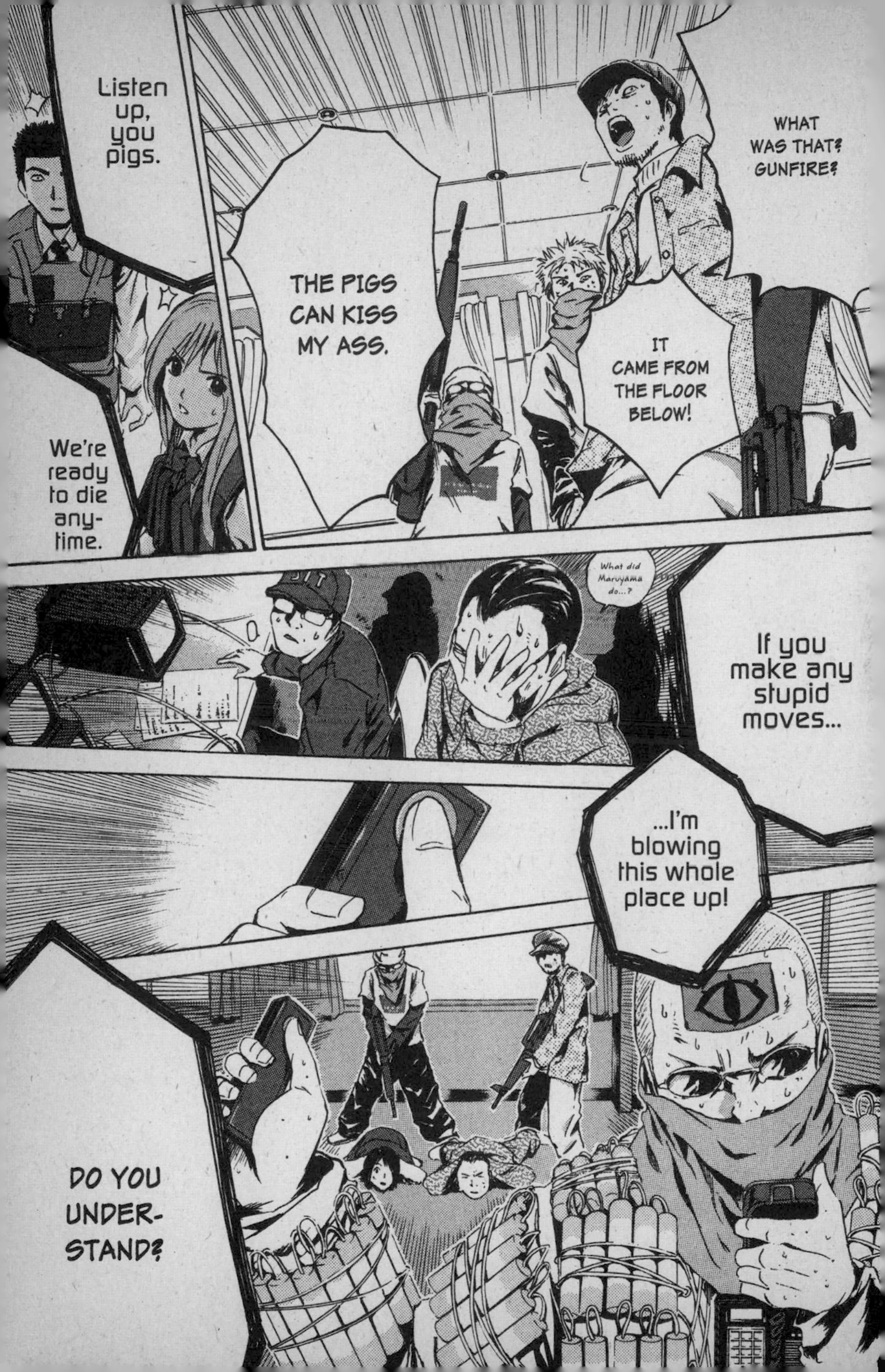
WHAT WAS THAT? GUNFIRE?
IT CAME FROM THE FLOOR BELOW!
THE PIGS CAN KISS MY ASS.
Listen up, you pigs.
We're ready to die anytime.
What did Maruyama do...?
If you make any stupid moves...
...I'm blowing this whole place up!
DO YOU UNDERSTAND?

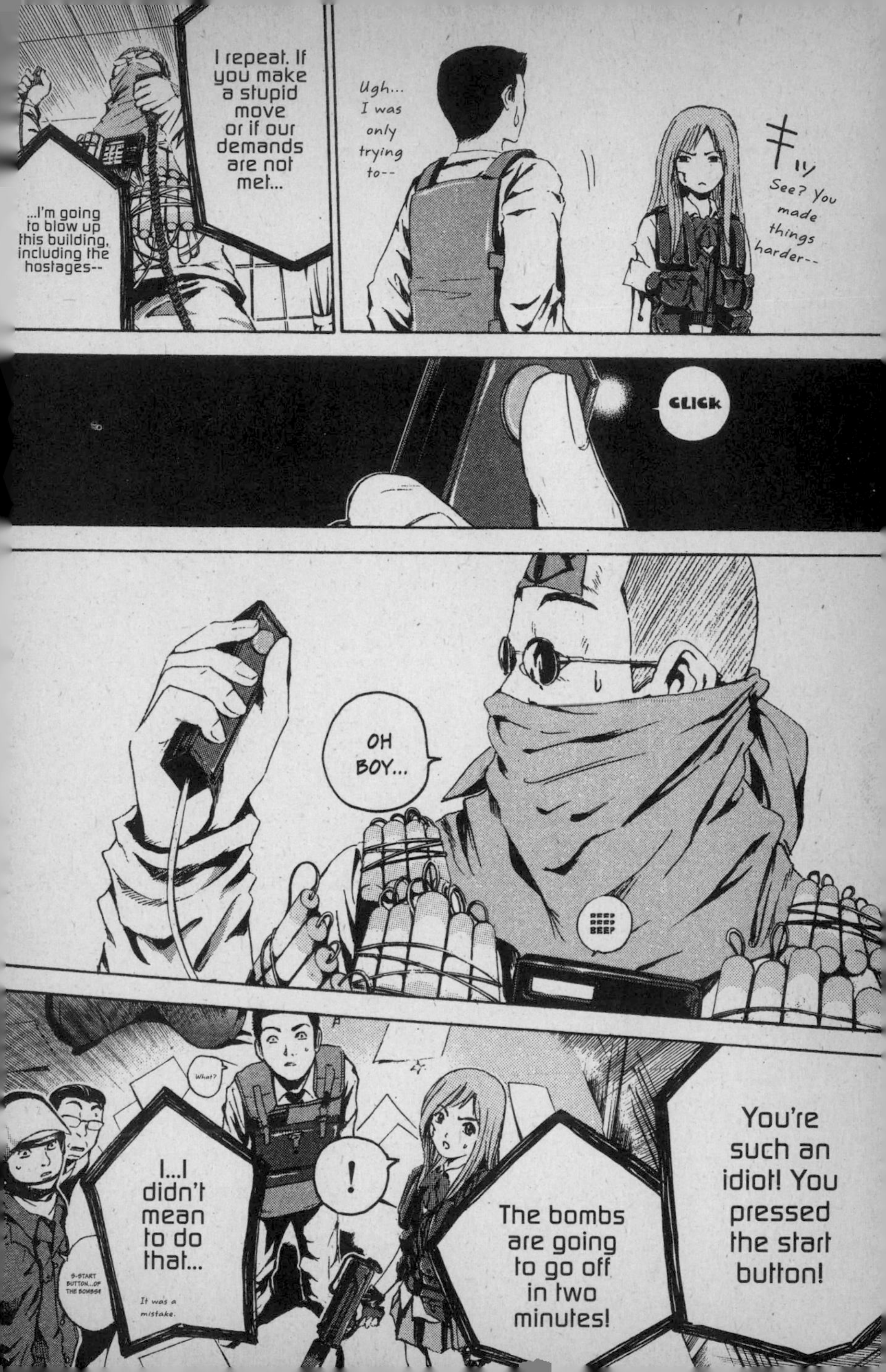
See? You made things harder--
Ugh... I was only trying to--
I repeat. If you make a stupid move or if our demands are not met...
...I'm going to blow up this building, including the hostages--
CLICK
OH BOY...
BEEP BEEP BEEP
You're such an idiot! You pressed the start button!
The bombs are going to go off in two minutes!
!
What?
I...I didn't mean to do that...
It was a mistake.
S-START BUTTON...OF THE BOMBS?

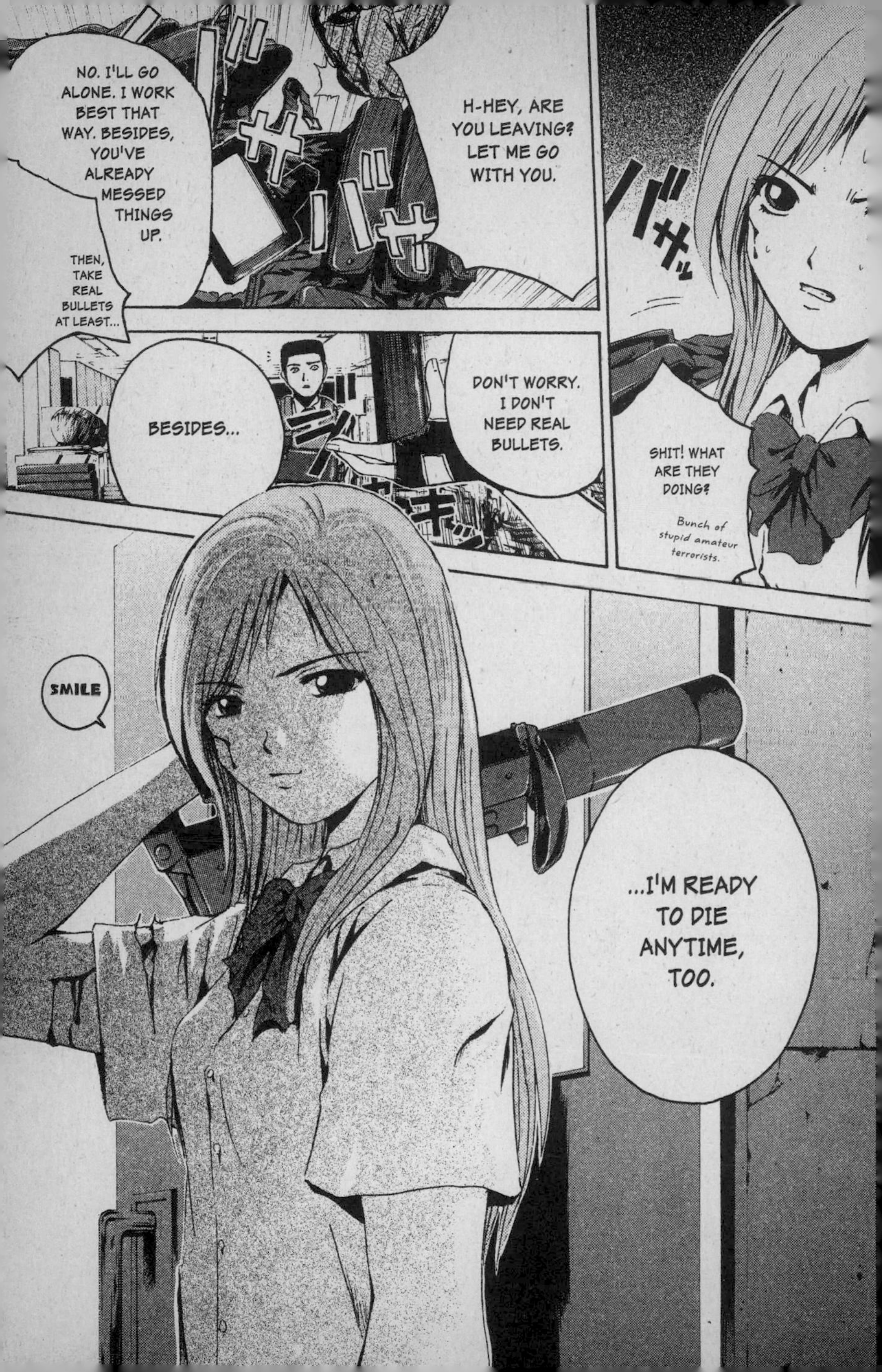
SHIT! WHAT ARE THEY DOING?
Bunch of stupid amateur terrorists.
H-HEY, ARE YOU LEAVING? LET ME GO WITH YOU.
NO. I'LL GO ALONE. I WORK BEST THAT WAY. BESIDES, YOU'VE ALREADY MESSED THINGS UP.
THEN, TAKE REAL BULLETS AT LEAST...
DON'T WORRY. I DON'T NEED REAL BULLETS.
BESIDES...
SMILE
...I'M READY TO DIE ANYTIME, TOO.

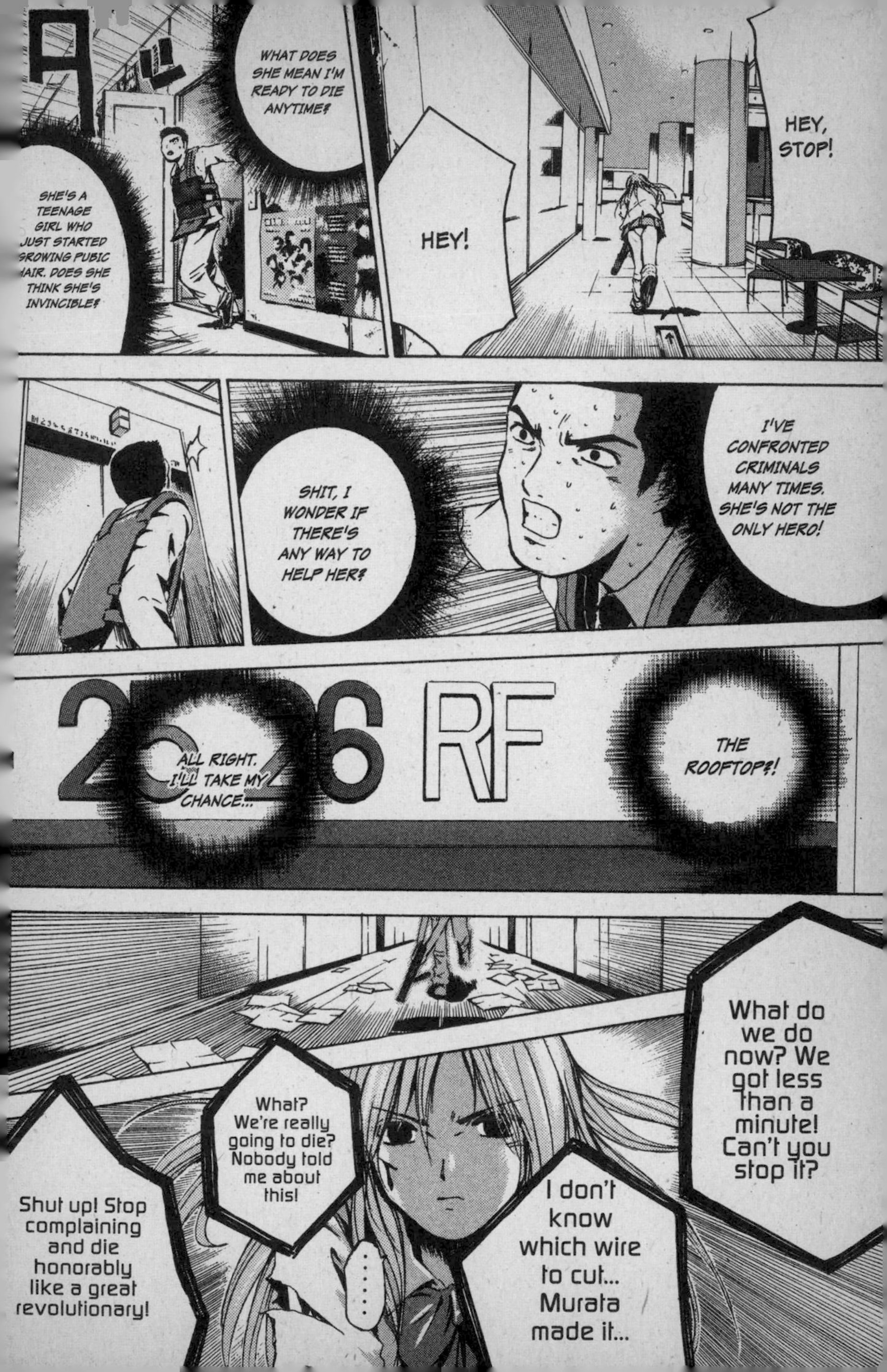
HEY, STOP!
HEY!
WHAT DOES SHE MEAN I'M READY TO DIE ANYTIME?
SHE'S A TEENAGE GIRL WHO JUST STARTED GROWING PUBIC HAIR. DOES SHE THINK SHE'S INVINCIBLE?
I'VE CONFRONTED CRIMINALS MANY TIMES. SHE'S NOT THE ONLY HERO!
SHIT, I WONDER IF THERE'S ANY WAY TO HELP HER?
THE ROOFTOP?!
ALL RIGHT. I'LL TAKE MY CHANCE...
What do we do now? We got less than a minute! Can't you stop it?
I don't know which wire to cut... Murata made it...
What? We're really going to die? Nobody told me about this!
.....
Shut up! Stop complaining and die honorably like a great revolutionary!

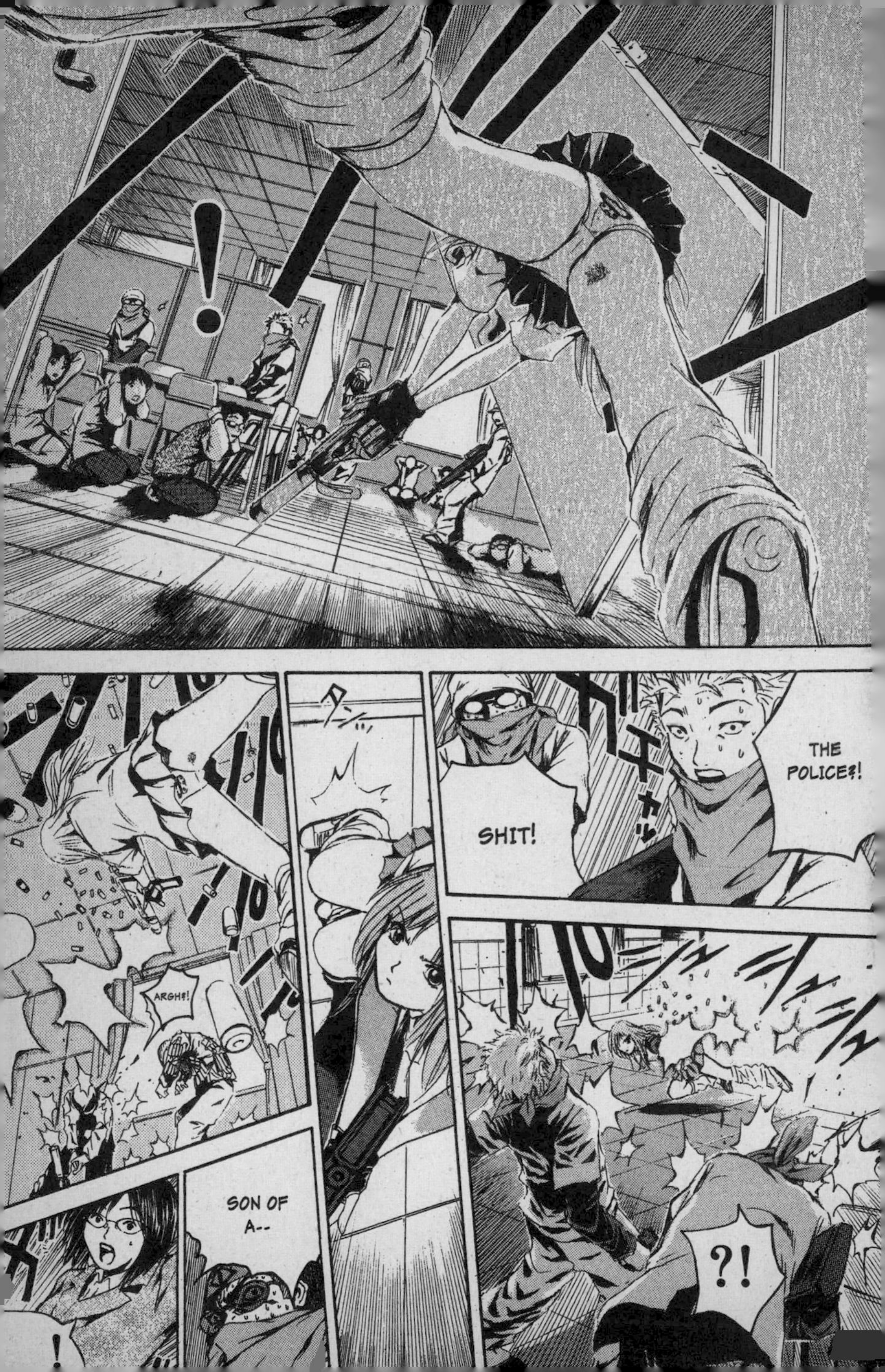
!
THE POLICE?!
SHIT!
ARGH?!
?!
SON OF A--
!

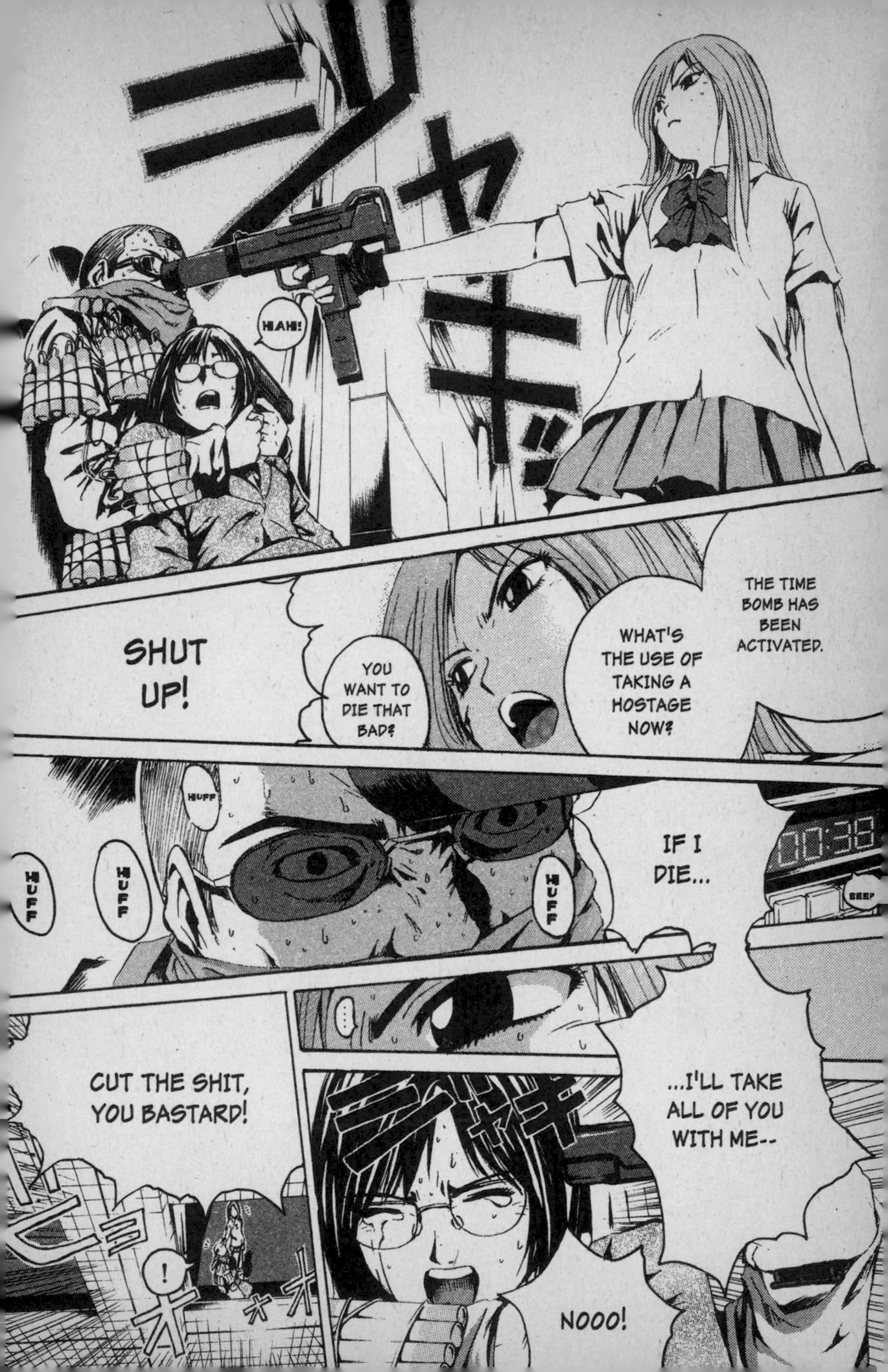

HAH!
THE TIME BOMB HAS BEEN ACTIVATED.
WHAT'S THE USE OF TAKING A HOSTAGE NOW?
YOU WANT TO DIE THAT BAD?
SHUT UP!
BEEP
IF I DIE...
HUFF
HUFF
HUFF
HUFF
...
...I'LL TAKE ALL OF YOU WITH ME--
NOOO!
CUT THE SHIT, YOU BASTARD!
!

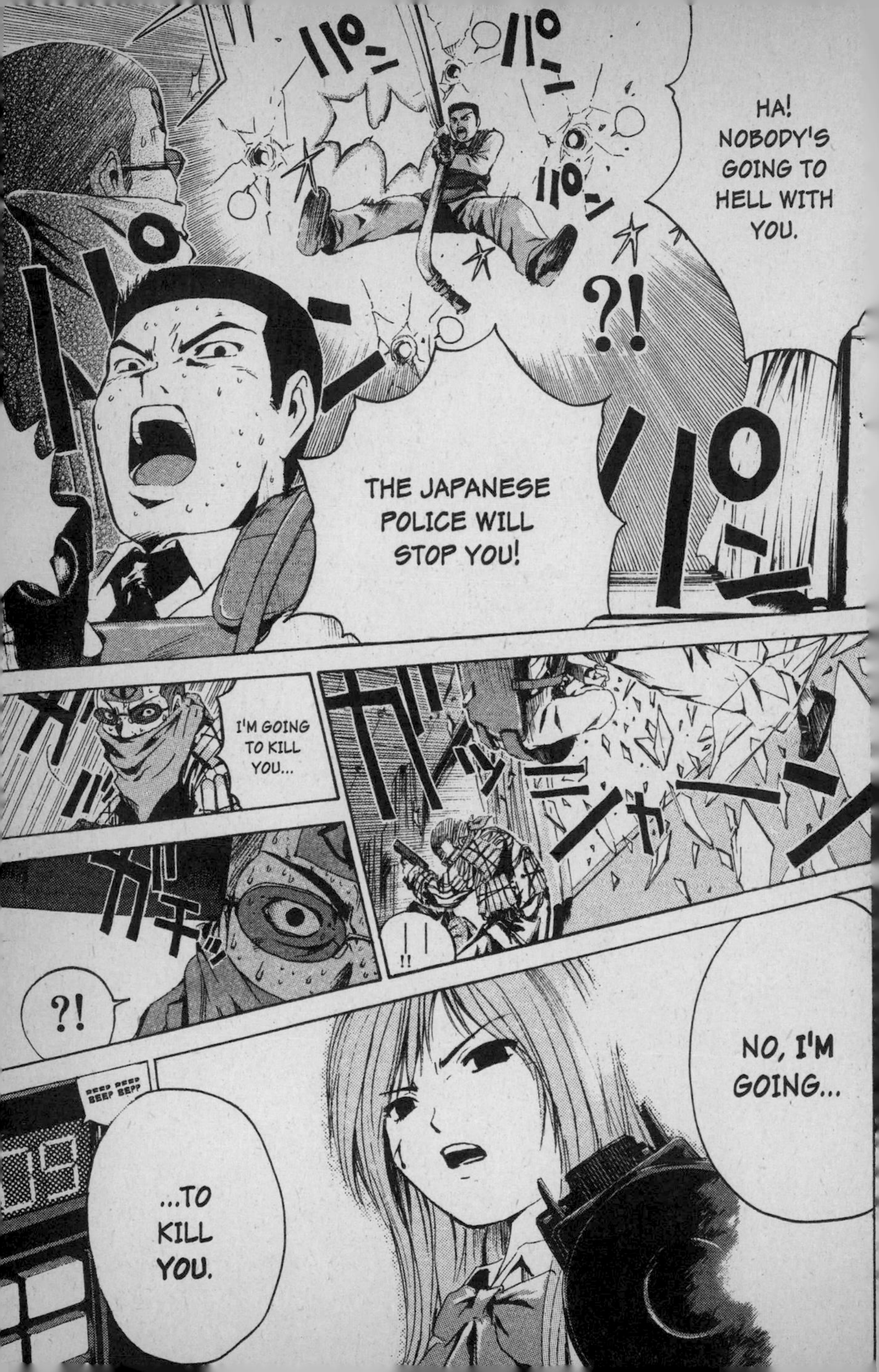
HA! NOBODY'S GOING TO HELL WITH YOU.
?!
THE JAPANESE POLICE WILL STOP YOU!
I'M GOING TO KILL YOU...
!!
?!
NO, I'M GOING...
...TO KILL YOU.

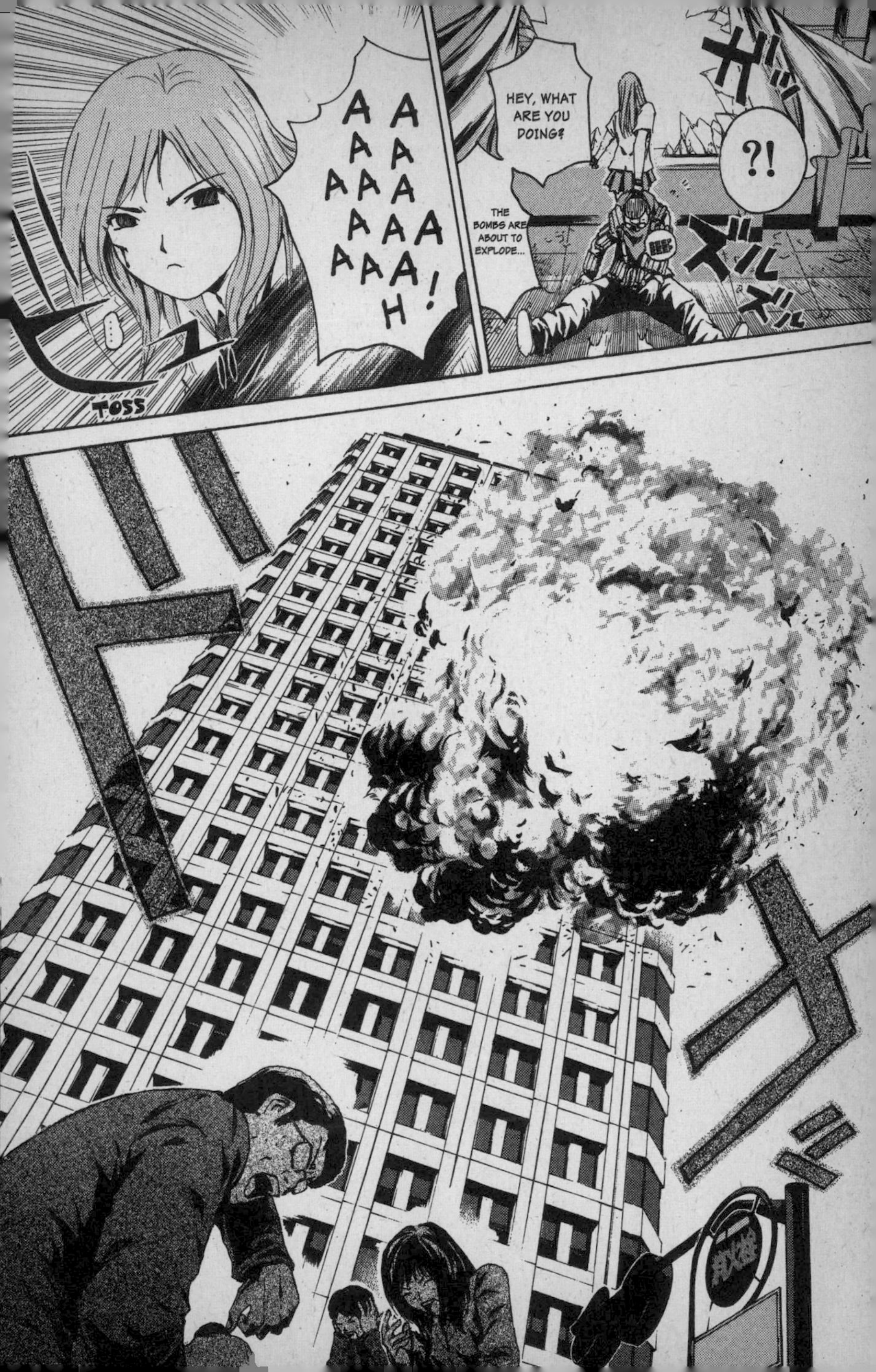
HEY, WHAT ARE YOU DOING?
THE BOMBS ARE ABOUT TO EXPLODE...
?!
AAAAAAAAAAAAAH!
...
TOSS

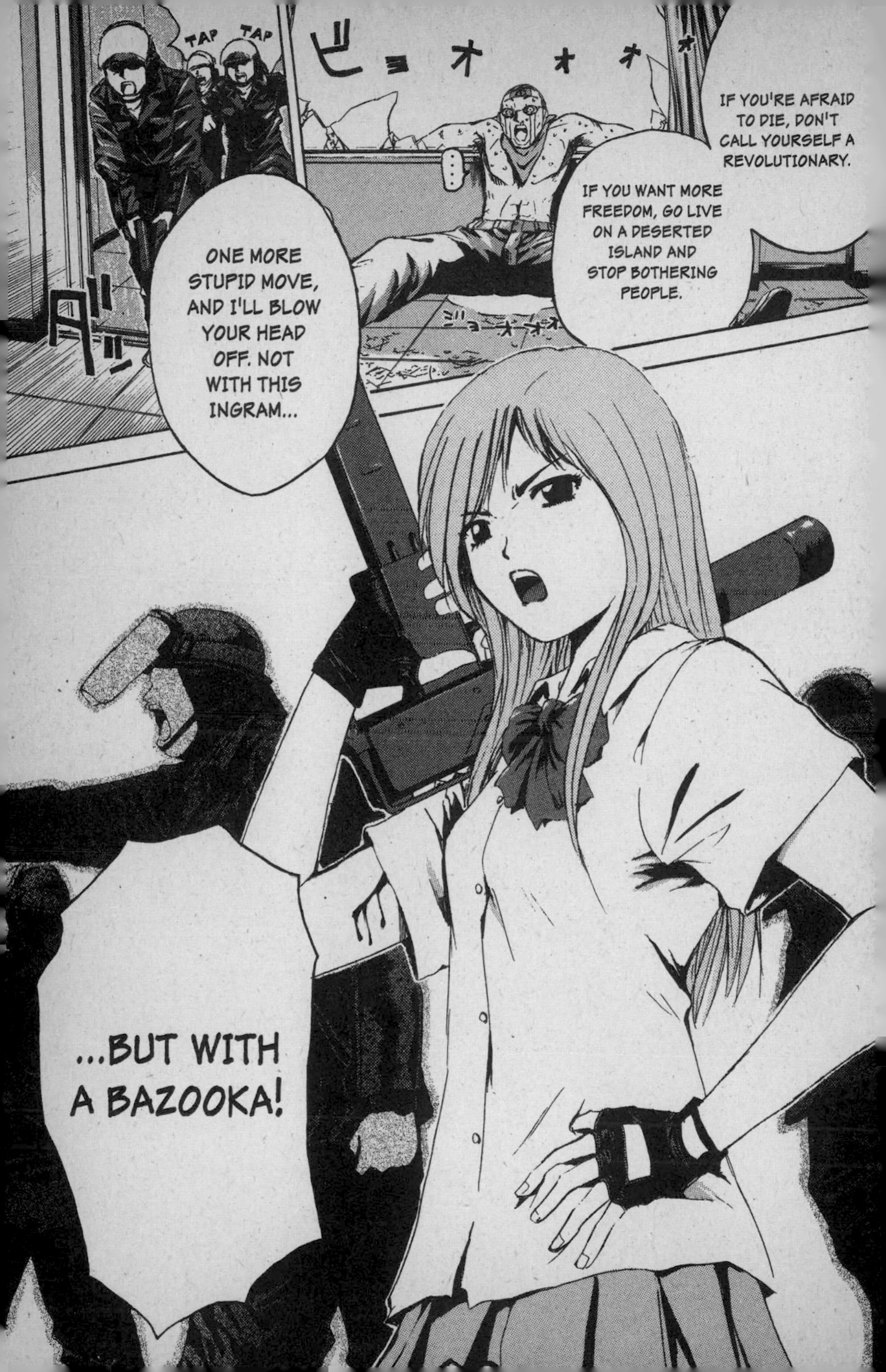
ビョオオオ
IF YOU'RE AFRAID TO DIE, DON'T CALL YOURSELF A REVOLUTIONARY.
IF YOU WANT MORE FREEDOM, GO LIVE ON A DESERTED ISLAND AND STOP BOTHERING PEOPLE.
TAP TAP
ONE MORE STUPID MOVE, AND I'LL BLOW YOUR HEAD OFF. NOT WITH THIS INGRAM...
...BUT WITH A BAZOOKA!

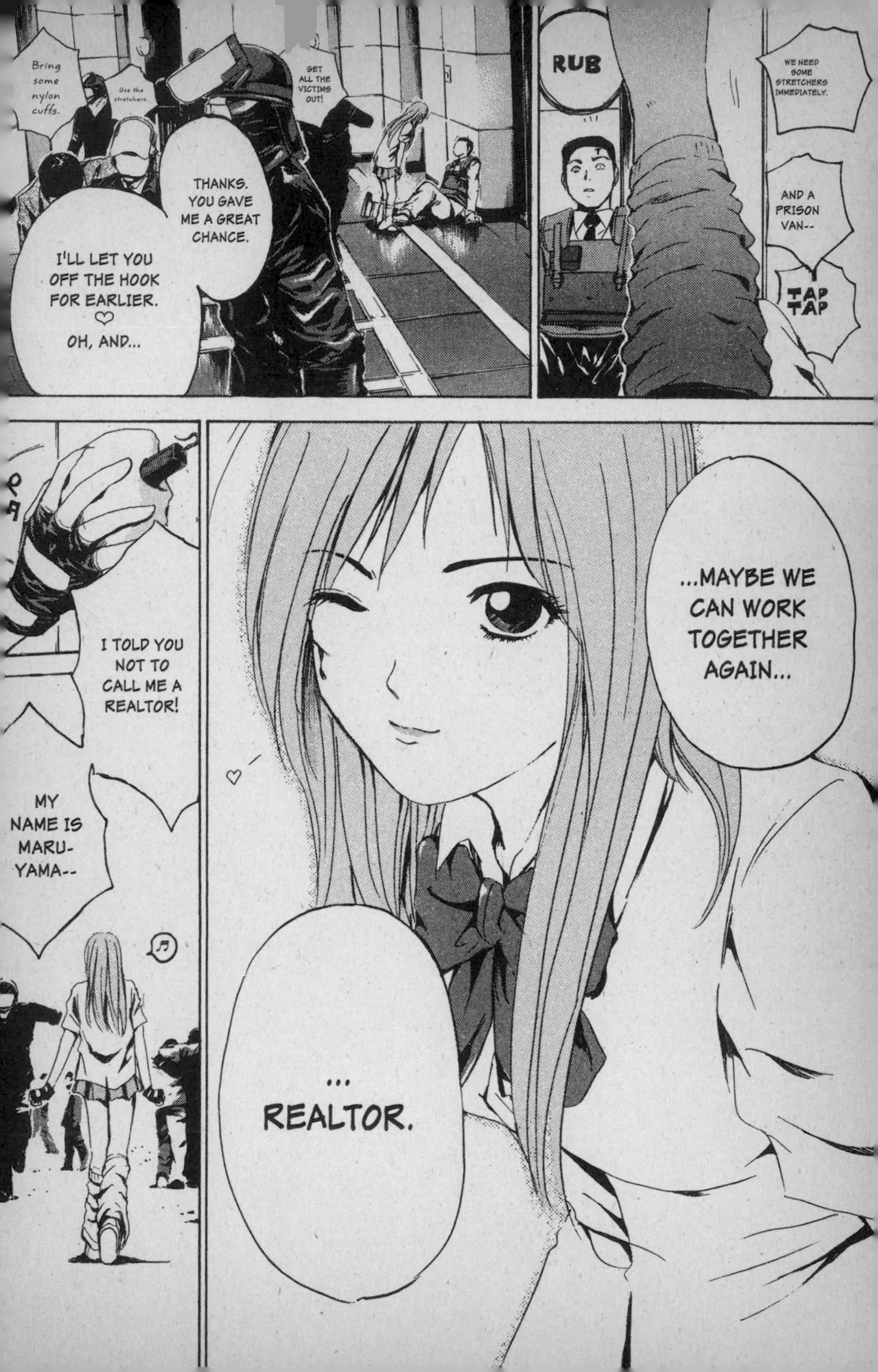
WE NEED SOME STRETCHERS IMMEDIATELY.
RUB
AND A PRISON VAN--
TAP TAP
GET ALL THE VICTIMS OUT!
Use the stretchers.
Bring some nylon cuffs.
THANKS. YOU GAVE ME A GREAT CHANCE.
I'LL LET YOU OFF THE HOOK FOR EARLIER. ♡ OH, AND...
...MAYBE WE CAN WORK TOGETHER AGAIN...
... REALTOR.
I TOLD YOU NOT TO CALL ME A REALTOR!
MY NAME IS MARU-YAMA--

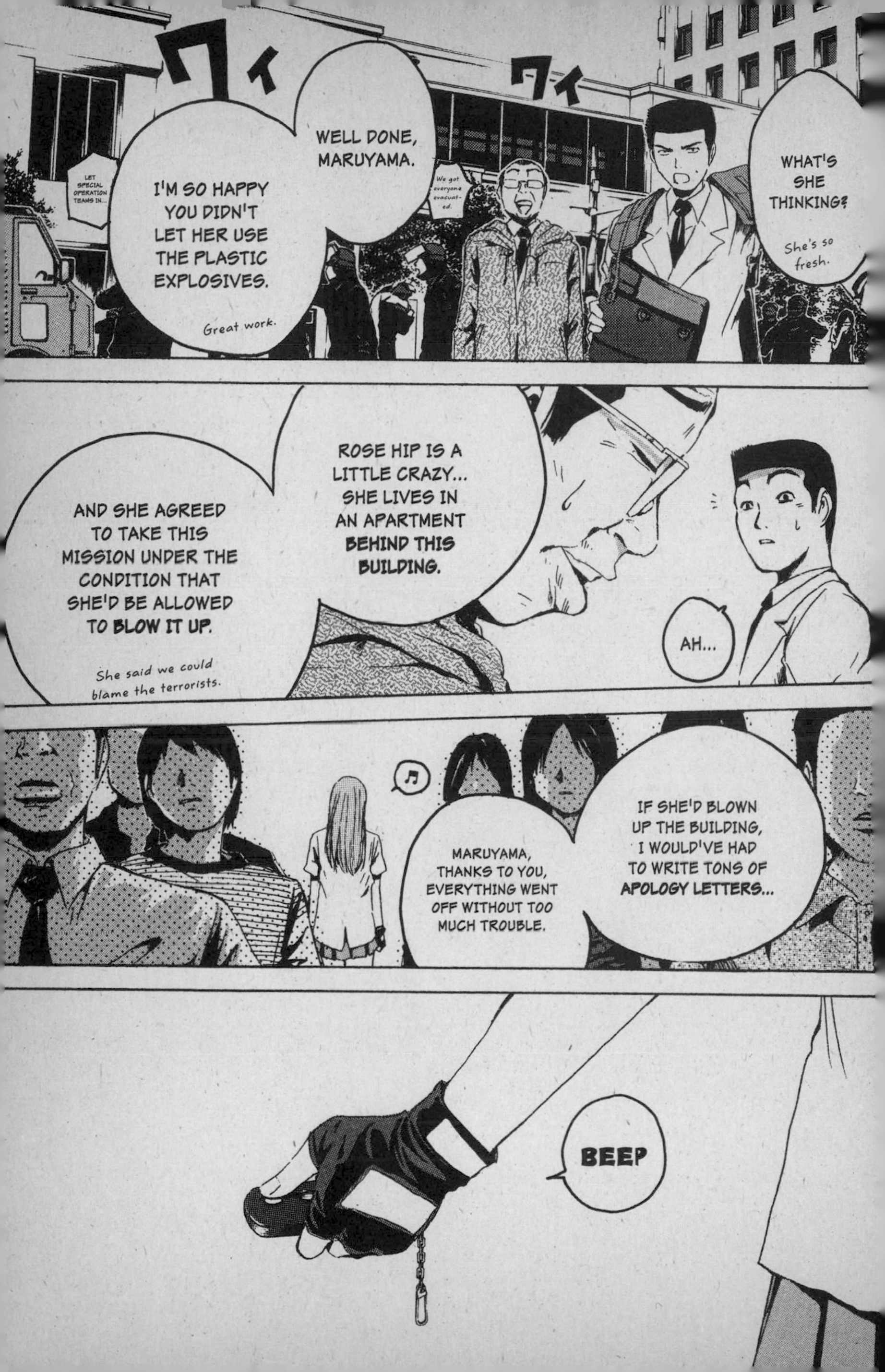

ワイ
ワイ
WHAT'S SHE THINKING?
She's so fresh.
We got everyone evacuated.
WELL DONE, MARUYAMA.
I'M SO HAPPY YOU DIDN'T LET HER USE THE PLASTIC EXPLOSIVES.
Great work.
LET SPECIAL OPERATION TEAMS IN...
AH...
ROSE HIP IS A LITTLE CRAZY... SHE LIVES IN AN APARTMENT **BEHIND THIS BUILDING.**
AND SHE AGREED TO TAKE THIS MISSION UNDER THE CONDITION THAT SHE'D BE ALLOWED TO **BLOW IT UP.**
She said we could blame the terrorists.
IF SHE'D BLOWN UP THE BUILDING, I WOULD'VE HAD TO WRITE TONS OF **APOLOGY LETTERS...**
MARUYAMA, THANKS TO YOU, EVERYTHING WENT OFF WITHOUT TOO MUCH TROUBLE.
♪
BEEP

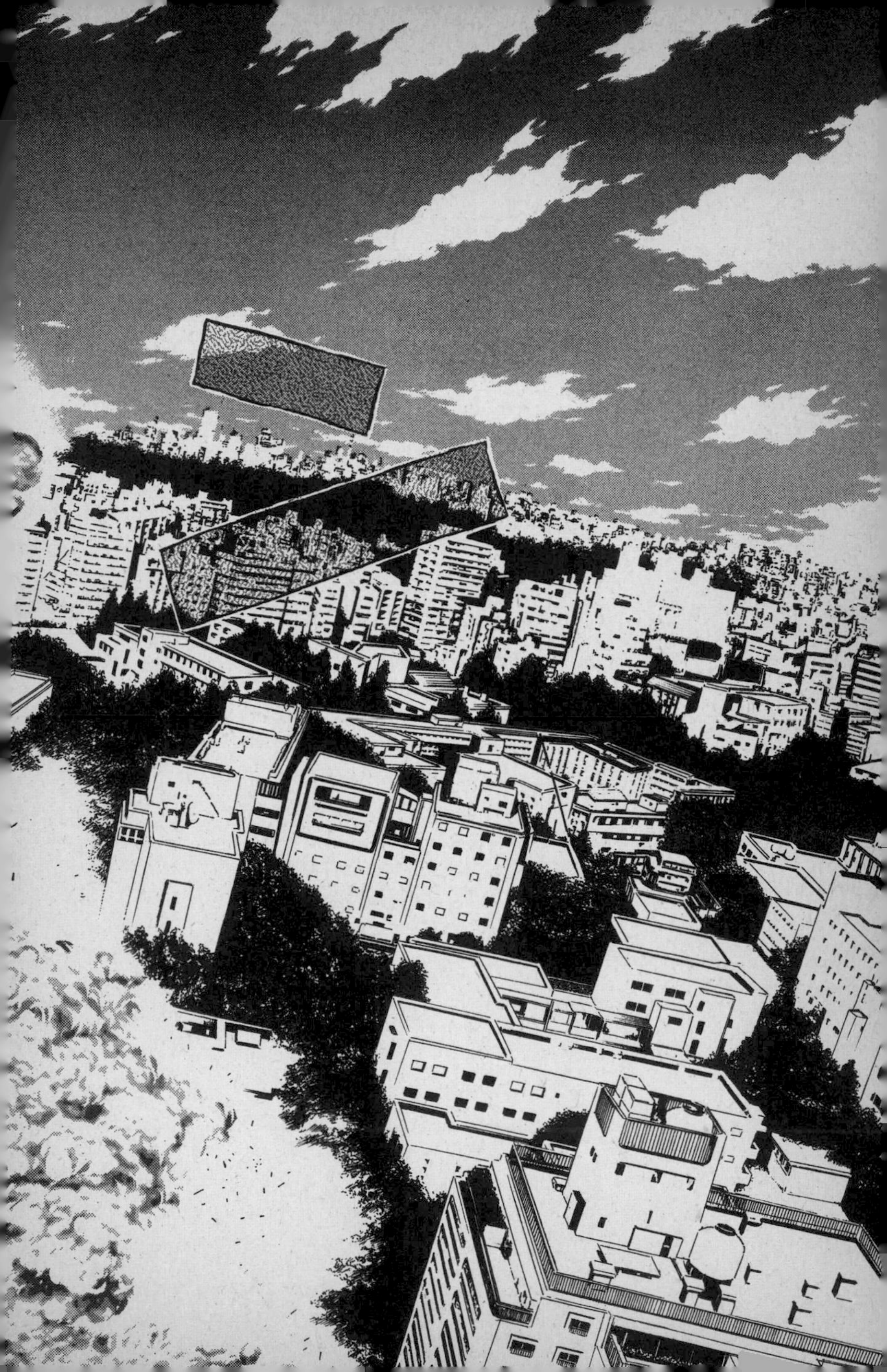

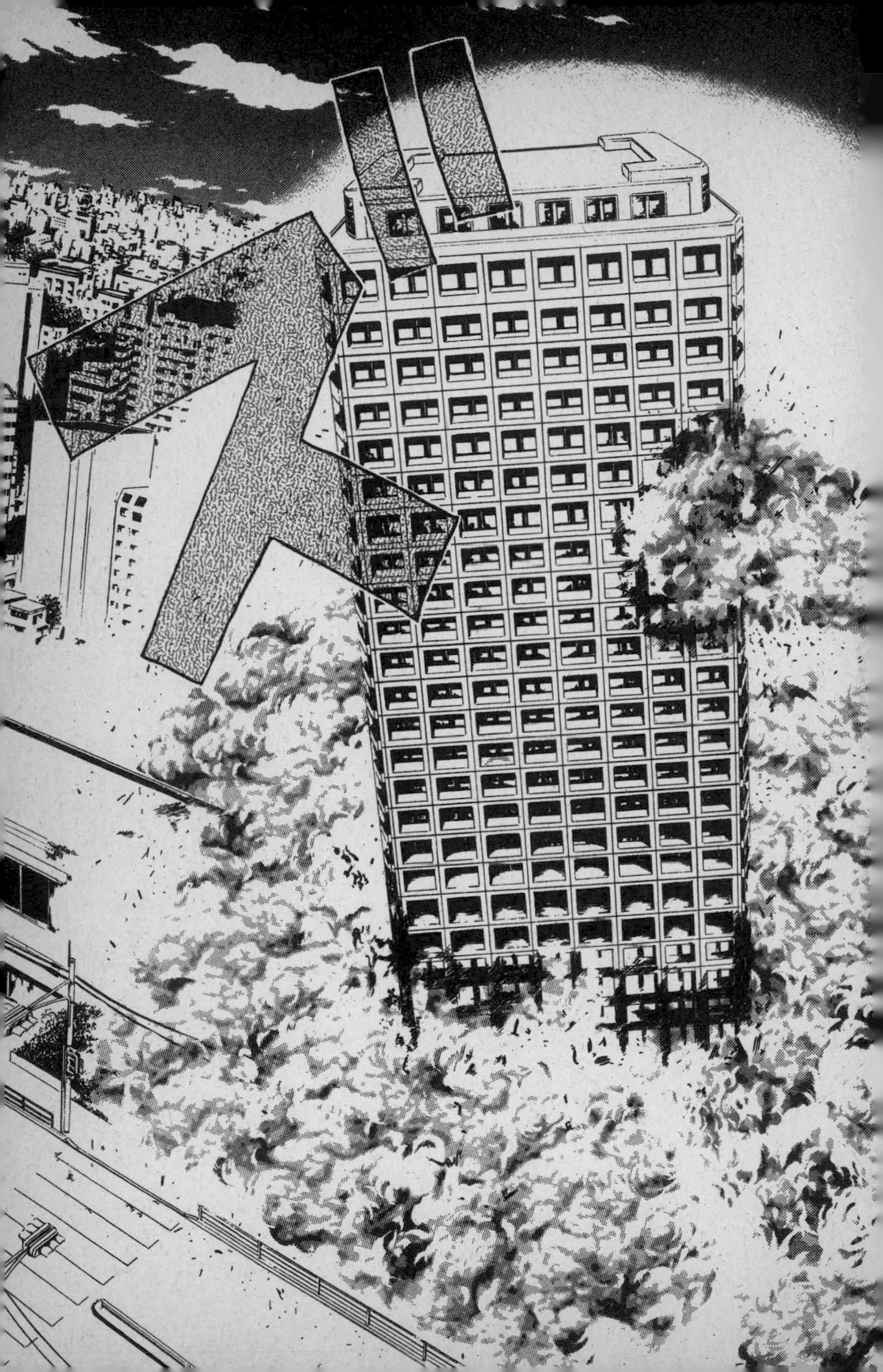

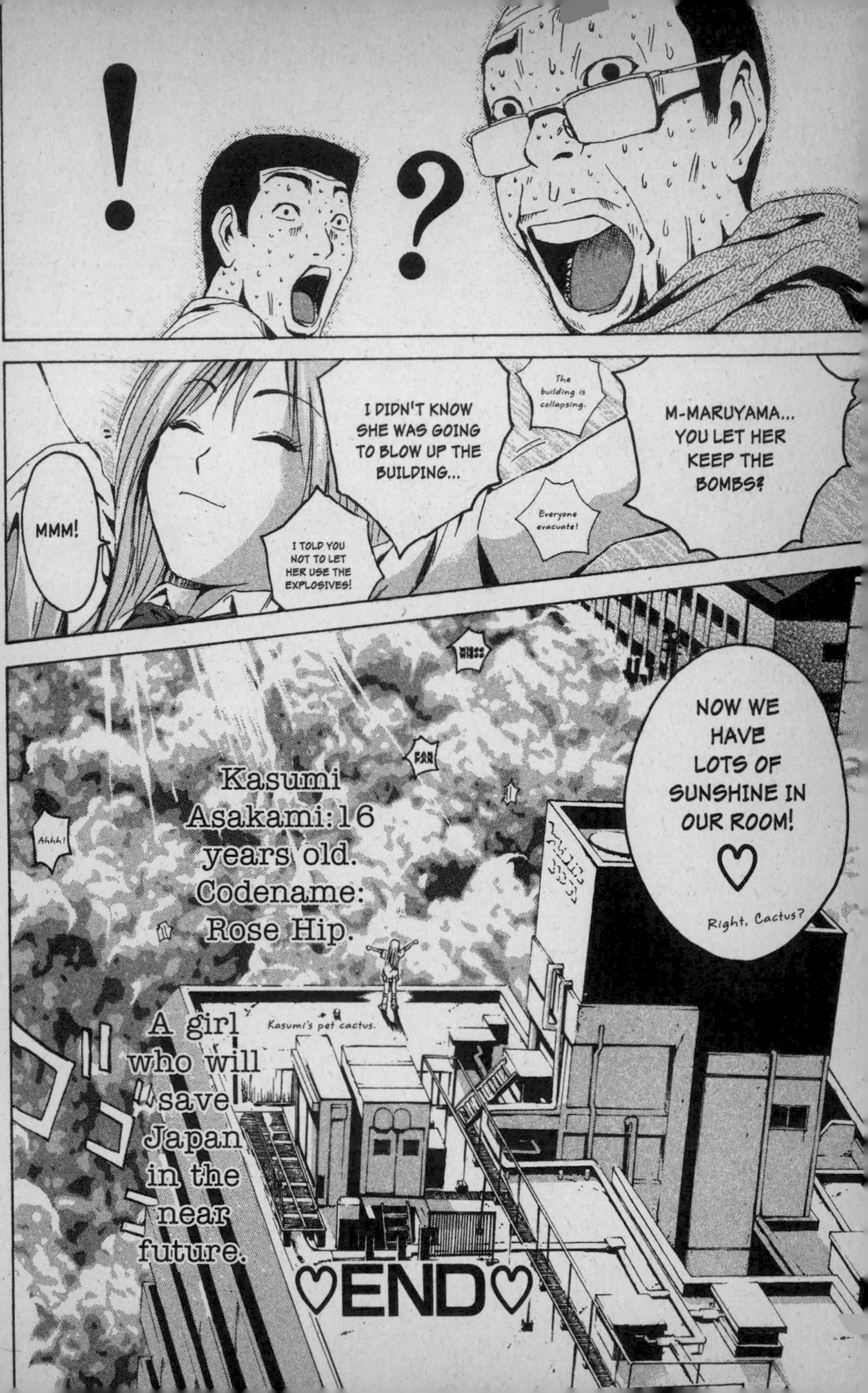
?
!
M-MARUYAMA... YOU LET HER KEEP THE BOMBS?
The building is collapsing.
Everyone evacuate!
I DIDN'T KNOW SHE WAS GOING TO BLOW UP THE BUILDING...
I TOLD YOU NOT TO LET HER USE THE EXPLOSIVES!
MMM!
NOW WE HAVE LOTS OF SUNSHINE IN OUR ROOM! ♡
Right, Cactus?
FAN
Kasumi Asakami: 16 years old. Codename: Rose Hip.
Ahhh!
Kasumi's pet cactus.
A girl who will save Japan in the near future.
♡END♡

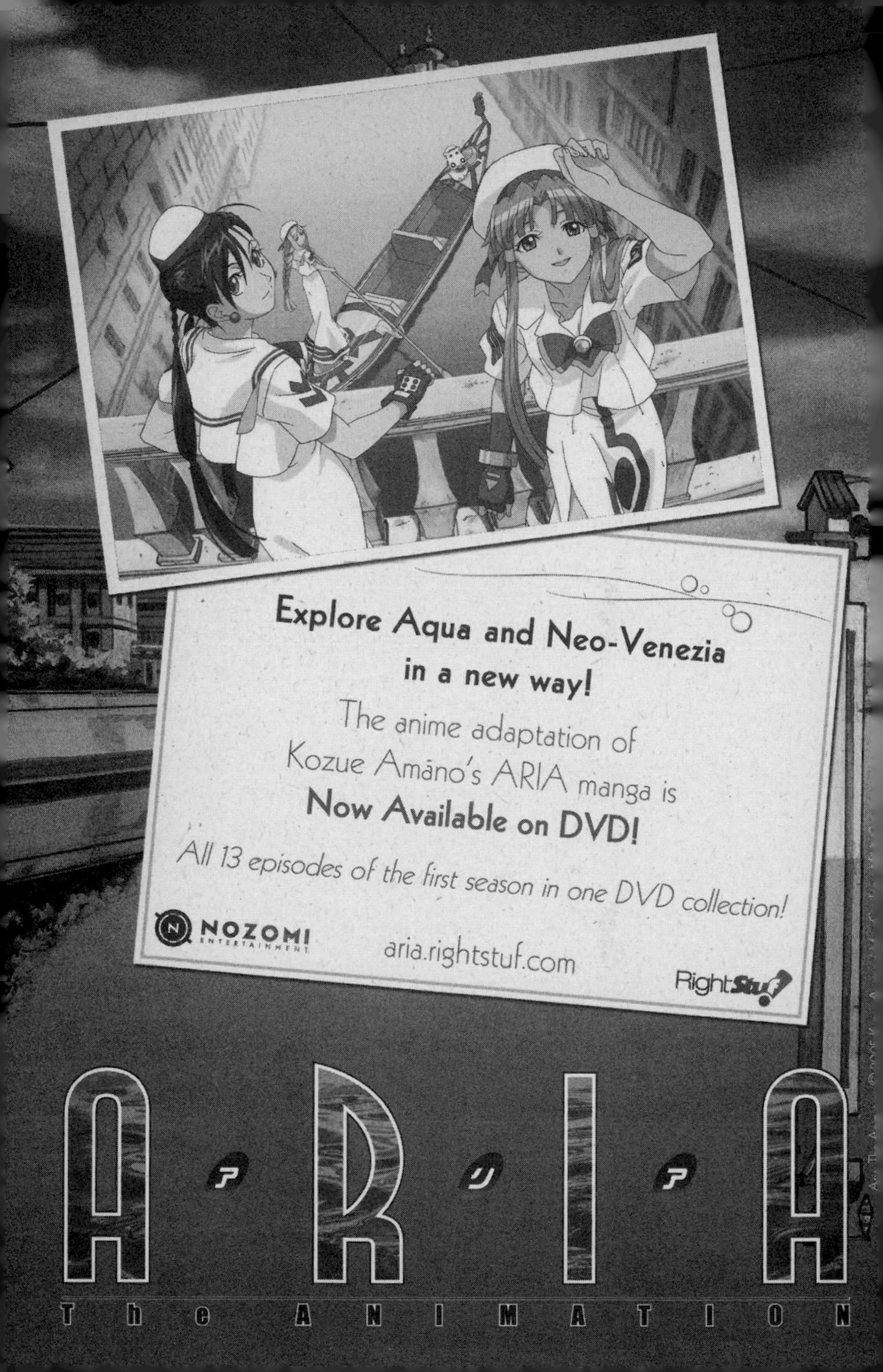
Explore Aqua and Neo-Venezia
in a new way!
The anime adaptation of
Kozue Amano's ARIA manga is
Now Available on DVD!
All 13 episodes of the first season in one DVD collection!
NOZOMI ENTERTAINMENT
aria.rightstuf.com
RightStuf!
ARIA
アリア
The ANIMATION

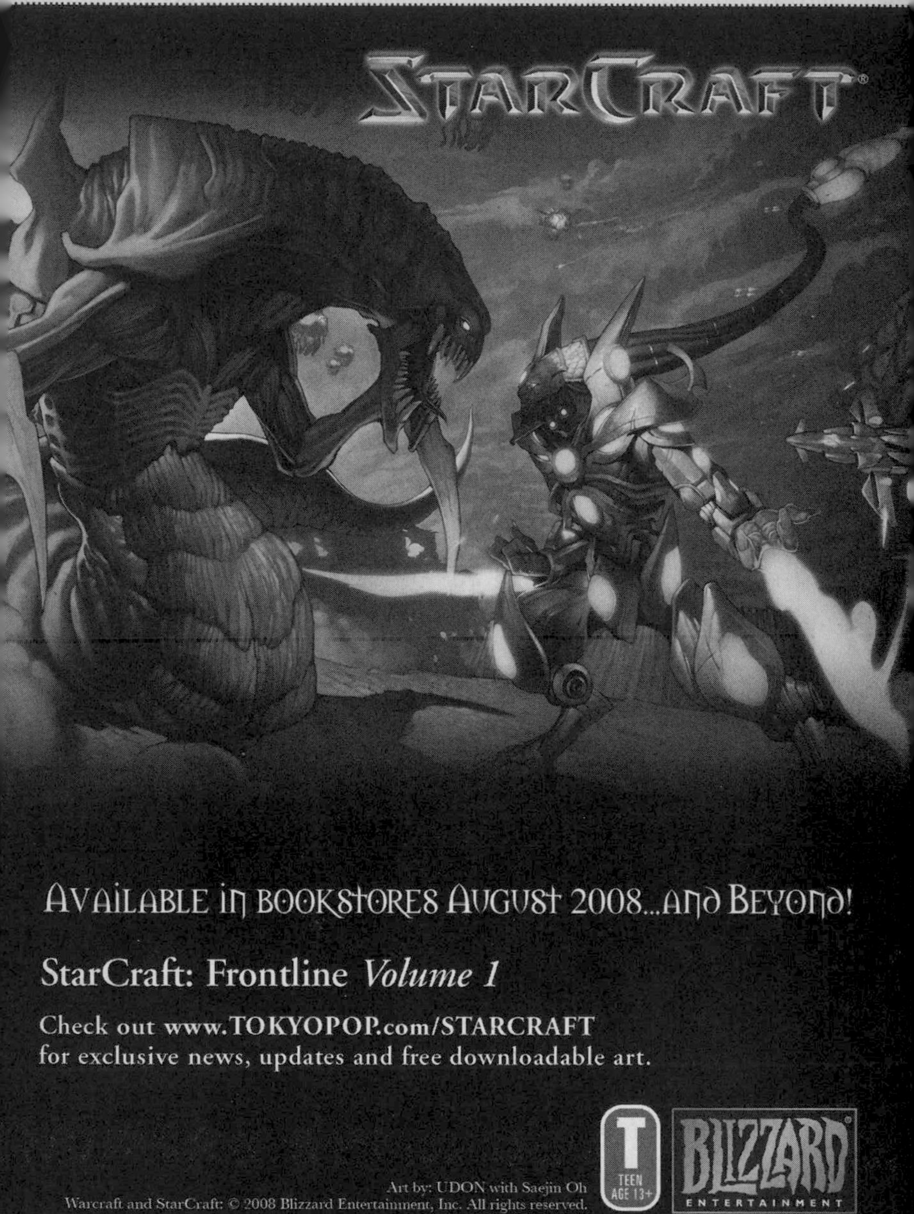
StarCraft®
Available in bookstores August 2008...and Beyond!
StarCraft: Frontline Volume 1
Check out www.TOKYOPOP.com/STARCRAFT
for exclusive news, updates and free downloadable art.
T TEEN AGE 13+
BLIZZARD® ENTERTAINMENT
Art by: UDON with Saejin Oh
Warcraft and StarCraft: © 2008 Blizzard Entertainment, Inc. All rights reserved.

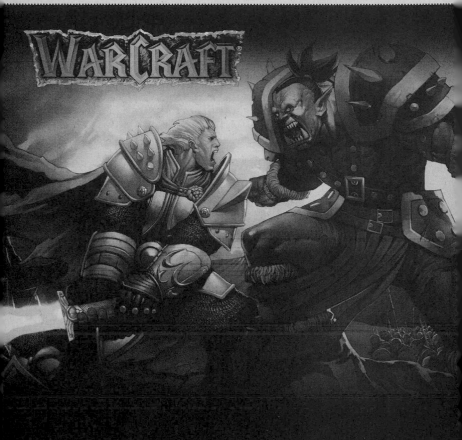

STOP!

This is the back of the book. You wouldn't want to spoil a great ending!

This book is printed "manga-style," in the authentic Japanese right-to-left format. Since none of the artwork has been flipped or altered, readers get to experience the story just as the creator intended. You've been asking for it, so TOKYOPOP® delivered: authentic, hot-off-the-press, and far more fun!

DIRECTIONS

1
2
3
4
5
6
7
8
9
10

If this is your first time reading manga-style, here's a quick guide to help you understand how it works.

It's easy... just start in the top right panel and follow the numbers. Have fun, and look for more 100% authentic manga from TOKYOPOP®!

THE MANGA REVOLUTION · LEADING 漫画革命 LEADING · THE MANGA REVOLUTION